Innocence of the Maiden

Praise for the SPEAR Mission Files

Blood Rage

"I love this series very much. It's everything I love about urban fantasy. [The plot]is very well thought out, with just enough twists and surprises to keep it thrilling and quieter moments for Danika to work through her feelings. On top of the creatures I'm used to seeing in books—vampires, werewolves, and other shifters—Young adds less common ones such as gargoyles and sprites, and it all feels organic. *Blood Rage* is at once a satisfying ending to the series and open enough that the author could come back to these characters if she feels like it. And I certainly hope she does."—*Jude in the Stars*

Moon Fever

"I love lesbian urban fantasy series when they are as cleverly written as this; it feels so real I wouldn't be surprised to meet a goblin or a gargoyle on my way to the bakery. The ending isn't exactly a cliffhanger, but it's open enough that expecting a third book seems reasonable, hopefully in the near future."—*Lez Review Books*

Both Ways

"[T]his sleek paranormal romance introduces Danika Karson, the best vampire hunter on the city's payroll…High points of this fast-paced novel include Danika's relationships with her mother and sister, the smoldering attraction that starts between Danika and Rayne, and detailed worldbuilding. This captivating story draws readers in immediately and keeps them hooked."—*Publishers Weekly*

"This book was nothing like I imagined and completely outdid my expectations. *Both Ways* is a wonderful read that spikes your heart rate and possibly makes your eyes well up. It is exciting and I cannot wait to see what the future entails for the characters."—*Hsinju's Lit Log*

"Honestly, if you're a fan of the genre, and enjoy pure escapist fun, get this book. You'll enjoy the story, root for all the good guys, cheer the downfall of the bad guys, and look on with interest at what happens to those in the moral middle of ambiguity. The action leads you from one thing to the next and you won't want to put the book down. At the end, you'll have had a good time and will want to see what happens next."
—*Lesbian Review*

By the Author

SPEAR Mission Files

Both Ways

Moon Fever

Blood Rage

Innocence of the Maiden

Visit us at www.boldstrokesbooks.com

Innocence of the Maiden

by

Ileandra Young

2025

INNOCENCE OF THE MAIDEN

© 2025 By Ileandra Young. All Rights Reserved.

ISBN 13: 978-1-63679-765-6

This Trade Paperback Original Is Published By
Bold Strokes Books, Inc.
P.O. Box 249
Valley Falls, NY 12185

First Edition: March 2025

THIS IS A WORK OF FICTION. NAMES, CHARACTERS, PLACES, AND INCIDENTS ARE THE PRODUCT OF THE AUTHOR'S IMAGINATION OR ARE USED FICTITIOUSLY. ANY RESEMBLANCE TO ACTUAL PERSONS, LIVING OR DEAD, BUSINESS ESTABLISHMENTS, EVENTS, OR LOCALES IS ENTIRELY COINCIDENTAL.

THIS BOOK, OR PARTS THEREOF, MAY NOT BE REPRODUCED IN ANY FORM WITHOUT PERMISSION.

Credits
Editor: Ruth Sternglantz
Production Design: Stacia Seaman
Cover Design by Inkspiral Design

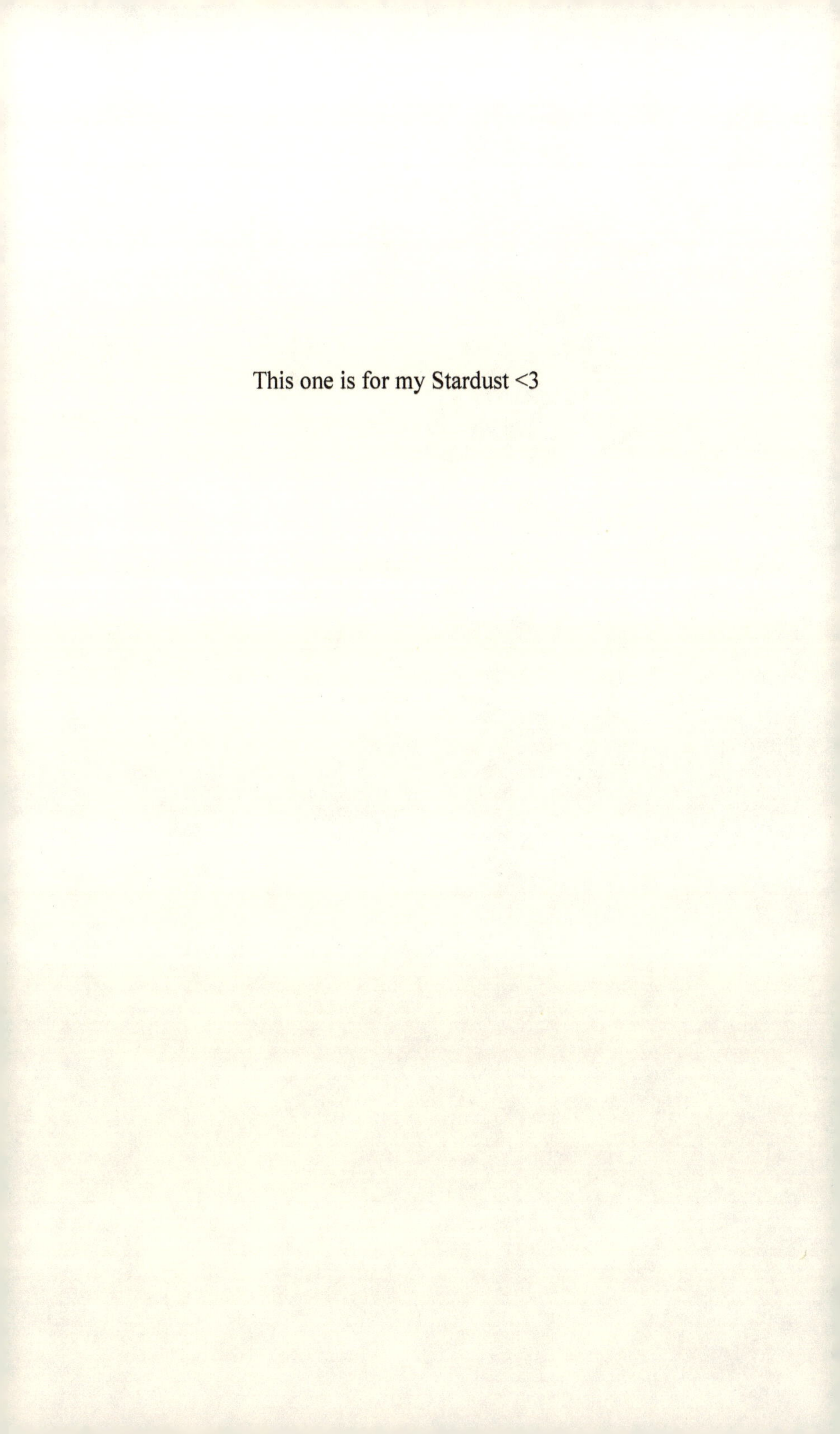

This one is for my Stardust <3

CHAPTER ONE

A soft glow of glittering silver particles fill the air. They shimmer like stars brought down to earth and float around me like motes of diamond dust.

So very beautiful, and all the more inspiring to know that *I* created this.

To my side, my mentor, Hyacinth Dixon, nods approvingly. "And you told me you had no gift for live spells," she chides.

I wriggle my fingers through the silver flecks of light. "I don't. But this is easy. A simple light spell? Anyone can do that."

"Yes," she agrees, "anyone. *Including* you. Now, would you like to try another?"

"Can I rest first?" I lift my hand appeasingly when I see her eyebrows arch enough to add further wrinkles to her forehead. "I know you had plans, but I haven't had much sleep lately. I'm tired. And I don't have the same aptitude for this as you."

"Poppycock," she snaps. "But if you wish, come, sit. I'll make tea. Fennel or hibiscus?"

"Breakfast?"

"Tina…" Hyacinth pauses her slow walk to the kitchen to throw a filthy look over her shoulder. "Builder's tea? You mean that horrible, milky monstrosity that barely contains real leaves?"

I smile. "It's not that bad."

She makes a strange *harrumph* sort of noise. "You have all the aptitude for our craft that I've ever seen in any witch, but your taste in foodstuffs will never cease to baffle me. All that meat and starch, what became of a delicious pea shoot salad on a warm day?"

Still grinning, I settle myself more comfortably on the sofa. It's a long, lumpy, elderly sort of thing, rather like its owner. But I've never sat on something more comfortable. "If it doesn't have steak in it, I'm not sure I want to know. Or at least some chicken."

"Tofu?" Hyacinth's voice takes on a hopeful edge. "I know how to make it beautifully, Daughter—you'd never know it wasn't the flesh of some poor animal."

"Texture no-no. Feels like rubber in my mouth."

Again that horse-snorting sort of noise. "I'll have you know my cooking is the finest in the city. You had best mind yourself before I turn you out on your ear." She ambles off, still grumbling under her breath.

Though I know Hyacinth would never, ever put me out anywhere, I do keep the rest of my comments to myself. Today has been a gruelling enough sort of day. The last thing I want is to give her more excuses to grill me harder.

"So, what do you want to try next? Can I do a ritual?"

The sound of water thundering into a kettle blots out her reply, then the rumble of it beginning to boil. I hear the clunk and clatter of mugs, cups, and saucers being manoeuvred around tall caddies containing all manner of loose-leaf teas.

"Hyacinth?"

Her face peeps around the arch of the kitchen. "Whatever for? After last year I think we both know that you're more than capable of rituals." Her voice becomes wistful. "I wish I could have seen it. A true force of darkness and evil chased away by the power of your protective circle. The Goddess is strong in you."

The praise means a lot, even if it's misplaced.

"All I did was *contain* an evil, Hyacinth. Besides, with that many willing *edanes* around me, I could hardly fail."

"Vampires?" she murmurs.

"And werewolves, and a gargoyle. Even a goblin."

She gives a slow nod. "To see so many peoples brought together to one goal. Beautiful. And yes, I'll grant you that the *fortis* of an extramundane creature is known to be especially strong. But *you* cast that circle."

I nod slowly. That circle rode on the strength of will emanating from each person present that night, including my own. Sheer force of will or *fortis* is a true force to be reckoned with and the powering engine behind every spell any witch casts. Still, there's nothing complex about calling on the Guardians.

Sometimes I still feel the tingle of all that energy condensed into a circle of power to keep bad stuff trapped and good stuff safe. A true highlight of my many years as a witch.

"Just doing my part," I murmur softly. "Besides, I owed her a favour."

"Well, you have repaid it tenfold. Perhaps more."

The kettle boils with a loud click, and I hear Hyacinth begin to pour out water. Then she comes shuffling back into the room, carrying a wide tray set with two teapots and two teacups with matching saucers.

I hop up to take it from her. "Let me."

She throws me a dagger-like look. "I am ill, not dead, Daughter. I can carry a tray. Leave me be."

So I stand back.

No, she isn't dead, but the vigour and liveliness I'm used to seeing in her is very much missing. Her steps have become slower and smaller over the past few days, her words softer. Her heavily wrinkled skin looks thin and pale beneath the long lengths of her curling grey hair. Her eyes, though…they retain all the life and vigour and love and mirth I've ever seen in them over my years in her presence.

I watch her set the tray on the coffee table before the sofa, then scoot aside the long, slender ferret snoozing on the winged armchair next to it.

The creature gives her a long, baleful look, then hops down with a yawn and a stretch. The gorgeous creature threads a quick figure eight around her ankles, then slinks towards the sofa.

Hyacinth makes a soft trilling noise at the back of her throat. "Thank you, dearest. I've already put out some food for you, so enjoy."

No answer from the ferret, but then, that's not unusual. Or maybe it is for this ferret, for she is a familiar. Yes, though she has the shape and mind of any weasel-type creature, she's also blessed with the power, understanding, and strengths of a witch's companion. And a name to match.

"Hey, Loki." I reach out to pet her head, slow and wary, touching only when given the eye contact that signifies consent.

Her fur is soft, warm, and silky and I enjoy a few peaceful moments of stroking before she leaves us for the kitchen.

Hyacinth sits and fluffs out the hem of her dress. Then she takes the smaller of the two teapots, using both hands to swirl it in slow, controlled circles. "We may practise a ritual if you'd like. Not the best use of your time, but it does no harm to ensure your skills are tip-top. No one wants a Mother who cannot lead a ritual."

I pause halfway towards grabbing my own drink. "Not this again, Hyacinth, come on—"

She swirls the teapot even harder. "Humour me. I know *you* think yourself unfit, but *I* know you'll remember your truth in time."

"But it's not about what *I* think, it's about the rest of the coven."

"Is it?" She peers at me, removing one hand from the teapot long enough to gently stroke the finely etched tattoo on her right cheek. "Because I know those girls. They will follow a strong leader."

I nod. "And fortunately, we have one."

For the first time in a long while, I sense irritation from Hyacinth. She puts the pot down and clasps her hands between her knees. "Tina. Daughter. What has happened to you? Why are you so shy of your own ability? Why do you doubt yourself?"

How am I supposed to answer questions like those? It isn't a simple *This is the problem*. There are dozens upon dozens of reasons, most of them buried deep in my past and out of reach, right where I want them.

"I don't want to talk about it."

"I know that. But perhaps through sharing I may allay at least a few of your fears." She studies me closely, bright eyes so keen and wise. "What happened to you? Before you came to me?"

Maybe it *would* help me to tell her, to unburden myself of the guilt I carry. Or maybe that would make it worse. Certainly nothing else has helped ease the pain of it all before now.

Still, I can see that she is watching me, waiting for an answer, so I decide to give her one. Or part of one.

"I'm too young." Already I sense her wanting to interrupt, so I keep going to ensure she can't. "Am I wrong? Most witches in Angbec have at least fifteen years on me, and all of them have far more experience and the knowledge to lead. I don't even have any lineage to speak of. In fact, I don't have any history here beyond the last two years. Nobody knows me. Besides all of that…" I sigh. "I'm not…enough."

Silence stretches between us. In it I hear the far, distant murmur of traffic outside the house, the soft ticking of the clock in the parlour. I hear my own breathing, abruptly quick and shallow, and underneath all of it, the whisper of the magic this house holds.

Hard to describe, but Hyacinth's house has always been *alive.* Much like a tree or a mountain, her home is a living, breathing thing, with a heartbeat and a presence. I hear it now, just a low murmur, like voices but not. Like wind in the trees, but not. Like the whisper of a loving protector.

Hyacinth runs a fingertip along the edge of her mouth. "Quite a litany of faults."

I shrug. "I've learned to live with it."

"You shouldn't. Let us begin with that last point, the one I believe is more important than anything else you mentioned."

"Hyacinth—"

"Do shut up, Daughter. Permit me to speak unhindered." Her voice is light and airy, but her expression is firm.

I close my mouth.

"You have lived in this city for five solars, yes?" She smiles when I nod. "I've known you for two of those, and that is more than sufficient to learn of you. To know and assess you. I invited you to join my daughters because I knew you had a place among them. I could *feel* your power even from a distance, though you tried your best to hide. And so I sought you out. Do you mean to tell your High Crone that she is mistaken?"

I side-eye her. "You hate that title."

"Perhaps, but it caught your attention. So, tell me, am I mistaken?"

I know this trap. Never would I dare tell Hyacinth that she is mistaken or wrong in anything. But in this instance, I don't know that I can avoid it.

"You're not mistaken…I'm just not the witch you think I am."

"That equates to the same thing."

I lean deeper into the sofa, rubbing my hands back across my tapered Afro. The tight coils snag on my fingers, and I realize it's time for a trim. No idea when I'll fit that in.

"You and the Willow Barks were the only coven to even notice me."

Hyacinth smiles. "Then perhaps every other coven is entirely populated with fools. What matter that there is no magic in your family tree? So what that your skill is a little…unrefined? Where do they think they started. Or I, myself?" She winks at me. "I started much like you—raw talent, minimal focus, just an aptitude for one small thing."

She flicks her fingers towards one of the potted plants on the sideboard, a lily, gorgeous but bare. As her fingers move, the stem extending from the spray of leaves at the base swiftly sprouts a fork. Then a bud. And another. A third, a fourth. Each bud twitches, swells, and blushes with deep purple before unfurling into the most magnificent of flowers in the space of mere seconds.

"A pretty skill," she murmurs, "though not exactly useful."

"I don't even have pretty skills."

Hyacinth sighs. "Your antics in this city since being here are more than enough." She goes on, "You may think yourself unworthy, but the covens do talk. Believe me, you and your skill are *known*."

The way she says that makes me abruptly nervous. "What do you mean?"

"Nothing you need concern yourself over. For now." Her words are tart and brisk, brushing away my concerns as though they aren't there. "The people who *need* to know you? They know of you. To the rest, lineage means nothing. The ability to create magic by harnessing our *fortis* isn't linked to our bloodlines. There may be prestige to coming from a well-known family, but not being such will never preclude you from stepping forward. In truth, none of the issues you highlight are issues at all. The only thing standing in your way is you."

"And my age?"

Hyacinth gives a big, roaring burst of laughter. From such a small, frail woman, the sound is startling—rich, bold, and full, pulled from her very depths. "Imagine a younger leader," she coos, "one with more than a handful of years in her before she simply dies and must pass on the mantle. Stability and consistency? Imagine that."

This time I can't help but join her in laughter. No matter what my fears may be, she has always had a wonderful way of making them seem less.

"Fine. I'll relax. A little. Good enough for you?"

"It will suffice. For now." She picks up her pot again and pours a generous measure of tea into her cup. The fluid is pale with a faint green-orange tinge and smells strongly of fennel. She sips delicately, then looks pointedly in my direction.

Hint taken. I swirl my own teapot, then pour, surprised to see the dark shades of a rich black tea. I give her a raised eyebrow.

"Chai," she says brightly. "The one concession I will allow you." She clicks her tongue. "Builder's tea? In my house? Ridiculous."

I grin and sit back with the cup in hand. Though my preference is something rich, full-bodied and laced with full-fat cream, so long as my drink is warm and so long as it's served in this place, I really don't mind what Hyacinth gives me.

CHAPTER TWO

We sit in silence for long minutes, drinking and enjoying each other's still, quiet company. No need to speak in a moment like this.

Hyacinth finishes her first cup before I'm halfway through mine and dumps the dregs onto her saucer. The faint drips of tea mingle with the murky clumps of wet leaves, and she studies them closely.

I watch. "I still don't understand how you see anything in there."

"There are no clear images as you might understand them, but more like to a single photograph, smudged with time. The shapes and symbols must be deciphered. Do you care to look?"

"Not especially. I'm more of a coffee person."

Still she gazes at the green-brown smudges on the bottom of her saucer. "You could learn much from leaves." Her forehead wrinkles with a frown.

"By staring into a wet saucer for hours on end?"

"So sceptical. But I have seen many things in these leaves, and so have other witches. You would do well to heed them."

I sip from my own cup. "Maybe one day. But I've got enough on my plate."

"Well, make it soon, dear Daughter. It would so please me to teach another how to read them."

"Another?" I sit a little straighter.

I had no idea any of my sisters had given much thought to reading tea leaves. I could see the older ones giving it a chance perhaps, but my younger coven sisters would likely put as much faith in the practice as I do.

I lean forward. "Who else have you been teaching?"

No answer. Instead Hyacinth frowns deeply as if the message she sees hidden in the damp mulch bothers her deeply.

"Hyacinth?"

She shakes herself, smiles, then she places the saucer to one side. With practised hands she pours a fresh measure of tea from her pot. After two more sips, she sits back in the big, comfy chair. Lazily, she dangles one hand over the arm and flexes her fingers through a short flutter of complex signs.

A moment later, silent and beautiful, a barn owl swoops out of the kitchen to glide through the room and land lightly on her wrist. Hyacinth brings the majestic bird around to face her and strokes the feathered head. "Will you fetch me my diary, my dear?"

The owl, named Seshat, hoots softly, then takes off again. I watch her huge, hooked talons on Hyacinth's wrist and flinch as they flex hard on take off. Yet, somehow, the bird never seems to hurt Hyacinth. In fact, none of the familiars do, though they all have the capacity to do so in the form of fangs or claws.

Moments later Seshat swoops in again, a small spiral-bound notebook clasped in her claws. She drops it on Hyacinth's lap, then lands daintily on the back of the armchair.

"Thank you." Hyacinth opens the book and starts flipping through the pages, muttering softly about the moon as she does.

I know what she must be looking for. "When's the next conclave?"

She pauses long enough to give me a quick side-eye. "Three nights hence. Sufficient time to make some decisions, would you not say?"

I find myself nodding absently. It *is* enough time, but I don't know if we'll ever be ready.

The Willow Barks have been my home since Hyacinth took me in as one of her daughters. The other members of the coven, my sisters, are as much family to me as my own birth mother. And maybe because of that, I sense that the next meeting of our coven is going to involve the same sort of bickering and infighting siblings are known for.

"You could pull rank," I murmur, mostly to myself.

Hyacinth frowns. "I *could* and in so doing destroy everything I've built for the Willow Barks over the last ten years. We are a coven governed by democracy and reason. I have no right to dictate what we should do."

"You're our Mother."

"As such, I *guide* you," she insists. "No parent should lead their child by the hand through all things. Their role is to *teach* a young one, furnish them with the tools to make informed decisions, and then allow them to do so. It isn't my place to do this for you, simply guide and support."

"And if we choose to merge the coven?"

A pause.

Her expression flickers to one of deep, deep sadness. It's fast, so fast in fact I might have missed it had I not been looking right at her. But as soon as it arrives, the expression is gone, replaced by one of calm serenity.

"Then we merge with another coven. It is as simple as that. My will does not override yours or that of anybody else."

Sometimes I wish it did. That would make things so much easier.

Our coven is tiny, and the recent upheaval in Angbec between vampires and werewolves and humans makes us vulnerable. The Willow Barks have a long, beautiful history in Angbec, but many of the members have long since passed on and have not been replaced. Now a mere handful of the once mighty coven remain, many of them old enough to be thinking of their next journey.

To protect my sisters, it would make sense to merge our coven with one of the many larger ones in Angbec. But to preserve our ways and our history? The only way to do that is to stand as the Willow Barks always have, proud and independent.

"My dear"—Hyacinth looks up again from her diary—"we have survived hundreds of years by being exactly like to our name. The storm may rage and howl around us, but we are willows. We are supple and pliable and flexible. We bend *with* the wind—we do not fight it. The mighty oak may stand tall and immovable against the gale, but under too much force it will crack and break. Not us. No matter how much we are battered hither and thither, we always spring upright to face the next hurricane. The next challenge. The next change. This will be no different."

I stare at my fingers. Then my teacup. Then her face. "How can you be so certain?"

"The Goddess has never yet led me astray."

Faith. Not quite the answer I was hoping for—could have done with something more tangible—but it will have to do.

Hyacinth finishes flipping through her diary. She tucks it into a pocket on her dress and then leans back for another sip of her tea. “Three nights from now, we vote on the future of the Willow Barks. I will meet you in the afternoon.”

I fight the urge to yawn. “Can’t. I’ve got work.”

“Morning then.” Her eyes twinkle. “But of course not too early since I know you appreciate your relaxed mornings.”

She really does know me well.

“I could, but it’s my turn to man ComDis this week.”

Hyacinth tilts her head to one side. “You know I approve of this…distress helpline…but can another sister not take over for one morning?”

I consider it. For about three seconds. “The only person free this week is Edith, and I’d rather not owe her a favour if I can help it.” When I spot the look of disappointment on Hyacinth’s face, I hurry on. “But no one ever calls, so I could still come. It just means that if my phone rings, I’ll have to answer, that’s all. We call it the helpline, but to be honest, it’s more of a *sit there and watch bad TV because no one really needs us* line.”

“Are you familiar with Murphy’s Law?”

A small smile tugs my lips. “Yes, but honestly, it’s been quiet over the last few months. Things have calmed considerably since the Werewolf Wars.”

“Very well.” And with that, Hyacinth grins. “I am a whetstone, dear Daughter, come rub yourself upon me.”

Tea spurts from my mouth as I attempt and fail to hold in my laughter. “Hyacinth!”

And then more of that laughter, loud and gleeful, rocking her frail little body from side to side.

❖

We practise several more live spells in the hours that follow. Not only that, but she takes me upstairs to do it.

Most witches, myself included, have a small space at home

dedicated to spells. Not least it keeps things subtle, but also, with our busy lives out in the mundane world, we often don't have the time or resources to give to elaborate spaces, ritual circles, books, candles, and offerings.

Not Hyacinth, though. A very much retired lady of leisure, Hyacinth has the freedom to do exactly as she wants, when she wants. And she does.

So, walking into her space brings on a mixture of awe and slight intimidation.

The first floor of her home is given over to comfortable living spaces: the main bedroom complete with en suite; another smaller, but still large, guest room; a bathroom; a study area. But above that, on the second floor, in an area that in any other house might be abandoned as lost attic space, Hyacinth has her spell space, her own sanctum sanctorum.

Hyacinth grins as she leads me upstairs, watching with amusement as I hesitate at the bottom of the next set of steps that leads to the second floor.

"Come, come now," she beckons me.

Still I pause. I've only been up there once before, and that was simply to knock on the door to get her attention. She didn't let me in, merely slipped through the door after opening it the merest crack and guiding me back down the steps.

"Why are we here today? Are you sure? You've never…" I can't quite get the words out.

"Must you question every decision I make today, Daughter?" Her voice is firm, but she doesn't seem angry.

I risk placing one foot on the bottom step. "No. But you're being very weird. More than usual, even."

"Why, thank you." Again she beckons, this time hiking her dress above her ankles as she walks up the stairs.

I don't bother explaining that my words hadn't been intended as a compliment. She likely wouldn't care either way.

Hyacinth moves slowly and carefully, but her steps are firm and steady. As she nears the door, her back straightens, as though she draws strength from the echoes of magic in her sacred space.

With a deep breath and a steeling of my nerve I complete that first step. Then the next. And the next. Soon I'm beside her at the top of the stairs, watching her reach into the side of the frame and root around before pulling out a key.

It's a long, ornate brass key, with frills and whorls around the handle. It looks like it might be used to open a box of wondrous treasures or enter some kind of treasured fantasy space.

Maybe it is.

Clearly sensing my reluctance, Hyacinth puts a gentle hand on my wrist. "You belong here," she whispers. "I say it, thus it must be so. Have no fear of this room—it is merely that, a room."

"Your sanctum—"

"Is always open to you, Daughter. Remember that."

She pushes the door.

A rush of warmth billows out at me, not dry, fusty, and uncomfortable, but like the reach of a tender, gentle hug. It unfurls over my face and hands, curling around my body to pull me close.

I can all but see the *life* of this room and all the magic that has taken place within.

Hyacinth steps inside, and as she does, candles spring to life on every shelf and in every corner. She sweeps her arms, and the thick, velvety curtains rattle closed on their large silver hooks. A faint glow emanates from the clean but bare floorboards, in the form of a perfect circle, marked with five clear points.

My mouth hangs open. I know I must look like a grounded fish, but I can't help it.

"It's beautiful…"

"Pish-posh." She flaps her hand around again. In response her altar lights up, tiny flames flicking into being on the end of each incense stick planted in her holder shaped like an open sunflower. The flames flare bright for split seconds before dying off into nothing, replaced by thin curls of sweetly scented smoke.

The altar stands against the north wall, draped with a rich green cloth embroidered with leaves in thin golden thread. It flutters in a breeze I can find no source for, and on top of it, a thick book bound in leather—vegan, no doubt—flops open to a plain, unmarked page. Also on the table are three large stones, a feather, a biro with the end gnawed off, and two small bowls roughly hewn from a rich, dark wood.

In the first bowl I spy a packet of gum, a handful of seeds, and a piece of quartz. In the second is a soft, round nest formed of hair, twigs, and soft white fluff.

"Is this where you kept Monty?" I gently play my fingers through the strangely delicate yet firm nest.

"Sweet little thing," she says, nodding. "I hope he is well now."

Monty is the name I gave to the tiny sparrow we found in the middle of winter, lying half crushed and frozen near the flower beds. Together we brought it in, fed it, then cared for the bird while it regained strength and health.

For some reason, the memory comes with a sweeping sense of nostalgia and…sadness? No, wistfulness.

Such a simple, wholesome thing to do.

I'd spend more time gawping at the room, but Hyacinth clearly has other ideas. She sits on the ground in the centre of her faintly glowing circle, legs crossed, hands resting lightly on her knees.

She gestures for me to copy, and I experience a quick twinge of embarrassment as my own knees temporarily lock up at the request for flexibility.

How old am I versus this woman, anyway?

She sits there, calm and serene, and makes a sweeping gesture with her hand.

"This is *my* sanctum, and I formally welcome you, Evangelina Marks. May you always find welcome, solace, and succour in this space."

I flinch just a little at the sound of my whole name. So rare that I hear it these days unless my mother is in a terrible mood. I barely use it, and no one in this city knows it. In fact, I'm not entirely certain how Hyacinth came to know it.

Not that it matters. I don't mind *her* using it.

I smile and try to find the right words in my memory to signify my acceptance and gratitude of the gesture. In the end, as my mind comes up blank, I simply quip, "So long as there's a comfy chair and a good book to read, I'm sure I'll find all three."

Hyacinth eyes me moodily but doesn't chide me. Instead, she leans slightly forward and gives me her own crooked smile. "Shall we begin?"

The candles all around us gutter for long seconds, throwing long shadows over her face. Through the dim, I catch the twinkle in her eyes and recognize the low level whisper of excitement running through her voice.

I let my gaze take in this magnificent space and feel more ready than I ever have done. “Let’s do it.”

CHAPTER THREE

Communing with mundane animals, growing plants, light, darkness, and sense-based spells. Basic things a witch might need day-to-day to make life a little easier.

Hyacinth demonstrates with round globes of white light, sending them dancing around the room in bright little displays enough to make my heart sing with childish delight. She generates flushes of warm and cold, fills the room with the scent of roses. Her hands flutter through complex signs and gestures that bring flowers blooming out of the floorboards or call the sound of twittering birds into the air.

Impressive little tricks and illusions that, though beautiful, are not so impressive to anybody who knows what a witch can truly do. But then, a lot of people don't understand what it is to *be* a witch.

Outwardly, we're no different to anybody else. We live, we breathe, we love, we cry. But at our cores, deep in our hearts, each of us with a link to the Goddess has a clear, inexorable sense of our place in the world. We see things others might not and are attuned to nature in a way most people have forgotten. Depending on which face of the triple Goddess we align with the most, witches are protectors, warriors, or sages.

But unlike the witches of common media, we don't throw fireballs, call down lightning, or fly about on broomsticks. No, we're simply women going about our day-to-day lives who happen to have a skill in directing our will at a problem strongly enough that the world bends to obey.

If I want light to appear in my hand, it is a simple direction of my intent, my *fortis*, to make it happen. If I want the air around me to boom with a sudden burst of sound, that too is easy to create. If I'd like the book at the other end of the room to appear in my hand, and if I direct my desire into making it happen, that book will gradually float towards me or, for those more skilled, move fast enough that it appears to teleport.

And so, for the third time in forty minutes, I beckon the thin, cotton-bound book towards me. With the other hand, I wipe away the faint prickle of sweat forming across my brow.

The book wavers, then bobs, like an uncertain baby bird, almost hitting several candles before wobbling up again to land in my lap.

Directly ahead of me, still cross-legged and comfortable, Hyacinth lightly claps her palms together. "Very good. Smoother than previous attempts, though still a little uneven. Why are you holding back? This is well within your capabilities. You must maintain your focus."

Of course, yes. Focus. Something I have either in abundance or not at all—there is absolutely no in-between. My brain can be messy that way.

"Sure. Focus. Yup. *Focus.*" I wave the book off my lap, directing it back towards the shelf.

Halfway there, Hyacinth snaps her fingers, and the book zooms off course and into *her* lap, far faster and more direct than my attempt. "I took the book from you," she murmurs. "Take it back."

"What?"

"Take the book back."

So I do. Or at least, I try. I reach out as I did previously, centring my desire into that one thought. The book wobbles. I push harder, more focused now, willing the thing to rise off Hyacinth's lap and towards mine. Another wobble. The book rises briefly onto its spine, then flops back down.

I frown. "Are you holding it?"

"I am."

"But you told me to take it."

The smallest of smiles lifts the corner of her lip. "Then take it."

But the book refuses to move.

Hyacinth isn't *physically* holding it. In fact, she hasn't moved at all. Her hands rest lightly on her knees, and her posture, though straight and proper, is relaxed and easy. But I realize in that moment that my will is in direct conflict with hers. And she is winning.

I sigh. "I can't fight you—you know that. You're miles stronger than me."

"In some things." Her voice takes on the faintest hint of disappointment, but she hides it with her next words. "You have all the tools you require to retrieve this book and place it back upon the shelf. I would like you to do so, please."

More flops and flutters from the book as I battle to lift it from her lap. I hear the strain as a faint buzz in the back of my head, building as a pressure above my eyes. I frown, even turn to face her more fully, and put my entire body into my attempts.

My fingers flex, my skin tingles, my heart *thud-thud*s against my ribs. The candles closest to me flare with tall flames that crackle with sparks of bright blue light. A gust billows through the thick curtains, bringing with it the scent of night blooming flowers from outside.

But the book remains firmly in place.

"Screw it." I stand and cross the small space between us. With a faint grunt, I snatch the book off her lap and carry it to the shelf. The thin book slides easily into the gap when I push it in. "There, happy?" Even to my own ears, my voice is petulant, and the tantrum is childish. But I'm tired now and ready to go on with the rest of my evening.

But as I look at Hyacinth, her half smile breaks into a full one. Once more she claps, but this time with real enthusiasm. Her eyes sparkle with pleasure. "Very good. A mite longer than I anticipated, but you made it eventually."

"What are you talking about?"

She stands and stretches her arms above her head. "You replaced the book on my shelf as I requested. And with that, our tutoring is over for the day."

I stare at her. Then the book. Then back to her. "But I didn't even use magic."

"No. You didn't." Slowly, Hyacinth walks over to her altar. She presses her hands together for brief moments, then starts to snuff out—not blow out—all the candles.

My mouth is already open with the intent to ask more, but the phone in my pocket, which has been quietly buzzing at me, on and off, for the past twenty minutes, begins to demand my attention again.

Two missed calls, one in progress. Several text messages. All from—

"I need to take this," I murmur.

Hyacinth gives me the briefest glance before nodding her agreement. She stands over her altar, grasping the chewed biro and laying the nib to the open page in that leather-bound book. In the still that follows, I hear the faint scratch of her words on the paper.

I carry the phone with me out of the room and back down the stairs.

As I go, the warmth and closeness of the room slides off me and remains behind. It leaves a faint but undeniable sense of loss in its stead.

Still, I can't afford to remain in the room to chase that relaxed, comfortable feeling. Hyacinth can't read minds—or at least I don't think she can—but I'd rather she not be part of the conversation I'm about to have.

I take the phone with me into the garden, accessible through a set of large glass doors beneath the stairs.

So pretty out here at night. Hyacinth's garden is a sea of flowers, herbs, and vegetables. How she finds the time to look after any of it is beyond me, especially in her increasingly frail state. But there's order, structure, and beauty here that comes only from a garden well-tended and meticulously groomed.

Directly ahead, a willow tree. Of course. The central feature of the garden around which everything else is arranged. It's an old tree, certainly older than the house, and stands tall, a beautiful sentinel over the entire area. Long, trailing branches curve out then down, delicately sweeping the soft grass with leaves and catkins.

On the left, vegetables, a fantastic, colourful selection that changes as the seasons do. Right now, the patch is full of beetroot, cabbages, aubergines, garlic, rhubarb, and fennel.

Behind the tree are flowers, mostly hyacinths—funny that—then peonies, lilies, dahlias, roses, alums, and lavender. I'm pretty sure hyacinths are only supposed to bloom in spring, but no matter the time of year, there are always some visible in this garden, a special little bit of live magic that my mentor takes advantage of just because she can.

Then, to the right of all that, the herb garden. My favourite.

Basil and coriander grow all the time of course, but this is the season for rosemary, thyme, bay, sage, and parsley. This year she also has coriander, dill, and oregano, and the entire area smells delicious.

I find myself walking along the neat paths she has made between the beds, bright white chunks of stone, which are likely chalk or limestone.

There is a bench at the far end of this area, one of my favourite places to sit, and though there are no bees at this time of night, I can hear the faint buzz of some insect or another. Several moths flutter through the growing darkness—those at least I recognize. I know there are spiders too, but I try not to think about those.

Once again the phone rings, and this time I see *Nikolette Mob* flash up on the screen.

The smile on my lips is immediate and impossible to get rid of. "Hi, baby." I press the phone to my ear. "Are you all done for the night?"

"Please, don't call me that. But yes. I'm waiting for you."

Oh. Well. Maybe not quite impossible to get rid of. "Sorry, I forgot." I clear my throat, falling into more serious tones to match those coming through the phone at me. She has always been a serious sort.

"Mm-hmm, well, don't. Someone might hear you."

"Over the phone?"

She sniffs. "I meant at your end. I take it you're still with the High Crone?"

"You can call her Hyacinth, you know."

"That's hardly respectful. Would you call the mayor *Jack*?"

I shrug. "Maybe. If I knew him. She's just a person, you know."

"But a powerful one. Please keep your voice down."

I roll my eyes, an instant later thankful she can't see me. "She's inside, I'm in the garden, we're fine. Anyway, I saw your calls. Is something wrong?"

"Not yet, just checking on you." Nikolette's voice resembles whipped honey—smooth, rich, and full. She speaks slowly, but not awkwardly so. My girlfriend talks as though she expects people to listen and means to give everybody the time to do so and comprehend. There is power and authority in her voice. And in everything else about her.

My heart skips. "Worried about me?"

"No. Just aware of how badly you keep time. We're meeting in an hour, and you haven't yet left. This is your reminder. I miss you."

"As if I need any prompting to remember to meet with you. It's been days. I can't wait to see you again."

"Please be on time."

"Of course. See you soon, love." I pause, wondering if I've managed to overstep the line again.

Long silence meets me down the line. Then a soft kissing sound. "See you soon." She hangs up.

I hug the phone to my chest, grinning like a loon, as I watch a tiny spider walk up the stem of a sprig of thyme. Fine. Just fine so long as it stays well away from me.

When I stand and tuck the phone back into my pocket, I find Hyacinth watching me from the house. She meets me as I walk back along the path, and her expression darkens.

"Take care she doesn't crush you underfoot, Daughter."

That skipping in my heart turns into an abrupt free fall. "What?"

"You think yourself subtle, but I recognize the signs of hidden love. I was not always an old woman." She wags a finger at me. "And if I understand right what I have been told, then you have chosen the most worthy of partners. But remember her desires will not always match with yours. And her *fortis* is strong."

"Stronger than mine?"

She refuses to answer, instead threading her arm through mine and leading me back to the house. "You do not have to keep secrets, by the way. Love is love in whatever form. It should be celebrated."

"How long have you known?"

"Long enough. It amuses me that you believe you could keep something like this from me."

"I'm sorry." I hang my head.

More silence, then a very soft "Whatever for?"

The fact that she wants me to say it out loud makes the sudden curl of shame even stronger. "I should have trusted you. I know you wouldn't think any more or less of me due to my choices."

She winks. "Certainly not from *this* choice." Her attempt to lighten the mood falls flat on me.

The desire to explain bubbles up inside me, like a natural spring breaking the surface. "This isn't my choice. I would have said something sooner. I would have shouted from the rooftops, but I—"

Hyacinth hushes me. "I know her and her family. Diana Byron is a fierce witch with unfeasibly high standards. It is little wonder that her granddaughter chooses to keep a precious creature such as you out of her sight."

That's one way to put it, I suppose, but certainly not the words I would use.

Being with Nikolette is…hard.

As if sensing my thoughts, my mentor gently pats my arm. "Do not think it a reflection on you, Tina. I believe she must make peace with many aspects of her own self before entirely welcoming you. There must be an immense level of pressure to meet the expectations of her family."

I play with the edge of her sleeve, like a child. "Sometimes I wonder what she sees in me."

Hyacinth pats the back of my hand. "I cannot speak for her, but if she has eyes in her head, she will see what an incredibly loving, kind, and powerful witch you are. Among other things."

"I guess."

"Believe me"—again she pats my hand—"you may be very good for each other."

"How do you know all this?"

A smile. "Anansi is an *excellent* spy when she wishes to be."

I spin in a sharp circle, seeking out the little traitor for a scolding. No sign of her, though. Just Loki lounging in the doorway and Seshat sitting silently in a tree.

Hyacinth has four familiars. *Four*. Safe to say Anansi is my least favourite.

My mentor catches my attention with a soft hand on my cheek. "Regardless, if you mean to keep your business private, then that is well. Just be certain it is for the right reasons and not due to fear. Fear only begets more fear."

I inhale deeply of garden's scents, sweet herbs and earthy vegetables, before stepping back indoors.

"I'm not scared, and neither is she. We're just being careful."

"As is ever your way."

"You say that like it's a bad thing."

She shrugs. "Life is shorter than any of us believes it to be. Short enough that to obtain what we desire, we must take risks and make difficult choices. These choices will inevitably be hard and may not always yield the results we desire, but often they will be the results we *need*. Remember that."

Another classic, cryptic Hyacinth maxim. I should be used to them by now, given how many she gives me on a regular basis. Instead of dwelling on it, I mentally stack her words on top of the rest of the odd things she says that I'm probably not supposed to understand.

"We're fine, I promise."

"Good." Hyacinth nods. "Then remember what I have said, and don't let your history prevent you from living out your future."

"And what's that supposed to mean?"

Her look becomes wry. "I know more than you have ever openly shared, but less than the whole truth. I hope in time you'll allow me past those tall, impenetrable walls you've built around your past."

I shift from foot to foot, my gaze now locked on a space over her shoulder. "There's nothing to tell."

"Mm-hmm," she murmurs, "remember, a lion dressed as a sheep can only fool the herd for so long."

Right. Seems like that's another one to add to the list.

I take her hand and gently squeeze it. "I'm heading off now."

A reluctant nod as she squeezes back. "I assumed you might. Perhaps I've pressed you too hard tonight."

I shrug.

"All I want is for you to achieve the potential you are destined for. Forgive me if I feel the need to remind you of what you are capable." She releases my hand and waves me off. "But that is for another time. Fare thee well and meet me here, as we agreed, the morning of our conclave. I will have a gift for you."

That pauses me in my hurried collection of my belongings. "A gift? Like what?"

She gently taps the side of her nose. "You'll know soon enough. But nothing before its due time. Meet me and I will give you the gift."

"Sounds like a bribe to me."

"Why can it not be both?"

I laugh, drawing her into a light hug.

Goddess, her body is so thin and small. She has never been a large woman, but now her bones seem almost airy, like a bird's. As I hold her, I worry that a strong enough puff of wind might blow her away.

"I'll see you in a couple of days."

Hyacinth presses her soft lips against my cheek. "Be well, Daughter. Walk always in the light of the Goddess."

I kiss her back. "And the Goddess fill your nights with life." An oddly formal farewell given that we're due to meet again in a couple of days, but this, rather like her strange maxims, is something else I've simply become used to.

I snatch up my bag and jacket, loop both over my arm, and make my way out of the house.

CHAPTER FOUR

I feel better than I have in weeks. Though traffic is heavy—some sort of werewolf march in memory of the riots a year back—I don't mind it at all. The radio gently plays one of my favourite songs, and I have the chance to enjoy my own company.

My fingers still tingle from all the magic we played with throughout the day. Not that too much of it was complex, but I don't really use magic all that much. Perhaps I'm getting rusty?

Working with the public and in such a visible role, I made the decision before moving to Angbec to keep my true nature to myself. Not that it would cause any problems, or at least I don't think it would, but I don't want to encourage my colleagues or my superiors to lean on my magic. Besides, anything that might rock the boat is also something I'd rather avoid.

Even five years on, a part of me experiences a flutter of nerves every time someone mentions my past precinct, previous colleagues, or even where I used to live.

I see a traffic enforcement officer waving my way. One arm is extended to stop the traffic on my right, while the other beckons me forward on a diversion.

Ahead the traffic splits in two. I can see some of the cars turning towards the outskirts, while the other line angles further into the more touristy areas of the city, places where all the bars, clubs, and *edane* delights can be found. One of them is visible even now, a club full of flashing lights and pulsing music with *Paltricks* written on the front in the form of a curvy, neon sign.

My nose wrinkles as I pass the bright lights, hinting at cheap drinks and the safe but very present thrill of being able to stand shoulder to shoulder with powerful and dangerous *edanes*. The club is vampire owned and open only after sundown, which makes sense, but what doesn't make sense is the name.

A parlour trick, sometimes also called a palm trick, has, for witches at least, been shortened to *paltrick*, the name given to a simple but flashy kind of spell. These paltricks take little preparation to perform and often use words as a focus. Some witches like to make those words flashy and impressive, using rhymes or even other languages. Others, like myself, keep it simple and basic, usually a two word phrase related directly to what we want.

The area we're due to meet in is entirely pedestrianized, so I'm forced to park several streets away. The area is largely empty, but I do spot one car relatively close with perfect, shiny paint and a lush leather interior. That thing probably costs as much as my house, and it belongs to Nikolette.

I take care to leave my own vehicle well away from hers and then walk quickly back to the narrow line of pavement between rows of tall Tudor age buildings converted into stores. One is a gaming shop, long since boarded up and closed with a single, subtle door of rough wood.

I don't enjoy meeting in this place, but at least it's neutral territory, one of those warded places, much like our sanctums, designed to put off nosy humans. I'd prefer to be outside, but I'll take what I can get at a time like this.

I reach for the handle, and a flood of magic fills my palm, subtle, invisible, but very much there. I answer with a pulse of my own, a little twist of *fortis* laced with a command. *Open.*

And it does.

Only the most determined of mundanes would be able to open this door, and even then they would need considerable mental strength to do so. A witch, however, can open it through the wards as easily as the cover of a book.

I slip inside and close the door firmly behind me.

The bottom half of the shop still homes shelving units, cabinets, and display podiums. Because it is so often used as a meeting place for the witches of the city, it isn't dusty as one might expect, and all of the furniture is in excellent condition. I even catch the faint scent of jasmine and gardenia on the air.

I walk through, faster now, knowing what waits for me upstairs.

I continue past the remnants of the checkout area and through the creaky door marked *Private* beyond. It swings loosely behind me, and I barely let it close before turning left and darting up the steps.

There are lights here, maybe electric but likely not, just the faint glow of some paltrick to illuminate the way. I follow them all the way to the top and round into the large space once dedicated to gaming tournaments. The large tables are stacked neatly and pushed to the edges, same with the chairs. Most are covered with white sheets, but two have been pulled down and brought to the centre with a pair of stools.

And there, waiting for me, is Nikolette.

Just like every other time I see her, my breath catches in my throat. I take a moment just to look, just to drink in every feature of her dark, regal beauty.

Her height is made all the more impressive by the shoes she wears, high in the heel and delicate. Long, long legs encased in wide-fit linen add to the illusion. The trousers are high waist and the blouse above them loose and flowing, but clearly finely tailored to her frame. It's olive green, a shade I know brings out the richness of her deep brown eyes. Her make-up is subtle and perfect, just like she is. And atop all that, her dark hair is long, thick, and glossy, framing her face with not even a single strand out of place.

She hasn't seen me yet, so I enjoy staring.

My own clothes are so casual and grubby, shredded jeans and trainers with a slouchy, baggy hoodie on top. I rarely dress up unless forced to, but for some reason, I find myself wanting to whenever I see her.

I move off the last step onto the tiled floor and feel a little ripple of cold dance up my body.

Nikolette's head whips towards me, and I realize she has cast something in the area to let her know if anybody is close by. No sneaking up on her, then.

I wave, both to let her know it is me and to flick some of the strange tingling magic out of my body via my fingertips. The sensation doesn't last long, but walking unexpectedly through a ward is often a very physical experience.

She crosses the small space to reach me, and nibbling my bottom lip, I watch her come.

By every Goddess of the moon and under it…she's so beautiful.

"Hi," I whisper.

"Oh, it *is* you. Good."

I glance over my shoulder. "Did someone else cross your ward?"

Nikolette follows my gaze out over the dim room. Her head swivels side to side, and she studies the area coolly before looking back at me. "Someone. I'm not sure who. Thought it was you, but then the presence disappeared."

"Well, I promise it wasn't me. I only just arrived."

"Yes. And you're late," comes the soft response.

I sigh. "Diversion around the memorial march. I had to take the long way."

She walks back to the table.

I dart after her, eager to be with her again, to wrap my arms around her.

"I thought you'd forgotten the time. Again." She tosses her head, making her glossy hair glide back over her slender shoulders. Always makes me wonder what she puts into those gently curling tresses to make them so shiny.

"Not this time." I sigh as the gentle scent of her designer perfume reaches my nostrils. "I wasn't kidding when I said I'd been thinking of you all week. Just let me hold you for a moment?"

Nikolette holds out her hands, but I duck between them and kiss her instead. I allow my lips to touch hers lightly, then more firmly, finally opening my mouth to treat myself to the sweet taste of her. Though she hesitates, it's only for an instant. Then she curls around me, all soft and gentle, hard edges smoothed away by my touch.

Her hand cups the side of my neck, thumb resting lightly on the base of my throat. I mirror the gesture and savour the faint pulse of her heartbeat beneath her skin.

"Our hearts beat as one," I murmur.

"May our goals forever do the same." And at last, she smiles. There it is. Though often strait-laced and serious, Nikolette becomes an entirely different person when she smiles. There is so much light in her, so much good and brightness. It's like staring into the sun, so radiant does she become.

"I've missed you." I whisper the words against her soft, full lips.

In answer she kisses me back, deeper than ever, gripping my hips and yanking me in close until our bodies could be mistaken as one. "When can I take you home?" she growls, nipping my bottom lip.

Another happy shudder ripples through me. Her need is so intense in this moment, I liken it to the billow of heat from an open oven door. If I step too close, I might be burned.

"Soon?" she insists. "Please?"

And of course, I know where she lives. Just as she knows my home. From the outside. But I've never allowed myself to enter.

Maybe it's a sense of propriety, maybe it's just nerves, but the idea of entering *her space* feels like a level of intimacy we've not quite reached.

I take the smallest of steps back. "You just want a chance to tip me over your sofa."

"And then some." She reclaims that step immediately, perhaps not even noticing that she has done so. "I want to tip you over my sofa, or into my bed where I can finally see just how good you are with your hands and tongue." Nikolette's voice is a silky purr.

Heat flushes my face and neck. I swallow down the sudden flood of saliva that fills my mouth. "I do want you." I concentrate on not stuttering. "I just…not yet."

Her left eyebrow lifts into a perfect, delicate arch. "You mean not until I finally let you be open about us?"

I look away. "That's not what I said."

"It's what you meant." She pulls away, and the loss of her lips on mine makes me shiver with sudden cold.

"I'm sorry." Instead of meeting her gaze, I allow my vision to track a mote of dust floating through the air. "I know it's difficult for you but…"

The purr becomes gruff. "But how can I invite you into my personal sanctum when I won't even be honest about what we are to each other?"

I keep my sights pinned firmly to the floor. Maybe if I do that, she won't be able to see how accurate her words really are.

"Tina?" When I refuse to lift my head, she tucks her fingers beneath my chin to do it for me. "Look at me."

I do. With effort.

Her stare is hot and intense, dark eyes slightly hooded as she drinks me in. I can all but *feel* the desire radiating off her.

Why is that so sexy? My body tingles again, not with a spell this time, just the sheer force of her need. This is a different type of *fortis*, more basic and lusty but still very much there and in the air. Her desire for me is a prickle against my arms and throat.

"I know you," she whispers. "I trust you. I want you—so, so badly. You must know that."

"I do, but—"

"Then please understand how delicate my situation is. I need more time to broach it with her."

Frustration hardens my voice. "You're a grown woman. I don't understand why you let her treat you like a child."

"I don't *let* her do anything." Some of the fiery passion leaks from her voice, replaced briefly by something younger, smaller, and meeker. "But I'll always be a child to *Yaya*. That's simply how my family works." She stares deeply into my eyes. "Please, Tina. Please? Just a little more time to bring it to her. Then you can shout about us from every rooftop."

Something about the pleading expression in her eyes melts away my resolve.

Instead of pushing the matter, I kiss her, long and deep, before pulling away. "Sit with me?"

At once she links her hand through mine.

Together we take the stools at the smooth, empty table and talk.

I tell her about my day, my time with Hyacinth, and the mystery gift she promises. Nikolette smiles and enjoys the tale before sharing the highlights of her own day, putting together new cover spreads for the magazine she edits. It's some high-fashion, glossy paged, advertisement heavy thing, but she loves it dearly. And the job suits her well—glamour and beauty, creativity and control, things Nikolette has always desired and excelled in.

Once or twice I've bought her magazine just to marvel at the decisions she made to turn that issue into a roaring, sell-out success. She is incredibly talented.

Outside, the bustle of the city continues without us, the murmur of both *edane* and mundane lives forming a quiet backdrop. The occasional shout or burst of laughter, toot of a car horn, or roar of a motorcycle engine. But it is all distant.

In our small, private space, Nikolette laces her fingers through mine and keeps her body pressed in close.

I long to do this every day, to spend time with her more openly but—

My phone trills in my pocket.

I look the question at her.

Nikolette sighs but gestures for me to answer, which I do after freeing my hands from hers and turning slightly aside.

"Tina Marks?"

"Hey Tae, it's me. I'm really sorry to call so late."

Only one person ever calls me *Tae* and starts their conversation with an apology. I raise a hand at Nikolette to keep her at bay, and answer brightly. "Chloe, are you all right?"

"Yes. Just…the conclave. Where is everybody?"

"You're at the sanctum now?" A sigh flees my lips when she answers in the positive. "It's not for another three days. You're far too early."

My coven sister gives a little gasp of surprise. "Oh no. I'm so sorry. I must have got the date wrong. I didn't realize—"

"There's no need to apologize." Again I raise my hand when Nikolette starts towards me.

But this time she ignores my warning and slides in beside me, curving her arms around my waist and pressing her lips to my free ear. "This is *our* time," she whispers, breath hot against my skin. "Hang up, put aside Willow business, and be *with* me."

I stand and step away, fighting to focus on the call. "Honestly, it's fine. You've done nothing wrong."

"But I'm not supposed to be here, really, am I?" Chloe's voice is so soft and forlorn I can't find it in me to be impatient with her.

"The sanctum belongs to all of us. You can go there whenever you like. Why not spend a few minutes there and relax before heading home? It would do you good."

Yet again Nikolette approaches me. She presses light, teasing kisses to my cheek and throat, and my insides turn to goo. I can't think with her touching me that way, can barely even breathe as the desire begins to curl through me.

I moan. Can't help it.

At the other end, Chloe stops her babbling.

Uh-oh.

I nudge Nikolette to the side with a light touch on her shoulder and quickly turn my back. "What was that, Chloe?"

An exasperated snort cuts the air behind me, but what else am I supposed to do?

Chloe is one of my Willow Bark sisters and knows nothing about me and Nikolette. I can hardly be expected to keep the secret while my girlfriend is trying to slip her tongue into my ear. Not only that, but Chloe is the youngest of our coven and prone to nerves. She needs near constant reassurance, which means I need to concentrate.

"I'm allowed to just visit the sanctum? Even without a conclave? Tae?"

I suck in a steadying breath. "Of course you are. Why not stay and soak in some moonlight? We're a few days off full, but it should still feel nice."

There's a pause and a rustling noise as if Chloe's moving around a tight space. "There's cloud cover today. Maybe I'll just go home."

To the left of me, Nikolette glares for short seconds before stalking towards the stairs. Her steps are hard and heavy, her back rigid.

"Um, whatever you need, Chloe, do whatever you need. I need to go—"

"But what about the conclave?"

Already several feet away, Nikolette reaches the topmost step.

I bounce on the balls of my feet, frantic to follow. "Just wait," I tell her, rushing now in my haste to be off the line. "Hyacinth will call us like she always does, and we'll meet like we always do. Is that all right? Are you okay? Do you need anything else?"

"I've disturbed you," she whispers, obviously mortified. "I'll go. I mean just—no, I'll go. I'm sorry. Truly, I didn't mean to interrupt your night. I'll go now. Sorry. Bye. I'm sorry."

I want to comfort and reassure her, but she's right. She *did* interrupt me—one of the few nights I have available to give to Nikolette, and now she's stomping away from me. "Bye, Chloe." I hang up and shove the phone into my pocket, scurrying to catch up with my girlfriend. "Nikolette, wait. Please."

She doesn't look at me.

"I'm sorry. I didn't mean to push you but—"

"One hour," she says, without looking back. "That's all I wanted. One hour of your time for myself. But between work, Crone Hyacinth, and those baby witches bothering you every three seconds, we never get time for us."

"I'm sorry—"

"Like usual." She doesn't even pause as she glances at her watch. "I'm heading home. I'm sure you're busy too, so I'll speak to you in a couple of days."

"But when?"

"I don't know. Soon." She spins on her heel and plants the lightest, most chaste of kisses on my lips. "Goodnight, Tina." And she walks down the stairs.

"I…you…let's meet at your house." The words are out before I can snatch them back.

The silence of the abandoned shop stretches between us, almost a physical weight.

Two steps from the bottom Nikolette whirls to face me, her dark eyes huge with wonder. With three long strides she is back in front of me again, her lower lip trembling. "Don't toy with me, Tina. Don't say that unless you mean it."

I can taste my heartbeat. It's filling my throat, my head, until my entire body seems to throb with it. Slowly, I reach for her hand and place it, palm down, on my chest. I want her to feel it.

"The Willow Bark conclave is in a couple of days. When we're done that night, I'll visit you at your home. If…if you'll have me?"

More of that silence stretches long and thin between us. I fear it might snap. That *I* might snap. That my sanity might shatter and go spinning across the building in so many jagged fragments.

Nikolette crushes her lips to mine, gripping my hips so strongly I imagine she has left small bruises. I allow myself to sink into her, wrapping my arms about her neck and letting her warmth seep into me. She tastes so fucking good. And the hot, heated rasp of her breath is loud against my mouth and cheeks.

"I formally invite you, Tina Marks, to my home. I offer you welcome, solace, and succour as well as very hot, very messy, rampant sex."

I can't breathe. My words are stuck. I want to go with her now, to fold myself into her and taste every part of her body.

Nikolette presses her forehead to mine. “Well?”

“I—” Nope. Lick the lips, moisten the tongue, and try again. “I accept your invitation, Nikolette Christie, and I…I…”

She grins.

“I hope that sofa is strong enough to take me.”

“Oh”—her voice drops to the filthiest of purrs—“it damn well better be. Because I doubt we’re going to make it to the bedroom.”

CHAPTER FIVE

The next two days are a blur.

There's no time to speak with Hyacinth, comfort Chloe, or even think about Nikolette—though I do find her appearing in my dreams more than once. Apparently, the promise of finally visiting her home—and experiencing *very hot, very messy, rampant sex*—is playing on my mind.

No, the city is abuzz with an energy I've not felt since the Werewolf Wars, and I can't figure out why. Almost like something that ordinarily keeps a lid on such feelings is missing.

I change into my civilian clothing while resolving to pull a few tarot cards when I get home. They might tell me something, they might not, but Hyacinth has asked more than once that I practise reading them. I agreed, but mainly because it was the only way to escape reading tea leaves.

On the way out, I catch sight of Sergeant Neil Hozier—short, broad, weary, and irritated. No, no...*Detective* Sergeant Hozier now. He's on the phone, and though I don't know who else is on the line, I can tell he's not pleased to be speaking to them.

"How many is that now?" Hozier snaps, clenching his free fist. "Three?" His eyebrows rise. "What, is it a full moon or something? I thought only werewolves responded to that lunar stuff." A pause and then, "Shit. Fine. Send in what you can, and I'll be on it this evening."

I push up on tiptoe, hoping to creep past him before my shift gets extended. Because yes, werewolves respond to the full moon, but so do sprites, goblins, and to a lesser degree vampires. Makes me glad to live in the city home to not only the Clear Blood Foundation, but SPEAR headquarters as well.

I might be a witch, but I'm just as vulnerable to *edanes* affected by the moon as anybody else.

"Is that you, Marks?"

Damn. The jig is up.

I stop and turn to face him. "Yeah, Skip?"

"You done for the night?"

I hold up my gym bag in what I figure is an apologetic gesture. " 'Fraid so. Did you need anything?" I struggle to keep the reluctance from my tone.

"Hmm"—he rubs at the non-existent hair on his chin—"actually, yes. We have another body in town. No ID yet or anything remarkable beyond the fact that they seem to be another unhoused type."

"*Edane*?" This time I try not to make my voice hopeful. SPEAR would handle the case then.

"Human." A rueful smile. "Sorry, Marks, this one is ours. I'll have some paperwork on your desk in the morning—you get started laying up investigation plans."

I sigh. "Come on, Skip, really? I'm a beat officer, not a detective."

"But you *should* be. You're smart, you're quick, and you're talented. I'll never understand why you took a step down when you moved here."

The tiniest fissure of guilt ripples through me. There are a number of reasons I stepped down. Just as there are many reasons I avoided joining an Angbec coven before Hyacinth found me. But he doesn't need to know about that. Nobody does.

"I wanted a fresh start, that's all."

"Well, you can start fresh with the paperwork in the morning. It'll be on your desk."

I sigh. "Fine."

"Make sure you get plenty of sleep." His voice becomes saccharine and sing-song as he walks away, chuckling to himself.

I stick my tongue out at his retreating back.

Fine. Another dead body? I can deal with that…so long as I get a good workout at the gym first.

❖

One. Two. One. Two. One. Two. One. Two.

I count the steps in my head, matching my breathing to the pounding of my feet on the treadmill. There's sweat on my forehead, my ribs, my back, my stomach, but I don't care. One ear is full of the rhythmic tones of early eighties reggae, the other free so I can listen to the beeps from the machine, the low murmur of sound from mounted TV screens, and the gentle chatter of people around me. My nose fills with the scent of dozens upon dozens of hot, sweaty bodies and their various energy drinks or protein shakes. It's an eclectic mix of *people* scents, sounds, and sensations so different from what I might experience with Hyacinth or even with the rest of my coven.

I find it important to come here at least twice a week, three times if I can manage it. Not so much for the exercise, though I do love the feeling of running, the sensation of movement and rhythmic pressure coupled with speed as I increase the pace on the treadmill. Even the clank of heavy weights hitting the mats and the chirpy calls of instructors guiding yoga or Pilates on the other side of the huge space are pleasant to me.

No, mostly I come here to ground myself in the affairs of people, as all witches should. We do have a duty, after all. And since leaving my old home and taking up residence in Angbec, I've tried to find ways to meet that obligation without going back to how things were. I don't need or want that level of responsibility, but I can still help. I can still look out for those who can't protect themselves within and beyond my job as a police officer.

But only if I immerse myself into the lives and habits of mundanes—non-magical, non-fantastical creatures, otherwise known as humans.

Through the one open ear, I hear a pair of young women discuss wedding dresses and high-heeled shoes. One man on the treadmill to my left seems to be in the middle of a business meeting, huffing and puffing while discussing rates of return, investment strategy, and high profile clients. Then another small group behind me, louder than all combined: a cluster of tiny, elderly ladies, cheering each other on as each in turn lifts a half pound free weight.

I tap the *up* button on the treadmill. The belt beneath me gives a shrill whirr, and the gears on the inside of the machine turn all the harder. The incline increases by two degrees, and the speed bumps up to what I consider a minor RPE.

I've had my warm-up, but I'm ready to sweat. I lean forward slightly and run.

Normally I'd run outside, around the sanctum or at least somewhere green, but the air just feels so *wrong* today. Whatever strange happening I felt earlier has chased me even here.

I run with my gazed fixed on a point straight ahead, my arms swinging, back solid and straight, core so firmly engaged I could probably bounce spells off my abs. The impact of each solid foot against the belt sends a shudder through me that I match my breath to.

One-two. One-two. One-two. One-two.

The TV ahead of me brightens, and I spy a green line at the bottom creeping left across the screen, indicating that someone is messing with the volume.

"*...today, as another body was found in the city tonight.*" It's a news programme, the announcer an older woman with a tight, sleek bun and a solemn expression. "*Information is limited at this time, though we understand that local police are treating this death as suspicious.*"

I pull out a single earbud so I can hear more clearly.

The newsreader glances at the papers in front of her and shuffles them importantly before speaking again. "*There is no sign of obvious* edane *involvement, but of course SPEAR agents have also been notified. Our reporter Nati Phillips is on the scene.*"

The image shifts to an exterior that I initially struggle to identify. Moments later I recognize the bare stretch of land where a fire raged more than a year ago and entirely decimated a night club. No one was harmed, but the building was condemned and speedily demolished. Nothing has been built there since, and the land has returned mostly to nature, with shrubs, scrubby grass, and wild flowers springing up in recent months.

Strangely beautiful, all things considered.

But now it's sectioned off with police tape, and I can see several of my fellow officers walking across it one measured step at a time, arranged in a long, even line.

The reporter gazes into the screen. "*Good evening, I'm Nati Phillips, and I'm live in Angbec city centre where an unidentified body was reported to police earlier this evening. Detective Sergeant Neil*

Hozier informs us they are treating this death as suspicious." The camera cuts away from Nati to feature Hozier himself, talking quickly with another uniformed officer.

When he notices the camera, he straightens his tie and seems to debate walking away before reluctantly approaching. He starts speaking before the reporter can.

"*I'd like to reassure all citizens that we are working hard and fast to identify both cause of death and victim. Though the circumstances are unusual, we do not currently suspect foul play.*" He fiddles with his collar. "*The Angbec police request that you remain calm and report anything suspicious in the usual manner. We are also—*"

"*My sources tell me that's three bodies found in the last day and a half, Detective.*" Nati's lips twitch ever so slightly. "*Is that correct?*"

I watch my boss, now cornered, think through his options. "*It's true that two other bodies have been reported to us in the last forty-eight hours, but I repeat, there is no cause for alarm.*"

"*No?*" Nati glances briefly at the camera. "*That's three bodies, Detective. All found in a similar area, in a very narrow space of time. Do you not consider that a pattern?*"

Hozier switches from fiddling with his collar to fingering his tie. He smooths it down with both hands, then tucks the shorter end inside his shirt. Then he pulls it out again and slips it back into the clip that supposedly secures both ends. "*Like I said, we're currently investigating and don't suspect foul play but—*"

The sound of the TV dies.

Several groans and mumbles of complaint spring up throughout the gym.

I look about, searching for the culprit, and spy a frazzled, shabby looking woman with curly red hair, tossing the remote control back behind the reception desk. She wears a T-shirt so long and baggy it might well serve as a dress, and equally generous joggers. She shrugs apologetically at the few folk glaring daggers her way, then returns to her stationary bike.

Pity. It would have been interesting to hear Hozier fumble his way through the rest of this interview. Maybe I *should* have gone with him. Not that I would speak to the press, but I could have offered him moral support.

He and I, though still entirely professional, have become somewhat closer since that ritual I cast for Danika, a SPEAR agent possessed by a parasitic interdimensional monster, to make a long story very short. He had been one of the people standing in the circle, offering his own *fortis* to help me call the Guardians. That makes him one of two people in my professional life who know anything of my ties to the witching world.

Oh well. Too late now.

Ten minutes later I begin the slow descent into my cool-down. The machine whirrs less frantically, and the belt's squeals lessen as my pace eases. I drag my wrist across my forehead to keep the sweat out of my eyes and focus on keeping my footing.

The interview with Hozier has long since finished, and the TV has been switched to a music channel. The latest offering is a loud, bass-heavy hip-hop piece with a video featuring plenty of women in high heels and bikinis. Pleasant enough to look at, despite the problematic nature of it all. One of the women presses her thick thighs together and swings her backside towards the camera. She squats low on glittering heels and rolls her hips with a coquettish look back over her shoulder.

I miss a step on the treadmill.

The belt keeps going, but I don't as I shoot off the end of it into a yelping tangle of limbs on the floor behind.

Snickers from my right. A murmur of concern from my left.

Someone reaches for me, trying to help, but I wave the hand away, too embarrassed to accept assistance.

It's been a long while since a music video, of all things, lit up my libido like a candle.

I lick my lips and think of Nikolette, but it's too late in the day now. Not only that, but I don't want to rush finally getting into her house. Besides, we haven't touched each other like that yet.

I limp back to the machine and slow it further, catching, from the corner of my eye, the red-haired woman watching me from near the doors. Apparently my yelp and fall was loud enough to draw attention from way across the room. She stares at me, checking me over, while I concentrate on climbing back onto the treadmill belt. By the time I get back into place to continue my cool-down, she and her quiet, intense stare have already left.

Chapter Six

When I wake the following morning, the first thing I notice is how much my hips hurt.

I knew the tumble at the gym would have an effect, but I don't enjoy the ache loitering in my right side or the new bruise on my calf. Stupid treadmill.

I fire a quick text to my mentor to let her know I'll be leaving soon. It's still early—barely even eight—but she's likely been up for a while already, waking with the sun like a bird.

I sip from a mug of sugary, creamy coffee while pulling together my clothes in preparation for tutoring and work. I don't need much, but with my plans for the evening ahead, I won't be returning until much later.

The smart speaker I have stashed near my bed clicks to life, and I pause to listen to the jaunty intro of *Wood, Woof, and Wold*, a podcast featuring a sprite, a werewolf, and a goblin. The charismatic trio meet weekly to discuss their favourite movies and how honestly the film industry has handled representations of *edane* life, following both the Supernatural Creatures Act and the Interspecies Relations Act. Both laws changed the country and cinema forever, and though I agree entirely with the rights and privileges they secure, I can't deny that a little part of me still enjoys the old films. Particularly those featuring witches.

I listen absently while sliding small chunks of avocado into my mouth.

The sprite, a loud and boisterous type named Redd, dominates the discussion, claiming that such representations are more problematic now than they were several years ago. "*I know a couple of witches,*" they say with a snort, "*and to say those old representations are awful is an understatement. We need to rip out the Hollywood culture and start all over again.*"

Grayson, a goblin with such a gruff voice he often needs to repeat himself, scoffs. "*And you think if we erased those examples from mundane history the same mistakes wouldn't be repeated? Why do you think humans teach about their petty little war back in the 1940s? It's an attempt to be a constant reminder to ensure they don't do anything else so stupid.*"

"*It doesn't work,*" Redd snaps.

"*But they're trying. And these films are the same. Besides, the wider public needs knowledge, and without educational materials such as these old films, what chance do they have?*"

"*Educational?*"

"*Perhaps you both have a point.*" Uriah, the sweet, timid, and soft-spoken werewolf, falls into the familiar role of peacekeeper. "*More recent representations are obviously more inclusive and honest, but there's no reason we can't learn from what humans thought of us in the past.*"

The podcast pauses for an ad read, and I check my phone again, while still chewing avocado.

No response from Hyacinth. Weird.

I dial her number and press the little device to my ear.

It rings. And rings…and rings.

Finally, her bright voice cuts in but only as a recorded greeting, instructing me to leave a message. I do, before tossing the phone onto the sofa so I can take a shower.

I wash my hair, condition it, and take the time to shave my legs and underarms. After a moment of thought, I put my foot on the side of the bath and reach between my legs to shave more delicate areas. Not strictly necessary, but always more comfortable on the day of a conclave. I don't know if we'll be sky-clad tonight, but if I have to be naked in front of other people, I prefer to look my best.

And I'm going to be seeing Nikolette tonight…

I let the thought fill me with giddy spikes of glee and take great care to leave everything neatly trimmed and tidy. Just in case.

I glance at my phone again once I'm dressed. Still nothing from

Hyacinth, but also nothing from the helpline. Which is good for a number of reasons.

First, that means Hyacinth isn't chasing after me yet. But more importantly, if the helpline is silent, that means there's no frantic stranger on the verge of some terrible emergency.

I appreciate the helpline and the value it offers to the women of the city, but it does, occasionally, prove inconvenient to run.

Wood, Woof, and Wold finishes for another week, and I bring the last few pieces of avocado out to the car with me. I've barely turned on the engine before my phone blurps with a loud, shrill note, rather like a strangled foghorn.

It makes me jump—not just the volume, but the fact that it's ringing with that sound at all.

I turn off the engine, dump the keys on the dashboard, and lift the mobile to my ear.

"Good morning, sister, you've reached the Comfort in Distress helpline. My name is Tina, and I'm here to help you."

A ragged gasp floats down the line followed by quick, shallow breathing. "Really? You can help me?" The voice is feminine, as far as I can tell, and pinched in a way that suggests panic. "I didn't know who else to call. My boss told me about this line—I didn't think it was real, but then I felt this horrible sensation all the way through my body, and I couldn't move at all. It took me an hour just to get to my phone. Am I going to die? Am I dead?"

"All right, it's okay, just breathe it out." I hold up my hand, even though she can't see me. "You're talking to me, so you're clearly not dead. I need you to take three deep breaths for me, can you do that?"

"Breathe?"

"Yes. Follow the sound of my voice and match your breathing to the rhythm of my words. We need to get you calm, or else you might hurt yourself. Now, slowly, with me, breathe in through your nose." I demonstrate loudly into the phone, relieved to hear the frantic woman follow me. "Good. Very good, and then out again. Nice and slow through your mouth, okay?"

She does, and the sounds of her gasps become a little softer. "I can do that, I can do that."

"Good. Then again. You're doing so well. In through your nose… hold for a brief second…then out through your mouth."

Again she obeys, and I take the opportunity to sneak a glance at the clock on my dashboard.

Damn. Murphy's Law indeed.

I concentrate on the call. "I want you to do that a few more times, and then, when you're ready, you can tell me what you need."

"You really can help me?" The gasps become pathetic little sniffles.

"I'm a witch of the Willow Bark coven. I'm here to do exactly that. Don't worry. I'll protect you."

The stranger bursts into tears.

❖

"Becca, I'm so proud of you. Do you understand? Not many people can go through what you've experienced and come out the other side as strong as you are. You're incredible."

Still sniffling, but no longer sobbing, my most recent client of the Comfort in Distress helpline chuckles softly. "You're just saying that."

I glance at my wall clock for the third time in as many minutes and feel a twinge of sadness tickle through me. I'm not going to make it to Hyacinth after all. I didn't even make it off my street.

"No, I'm proud of you and you should be too. Remember, it's no small thing to reach out the way you have today."

As soon as I'd got Becca talking, I'd left my car to return to the house. I'd set my smart speaker to play calm, soothing music and attached my Bluetooth headset to my phone. Then I'd sat down to listen.

And Becca talked. And talked. And *talked.*

She told me about the strange sensations filling her body for the past week, feelings like bubbles or fizzing or trickling. She explained the fights with her parents over university choices and her desire to leave home. She shared how the last shouting match ended with picture frames leaping off the walls as though hurled by invisible hands. And she ended with how that strange feeling in her body burst forth from her skin in waves of magic that put holes and dents in the walls of the family home.

Despite my initial reluctance, I'm glad she chose to call the helpline. New witches, especially young ones with no guidance within their families, sometimes discover their gifts with *fortis* incredibly late, usually in times of great stress. And the thought of any young woman going through all that without help or comfort is enough to bring tears to my eyes.

Makes me glad I chose not to give this shift to Edith.

"Thank you, Tina. I don't know what I would have done if you hadn't picked up the phone."

I smile. "My sisters and I run this helpline in shifts. If it wasn't me, it would have been one of them, but one of us will always, always be there. Now, do you remember what you need to do next?"

"Stay in a quiet space. Settle my mind. Remember my chants. Then go talk to my parents."

"Perfect. And…?"

"Oh, remember that there will always be a sister on the other end of the line." She pauses. "You…are you really all sisters? All those women you talked about?"

"Not by blood, but the connection among witches is so strong we liken it to siblings. We're all connected. We all love each other. We all help each other. We're family."

"Do you think we'll get to meet one day?"

I hesitate. My desire to help this girl is strong, of course it is, but I don't want to lead her down a path she's not yet ready to handle. "If the Goddess wishes it."

Some rustling down the line, as though she's shifting her position. "There's a Goddess too? Wow."

"Sure is. And when you're ready, maybe we can teach you. But for now, you need to handle your family. Are you ready?"

Becca takes a deep breath and releases it slowly. "Yes. I am. Thank you so much, Tina. You're incredible. I wish you really were my sister."

"You're going to do just fine. Remember, I believe in you. And I won't end our call—that's for you to do when you're sure you're ready."

"Okay." More rustling, then the creak of a door opening. "Okay. I can do this. I've got this. Here I go." Another deep breath and slow exhale. "Bye, Tina."

"Goodbye, Becca."

She hangs up.

I pull the Bluetooth headset off my hair and flop back onto the sofa with another glance at the clock.

Well, so much for meeting Hyacinth. Even if I drove there now, I'd have to leave her house immediately just to be ten minutes late to my shift.

I call her.

Once more it rings out before sending me to her voicemail inbox.

"Why did you have to mention Murphy's Law? As soon as I got into the car I had to handle a call on the helpline. Poor girl was frantic, and I just couldn't leave her. She talked for hours. Anyway, I'm sorry I missed you. I know you had a gift for me, but maybe I can take it at the conclave instead? I'll get there early, how's that? Then we'll have time for a chat before the others arrive. Again, I'm sorry, but I promise, I'll make it up to you. See you tonight."

"What a day." I heave another sigh and stare again at the neatly typed page in my hand. "Stefan Hood. Penny Randall. Kenneth Zamiri. Sean McLachlan. Morton Bluett. Dallas Goldingham." So many of them. How can there be so many? Brothers, mothers, daughters, cousins, sisters, fathers…All of them missing or dead. Or both.

I've been here for hours cross-referencing the three latest dead bodies with the missing persons backlog, looking for a match. Nothing so far and there are still several more pages to get through. Not the most exciting way to spend a shift, that's for sure.

I need a coffee. Or an energy drink. Anything to wake me up and make it easier to stare at all these gleaming white pages covered in tiny black text and—

"Marks? Damn it, woman, get your head out of the clouds and answer me."

I sit up hard, and multiple stacks of paper slip to the ground. Crime scene reports, evidence trails, and witness accounts slide together into a pool of administrative pain and suffering.

"What? Huh? What?"

"You didn't hear a word of that, did you?" Looming beside my desk like a winter storm is Hozier, and he looks more fatigued than he did last night. I wonder if he got any sleep after that awkward interview.

More paper hits the ground as I scramble to my feet. "Sorry, Skip, I was just…"

He eyes me suspiciously. "You were away with the faeries. I've been calling for ages." His eyes suddenly widen. "Wait, is it okay to say that?"

"Huh?"

"Faeries." He leans in slightly and drops his voice. "That's not an insult or anything, is it?"

I roll my eyes. "Skip…"

"Sorry, sorry. I just like to be respectful. Anyway, was I wrong?"

No. And I can't deny it, so I don't try. Instead, I focus on straightening my uniform, noting with sudden confusion that one of my epaulettes is missing. There's no sign of it on the ground, my desk, or even my chair, and as I scan the area, I feel Hozier's gaze grow more intense on me.

A sigh. "You'd forget your head if it wasn't screwed on," he murmurs. "It's over there."

I follow his finger towards the desk housing the printer, scanner, and stacks of fresh paper. There, on the top of the printer, is the missing adornment, complete with number and button hanging loose.

"Sorry, Skipper. I think there's a sewing kit somewhere around here. I can—"

He raises a hand. "Fix it later. I was asking what you're still doing here."

I hope my gaze is as quizzical as I think it is. "Working?" I gesture to the mess on the floor. "I thought you wanted me to find potential links between the bodies and the never-ending list of missing persons."

"I do. And you will *if* there's a link to find. But you won't find anybody if you don't get some rest. You do realize what time it is?"

A shrug. "Six thirty?"

Hozier stares, his lips slightly parted. "Try nine fifteen."

Oh. Oh no, no, no.

I rub my face with both hands, dragging on my face as I realize what I've managed to do. This morning's hotline call has really thrown off my day. Yet again, I've blown off Hyacinth, and now I'm adding my coven to that list, as well as—

"Nikolette." Oh no. Oh no, oh no, oh no. Not today. Today of all days.

I drop to a crouch and start dragging papers together. They're a mess, once neat piles thrust together without care or reason, but they'll have to wait. I should have been at the sanctum more than an hour ago.

"Tina—"

"Sorry. I'll fix it, I swear, but I need to go. I'll sort it in the morning."

"You're not on shift until midday."

"Then I'll come in early." The edge of one of the loose sheets lays open my index finger. I mentally connect that motion to the brief stab of pain only when a bright floret of blood blooms across the otherwise pristine page. I suck the edge of the damaged finger, dump the entire pile on my desk, slam an elastic band around the mess, then tip the stack into the biggest drawer on the left of the desk. Then, with both hands, I scoop the rest of my desk paraphernalia in on top.

Hozier leans back with his arms crossed. "So that's how you keep your desk so tidy. Do you do this sweep-under-the-rug routine every shift?"

"Shh," I hiss back.

He narrows his eyes at me, but I barely see it as I check my phone. I need to check how much trouble I'm in.

Seven missed calls. Twelve text messages. Two voicemails.

Yup. I'm in trouble.

One of the voice messages is from Nikolette. All the text messages are from her too. The missed calls seem to be from my sisters, though I can't be sure without a proper check. But who else would call that many times in such a short period?

A little lump of distress fills the back of my throat just as a gentle hand settles on my shoulder. I flinch, but it's only Hozier, his eyes wide with concern.

"Take a breath, will you? Whatever it is, take a second first."

"But—"

He shushes me. "Slow down. Breathe. Do you need help at all?"

Of course I do, but this evening is going to be awful enough without a man sticking his nose in.

"No, Skip." I smile brightly, pouring all my effort into appearing soothed. "I've got it. Promise."

No way of knowing if he believes me, but he does release my shoulder. "Set alarms or something, will you? This is the third time in as many weeks I've had to chase you off this desk. We don't pay overtime, you know."

I certainly do know, but thankfully, this job has never been about the pay.

I nod because that's what he seems to want, then dart away from my desk towards the changing rooms. I'm nearly out the door when he calls me again.

"What?" None of the polite sweetness in my voice this time.

Hozier flicks his gaze towards the printer.

Hint taken. I hurry back, grab the fallen epaulette, then dash away before he can say more.

CHAPTER SEVEN

In the changing rooms I stop in front of my locker and heave the door open. My rucksack tumbles out, followed by my civilian clothes and trainers. They all land on my feet, which are safe only because of my thick uniform boots.

I spend a silent moment considering if I should bother changing. Nikolette won't mind—she likes a smart uniform.

Another glance at the phone makes me think better of it. Tonight, perhaps above any other night, my sisters need no reminder of my loyalty to anybody other than them, and I need to visit them first.

My phone lights up. Though silent, it demands my attention by brightly flashing an unrecognized number at me. I jam it between my cheek and shoulder to talk while I change my clothes.

"Tina Ma—"

"Where are you?" The voice cuts over me, hard and irritated. I know it well. Unlike Chloe who is soft and sweet, this is Iris. She's one of the more experienced witches of the coven and old enough to be my grandmother. Nowhere near as gentle and congenial, though. "We've been here for an hour, and I'm cold."

I make my voice as apologetic as I can. It's an effort. This woman irks me. "On the way, promise. Just tell Hyacinth that I—"

"She's not here."

I pause, one foot half raised. "What?"

"She's. Not. Here. We're waiting here like fools, and she won't answer her phone."

A tiny pulse of cold washes over my skin.

I switch the call to speaker, then scroll more carefully through my messages and missed calls. Plenty from my coven sisters. More from Nikolette. Nothing from Hyacinth.

"Have you called her?" I fit my trainers before realizing I have them jumbled left and right. For Goddess's sake.

"I *told* you, we've tried, but there's no answer. I was going to send one of the others to check, but you're the only one who knows where she lives. Where is she?"

I swallow past the little lump forming at the back of my throat. "I don't know."

"Great. Just great. How are we ever going to get this done? Are *you* coming?"

"Of course, but I can't stay long—"

Iris splutters. "What do you mean, *you can't stay*? We've got stuff to do."

And *I've* got a date. But I can't tell her that, so I mumble some sounds that I hope convey urgency and regret.

My phone buzzes against my cheek as a second call tries to interrupt. When I look, I spot the name *Nikolette Mob* blinking at me.

I wince. "Gimme a second." I cut off her disgruntled cry and tap the screen to switch between calls. "Nikolette? I'm so sorry, I'm coming, I—"

"I suppose you got wrapped up at work again?" The words are a question, but her tone is not. Her voice is soft and deep, smooth and delicious, just like the rest of her. But with all of that is the tiniest edge of frustration. Just like in the gaming store.

"I'm so sorry. I won't be long."

Nikolette sighs. "And the Willow Barks? I thought today was your conclave."

"Yes, them first, but then—"

"Tina…I thought today was the day. I thought you were finally coming here."

"I am—"

"But your coven comes first. I understand."

Finally, I get both trainers on and bound to my feet. "That's not what I said."

"No, but it *is* true. I just hoped that…" She clears her throat. "Don't worry about it. I know what responsibility is about. Do what you need to do."

"Nikolette—"

But she's already gone.

"Fuck."

The phone directs immediately back to my coven sister. "Did you just put me on hold? What are you playing at? Do you understand how important tonight is?"

I fight to keep my tone light. "Iris, I need you to go ahead without me."

Long, heavy silence fills the phone line.

"Hello? Iris?"

"Pathetic," she whispers. "What could be more important than this, the future of our coven? Goddess only knows what Hyacinth sees in you. I'll never understand why she chose you for special treatment."

I swallow hard to moisten my suddenly dry lips. "I'm sorry, I—"

"Forget it. I'm more than capable of handling this without you. Though if you *do* see Hyacinth, maybe let her know we're waiting for her." She hangs up too.

CHAPTER EIGHT

The car journey feels years longer than it truly is. I use the time to think, plan, and attempt to make a choice, while silently pining for a marked police car with the flashing blue lights. Not that roads are busy at this time of day, but drivers are more inclined to make way for an officer of the law.

I leave the station behind and make my way towards Mendyke in the east. Then, after two streets, I turn back on myself and direct the car towards Cipla instead. A mere mile later I stop and pull over to the road's edge, mindless of the double yellows insisting I shouldn't.

What do I do? Which way should I go? To whom? And where is Hyacinth?

She has been mysteriously absent for the entire day, having neglected all my messages and texts. I don't remember her mentioning a meet out of the city or anything that would make her unreachable. In fact, she should be furious by now since I've missed our morning meeting, my proposed pre-conclave meet, and now I'm late for the conclave. I'm surprised she hasn't called me herself.

Ahead, the road forms a fork, the left side continuing into Cipla while the other angles back towards Mendyke.

Then the loud blast from a horn behind draws my gaze to the rear-view.

A lorry. A big one, wide enough that, even hugging the curb, I've blocked the road too much to allow passage. I can see the driver waving at me, no doubt swearing.

Slowly, I put the car in gear, depress the handbrake, and roll forward, hoping I've made the right choice.

❖

Mendyke is a beautiful area. The houses are tall and wide with extensive rear gardens and fancy front drives, often filled with trees. Some of them even have willows.

It's quiet and peaceful as I drive through, so much so that it would be easy to forget the amount of power behind each closed door.

Though there aren't many, I know some werewolves live in this area, as well as many aged vampires. Apparently the hustle and bustle of central and western Angbec is too much for the older ones.

My route takes me towards the rear of the district where a large river forms a wide loop before cutting out of the city and into the countryside. It is a gorgeous natural feature, made still more beautiful by its history.

Earth science was never a subject I studied much, but I know enough to recognize that the flow of the river has been strong enough over the years to create the feature I'm aiming for: a curved pond, entirely cut off by the main river, surrounded by a mix of young and old willow trees. An oxbow lake, I think it's called.

It's public land, but not many people go there beyond the brave souls who occasionally walk their dogs. Maybe the area has a reputation. Or maybe the magic we use to keep away nosy civilians is simply doing an excellent job. There are several spots like this all over the city, some unofficial and slightly frowned-on, but most are well-known and formal, buildings or spaces filled with wards to discourage prying mundane eyes, similar to the one Nikolette and I used in the abandoned gaming shop.

I park more haphazardly than I would at any other time and leap out of the car. Several steps away, I remember to lock the vehicle, then duck down the narrow path between two homes.

The passage leads into a large field, over a short bridge that crosses one snaking path of the main river, then onward towards the sparkling glistening in the foliage that I know marks the crescent-shaped pool of water.

Voices. Low ones. Angry ones. Bored ones.

I dart towards the trees, push through the hanging curtain of willow branches, and feel my heart sink. Our coven may be small, but there are certainly more than two of us. Unfortunately only two have chosen to remain.

One of those is Iris, utterly naked and spinning on her heel to glare daggers at me. "And look who has finally deigned to grace us with her presence."

"I'm sorry—"

"The others left. We have lives too, Tina."

"I know, I know. I thought Hyacinth would be here."

She raises an exasperated hand. "So did we. She's your *mentor*, where the hell is she?"

The resentful stress on the word *mentor* forms an almost visible miasma of green jealousy around her body.

"I don't know."

Iris grumbles under her breath. And then, "Isn't she the one who called for this vote in the first place? You'd think she'd be here to see it through. Though what we want clearly doesn't matter."

I step forward. "Come on, Iris. Anything and everything Hyacinth does is to protect us. You know that."

"From what?" She spreads her hands in a confused gesture. "For weeks she's talked about *danger* this and *uncertainty* that but now we have the chance to *do* something about it, she can't be here? We already know what we want. If she doesn't want to lead us through that, then maybe it's time for a new Mother."

"Give it a fucking rest, Iris." Kiara speaks up, younger and abrasive, the second of the pair standing before me. She too is naked and stands with one hand planted on her outthrust hip. "You're not Mother, so get over yourself and focus. We're too small to exist alone. We *need* to join another coven. Ever heard of safety in numbers?"

"Have *you* ever heard of identity and preservation? Any other coven we joined would swallow us whole and leave nothing left of what we are."

I grind my fingertips into my eyes. I'm so very sick of this debate, largely because both sides have valid points, and we've been talking in circles for weeks.

Is our safety worth potentially losing decades of history and tradition?

Is preservation of our past worth risking ourselves?

I wish I had the answers.

I raise my hands to make myself mediator. "Did you at least discuss which coven we might join?"

Iris rolls her eyes. "Choosing between the weakling Acorns, the fanatical Elms, the eccentric Chestnuts, and none of the above isn't much of a choice."

Several seconds pass before I realize I've cast my gaze downward at the mention of the Elm Stems. They *are* a powerful coven, but vastly different to us.

I try not to think of Nikolette.

"Fine." I brighten my tone. "That's progress. How about I find Hyacinth, put the options to her, then we cast a vote on those four?"

They exchange frustrated looks. "That's what today was supposed to be," says Kiara. "And with you sitting on the fence and Hyacinth abstaining, we're at an even split."

I stand a little straighter. "She's not voting at all?"

"Not last I heard. She wants us to decide for ourselves."

But…if she's not voting, that means my sisters are waiting for *me* to break the tie.

The very thought makes my skin crawl. I'd rather crawl into a hole and never see daylight again than make a decision like that.

I give myself a little shake. "Then go home. We can't do anything now."

"Of course we can." Kiara stares at me. "Chloe and I want to merge. We already talked about it. A merge is clearly the best way to protect ourselves and—if it's so important—it means we have other sisters to teach the way of the Willow Barks."

Iris rolls her eyes. "No. If we join a larger coven we'll be assimilated and lost. Edith and I would much prefer that we go our own way as we always have. If we're so worried about numbers, perhaps *we* should recruit sisters to *us*. Tina, I refuse to believe you're so naive that you can't see the sense in that."

I back off, both hands raised. "Without Hyacinth here we shouldn't be voting on anything. Please, just go home."

They share another exasperated look, but miraculously they don't argue. Instead, they give the smallest gesture of obeisance to the sanctum by touching their fingertips to their foreheads, then turn to grab their clothes. Edith takes her time putting her underwear back on, then wriggling into a long floral dress.

Kiara simply steps into a loose pair of bib overalls and pulls the straps up over her bare shoulders. She doesn't even bother with shoes. "Goodnight, Tina."

The air buzzes with the tension set to snap like an overstretched hair elastic.

I wave sheepishly at her retreating back. "See you round."

Iris slides her feet into a pair of black loafers, then glances over her shoulder. "May the Goddess guide and protect you."

"And the Goddess fill your nights with life."

Then they're both gone.

My knees give a little wobble, so I allow myself to sink into the soft, lush grass. The scents of crushed clover and wild garlic spring up around me, and I dig my fingers deep into the varied hues of green. My heart is fluttering faster than I'd like as I sit beneath the quiet of the trees to let my pulse settle.

The wind sings through the long, drooping branches of the willows we are named for, and soft white flecks of catkin fluff drift down around me.

It makes sense that Iris is so riled up at this debate. She is powerful and old, maybe even older than Hyacinth, with a family full of well-known witches. Very likely she is the matriarch of her own family and has never had to deal with political obstacles before.

Then there's me, right in her path, a relative newcomer, with no witching family and no history. Not only that, but I've somehow caught the eye of our coven Mother and been swept into her powerful arms to learn hints, tips, and tricks any other witch would perhaps give up her book of shadows to learn.

So I do understand her vague animosity towards me. That doesn't make it easier to deal with, though, and without the buffer of Hyacinth close by, it was stronger today than usual.

Hyacinth. My mind drifts to her kindly face, soft voice, and gentle hands.

Where *is* she?

I should stop by her house. It would only take a couple of minutes, and then I could—

A little chirrup from my phone brings my mind back to the present.

A message from Nikolette. Uh-oh.

I take my feet slowly, brushing leaves and dust off my legs.

A tickle against the back of my wrist draws my gaze, and I can't help but shriek at the sight of a spider crawling down my arm.

"Ew, ew, no, ew, get off, get off!"

I dance around, waving my hand about, slapping at my wrist. I must look like a right fool, but I don't care. Sure, we are tasked to do no harm to any, including Gaia's smallest creatures, but spiders can get well and truly fucked.

My mad flailing sends it sailing off into the darkness, and all the peace and calm I managed to gather to myself is gone.

Never mind. At least I can settle one concern by visiting Hyacinth.

I leave the quiet meeting place behind, still brushing down my clothing in case any other creepy-crawlies have decided to hitch a ride.

Chapter Nine

Back in the car, I give myself another pat-down. Nothing. Just a few more pieces of catkin clinging to the tight curls of my Afro.

Good.

And not only that, but I've mentally planned my roundabout route to Nikolette's house. I'm not worried exactly, but after the tension of that conclave meeting, the last thing I want—or need—is for my coven sisters to see me visiting an Elm Stem. If I have to drive a few miles out of the way to arrive unseen, I'm willing to do that.

Hyacinth will just have to wait.

En route, I also practise how best to apologize.

I arrive at Nikolette's grand, expensive tower block after a quiet twenty minutes of driving. There aren't many spaces, but I squeeze the car into the last, probably too small, gap and ring the buzzer for her apartment.

The building towers over me, most of the windows dark except for the line of smaller ones marking the interior stairwell.

The intercom crackles. "What?"

I chuckle and decide to believe it isn't a nervous reflex. "I'm here, Nikolette."

"Where is your key?"

For a second I have no idea what she's talking about. Then, at the back of my mind, a memory kicks in: a hopeful and playful Nikolette pressing her door keys into my startled hands. *Just in case you want to surprise me one day*, she'd said.

"I…left it at home."

Silence. Then a soft click and a whirring sound as she unlocks the door from her place on the third floor.

I slip through and head straight for the stairs. The lift is better than most, bright and spacious, with soft music and a playful *ding* on every floor, but I don't like cramming myself into a moving box. Besides, three floors isn't far, and the quick burst of cardio is a good way to distract from the sense of panic creeping up my spine.

Nikolette sounded furious.

I feel her wards before I reach her door, which I note is ajar. This ward is simple, structured like the one she cast in the gaming shop, so there's no hiding my arrival.

In the open door sits a large Maine Coon, fluffy and stiff. I pause, and the huge feline considers me closely, eyes narrowed.

"Um, hi?"

Nothing. Not a hiss, mew, or chitter, just a cold, narrowed stare, ears turned slightly back, tail tip flicking.

I wave nervously, wondering if I'm being assessed and measured before entry. "You must be Nikolette's familiar, right? Hi. I'm Tina, and I—"

The cat hisses.

Right. I'm in bigger trouble than I thought.

And then, "Princess, stop it. Of all the people I need protecting from, you can bet Tina isn't one of them." Nikolette's voice floats through the open door. Her words are tight and clipped, sharp enough that I flinch without meaning to.

I position myself on the side of the hinges, then press my hand flat to the door. It opens slowly, grudgingly, making a space wide enough for me to eventually hop in over the cat.

Still, Princess doesn't move.

Bloody thing. Worse than Loki, and that little diva barely tolerates me.

At once, the scent of oud oil laps against my senses, and I wish I had taken the time to pack some sandalwood or lavender.

I shove the door shut behind me, noting with no small measure of satisfaction that it has lightly bumped Princess across the threshold and left her trapped outside. Good. As a familiar, I'm sure she's great—as my girlfriend's pet, I know damn well when I'm not wanted.

I toe off my trainers and socks and leave both pairs heaped near the mat, bypassing what looks like the bathroom and two bedrooms on the left and right of the corridor respectively. There's no visual sign of Nikolette, but I can feel her.

Gloom greets me through the last door which appears to be the sitting room. It's not a murky gloom, just the relative dim of a room lit by too few candles. I see them on a wide table, with place settings for two. They're tall, yellow tapers, listing dismally sideways in a pool of their own melted wax. In the chair behind them, hands steepled beneath her chin, is Nikolette.

Her hair is pristine, soft, sleek, and glistening in the flickering light. Piled high off her neck into an elaborate coil at the top of her head, only a few wispy—but clearly intentional—tendrils curl free. Her dress is green, olive green I bet, because I know damn well how perfectly that colour suits her skin tone. It's cut low in the neck and high at the thigh, showcasing one slender leg peeping through the split that reaches her hip. No shoes, though, those are slung carelessly beneath the coffee table, forlorn and forgotten.

With effort I put aside thoughts of my own mucky outfit, probably spotted with blood from my paper-cut finger.

She looks at me, at last. And my breath catches in my throat.

So, so beautiful. And so, so pissed.

"Hi." I wave a hand awkwardly. "You look amazing."

"I looked even better three hours ago. What happened?"

I gaze at the floor. Why? How can she make me feel as tiny and naughty as a schoolchild turning up to class with the *My dog ate my homework* excuse?

"Missing persons." My tongue feels thick in my mouth, as if even my body recognizes this is a daft excuse. "Still missing from Vixen snatching people off the streets. And then the dead bodies. Three in two days. We're catching up."

She exhales deeply, somehow more elegant and beautiful than before. "Fucking vampires." Her words are a soft hiss. "And what good are SPEARs if they can't keep a few bloodsuckers under control?"

"I don't think it's vampires. And the victims are all human, so we can't pass them on to SPEAR anyway. These deaths fall under the jurisdiction of the Angbec police—"

Nikolette stands. The motion is graceful and smooth, but sharp enough that it cuts me right off. "I. Don't. Care. I'm tired. I'm so, so tired, and I just wanted to hear what you came up with before I went to bed. If that's the best you've got, we're done. Goodnight."

She sweeps away from the table, her dress forming ripples on the ground as she goes.

"Wait." I move to slip in front of her. "Please wait. I'm really sorry."

"Of course you are, you're always sorry. But that doesn't change anything. I'm tired, Tina. I'm so tired of wanting you so badly and never getting to have you."

I hang my head.

"We had plans." She gestures to the dress. "Plans *you* suggested. You agreed to come here and be with me. *You* did that. That was *your* idea. And you couldn't even show up. If you got cold feet, all you had to do was say so."

I hold my ground in front of her. "That's not it. I just got wrapped up at work. I'm not denying I'm a shitty keeper of time and I should have done better, but don't you think we should talk before going to bed angry?"

Her eyes widen ever so slightly. "You can go to bed angry. I'm not. I'm going to bed tired, fed up, and alone." A note of ice enters her tone, no doubt in response to my little gasp of surprise. "If you can't be here on time, why should I let you stay the night? You couldn't even remember your key. I suppose it's on some shelf somewhere in your shit tip of a house."

"But we always spend extra time together after a date night."

"We haven't had a date night," she snaps back. "And I've spent more time cuddling Princess than I have with you over the past few months. A quick snog and a fumble in that horrible, closed shop don't count."

As if to emphasize the point, a soft *flumpth* sounds from somewhere behind me. Then, tail up, steps light and dainty, Princess saunters into the room. She throws me a filthy look, then darts up and into Nikolette's arms.

I eye the cat. Then my girlfriend. How did she get back in? We're on the third floor.

"The last few months have been awful. I know that. But it isn't my fault. You know what it's been like at work and—"

"I'm not talking about the police. Or the missing persons, or the vampires, or the werewolves, or that insane ritual you pulled last year.

You realize the air is still thick with whatever you called down that day?"

My inner defences slam to attention. I can't help it. And after the pride and wonder Hyacinth has repeatedly expressed at my exploits, this response stings all the more.

"I didn't call down anything. I *contained* it. Besides, would you have left a SPEAR agent to die?"

She sniffs. "You might have your little fangirl crush, but my tastes run far more refined. From what I hear, that agent is arrogant, undisciplined, and entirely overrated. And they fired her, so she can't be that important."

"She quit."

"That's worse," she fires back. "Anyway, SPEARs are more than capable of looking after themselves, and they certainly wouldn't kill one of their own. You're so gullible."

"It was dangerous."

Nikolette tosses her head. "So? That's their job. They're more than fairly compensated for it. They shouldn't need us to step in and wave a magic wand over it all. But you did it. You ran to them like a good little puppy." She lifts her hand against my attempt to speak. "*And* I seem to recall you wanted to keep your witch life separate from police work. How many people know about you now?"

My head aches. I press my fingertips to my temples, but that does nothing but make my skin tingle. "It's fine. Hozier is a good person. He won't give me away."

"And the SPEAR agent? The vampire she hangs out with? And every other member of that unit? And a goblin if I remember right? Trust you to inadvertently owe a goblin a favour—you'd better hope *that* won't come back to haunt you."

"It won't."

"You can't know that. It's a risk." Nikolette lowers her arms and lets Princess slide to the floor. When she faces me again, her eyes blaze with an undercurrent of fury. "One that jeopardizes you as well as me."

"It has nothing to do with you."

The air in the room seems to become colder. Thicker. I couldn't put my finger on exactly what, but suddenly it's hard to breathe. Each breath I draw in is like fighting against an atmosphere that's too thick to be inhaled.

"Everything you do reflects on me. We're dating. How soon before I end up on the police force radar? Or before someone learns about us?"

I sigh. "You're worrying over nothing, I promise you. Hyacinth already knows, and nothing bad has come of that."

"You told her?" Her voice rises several octaves. "After everything I've said, after you agreed to give me time…How could you?" The hurt in her voice is far worse than the anger.

At last I manage to look her in the eyes again. "No. I would never. You asked me to do something, and I agreed. I haven't told a soul."

"Then how does the High Crone know?"

I give a helpless shrug.

Hyacinth is insightful and intuitive. The reality is that sometimes she just *knows* things. But I doubt that will satisfy Nikolette.

She crosses her arms. "And how does she feel about you bedding down with the enemy?"

"For Goddess's sake, Nikolette, please." I rub my hands across my eyes and, again, open my mouth to say the same thing I have several times in the past. "I'm a Willow Bark and you're an Elm Stem, but we're *not* enemies. We never have been. Our covens are just…different."

Nikolette stares at me. Her eyes brim with an emotion I can't quite place, but it makes her mouth draw thin and her nostrils flare. "Different? Interesting. I'm sure I've heard some other words in the past."

"Not from me."

"No. But your sisters? I know what they think of me." She grits her teeth. "Aggressive. Dangerous. Arrogant. Bigoted."

I hurry over to her, try to take her hands into mine. She resists, but I reach out again, finally snagging her fingers to cup them to my chest. "No. That's not true. Please, that's not what I think of you at all."

"Do you know why I've insisted we keep quiet about us?"

"I thought I did. Until you asked like that."

Nikolette stares at our interlinked fingers. "All my life I've known what I was growing up to be. If not Mother of the Elm Stems, then certainly Mother of another coven. Every witch in my family has done that for generations. We are taught, from early on, that nothing must get in the way of our final goal because that's what we're supposed to do."

"I know all that, but—"

"But you don't *understand*." Her voice hardens. "I'm fighting, constantly, against everyone on *every* side. You think I don't know what other covens think of the Elm Stems after the failed vampire coup? Of course I do. But I also know that the pride of my family won't settle for anything less than perfection." Her voice cracks. "*Yaya* won't settle for anything else than perfection. And as far as she's concerned, the praxis and traditions *she* upholds are the only ones that matter. You would rank so far beneath her that you'd basically be human."

Her words only reaffirm that I never want to meet her grandmother if I can help it.

Aloud I murmur, "But we *are* human."

Again, that odd twist in her lip. "Are we?"

I stare at her. "We have a connection to the Goddess and a powerful handle on our *fortis*, but we're still human, Nikolette. We're not...better than them."

She looks away.

I step around her body, trying to catch her eye. "Nikolette, we're not *superior* to mundane humans, we're just different."

"Different. Fond of that word, aren't you?"

I ignore the razor blade of sarcasm. "Being different doesn't elevate us. We walk among humans, we live as them and with them. We help them. That superior attitude has historically led down a dark, dark road."

Quickly she backs off several steps to bend and pet Princess. "Fine," she mutters. "Whatever."

Something inside me runs a little cold. Of all the beliefs the Elm Stems hold, I thought *that* was one we both agreed was nonsense. After all, the attitude of us and them, weaker and stronger, superior and inferior is how some of the most horrific events of human history came to pass.

No. Not tonight. We have enough on our plates.

"Fine." I raise my hands, palms out. "Forget all that. How do we salvage the remains of our date?"

"We can't. It's late, we both have work in the morning, and I'm not in the mood to babysit you right now."

"Excuse me?"

Nikolette straightens. "Come on, Tina. Tonight is another example of you struggling to keep up with even the most basic aspects of adulting. You forget meetings, you can't be anywhere on time."

"I—" The words stick in my throat. "You can't—" I swallow hard and fight to control the heat rising up the back of my neck. Not today. Not now. "I'm sorry."

"You're always sorry. But that doesn't change anything, does it? I'm constantly calling you to keep you on track, prompting you to make even the most basic of decisions. It's like taking care of a child, and frankly, I need a break."

That heat billows up and morphs into a torrent of words I have no hope of keeping back. "That so? Well, *I'm* sick of scrambling to keep up with your mood swings, and hot–cold attitude. You want me, but you can't tell anyone. You invite me to your home, but I'll never meet your family. Are you honestly so whipped by your grandmother that you can't be seen slumming with the riff-raff? Am I such a risk to your future prospects?"

The second the words are out, I want them back. That angry heat, now expired, vanishes into nothing, and I slap both hands against my mouth. But the damage is already done.

There is a glint in Nikolette's eyes that I've never seen before, a curious sort of sharpness that would no doubt lacerate if it was made tangible.

"Ambition isn't a dirty word, Tina. Striving to move forward, to improve, to evolve—these aren't bad things. They're what we are supposed to do. Or would you prefer we all do as *you* do? Stumble through each day like a baby, wasting the opportunities just dropped onto the silver platter at your feet?"

I struggle to catch another breath. It's too hard, and I back away from her slowly until the backs of my knees hit the edge of her sofa. I lower myself into it, letting the soft cushions hold and support me. "Okay, maybe we should both calm down—"

But she can't seem to stop. "How many witches can claim one-to-one training from the High Crone? Do you have any idea how much more powerful you could become?"

"I don't want power."

"But you *do* have it. It's right there, in you, waiting to be used, and you're wasting it."

I look down at my bare feet on the pristine hardwood floor. Even the fluffy rug slightly off to the right looks perfect and barely touched, as if there for show rather than to be used.

"Why are you saying this?" I can't look at her. I can't look at anything. I keep my gaze pinned to my feet, my toes, the tiny textured indents where a hole in my sock pressed tight against my skin before I removed it. "I…we…" I suck in a deep breath. Hold it. Release. "Fine." Abruptly, I'm on my feet.

Princess hisses as I dart by, but I don't care. I'm heading back to the door.

"Fine." I'm shoving my trainers back on. No socks, I simply grab those and stuff them into my pocket.

From behind, I can hear Nikolette's soft footsteps, then the pause as she stops in the doorway.

"Fine." I say it again, largely because I don't know what else to say. What *can* I say?

I retrieve my coat and bag and sling them over my shoulder as one before yanking on the door handle. "Fine."

The door doesn't budge.

A faint prickle, like the brush of coarse, dead grass against my skin. A spell.

"Open the door," I whisper.

Nikolette chuckles. "So, ready to leave? I thought you wanted to talk*?*"

"Open," I snap. Not at Nikolette, but at the door. "Now."

The prickling sensation intensifies into a full body tingle, then dies out like a lit candle wick shoved down into its own melted wax.

The door blasts open in front of me, hard enough to slam into the wall.

Princess hisses and raises a paw to me, but I pin her with a glare of my own. "Don't even think about it," I tell the furious cat.

She steps away, but not without another violent hiss.

I look back at Nikolette. I want to say something, anything, but the words are all tied up at the back of my throat. Instead, I shake my head at her and dart out of the flat.

She doesn't follow.

CHAPTER TEN

I barely acknowledge the drive home. One moment I'm stomping down the stairs in Nikolette's building, throwing open the door to a dark and rainy street. The next I'm in my own home, swaddled in a Slanket with a packet of chocolate biscuits in one hand. There's something horribly self indulgent about eating the sweet treats straight from the pack, but the same could also be said for a blanket with literal sleeves.

I try not to think too much as I shovel an entire biscuit into my mouth. The sweetness crumbles between my teeth, and I focus on the delicious richness of chocolate, until it stings a filling in my rear right molar.

The bleak, yawning, emptiness of the house rolls over me. It's cold too—since I hadn't intended to be here tonight, I hadn't bothered to turn the heating on. This Slanket is a practical addition to my current outfit as well as a comforting one.

At times like this I almost wish I had taken up Hyacinth's offer of a familiar. Not that I particularly want a pet in the house, but familiars aren't really pets.

A small smirk draws up one corner of my lip when I try to imagine Princess allowing head scritches or belly rubs. That cat would sooner tear out my throat than allow something as domestic as that. Even Loki thinks such contact is beneath her, though she will occasionally allow me to scratch the top of her head with one fingertip.

No, familiars are companions and protectors. They are eyes and ears when a witch may have none, and they are a connection to whatever force it is we draw magic from. Sometimes they are a conduit, other times an aid.

And other times they're simply an *almost* animal in one's home.

No. It might be lonely tonight, but I don't want a familiar.

I risk a glance at my phone.

The screen remains stubbornly blank. No message. No call. No notification from the hotline. Hell, not even a notification of some exciting news article or short video I absolutely *have* to watch. Just nothing. Emptiness. Loneliness.

Ugh. That's enough of that.

I turn on the television.

News. Cartoon. Reality TV. Game show. Another game show. Or is that reality TV again? Or both combined? Hard to know. Local news. World news. Cricket. Tacky daytime soap.

Flicking through the channels is pleasant, even if I don't land on anything worth watching. Somehow, seeing the multiple images flash by over and over is relaxing, soothing in a way I didn't expect. Maybe because channel-surfing matches the rhythm of my mind, flicking back and forth, on and on, to and fro between work, Nikolette, the Willow Barks, dead persons, Hyacinth…it never ends, my mind is awhirl with thoughts I can't make head or tail of.

Hyacinth. I never managed to look for her. Guess it will have to be tomorrow. I'm in no state to head to her house now.

I gobble another biscuit. And another. And another.

My phone bleeps.

Both biscuit packet and remote hit the ground as I dive for the phone. Crumbs rain from my chin and into my bra, but I don't care.

A text message.

The number is one I don't know, the message disappointing.

Tomorrow? 9pm? Confirm.

That must be Iris. Or Edith? I really should save their numbers.

Grudgingly I tap out a response.

Yeah, 9pm is fine. Will find Hyacinth.

The answer to that does nothing to improve my mood.

Good luck.

I roll my eyes and toss the phone to the side. That's quite enough of that.

First thing tomorrow, I'm going to find Hyacinth.

After renewing the prescription for my medication. And pulling my laundry from the machine so I can finally hang it up. And finding my keys to Nikolette's flat. And ironing the freshly washed white shirts of my uniform—

Oh! And popping into the station to finish cross-referencing the missing persons files with the bodies found in town.

And sewing the fallen button back onto my epaulette.

I'm still half making the list in my mind as sleep rolls over me and claims me fully.

❖

As I leave the house the next morning a sense of generalized unease arrives and stays with me. I've already called Hyacinth several times since waking and not received any sort of response.

It's not odd for her to vanish for days at a time. Sometimes even weeks. But to do so right before a conclave? And when she has clear meetings and responsibilities in the city? No. That can't be right.

Something nags at the back of my mind, twisting and turning itself into knots that I must untangle before I can see it fully. But the closer I look, the more I consider it, the tighter the knots become.

The day is bright and sunny. The radio spits out talks of new initiatives pouring from the Clear Blood Foundation, including discussion of a brand new drug designed to make werewolf transformations more manageable. Fascinating. Of course it won't work, werewolves just aren't built that way, but the research coming out of the R&D department has never ceased to amaze me. And I could be wrong—the Life Blood Serum changed everything, after all.

Life Blood is a wonderful, powerful chemical Angbec has been able to add to every blood donation since its official release, a chemical that keeps the blood fresh and viable, meaning that even if it isn't suitable for medical work, it can be offered to vampires as an official, ethically generated food source.

Who knows what the world would be without a means to feed vampires? At the very least I'm sure witches would have far more to do than simply help and guide humans from the background.

I turn up the radio.

Several broadcasters debate the cause of death for the bodies found over the last couple of days, but there isn't much news, just speculation and heresy, which I know to be the case because there are no leads. Unless something turned up in the middle of the night, of course, but I doubt it.

I stop the car and turn off the engine, then stop to think about why. It's only when I look around that I realize I've driven all the way to Hyacinth's home without even thinking about it.

Talk about autopilot.

I hop out, lock up, and look up at the tall iron gates across the front of the property.

Like many of the larger homes in this area, Hyacinth's three storey beast has a gated front and a driveway large enough to fit three cars. The gates aren't electric, but they do form a clear line between the public right of way and the grounds of the property. I never park in there, not least because the larger gate is often locked, but also because something about the clean, red bricks of the drive makes me wonder if they've ever been driven on. Certainly, Hyacinth has no car of her own, just an ancient bicycle with clickety-clackety wheels and a horn in the centre of the handle bars that sounds like an angry goose when squeezed.

I stare in, looking for some sign or signal that she's there.

But the only person I see is a lone figure at the end of the road, marching quickly around the corner to vanish from view. The corner leads to a dead end with nothing but a turning circle for the cars mistakenly driven into this extravagant cul-de-sac.

More curious than that, though, is the fact that the smaller gate to Hyacinth's home, designed for those on foot, is hanging slightly open. This one is never locked, but Hyacinth is always so insistent about seeing it shut when not in use.

To preserve the outward grandeur and aesthetic of the house, she often says.

I push through, and at once, a hot gust of air billows up from nowhere and batters my face, driving against my skin like a localized storm. It burns blistering hot for all of a split second, then cuts short, like a fan suddenly switched off at the plug.

A spell. But one I've never felt before. Something about it is spiky and sharp on my skin, and though I can't place it, I know it was incredibly powerful. But now, it's gone.

There's something underneath it too, a second casting that might be a spell but is more likely to be a ward. Again, something I've never felt before. This one is soft, though, like fur or velvet, very different in tone to the spell that expired.

Double weird.

It isn't unusual to experience spells I can't recognize here—Hyacinth is infinitely more powerful than me. But even knowing that, understanding that she cast *something* here that I can't place, maybe even two things, makes me uneasy.

I wait on the drive, hoping for some sign that Hyacinth is close enough to have dismissed the spell I felt so strongly.

Nothing.

"Hyacinth?" My voice seems to drop out of my mouth and fall flat against the ground as though the air is too weak to carry it. Like speaking into a vacuum. "Hyacinth, did you do that? What was that spell? It's gone now, did you know?"

No answer. Nothing but the faint whisper of something soft and hairy against my cheek.

I turn. Scream. Flail like a bird about to take flight, flapping and brushing at my shoulder.

The huge, hairy spider sails away, propelled by my frantic thrashing. It lands lightly on the ground near my feet, then scuttles back a step or two before looking up at me, actually *looking* at me, with apparent concern.

It. Is. Enormous.

The rational part of me knows my fear of the many-legged beasties may well make it seem bigger than it is, but this thing is truly vast, even for a pseudo-tarantula. It is easily the size of a serving platter and certainly wouldn't fit under any drinking glass I own, even with the legs scrunched up. As clearly as my own hands and clothes, I see the hairs on every long leg and the little claw at the end of each.

"Anansi, you mad creature," I yell. "What the hell did you do that for?"

The spider waves two legs at me, actually waves, as if *I'm* the one with the problem.

"Stay the hell off me—I've told you a million times."

More leg waving, then the hideous arachnid turns about and scuttles towards the house.

I really, really, *really* don't want a familiar.

I brush off my shoulders again, shake out the tension, then keep moving.

The red bricks are bright and hot, throwing back the warmth of the early morning sun. Small tufts of green show in some of the cracks, and beyond that, near the front door, a hanging basket swings to and fro. Beneath it, several wilted flowers and leaves litter the bricks. And behind that, the two glass panes to either side of the heavy oak door are textured, frosted, and gloomy.

"Hyacinth?"

Still no answer.

She must know I'm here by now, right? If my arrival is what triggered the end of that spell, then she would know. And no doubt Anansi has scurried off to tell her of my presence. After all, that's what familiars do.

I touch the front door, meaning to knock with the huge brass ring in the centre.

It swings open.

A chill chases through me.

"Hyacinth, this isn't funny. Where are you? We've been looking for you."

Inside, the house is cold. And dark. And…lifeless.

I stumble, taken aback but the strange sensation. Only days ago I marvelled at the life in this house. I walked through it and felt it breathe with me, felt the pulse of it hum in my heart and bones. I heard it speak, whisper to me like a cool breeze through the trailing branches of an old willow tree. Now?

The breathing has stopped. The pulse is still and silent.

I walk through the house, checking every room on the lower floor while worry rapidly begins to morph into panic.

Where *is* she?

And why is there a meal, half eaten, out on the small table in her sitting room? Half a sandwich lying on a plate beside an apple core and the naked stems of several sprigs of grapes. A pot of tea, the loose leaf diffuser still full with browning leaves.

I lean in to take a sniff. Fennel.

The top half of the sandwich jerks across the plate.

I glare at it, educated enough by my earlier jump scare to recognize what this must be.

"Anansi? Stop mucking about. No need to match your namesake, okay?"

But it isn't the spider. A long tail flops out the side of the sandwich, followed by the tiny, furry body of a truly adorable white and brown mouse. A mouse still munching on a corner of the crumbs dropped from the sandwich.

Ah, the fourth and final familiar. I smile. This one, at least, I can get behind. "Hey, Dink."

The mouse twitches his whiskers at me, pausing briefly to rub dainty paws across his face.

"Where are the others?"

No answer, of course, just more whisker-twitching and nibbling of crumbs.

"You coming with?"

The mouse hops forward a step or two and regards me closely. Then he turns about on the table to continue munching crumbs.

Fine. I don't need the company. I know my way around.

From the ceiling and near enough every wall are hooks and pins from which hang drying plants. The cool air is filled with the scents of thyme, lavender, rosemary, honeysuckle, vanilla, sage, mint, and so many other plants. I can name them all and reel off the properties of each, both as a food, and as a spell component. There are also crystals, stones, and minerals on near every flat surface. Feathers, small sprigs of flowers, incense sticks.

Walking through Hyacinth's home has always resembled walking through a New Age bric-a-brac store.

Near the stairs I can just see through to the pantry, the door of which is open. Hanging in there are thick slabs of meat, probably beef, glistening with a coating of salt.

"Hyacinth?"

I call again, but with every step I take, it's clear that she isn't here. No one is, except the familiars.

I move up the stairs, my hands in my pockets, careful not to touch the walls, banisters, or anything else. Maybe it's police training, maybe it's nerves, but something inside screams that I mustn't touch anything.

She's not in her bedroom or its fancy en suite. I can't see her in the bathroom, the spare bedroom, or the study.

Well, then there's only one place left to look.

I stand at the bottom of the steps leading up to Hyacinth's spell space.

Unlike a few days ago, the feeling I get from the narrow steps is one of emptiness and dread.

I take the steps slowly, swallowing back fear, licking my lips to moisten them, gaze fixed on the handle at the top of the stairs.

When I reach it, the rising feeling of dread crests and breaks, engulfing me fully.

The door is ajar.

"Hyacinth? Please…are you here? It's Tina."

Nothing, just the laboured hiss of my own breathing and the dead, stagnant silence of an empty house.

Then a loud, shrill blast of sound cuts through the silence.

CHAPTER ELEVEN

My phone. It's my phone.

I recognize the sound too late to save my racing heart and slump back against the wall with my hand on my chest. It continues to ring, the sing-song instrumental of some pop track from thirty years ago. It's the tune I use for numbers I don't recognize, though by this point I think I know who it might be.

I wrench the little device free and crush it against my ear. "What?"

Iris splutters and coughs over her anger. "That's no way to answer the phone, is it? I thought that you—"

"I'm looking for Hyacinth, what do you want?"

A pause. "Have you found anything?"

"I'm at her house now. She's…gone."

The following pause is longer. "Do you know where she is?"

I shake my head, realize she can't see me, then add, "No. Her familiars are here, though. I don't know what's going on."

Iris sniffs loudly. How is it possible to put so much disdain and irritation into one tiny sound? "She can't exactly walk around Angbec with a giant spider, a mouse, an owl, and a ferret, can she? That doesn't mean anything. Anyway, what do you mean she's *gone*? Gone where?"

"I don't know."

My hand hovers near the handle to the spell space. It's unlocked. Open. I could just step in. I could invite myself into the most sacred of hallowed places and start rooting around. But for some reason, doing so while talking to Iris feels even more disrespectful than the act itself.

I keep myself steady and wait.

"What do you mean you don't know? There must be something.

She wouldn't just leave. We had a conclave last night. Is there a note on the fridge? A message on a mirror? A letter taped to the door, something?"

"Iris…"

More soft sounds of irritation. She exhales a heavy breath. "I tried to arrange another gathering for this evening, but nobody is willing to do so without the call of a Mother."

"Like I said, she's not here and I—"

"*You're* there, though." Her voice becomes abruptly soft and saccharine. "Why don't you give *me* the address? I could come by to help you look. And while I'm there, I could use the calling stones."

I squint slightly. "You want to come here?"

"Who else is going to do it? You?" she scoffs, rather unkindly. "Give me the address, and I'll pop over. It's about time I learned where Hyacinth lives anyway. I don't understand why you're the only one who knows."

"I…" Unease bubbles up inside me. "No."

"Why not? I'm the eldest and strongest of our sisters. If anyone should have access to Hyacinth, it's me. Who else is going to act in her stead?"

It makes sense. Almost enough sense that I open my mouth to speak. But at the last moment I snap my lips shut.

Iris doesn't know where Hyacinth lives. That means Hyacinth doesn't *want* her to know.

"No."

An explosive exhalation ripples down the line. "Listen, you little brat, tell me where you are, right now. You've no right, and no matter what fancy little relationship you think you have with our Mother, you're not the one in charge. You don't have the power, the *fortis*, or the experience for whatever it is Hyacinth has been showing you, so give me that address, right now."

I stare at the phone, pleased to finally understand Iris a little better.

Slowly and clearly, I decide to take the diplomatic route, though my stomach roils with sudden rage. "If Hyacinth trusts you enough to give you access to her home, then she can do that in her own time. I've been gifted with the knowledge and don't appreciate you demanding I break that trust."

More heavy breaths. Then a gasp, as if Iris is fighting to regain control of herself. "Tina, please. This is odd, isn't it? Hyacinth wouldn't just disappear. What if she needs help? What if she's hurt? I could help you find her. I could—"

"I'll let you know if I find anything. In the meantime, if you want to call the others so badly, use a phone. You clearly know how."

"Wait, Tina, I—"

I hang up.

In the stillness that follows I look to the door of her spell space and steel my wavering nerve. Because Iris is right.

What if Hyacinth *does* need help? Or is hurt?

Something is clearly horribly wrong—the state of this house is enough to make that plain.

If Hyacinth was planning anything, it would likely be from within the safety of her spell space. That means, like it or not, I need to enter and have a look around.

Slowly, I place my hand on the flat of the door and push it all the way open.

First thing to strike me is the dark. So, so dark. The thick curtains are pulled tightly shut like the last time I was here, though this time they block sunlight instead of moonlight. But unlike last time, none of the candles are lit, nor do they spring to life as I open the door.

I press my hand to the left wall, then the right, searching by touch for a light switch. There must be one, right?

Eventually I find it and give it a single click.

Nothing.

Again.

Still nothing.

Great. With no choice but to let my eyes adjust to the gloom, I wait in the doorway with my toes just hanging over the threshold and allow myself to feel.

This room…the space so vibrant, energetic, and alive mere days ago has become a shadow of its former self. There's still energy here, a faint echo of power and magic, but nothing like what it should be. It's the broken and crumpled flakes of a discarded snakeskin, rather than the real thing.

This is Hyacinth's primary casting space, home of hundreds if not thousands of little rituals, spells, offerings, and worship. It should be all but singing with her power and memory.

But I can't feel any of it.

After several seconds, I can pick out the fuzzy shape of furniture in the space. Still gloomy, but enough to make it safe to step forward, straight forward and to the window in the far wall looking down onto the garden.

The curtains rattle on their hooks as I draw them back, and at last, bright, glorious sunshine spills into the room. Then more, as I follow the walls, opening more curtains as I go. Soon, the entire space is lit, and I can see clearly enough to avoid the slightly sloping ceiling.

The floor is still dusty, not with dirt, but with the remnants of herb mixes and fine, crushed salt. Each of my steps has a crunchy, grinding sound to it as I move about the space. Near the centre, there are traces of chalk too, as though Hyacinth had been drawing on the floorboards.

Did she cast a circle here recently? I recognize the signs and wonder if the leftovers are linked to what I felt as I entered the house.

Peering down, I can see the faint traces of a circle of protection, the same type I used so many weeks ago to help my SPEAR friend with her little monster problem. These circles are designed to form an impenetrable barrier against spirits and other unknowables visiting our world. They keep stuff you want in on the inside, and the stuff you want out on the outside.

There's no way of knowing which one this particular circle was supposed to do, but the fact that it's here bothers me. What on earth was Hyacinth calling into her own home that she needed a protective circle?

Her altar is just as I remember, draped in that beautiful cloth with the golden embroidery. Like before the stones, the bowls, and the book are still there. This time, however, the book is shut, and I see the faint swirls of beautiful circular patterns on the front.

I know this is Hyacinth's book of shadows, a record of all of her spells, rituals, thoughts, and desires. Some traditionalists—boring people—might call it a diary or a journal, and while I know that's kinda what it is, I much prefer the name we use.

Long seconds I stare at it, alarmed that I'm even considering what I'm about to do.

But what else is left to me? There is no sign of Hyacinth anywhere, and she hasn't picked up her phone in over a day now, maybe more. Nobody knows where she is. Perhaps, just maybe, there is a clue within this book.

"Mother and Goddess, forgive me," I murmur and hover my hand over the stiff front cover.

A sense of defiance oozes over me, disdain and distrust. I know it comes from the book.

"I'm sorry," I find myself saying aloud. "But I have to know. Please?" I let my fingertips touch the cover.

It resists at first, as though sensing I'm not the owner. Then the resentful feeling flitters away, replaced by gentle acceptance.

Slowly, I open the cover.

As expected, a journal. The first few pages are old, almost as far as fifteen years back. Hyacinth's writing is tight, neat, and precise, formed with care and attention to form and order. The entries begin regularly, and though I don't read them in full, I catch a sense of worship and praise, hopes for a bright, golden future, and inner emotional turmoil.

I move away from those pages as fast as possible. Somehow spying on her innermost thoughts seems even worse.

Instead I flip forward, trying to find more recent pages. As I move through the years, I find inserts and scraps of other paper. There are flowers in there, pressed between sheets of tissue paper, and even the odd feather. A long length of bark peeps out from between a double spread near the middle, and I use that as a bookmark to reach that section.

The first thing I see is my name.

> *So strange that this young witch should appear from nowhere with no sign or herald.*
>
> *Tina Marks. Interesting.*
>
> *I must watch her and learn more. She may be just what we need.*

I flip away from that page super fast. I don't want to know what Hyacinth thought about me before we met. Maybe later, when we can talk about it properly, I'll have that discussion—what did she mean about *what we need*?—but until that point, there's no need for me to dig.

More pages on, representing maybe a year of time, there's another interesting passage.

> *We all have a role to play, whether we wish it or not.*
>
> *I have a role, she has a role, if only she would accept it.*
>
> *I never before met a child less willing to be what she should, but she must learn to trust herself again.*
>
> *The Maiden must eventually mature into the Mother. That is the way of things.*
>
> *When she accepts, as she must, when she recognizes her true potential, I'll be ready to pass the staff of the Mother to the most capable hands I've ever known.*

My fingers tremble on the pages.

What is she talking about? *Who* is she talking about?

I flick forward again, but I'm nearing the end of the written sections now. There are plenty of pages after that, but they are smooth, plain, and untouched.

The last entry has no date, but from context I guess it is earlier this week. I snatch up the book and hold it close. I have to because the words are a sprawling scrawl, lacking any of the neatness and precision of earlier pages. With it is a ring of wood, plain, narrow, but quite beautiful. It is dark and smooth, probably walnut or mahogany, fixed by a tiny thread taped down to the centre of the notebook.

> *The sickness spreads faster than I anticipated. I no longer have time to wait for her. Within the next two days I must reveal all.*
>
> *I only hope I have prepared her adequately for the truth. And that she will forgive me.*
>
> *Tina. My dearest Daughter, I am so very sorry.*
>
> *I must also give her the ring. I have no use of it now.*
>
> *Perhaps I can disguise it as a gift and later leave instruction on how she can—*

The passage ends abruptly. So too do all entries to the book.

What the hell?

I inspect the ring nestled within the pages. The diameter is wide enough that it might fit my middle finger, and despite being wood, I'm sure it would be very comfortable. On the inside is a line of script, etched delicately with a wood burning tool. I can't read it, but the symbols are curving and sweeping. Outside, the ring is plain, decorated with nothing but the natural grain of the wood.

She's right. I *do* like it. Not that I wear a lot of jewellery, but this piece speaks to me on a level I'm not sure I understand.

I fight the urge to slip it on my finger, choosing instead to wait until it is handed to me. After all, a gift isn't a gift if it is taken before its time.

Instead, I turn the book back to the front and close it.

I knew Hyacinth was ill, of course I did, but I had assumed it was nothing more serious than a summer cold. Is something more sinister going on? Why didn't she tell me?

Instead of answers, this book of shadows has given me more questions, and the creeping unease I felt earlier returns harder and stronger than ever.

What illness? And reveal what? To whom? The second part of the entry certainly refers to me, but the first? Was that intended for me too? Who does she crave forgiveness from? Where is she? Why is this room open? Where is she? What were those spells I felt on entering the property? Where? Is? She?

A loud crash from downstairs shatters my thoughts and drags me round in a circle towards the door. More thudding, thumping, then the shrill shriek of *something* beneath me.

Whatever is going on, someone is hurt.

CHAPTER TWELVE

I hurtle back down the steps, leaping down them two at a time. On the first floor I whirl around the corner, then dart down the next set, using the banister to keep my balance. Preserving the scene be damned, I need to get down there.

As I hit the bottom step, a metal tray shoots across the ground in front of me, skidding to a stop against the plush rug forming a line towards the sitting room.

Another loud yowl fills the space, and then a tiny streak of fur and teeth rockets across the hardwood floor. After it swoops a large owl, wings outstretched and silent as it sails through.

"Seshat?"

The owl ignores me, drawing up both legs, claws extended, in preparation for a strike. Only then do I recognize the little ball of fur she follows, tail lashing for balance as he struggles to find a hidden spot beneath the cabinet near the pantry.

"Wait, Dink?"

With a little tail flick, the mouse vanishes into the gloom beneath the cabinet. Thwarted, the owl cuts upward from a daring dive, beautiful wings grazing the handles as she banks in midair.

"What are you doing? Quit it, the pair of you."

As if in mockery, from beneath the same cabinet, Anansi abruptly scuttles into the open, causing me to leap several paces back up the steps. The spider waves two sassy legs at me, then sprints towards the kitchen where yet another barking sort of scream cuts the air.

The animals have gone nuts.

In the kitchen, carnage. Saucepans and frying plans have been loosed from their hooks and strewn across the floor. Several pots of tall utensils like wooden spoons and ladles are on their sides, spilling their contents like guts.

Two smashed bowls and a teacup form a pile under the sink, and a puddle of oil oozes from the cracks of a toppled jar filled with garlic and red peppers.

On a high shelf running above the sink, a furious, hissing ferret glares down at me, back arched, mouth open wide to show pointy teeth.

"Loki?"

I turn in a slow circle, trying and failing to sidestep the rising feeling of dread.

The animals are acting like, well, animals.

But they're *familiars*—they shouldn't be chasing and destroying things. Certainly not each other.

A low shadow slips across the ground again, and I dive after it.

Just in time, as Seshat's soft, silent wings ghost across the top of my head.

The mouse she chases wriggles madly in my hands, and I grip as firmly as I can without crushing. "Dink, get a grip," I tell the terrified rodent. "And you, you know better, Seshat."

The owl swoops around and lands on the curved arm of the tap above the sink. She regards me with an intense, regal gaze, and from the corner of my eye, I see Loki gather her legs beneath her in preparation to spring.

"Okay, stop, all of you. Hyacinth wouldn't put up with this—look what you did to her garlic oil."

The mention of their mistress seems to bring a sudden stillness to the room. A return of the senses, almost. Dink finally stops wriggling in my hands and simply sits, while Anansi climbs up the side of the nearest cabinet to rest near a wooden chopping board. Seshat turns her head to regard me coolly, and Loki twists mid-jump to land crouched and easy on the ground.

I sigh. "All of you, what the hell? Where is Hyacinth?"

Again, the sound of her name seems to send a charge through the room, and Seshat hoots at me. The soft brown and white feathers of the barn owl rustle and quiver as she hops lightly off the curve of the tap and down to the sideboard.

Again I look around.

No food. At least not that I can see. And barely any water.

How long as Hyacinth actually been gone?

Slowly, I unfurl my fingers from around Dink. "Can you show me anything, or lead me to her? Did she leave any message behind?"

I *feel* Seshat move more than anything. Her flight is too silent and her motions too swift; but that faint gust on my right side gives me warning and I spin away from her, clutching Dink to my chest again.

The owl hoots again in disgust and anger and cuts another curve to fly out of the room and across the landing towards the open front door.

"No—!"

But it's too late.

Seshat spreads wide, beautiful wings and soars out into the sunshine beyond. I dart after her, hands still tight around Dink, and between my legs shoots a blur of black, white, and brown: Loki. She darts through the open door, across the drive, and slithers through the narrow gap between the bars of the gate like a furry eel. A moment later she's gone too.

Dink sits peaceful and quiet in my lap as I drive the car onward. He seems far calmer now and much more like himself, resting and watching with the uncanny intelligence all familiars seem to possess. More than once I catch him staring up at me, and I fight the urge to defend myself from the apparent disappointment.

A glance at my phone tells me I've been at this for an hour, a whole hour driving back and forth, peering under cars, staring into trees, scanning rooftops.

There are more text messages on my phone too. I can just see the flashing letters of *Nikolette Mob* before I return myself to the more pressing matter of the runaway familiars.

Both Loki and Seshat have vanished without a trace, and I don't know how much longer I can look before admitting that they're gone.

I put the urge to panic aside and instead drive back to Hyacinth's house. This time I park right outside the tall gates and let myself inside. It's mid-morning now, and I've managed to achieve nothing since being here. Nothing except increasing the fear and unease boiling through me non-stop.

I'm going to need help.

I hurry back up to Hyacinth's sanctum while Dink claws his way up my clothes and rests on my shoulder, tucked in close to my ear. His tiny body and negligible weight are a strange comfort as I march over the threshold. No time for pause or uncertainty this time—I need help.

The altar seems suddenly larger and more imposing now that I intend to use it. That's silly, of course, nothing in this room has changed since I was here an hour ago, but the act of leaving and returning has made even more obvious how still the place is. How…dead.

My mouth is dry. There are butterflies doing loop-de-loops in my stomach.

I stand before the beautiful green cloth with its delicate embroidery and toe off my shoes and socks. They make an untidy pile to one side as I kick them out of the way of the space where I slowly drop to my knees.

"Draw," I murmur, pointing at the curtains one by one. They close slowly, as if reluctant to obey my command. As a dim faux twilight falls on the room, I point next at the candles on the altar. "Light." Bright orange flames burst into being, before dying down to more reasonable levels on each charred wick.

Concise. Simple. Just the way I prefer my paltricks to be.

In a corner of the altar, untouched, are three stones. Roughly the size of an egg, though more evenly shaped, each stone is made of a different material. Each one represents something different, but I'm too flustered now to remember what. What I do remember, however, is that they can be used for communication. Not like a phone or a walkie-talkie, but more as a means to express a predetermined message or confirm an existing idea. More than that, they can reach out to several people at once, if the people are linked in some way. Like the sisters of a coven.

The stones are warm to the touch as I pull them close, despite resting on the shadiest part of the table. One smooth, black, and shiny; the second brown, striped, and grainy; the last faintly blue, clear, and glistening. Obsidian, petrified wood, and celestine.

My fingers shake as I gather them into the centre of the table.

I don't want to do this, to open myself up and expose even the smallest part of my mind to people perhaps as much as five miles away.

I clench and unclench my fingers, wondering if I can even remember how the spell is done.

I find myself looking over my shoulder for guidance, but of course I am alone. No comfortable hand on my shoulder, no playful admonishment whispered in my ear. Then again, I know what she'd tell me anyway.

Hyacinth Dixon would assert that I already know what to do. That I must trust myself. That I must believe in my ability to be guided by the Goddess and whatever other platitude she happened to be feeling that day.

Dink nibbles at my earlobe.

"You're cute," I tell the little rodent. "Will you stay with me while I do this?"

His whiskers twitch against my cheek as he remains calm on my shoulder.

Guess that means *yes*.

I don't know exactly how Hyacinth uses these stones, but I've never excelled at directly copying her anyway. Her incantations are pretty and well formed, always with a clever rhythm or rhyming scheme that makes me think of Shakespeare or Milton.

But I don't need to copy her. I've always had my own way of doing things, and despite my internal protestations, the fact is that I know *exactly* what to do.

I arrange the stones into a line, with obsidian the furthest away followed by the wood, then the celestine. I lay my hands flat on the table to either side, thumbs meeting beneath the celestine while my other fingers angle towards the obsidian. I imagine the formation of my hands to be an arrowhead and the line formed by the stones to be the shaft of the arrow.

Then, and there's no other word for it, I take a breath deep to still my body and *reach*.

There's nothing physical about the motion—it's all internal. Every part of the action is drawn from within, from my connection to the Goddess, the strength of my will, and my learned ability to pour that *fortis* into action. I want to talk to my sisters. So I *will* talk to my sisters.

My fingers begin to tingle. Clearly I've tapped into something.

"Sisters," I murmur into the stillness, "those hearts linked by the grace, strength, and flexibility of the mighty willow and the will of the triple Goddess, hear me."

Nothing.

Did I do it right? Did I misremember after all?

Then an answering tingle arrives at the back of my ear. It's small and soft enough that I might have mistaken it for Dink, except he chooses that moment to scuttle off my shoulder and down my arm to the table. His sleek fur puffs out, and through that I realize that magic is afoot.

In their simple line formation, the stones begin to shimmer and glow, not enough to light the room, but certainly enough to be visible even to the untrained eye. But to my eye, one well used to watching the motions of *fortis* made manifest, I see a shimmering gold thread snake out from the piece of obsidian. It forms a tiny, delicate arc towards the petrified wood and bounces off it into another arc, then the same motion off the top of the celestine before arcing again. This time it bounces harder and further, straight off the table and into me where it strikes my chest.

The sensation is gentle and barely there at all, like someone has prodded me lightly with the tip of their finger.

From the top of the obsidian, more golden lines arch out to touch my fingers before springing off into the table and out into the room. Some vanish into walls, others into the floor, but each of them moves in a direction I know, with sudden certainty, represents each of my sisters.

I sigh, relieved and concerned at how easily a spell of this nature has come back to me.

I guess some things can never truly be forgotten, only hidden.

I remain on my knees watching, thinking, waiting for a response.

There. A presence. An *arrival.* I can't hear my sisters, of course, nor can they hear me—it's not that type of magic. But they can certainly *feel* me. And now I can feel them.

I return to my probing, and I sense excitement, then curiosity, followed quickly by…disappointment.

Oh well. I should have expected that, but it still hurts. I struggle to maintain my focus.

"I know I'm not Hyacinth." I speak aloud, more for myself than my sisters. "But we have to meet. Something is really wrong at Hyacinth's house, and we need to figure out what to do. Can we meet this evening? The same time as yesterday?"

Though my words don't carry, the intent does. I form the image of our meeting place in my mind's eye, picking out all the details of the space beneath the willow trees: the gentle lapping of the water, the soft breeze through the dangling branches, the scent of clover underfoot, even the faintest taste of salt on the air, blown up from the ground as residue from past rituals.

Four minds touch briefly against mine, agree to meet, then whisk away again.

The golden glow around the arrangement of stones and my fingers begins to fade. First from my fingers, the golden threads retreating back into my hands in a glittering shimmer of light. Then the one leading to my chest springs back and begins a reverse path back across the stones, celestine, petrified wood, then back to obsidian again. It gathers into a single point on the crest of the obsidian, then with a last glimmer winks out.

The tingle fades, my intent ebbs, and slowly I peel my hands away from the table.

I did it. I really did it.

My relief is palpable. No errant flashes of *fortis*, no accidents, no danger, just a calling performed quickly and simply.

From the corner of my eye, I spot a long, slender, furry leg extend across the surface of the altar. Then another. And another, and another, and another, and—

I throw myself backward, knocking the altar and jostling the stones across the fabric. Dink squeaks indignantly, and Anansi finishes her slow, methodical hike across the table.

"Damn it, Anansi!"

The spider stops. Stares at me, I think.

Part of me wonders what she sees through those many eyes, yet the rest of me recoils at the thought of the creature coming anywhere near me.

But then I realize the truth of it all.

Dink has already latched on to me, staying close and riding on my shoulder. Seshat and Loki might be gone, but a witch's familiar won't last long without their witch. Or rather, without their witch, the animals quickly revert back to their plain, mundane selves and cannot be considered companions any more.

Without Hyacinth…

I remember seeing Dink eating crumbs at the table downstairs, Loki gathering her back legs beneath her to spring an attack on an unsuspecting Seshat. No familiar in their right mind would attack another, not knowing they have a witch to serve.

Still on my hands and knees, I stare at the spider and for the first time consider what all this really means. If the familiars are beginning to revert that must mean that—

"No."

It can't be. I won't think that way. I refuse.

This is a horrible misunderstanding, and soon Hyacinth is going to show up and wonder what all the fuss is about. She'll laugh and joke and fuss and apologize, and I'll feel like a fool for ever suspecting anything else.

Yes. That must be it.

In the meantime, though…

I look down at the spider and the mouse and feel my insides lurch.

They're going to have to come with me.

Chapter Thirteen

I've packed up Hyacinth's house. There's not much more I can do there now. With half the familiars gone and no sign of the mistress of the house, I can't see much point in loitering. Plus I need to get to work.

After several minutes of searching, I realized that the key to the spell space was missing. No stranger than anything else, but a quick grasp of the handle and a whispered "Lock" solved that problem. Then I took myself downstairs to clean up the kitchen as much as possible.

The garlic oil was ruined, as was my mentor's favourite teacup. But least there were no more half-eaten sandwiches or vaguely rotting tea leaves lying around.

Now, back in my car, I want to drive on, but I can't because I'm all but smeared against the driver's side door. The vehicle has never felt so small. It isn't a large car, but by no means is it cramped or uncomfortable. Except for today.

Dink perches on the dashboard, rear legs bunched up, tail curled around them. Anansi sits on the passenger seat. The giant spider is still and calm, giving no sign at all that she is even aware of my presence, but my skin crawls at the sight of her. Even the thought of switching gears to take off sends a shiver of nausea through me as I realize how close my hand must get to her hairy, bulbous body.

I lick my lips. "Don't move," I mutter. "Don't even twitch, you understand?"

She faces me. I squeal.

"I said *don't move*." A little whimper slips out of me. "Why, Goddess, why? Why did you have to be a *spider*? A moth, a butterfly, a cricket, anything but a spider."

Slow, oh so slow, I reach towards the handbrake. Nothing. Good.

I ease the handbrake down, push into first gear, and ease away from the iron gates…to slam my brakes on an instant later.

There's a woman. Red haired, wide eyed, and startled, she whirls round and bows over the front of my car with both hands splayed on the bonnet. I can't tell if I've bumped her or not, but I certainly scared her as much as I scared myself. I didn't even see her.

I jerk the handbrake back up.

"Are you okay?"

She doesn't answer.

"Hello? Miss?" I climb out of the car, ignoring the *ka-chunk* as it stalls, still in first gear.

The door hangs open as I scoot around it and rush round to the front.

She's not moving. Just standing there.

Did I hit her? Maybe she's in shock.

"Hey." I snap my fingers close to her face. "Hello? Are you okay? Say something."

Then I feel it. Oh so faint, as if repressed, but very much present. A kinship. Knowing. Understanding. *Sisterhood.*

Her head snaps up. She feels it too. "I'm sorry, I—"

"Don't worry, it's fine. Did I hit you? I wasn't going fast, but you weren't there, then all of a sudden you were—"

"No, no. I'm fine." For the first time her eyes meet mine, and I find myself startled by what I find there. Her eyes are different colours. One is bright, brilliant blue, almost sapphire. The other is brown, like mine. Both are wide beneath her sparse red eyebrows as she backs off a step. Then another.

"Wait, you might be in shock or something. Can you hold still for just—"

"No." The single word holds a slight edge of panic. "I told you, I'm fine. Please don't worry about me." Another step back and then she's out of reach, turning on her heel to quickly walk away.

I hurry after her. "But what are you doing here? I've not seen you before. Are you new? Did you call the helpline?"

She keeps her head down and continues to walk. "I shouldn't be here."

"No, it's fine. There's a lot of us around here. Do you need help?"

Still she refuses to look at me. "No. I…I took a wrong turn. This isn't where I was hoping to be. I'm leaving now, I swear."

"But—"

"I'm going," she snaps. "Please leave me be." And she increases the pace.

Everything I know tells me to follow. Every instinct, habit, and even law. A civilian walking away from the scene of an accident? Even if I didn't hit her, surely I have a duty of care to be sure she really is all right.

But as she scurries out of sight, I think of my own life, my own closet-based skeletons, and force myself to stay back. After all, I'm a witch with plenty of secrets I prefer to keep under wraps. I can't begrudge a fellow sister a few of her own.

Funny, though. I'm pretty sure I've seen her before.

I enter the station with Dink riding on my shoulder, half hidden inside my T-shirt. I can't see Anansi, but that's just fine. I know she's there, deep inside my rucksack that I hold by a single strap at arm's length.

A wildly gesticulating woman stands at the front desk, facing a constable who looks bored and ready to finish for the day. She is tall and dressed in motorcycle leathers, with the helmet looped over her forearm. Her long locs are caught up in a high, messy pony, and her expression is dark and irritated.

I soften my steps and cut to the right, meaning to sneak through the cafeteria to reach the changing rooms.

"Hey, Tina?"

Damn. No such luck.

I spin about as casually as I can manage, letting the rucksack slip from my fingers. It meets my foot as it falls, and I boot the whole thing through the door using the low table and planter nearby for cover.

"What's up, Shelly?" I stay close to the door, for the first time in a long while wishing I had long hair, or at least hair to my shoulders.

The constable points at the woman in the leathers. "I know you're not clocked in yet, but see this one off, will you? I can't leave the desk."

"*This one*?" The motorcycle helmet swings wide as she gestures with both hands. "Well shit, did someone eat all the best doughnuts before you could get close?"

I roll my eyes. "Danika? Come on, it's too early for this."

She grins at me, showing off a new scar on her chin. I bet there are plenty of stories connected to that. "Joke's on you—I've not been to bed yet. Anyway, I need help and I—"

Shelly clears her throat. "And I already told you—we can't just give out information to civilians."

"And *I* told *you* I'm not a civilian. I work for the mayor."

Oh. This again. I hurry to the desk and give Danika a meaningful side-eye. "I've got it, Shelly. Do me a favour meanwhile, and tell Hozier I'm in, please."

She nods, though not without another glare at Danika, who simply smiles sweetly and blows a mocking kiss.

I give her a shove. "Come on, you. Don't know how many times you need to hear it, but you can't just come wandering in here demanding stuff."

"Oh, but you guys have the best toys. Learn to share."

I bite back a snort of laughter and make a great show of carting her out of the station. I march Danika out the door, down the steps, and to the side, where she promptly begins to giggle.

"Oh no, Officer, please, please don't cuff me," she cries. "Have I been naughty again?"

"You are such a pain," I murmur, angling us both towards the gate at the side of the building. I punch in the security code. "Get in, keep your head down, and be quiet."

Danika gives me a curious look, but nods and slips through without another word. I don't bother watching. We've done this enough times now that she knows where to go.

I make my way back inside, wave once at Shelly, then snag my rucksack on the way through the first door. Once more I hold it as far away from me as possible as I march down the short corridor and through the double doors for the cafeteria. This area is open to the public to a small degree, so I don't loiter.

I take the door on the far side marked *No Public Access* and wind my way towards the changing rooms.

Only when there do I remember the state I left my locker in last night, and I flick out the rumpled shirt. Oh well. I trade that one for the one in my bag, carefully place Dink inside the locker out of reach, and then begin to dress. The smart utility trousers, with multiple pockets. Belt with loops and catches for my baton, torch, and other peripherals. Long-sleeved white shirt with buttons I struggle to fasten, under a body vest that I probably don't need to wear yet. The hat I pull off the locker hook and rest on the bench running down the centre of the changing room.

"Anansi?" I make my voice a low whisper.

My rucksack shifts and then the huge spider crawls out.

I look from her, to the hat, then back again.

No. I can't do it. I just can't.

Before she can climb in, I grab the hat and slam it onto my head. "No, I'm sorry, you'll have to stay here. I can't have you inside there just…resting on my head." I fight to hold back the shudder of revulsion, fail, and shrug at the spider.

"You can have the run of the place, though. Just don't be seen and try not to get squashed. Can you handle that?"

No response, of course, unless I can count the vague twitching of a middle pair of legs as an answer. The spider crawls softly, silently away, and I swap Dink from inside my locker to a pocket on my stab vest. It's snug, but he's small. He should be fine in there.

Everything else gets crammed into the small space, and I dart out to the main office.

CHAPTER FOURTEEN

Danika is already there, ambling up the steps from the interrogation rooms as if she owns the place. Normally I admire her confidence, but today is just not the day.

"What do you need?" I mutter, unlocking my desk drawers.

She tuts. "*Good morning, Danika. How are you?* Oh, I'm fine, thanks. Busy night, though, hunting for redcaps in the attic spaces of the shopping centre in Cipla. *Oh, redcaps, really? Aren't they really mean?* Sure are. Savage little bastards with teeth like fucking needles and—"

I roll my eyes. "Okay, okay, I get it. Sorry. I've had a rough morning."

"Sounds like it. Why is there a rat in your pocket?"

I sigh. I know she's trained to be observant, but if I can't keep Dink hidden for longer than five seconds, we're going to have a problem.

"He's not a rat, he's a mouse. His name is Dink, and he's a familiar. I'm…familiar sitting."

"Dare I ask?"

"Best not." I sit down and let Dink loose to sit on the desk. May as well, there's no one else around just yet. "What can I do for you?"

"Orthon Blue or something like that. Missing persons. We—I mean, SPEAR is still dipping their hand in to help, but Jackson thought maybe I could cross-reference the names you have against a list of his researchers."

I nod and start pulling papers out of the drawers. "Still a load missing?"

Danika shrugs. "They're dead." Her eyes widen at my gasp of surprise. "What? It's true. It's been too long, and for there to be no sign of them at all is weird. Besides, I said *dead*, not *gone*. We still don't know how many of them were turned into vampires or werewolves last year. I'm positive not all of them died."

I only know half of that story, and given my own problems right now, I don't really want to dig into it. I shove the entire stack of mismatched papers into her hands. "Go nuts. Some of the names we're ticking off simply because we don't have the resources to look. Others we've passed to SPEAR. But that's the list I was given."

She takes the papers but doesn't look at them, instead tucking the stack under her arm and studying me closely. "What's wrong?"

"Nothing."

"Bullshit," comes her calm response. "There's a mouse on your desk, a haunted look in your eye, and your shirt is on inside out. Something's up."

I glance down at myself. Oh. Guess that's why the buttons were such a struggle.

I want to tell her. Sure, witch business is private, but none of my coven want to speak to me, and Nikolette, the one person I'd usually speak to is…well. But that doesn't leave me with anybody else.

"I…my mentor is missing."

Danika cocks an eyebrow and gestures to the papers under her arm.

"She's not on that list, but she missed an important meeting last night and hasn't answered her phone for a day. Then I went to her house this morning and she's not there."

As I say the words, I remember the strange witch outside her house. What on earth was she doing there? And why was she so familiar? I force my memory back to that awkward encounter and examine as much as I can remember. Hair. So much thick, red hair.

I look up as the memory reaches me. "The gym."

Danika arches an eyebrow. "At the house? What?"

"Nothing. I just remembered where I saw someone, that's all."

"Ooh…" The SPEAR agent offers me a roguish grin. "Maybe they're following you. Anyway, like I was saying—at your mentor's house—are there any signs of forced entry? Struggle? Theft? Marks of vampire entry? Fur? Scales? Feathers?"

I smile. Danika really *is* a SPEAR. Even if she works directly for Mayor Cobé now, nothing will ever change her core. I guess some truths just can't be denied.

"Nothing like that," I assure her. "She's just *gone*. I wouldn't worry except…" I pause, unsure of how to go on. In the end I settle on "She's close to me. A mother figure in my life. She goes off on her own all the time but not without telling me. And certainly not when due to meet with me."

Danika perches on the end of my desk. "And you can't look because, what? Civvie Bashers"—that would be mundane police officers—"don't have time for extracurriculars?"

I watch Dink nibble on a corner of my in tray. "I don't have any proof something is wrong beyond"—I lower my voice—"witch stuff. So I can't even report her missing to the department."

She gives me a sharp look, then nods. "Want me to look? I *do* owe you."

Slowly, I shake my head. "I…no. Thank you, but I can't involve you in this. It's coven business. I have to handle it myself. Besides you have enough on your plate. Orthon Blue, did you say?"

"Something like that."

I smile. "No Orthon, but there was a Morton Bluett. Maybe that's who you want?"

Her eyes widen. "I can barely remember what I had for breakfast, and you can just pull that name out your arse?"

"You probably didn't *have* breakfast, if I know anything about you. But yes, that name is in the list somewhere. Check it out. Take a copy if you need—I'll be starting my beat soon, and you need to scram before you're seen."

Danika playfully punches at the air. "I can take them."

"Oh, I know. That's what I'm afraid of."

She chuckles as she makes her way to the photocopier and starts selecting pages to copy.

I sit back in my seat and fiddle with the sleeve on my shirt. Yup. Definitely inside out.

I consider going to change it and pause when I feel my phone rumble against my thigh.

Text message.

The screen, when I look, shows another missed call to match the one from earlier and even more text messages. All from Nikolette.

Something inside me turns a little nervous circle. What could she possibly have to add after last night? Is she calling now to make it official? To dump me formally and then move on with her life, being tall and glamorous and gorgeous and, let's be honest, entirely out of my league?

I still don't understand why she ever gave me the time of day, not least because we're just so different. Opposites might attract, but they also fight like cats.

I risk opening the earliest one.

We need to talk.

Call me.

Well, I should have expected that, really. Nikolette is nothing if not brisk and forthright, a marked contrast to my shy bumbling. Problem is, that doesn't tell me a great deal about her mood. The next one tells me less.

Don't ignore me. We need to talk this out.

The third, sometime in the early hours this morning, makes me sit a little straighter.

I'm sorry. I overreacted. But you can't ignore me forever.

Let's talk. Please.

That's not like her at all.

I risk opening one more message and almost drop the phone.

Tina, please, don't shut me out. I've been thinking all morning and I'm sorry. I shouldn't have said what I said.

Please, can we talk. Please?

I mouth the words as if to feel them out, as if only by half-speaking them I can be sure they are real.

Danika finds me like that, still mouthing the text message, as she dumps the papers back on my desk, narrowly missing Dink. "Thanks," she says brightly, "I only copied a page or two, but you're right, it was Morton Bluett. Goblin weapon smith and researcher for Clear Blood."

"Glad to help."

She leans over the desk. "Are you sure you don't want me to look into this woman? Your mentor, what was her name again?"

"Hyacinth Dixon, but no, it's fine. This is coven business. We need to look after it ourselves. You go hunt for your goblin."

With a shrug, she backs up and finishes tucking her copied sheets into a pocket on the inside of her jacket. "Suit yourself. You know where I am if you want me." She smiles, nods, and heads back towards the stairs leading down to the *edane* holding area.

I barely see her leave as I turn my gaze back to the phone and the messages listed on my screen.

Slowly I begin to tap out a message of my own.

I'm sorry too, I

No. I don't like that. Delete it. Start again.

You really hurt me last night. I don't think you realize how it feels to

Ew, no, that's worse. Delete that too.

I lower my head to the cool wood of my desk, letting it soothe my abruptly aching forehead.

A tiny weight passes over my wrist, and I turn my hand to let Dink sit on my palm.

Dink. I find myself smiling at the bizarre antics of my mentor.

Anansi, Seshat, and Loki. Powerful Goddesses from their varied pantheons known for wisdom, power, and protection. And Dink. *Dink*?

The fact that Dink is the only male of the four familiars isn't lost on me either, but I still find it funny that Hyacinth would name her helpers in such a way. Maybe she's trying to tell us something.

Several minutes later, my beat partner for the day arrives, a short, prematurely balding man, with probably too many piercings to be considered safe in a job like ours. He waves a hello at me and wanders off to the male-gendered changing rooms.

That's my cue. I carefully place Dink back into my pocket and tuck his tail in around him. Then I scout the room. It's large and quiet right now, and Anansi is nowhere to be seen. The crafty little creature could be anywhere, and I have no way of knowing.

Well, hopefully she's doing as I asked and staying well out of sight. She'll be safe here, after all, so long as she doesn't crawl across anybody's desk. Then again, given her namesake, I'm not sure I can count on that.

Fifteen minutes later and we're ready to go, PC Tina and PC Vince, on the beat to ask questions about a trio of vaguely suspicious deaths. Goody! Still, it's good to get away from all that paperwork, even though I know it will be waiting for me when I get back.

Vince gestures me ahead of him out of the station, and we begin the long looping walk that will take us through all the trouble hotspots in the local area.

Given everything else that has already happened this morning, I can only hope that this is a slow day.

CHAPTER FIFTEEN

This is not a slow day.

Maybe the general population is starting to feel the moon because after picking up one intoxicated person, assisting one fallen cyclist, directing three lost tourists, and convincing one bemused werewolf to stay out of the sewers, I'm more than ready for my break. No one has seen anything or heard anything about our mystery bodies, and if we find many more dead ends, we'll have to widen the canvassing area.

Vince gestures to an empty bench beside a small but popular water feature and opens up the carrier bag containing our lunch.

Yummy—ham and cheese baguettes and a pack of spicy crisps. I open those up first and slot half of the crispy slices into the sandwich.

"Do you always do that?"

I pause, the bread half raised to my mouth. "What?"

"The crisp thing. Every shift we're paired for I grab you a sarnie, and every shift, no matter the flavour, you shove the crisps inside it. Does it even taste good?"

I nod and take a huge bite to demonstrate. "You should try it."

He leans back against the sudden spray of crumbs. "If you say so. Which way do you want to go after this?"

"Industrial estate. If we do that first and walk through, we can then scoot round and pop out at the bottom of West Side. Then it's a straight shot through the tourist trap." I cut a glance at the clock in the tall tower off to the right. "It's about time for the first lot of trains and coaches to drop off, and if we time it well enough, we can put ourselves in the right place."

"Hmm." He chews thoughtfully. "And here I was thinking we'd have a quiet shift. Didn't know you wanted to go looking for trouble."

"Meaning?"

A shrug. "Most lids around here stay away from the bus and train stations at busy times. The go-go buttons"—transport police—"are already there, and they can deal with whatever kicks off. You, though, you want to be right in the middle of it. You're not much like the others."

"Thank you?"

"Heard you transferred over. Where were you before this?"

I wave a vague hand around. "Just a house down south."

"Oh yeah?" Another bite. "You don't want to tell me, just say."

"It's not that, I just…yeah. Fine. I'd rather not, if that's all right. I moved for a reason."

His eyes grow lively with curiosity. "Well, now you done whetted my beak for it. Go on, give me a clue. Dirty dealings? Crooked skipper? Guv kept putting his hand on you? Too many missed promo opportunities?"

Another savage bite of the sandwich stops me from saying something I shouldn't. I take my time chewing, using both sides of my mouth, while Vince all but vibrates with excitement beside me. Only when happy I've suitably pulverized my mouthful do I allow myself to swallow and thus clear my mouth.

"Nothing like that. I'm just a private sort is all."

"I know that's the truth. No one has anything to say about you, not even Skipper. Sure he had a word or two about when those vampires broke in and wrecked the place, but beyond that…" He trails off, as if waiting for me to fill in the gap.

I don't.

Instead, I munch on my sandwich, turning my gaze out and over the space before me. This area is touristy, but mostly arty, with weird interactive sculptures and long, scooped out benches shaped like heads of lettuce. No idea what was in the minds of the city council when they decided on this, and maybe that's what turned this area into such a weird blend of shops and empty units.

Certainly nothing like where I came from, Vince is right about that.

But then, there's nowhere like Angbec that I've ever heard of.

Angbec: the hive of unusual activity and the forefront of all human–*edane* relations in the country.

Which is exactly why I came, leaving Mama in our oversized home to take on a small, cramped terraced house in the middle of a dense residential street. I miss the old place, but our town simply lacked the numbers necessary to remain hidden. At least here, I'm one among thousands.

At my side Vince gives an abrupt gasp and leaps to his feet. I follow, dropping my sandwich, primed and ready for some sort of emergency I need to spring off towards. He slaps a hand to his mouth.

"What? What is it?"

"There is an *enormous* spider on your back right now. Don't fucking move."

No. Oh no, no, no, oh no.

I can't feel anything at all, but the horrified look on Vince's face tells me it must be true. Then, as if to add weight to it, Dink peeps his tiny face out of the pocket on my stab vest.

So, Anansi came along for the ride, after all.

Slowly, Vince draws his baton from the sleeve on his belt.

"Wait, what are you doing?"

He readies himself. "I think I can flick it off you. Jesus, it's massive, what the hell?"

I spin around to face him, immediately terrified that he'll hurt the innocent creature. Yeah, gross but certainly innocent.

"Stop, stop, don't do anything."

"But it's moving up your back—"

"Shut up, just shut up a second."

I still can't feel her through the stab vest, but just knowing she's there, knowing she's *on* me makes my skin crawl something awful. Then my mind drifts. How long has she been there? Where was she before? Was she *inside* my clothes? On my skin?

The panic starts to rise, but I punch it down with a savage mental fist.

Think. Think, think.

I back away from Vince, my hands still out towards him.

"What are you doing?"

"Shut up. I've got this. Just don't hit me with that damn baton."

The urge to scream, to pull off and shake every scrap of clothing, nearly robs me of my senses. It's only when Dink peeps his head out of my pocket again that I begin to see clearly.

Familiars. They're just familiars. Cool, intelligent, and powerful little creatures sent to help. And that must be it, right? Anansi is here to help.

The backs of my legs bump up against another bench, and the sharp jolt gives me an idea. A wall, a tree, a fence, anything.

I look around, careful to keep my back away from Vince, who is still watching me like the scene from a horror movie.

A sculpture. Short and squat with curves, dips, and holes like a floating piece of metallic Swiss cheese. I keep backing up until my arse butts up against it, then slowly drag my body down the shiny surface.

There's a tiny skitter, the soft brush of hairy legs and claws against the back of my neck, and then nothing.

I scream. Can't help it. I scream, whip off my hat, and leap forward again, dancing around in front of the statue like a woman possessed.

"Is she off?" I yell at Vince. "Did I get her? Can you see her? Where did she go?"

"She?" he mutters back, scurrying over to look me up and down. "Got attached to the creepy thing, did you?"

My mind is too busy to worry about what I've said. Instead I spin about and use the shiny surface of the sculpture to show my reflection. Nothing. No sign of Anansi at all, just my own distorted, petrified face.

I bend low with my hands on my knees. "Oh Goddess."

Vince wriggles past me to look at the sculpture. He looks up, down, across, and into it, his baton still raised as if to strike.

From the corner of my eye, down low on the ground I spot the telltale flicker of many legs diving for cover.

"Vince—"

"What, I need to find it. That thing probably came in on a plane from who knows where. There's nothing native to this country that looks like that. What if it's venomous? We need to find it before someone else does."

Of course, that makes sense. Anansi, though shaped like a tarantula, is much larger than one. More than that, her colouring is entirely off. I have no idea what species she is, but Vince makes a damn good point. A point that makes my skin crawl all the more.

"Well, I…it…I mean, they don't like being around people much, right? Maybe it hid?"

"But we still need to find it," he insists, now beginning to scout along the ground.

Anansi inches closer to my foot. Goddess, no, Vince is so close now, scanning closer and closer. He's going to find her if I don't do something right now.

Only one thing I can do—I drop my hat, letting it flop down on top of her, feigning a fumble with my trembling fingers.

"Oops."

But Vince doesn't even look at me, just grabs the hat by the rim and thrusts it back at me as he continues to search.

I take the hat carefully, peering into the lined interior, hoping, praying, but also dreading what I'll find.

"Oh, good…" Yup. There she is, one huge, hairy spider, clinging to the silky lining inside the hat with her legs slightly splayed.

I close my eyes and beg for strength for the triple Goddess. It's the only way I'll manage what I'm about to do next.

Beside me, Vince springs to a full stand and whirls to face me. "Tina?"

I slap the hat onto my head. "Yeah?"

Oh no, no, no, I can feel her moving, eight delicate legs finding balance in my hair. It's not uncomfortable, and she certainly isn't heavy, but I sense every motion, every step, every wriggle, large or small.

Again my stomach writhes. The sandwich threatens to reappear.

"It's gone." Vince looks about a little more, but half-heartedly now. "How can something so big move so bloody fast? And where did it go?"

Just voiceless shakes of the head. I can't speak. I don't trust myself to try. Instead I simply stand, one hand pressed to my belly, the other to my chest.

Just breathe in. Breathe out. And in. And out.

"Do we need to report that to pest control or something? I know you didn't see it, but I'm not kidding—I've never seen such a big spider in my life. Looked like it belongs in a movie."

"Uh-huh." Even to my own ears, my voice is a painful squeak. I angle the hat to give Anansi as much space as possible while my innards coil into horrified, disgusted knots.

Is the hat moving? I feel like it's moving.

Vince scours the area around the sculpture for a few more seconds before backing off, scratching his bald head. "Weird. Very weird. You keep looking here, I'm going to check if it scuttled off that way."

I barely see him go. My knees give a horrid wobble, and I drop down onto the nearest bench, gingerly pulling the hat off to rest it upside down in my lap.

Anansi waggles her legs at me.

"By every Goddess of the moon and under it, what are you playing at?"

More leg waggling.

"Do you want to get crushed? I should have left you at home, I just knew it. This is an actual nightmare—" I slam the hat back onto my head as Vince jogs into view. Eight hairy legs mash into my skull, and I might swear I also heard a hiss or a squeak of pain.

"Nothing." Vince pauses and screws up his face. "I checked with Skip, and he told me to stop being such a bloody baby and get back on the beat. So, I guess that means just leave it."

"Yup. Yup. That's fine. Leave it. No problem at all. Let's get a move on. We should try to reach the bus station before the crowds trickle in."

Though he nods, Vince continues to scratch his head as he walks. "What on earth?" he murmurs softly. "Why would such a thing even be out here?"

Why indeed?

CHAPTER SIXTEEN

We reach the back of the shopping centre and the wide stretch of three roads that criss-cross each other towards the car park, bus station, and string of smaller stores. I've just about managed to keep my cool, but I know too much longer with a literal spider on my head is going to do terrible things to me. I *need* somewhere to put her. Anywhere. Just so long as it's safe, private, and a place I can return to once my shift is over.

Instead of watching the streets and the people, I find myself watching the buildings, scouting out somewhere I can duck in for a moment or two.

We've completed our first circuit of the area and are looping around to patrol past the bus station again when Dink once more pokes his furry head out of my pocket. He scents the air delicately before scurrying up my vest and into the neck of my shirt.

A quick glance left shows me Vince hasn't noticed a thing, but there is one man, standing outside a pizza place with the shutters down, who looks at me curiously as we pass.

The mouse curls up against the base of my throat, tail flopping out over the collar. I stuff it back in with a grimace, once more scanning the area around me for anybody who might be looking.

Nobody.

But I do spy a small, nondescript, wooden door in the line of buildings on my left.

My heart gives a little leap of hope.

I stop in front of the door, stooping as if to retie my laces.

When Vince looks back at me, his head cocked with curiosity, I make a great show of pausing, then place my ear to the door. "Hear that?"

"No. What's up?" He walks back to me and looks at the door with surprise. "Wow, how long has this been here? I don't think I've ever noticed this door before."

Good. He's not supposed to.

I tell him, "It's just an old gaming shop, but sometimes people struggling with addiction take shelter in here. And I thought I heard something. We should probably take a look."

"You sure? Doesn't look like anybody has been in here since the place shut."

I straighten and grasp the handle. My body tenses as I wait for the familiar blossom of *fortis* to greet me, but as I push the door open, nothing happens. Odd. Are the wards gone?

Dink turns another excited circle inside my collar. I wish he'd stop—he has claws, and they itch as they scratch me. On my head, Anansi squirms her legs against the tops of my ears.

Never mind that I have to get inside. I *need* to get her off me. Now.

Vince peers into the gloom beyond the door. "Weird. You'd expect this to be locked."

I don't have the brain space to make up an appropriate lie. Instead I march through into the cool quiet beyond. "You search down here," I tell him without pausing. "I'll do a quick sweep upstairs."

"Sure, I guess." He eyes the empty space with an air of quiet interest, still muttering about how he never knew it was here.

Like a few days earlier, I walk past the display podiums, shelving units, and cabinets, but something doesn't feel right.

The glass in two of the cabinets is broken, shattered pieces strewn across the floor. There's even a food wrapper and a grubby pair of jeans draped over one of the podiums.

I feel a prickle of annoyance at whoever came here after me and Nikolette. The least they could do was keep this space tidy. And replace the wards. Though I don't know why any witch would remove them in the first place.

And what's that smell?

No time. I head straight through the checkout space and the creaky door marked *Private*. I barely let it close before sweeping the hat off my head.

Anansi immediately jumps out, landing lightly on the floor and scuttling towards the stairs.

"No, no, no, you daft thing, where are you going?"

But she doesn't stop, simply folds herself into an impossibly small gap at the bottom step, only to reappear again near the top several seconds later. Her body oozes out of the hole in the floorboards legs first, followed by her body that pops out so sharply I swear I can almost hear it.

There's sweat on my forehead, filling my underarms, dampening my palms.

I rub my hands against my thighs, reposition the hat, and take the stairs. "Anansi? Get back here, I need somewhere safe to put you. Anansi?"

Then Dink crawls out of my collar. He scrambles across my stab vest, over my belt, and down my left leg before flumping to the floor and darting off after the spider.

What is wrong with these two?

"Guys, come on, please!"

I hurry after them, trying to keep my steps light and my voice low.

I manage it fairly easily until I round the corner off the steps into the upper game area with its covered tables and low stools.

My mouth drops open. "What the hell…?"

The space is a veritable junkyard of needles, old clothes, moulding food, faerie dust cartridges, and empty, shredded blood bags.

My mouth still hanging open, I walk through to take in the devastation. So much mess, so much grime and filth, with horrible signs smeared over the walls and the creeping scent of what I hope isn't excrement.

The urge to cover my nose rises strong within me, but I can't. I can only stare.

In any other place, at any other time, I might have assumed I'd stumbled onto a den. They aren't common, but it's not unknown to happen across a hotspot for humans seeking vampires to share their blood, or a quiet space to snort the fine green dust said to give a user the most glorious of highs.

So sad that mundane and *edane* alike are occasionally driven to the sort of life that ends in rehab if they're lucky and death if they aren't.

The last time I helped a team pull one of those places apart, I struggled to get the smell of rot, pain, and despair out of my hair and clothes. That was also the last time I'd ever worn my hair long.

But this place isn't a den, not with all its wards and protective barriers, designed to keep exactly those people out.

But the wards are gone…

Sickness rises in my stomach as I take another step.

Bloodstains dot the tables and stools, spilled from medical blood bags I recognize as stores from the Clear Blood Foundation. Gang signs, known for their links to werewolves in particular, are scrawled over the walls. Piles of clothes, old shoes, and towels are heaped up in corners as if to serve as lumpy, makeshift nests for passing out in. There's even a dark slick of black ooze against one wall that I'm pretty sure means a vampire has died here.

Ahead of me, Dink and Anansi have stopped beside a table with jagged, broken legs stabbing up at the ceiling.

Slumped against it is a figure with the head bowed, face hidden by a scraggle of tightly curled grey hair.

"Hello?" I call softly. "Sir?"

No answer. Hardly surprising, though. The amount of faerie dust apparently used here would be enough to knock out a mature male gargoyle. Maybe even a female.

"Can you hear me?" I hurry closer. "Sir?"

I hope it isn't a fang junkie. The last thing I need is the complicated paperwork related to transferring a murder case. Hopefully it's just some poor soul who took a little too much.

The two familiars dart aside as I reach out and grasp the figure by the shoulder.

A shock of static fizzes through my fingers, and I let go, but even that brief touch is enough to know that I'm far, far too late.

The body is limp and cold. Rigour has apparently been and gone, and it slumps to the side as my touch disturbs it. One arm twists awkwardly beneath the limp body, while the other flops outward, palm up and exposed.

Great, just great.

I turn, as if to run for Vince, but movement from Dink catches my eye. As I watch, the little mouse scurries over the body, under the long hair, and out the other side to hurry down the outstretched arm. He stops at the upturned palm and curls up there, smoothing his whiskers with both front paws. Then Anansi joins him, resting on the join of the wrist and waving her middle legs.

Only then do I see what they seem to be gesturing at.

The hand wears a ring on the pinkie finger. It is narrow and plain, entirely unremarkable but for the fact that it's made of wood and that it appears to be an exact match to one I've seen already today.

I stare at the two familiars. A tremble settles into my lower lip.

"No. No, no, no."

Again I reach out, this time to push back that long grey hair, to expose the face beneath.

"Oh no."

Not an addict chasing a faerie-dust high. Not a fang junkie. Not even a plain and simple unhoused person seeking a roof under which to spend the night.

A tear slips down my face as I gaze at that familiar face, the wrinkled forehead, the high cheekbones, the tiny tattoo etched beneath the right eye.

"Hyacinth…?"

CHAPTER SEVENTEEN

It takes several seconds to pull myself together, still more to stop my vision blurring and dash away the tears. I sit back on my heels, hands pressed to my knees, fighting, struggling to think.

What happened? What should I do? Who did this?

The questions whirl around my mind, more and more, faster and faster until there's nothing but white noise and screaming between my ears.

Anansi skitters towards me and stops beside my knee.

For the first time, probably ever, the sight of a spider so close to me does nothing.

She taps side to side in front of me, waving her front legs as if to catch my attention. As soon as I gaze her way, she scurries back to Hyacinth.

She wants me to look at the body.

Oh Goddess, the body. Not Hyacinth any more but *the body.*

I fight the urge to scream.

Her face is peaceful and slack, eyes closed. At the very least it doesn't look as though she died in pain, an assertion that vanishes the second I turn her body a little more.

Black, dried blood is caked all over her clothes and on the floor beneath her. It's too old to be damp but fresh enough to be sticky, with vaguely dusty edges that crack as I shift her around. Her pretty tunic is shredded, decimated by many, many hacking slashes, as though from a knife. Through the gaps, I catch glimpses of the horrible wounds in her skin, choked with dried-up blood.

"Vince…" My voice is a strangled whisper. I know I need to do better than that, but I can't gather the breath. "Vince?"

My throat locks up. Head begins to pound. Mind fills with the memory of petrified screams, desperately running figures in the gloom, and the unforgettable scent of spilled blood.

No. No, please, not again…

Movement on my left draws my eye towards a door in the far wall. I hadn't looked there before, but I recognize it as the way to the fire escape Nikolette used, while I utilized the front door. Couldn't be seen together after all.

There's a flash of motion, a flicker of red, then the patter of light, quick footsteps retreating.

"Vince!" This time my voice is loud and powerful, more than is human, a shout that carries with it the weight of my will.

I hear a yelp from downstairs and an answering call of my name.

"Front door," I bellow, already on my feet. "Murder suspect attempting to flee the scene."

"Murder? What the fuck?"

"Go!" I roar back, then sprint across the room and headlong into the door.

It slams open into the near wall and bounces back at me. But I'm already through. Before me, a door to the right leads to the bathrooms, and on the left, a staircase dog-legs its way down to the ground floor.

That same flash of red flickers out of sight.

I run, pounding down the stairs two at a time, half slipping, half sliding, one hand gripping the banister rail while the other fumbles for my shoulder radio. "DA39, this is Moon-E3, pursuing suspected C84. Old gaming store on Belmy Road. Moon-E3 and Hawk-F7 in pursuit."

The radio crackles to life beneath my hand. "Moon-E3, this is DA39, repeat?"

I hit the bottom of the stairs just as the fire door slams shut ahead of me. I barely pause, simply kick the damn thing open and dart out into the rear yard.

It's dim back here, a bare square of concrete and empty pallets hemmed in on all sides by the tall buildings. Diagonally and to the right, the flash of red I now recognize as hair struggles to climb over a low wall separating this yard from the narrow passage which leads to the street.

"Stop, police," I bellow, leaning into a new sprint. "Stop now!"

They don't stop. They fumble their way over the gate, tumble down the other side and presumably into the alley.

I hear another door crash open from inside the game shop. Vince is moving at last.

Good, because we're going to catch this guy in a pincer movement.

One hand planted on top of the wall gives me stability as I vault over it, scooting my feet up high to clear it with plenty of room to spare. Muddy puddle water splashes up my boots and across my ankles as I land and take off again, with only the slightest of pauses to catch my balance.

"Moon-E3, this is DA39, repeat last call."

The figure ahead of me darts left out of the alley.

"Suspected C84." I dodge around a large industrial bin. "On foot. Blue jeans. Baggy knitted jumper. Red hair." Hurdle a small slick of what I hope is spilled milkshake. "Leaving empty game shop onto Belmy Road."

"Ten-four, Moon-E3. Incoming backup. Two minutes."

Oh, we're not going to need two minutes.

I burst out of the alley in time to see the figure haring up the street, an awkward, slightly tilting gait. Just ahead, the door to the shop opens and Vince tumbles out of it, one hand still on his radio. I belt past him with a sharp "Move!"

And then I'm running again.

I squint at the scene ahead, gaze fixed on the back of the figure retreating before me. To the left and right are civilians, most oblivious, a sparse few watching with interest as I streak past. No time to stop, no time to take care.

An elderly couple just about swing out of reach as I hare past them, a man pushing a pram doing the same. I barely look, hardly see, certainly don't pause as the subject of my chase begins to slow.

Far behind, I know Vince is there, hot on my heels, but he'll never catch me. I'm fuelled by rage, by grief, by a savage burning desire to discover who would dare do this.

The figure ahead reaches the busy road that cuts in front of the bus station. They pause, seemingly caught up by indecision.

I don't.

With a great leap, I launch myself at the stranger and tackle them around the middle, taking us both to the ground in a tangle of limbs. I just have the presence of mind to shield their face with my hand and then we're tumbling over and over off the lip of pavement and into the road.

There are screams. Shouts of alarm. The honk of a car horn.

I realize then that I've rolled us both into oncoming traffic and that a double-decker bus is leaning into a frantic attempt to brake.

Someone is screaming. Maybe it's me. I can't be sure, but I hook my legs around the suspect and throw myself backwards, barrel-rolling us onto the kerb.

Metal squeals as the brakes work hard to save us, and several shouts come from petrified onlookers.

The figure in my arm wails frantically, and I grip all the harder, winding my legs around their knees. I grab their hands in mine and wrench them behind their back. "You're under arrest," I hiss, putting my face close to all that curly red hair. "Fleeing the police. Breaking and entering. Murder."

"No, no, please—"

"Shut up. Vince?"

He arrives ever so slightly out of breath, one hand already tugging solid handcuffs off his belt. He bends beside me and grips one of the flailing wrists, slamming the first cuff in place with a practised slap. "You don't have to say anything right now, love," he murmurs, "but it may harm your defence if you don't mention something when questioned that you later rely on in court."

"Please, please—"

I tighten my grip. "Pay attention." My voice is an ugly snarl, but I don't care. I can barely see through the rage blinding me. There's nothing but layers upon layers of red.

Vince clicks the second cuff into place, then uses both hands to heave the suspect up, out of my grip, and to their feet. "Anything you do say may be given as evidence. Do you understand the rights I've read to you?"

At last I stand. Somewhere in the back of my mind I register pain in my right leg. Maybe I twisted it during the tackle or something. Who knows? Who cares? I limp around the slumped, whimpering figure and plant my hands on my hips. "Well? Do you understand?"

A familiar flash of knowing fills my senses. Kinship. *Sisterhood.*

The figure finally meets my gaze, and for the second time that day I find myself staring into mismatched eyes, one blue, one brown.

Something in my gut twists like an angry knife.

"Please," she whispers, "you don't understand. I haven't done anything wrong."

The woman from before. From outside Hyacinth's house. That I almost hit with my car. The one I thought I'd seen before. The witch.

I glance at Vince, but of course he has no clue.

On my shoulder, the radio gives a hiss of static. "Moon-E3, this is DA39. Reinforcement closing on your location, please confirm?"

I let out a slow, measured breath through my nose. "Hey DA39, this is Moon-E3 and Hawk-F7. We're at the bus station. Suspect in custody."

"Ten-four, Moon-E3. Bring them in."

Slowly, I eye the woman from top to bottom. Her hands are shaking behind her back, her shoulders hunched and tense. She refuses to meet my gaze, staring hard at the floor without speaking.

I fight the urge to slap her across the face.

Damn right I'll bring her in. Can't make any promises as to what will happen after that, though.

Chapter Eighteen

The next hour is a blur of motion. Rubber-neckers at the scene getting in the way, trying to look at what is going on. Two marked cars screeching to a halt close by and disgorging five of my fellow officers. Vince holding tightly to this strange woman while I pace back and forth in front of her, anger and confusion pulsing inside me.

It takes so much effort to keep my hands to myself, my voice to myself, my thoughts and anger to myself.

Who is this woman? What was she doing inside the shop? What *happened* to the shop? What was she doing outside of Hyacinth's house? What coven does she belong to?

Along with everything else going on, I can't help but remind myself that she's a witch. She should have been able to feel the wards in that building and surely would have known what they were for. More than that, if she's local to Angbec, then there's no way she couldn't recognize Hyacinth. Everybody knows Hyacinth.

Knew. Knew Hyacinth.

I sit in the front passenger side of the car Vince insisted I climb into, saying that he and a couple of other officers would secure the scene back at the shop.

I don't have it in me to argue.

That's how I find myself back at the station standing outside the interview rooms, waiting for a chance to go in.

Sergeant Hozier meets me there first.

"What are you doing?" he murmurs.

"I'm going to question her. I need to know what she was doing. Who is she? What was she doing there? Why did she kill Hya—that woman?"

Hozier eyes me cautiously. "No. You're too high-strung and stressed out. I don't know what happened out there, but I'm not letting you into this room."

I gape at him. "But—"

"Who is she?"

I shake my head, as if that will help me clear the fug at the sudden subject change. "I don't know. That's why I want to go inside. I need to ID her and—"

"Not the suspect. The woman in the shop."

"She…" I pause.

He puts a hand on my shoulder. When I flinch away, he backs off two full steps and shoves his hands into his pockets. "Sorry, I just need you to know I support you, Tina. I would never, ever say anything about what you are and what you do. I don't really know *what* you do, but I *do* know you're on our side."

Immediately my gaze flicks to the floor. "Skip—"

"*What* you and your witch friends get up to is none of my business, until it becomes my business. So I have to know, right now…Is this my business?"

I can't look at him. "I—"

"Tina." He leans in close to drop his voice to a whisper. "We can't solve a murder without all the facts, and this is the fourth body. You know this connects you to the other three, right?"

I hadn't considered that in the whirlwind of events, but he's right, of course. Four people turn up dead in a short amount of time, all located relatively close together? The facts of one can easily affect the others.

With effort, I raise my gaze and look him dead in the eye. "I've no idea who the suspect is. I've seen her once before, but that's it."

He frowns.

Both of us are so deeply aware of my avoidance of the question. But will he break first, or will I?

Hozier moves to bodily block the door. "You're not going inside. I have plenty of people out here to help, and you need to take five. Go see the first-aider."

I give him a curious look.

"You're limping. Did you fall when you were running?"

I think back over the chase. It seems so long ago now. Maybe when I tackled her, or hit the road. But he's right—I can feel it now, a twinge of pain up my right leg that only intensifies now that I have my mind on it.

"I need to know—"

"No, you don't." Hozier pins me with a firm look. "You *need* to see the first-aider, then clock off for the day."

"But—"

"Clock. Off." His voice hardens. "Come in tomorrow, fresh and rested, and we'll talk then."

No point arguing with that voice. I haven't heard that tone directed at me over much, but now is the time to cut my losses.

Still grumbling, I make my way to the first aid office and wait for the officer to show up.

They're a tall, round-shouldered figure with their own barely visible limp. "Hey." They slip into the room and shut the door. "I'm Chris. Skipper says you need looking at."

I pull up the leg on my trousers, surprised to find dried blood forming a trail down the side of my calf. "Guess I hurt myself."

"Mm-hmm." Chris begins pulling antiseptic wipes and bandages off the shelves. "Get your leg out of those, so I can have a proper look."

Belt first, button, zip, then I pull the trousers down enough to pull out my leg. The whole thing, from the thigh down to just below my knee, is an angry patch of shredded skin. I must have hit the ground hard. I didn't even notice.

Chris whistles softly through their teeth, then gestures for me to lie down on the examination bench. When I do, they begin to look me over, gently cleaning up the wound, a portion at a time.

Soon, a little pile of bloody wipes lies on the ground, and my skin is singing with pain. Manageable, of course, but the stinging sensation from the wipes is hard to ignore.

Fortunately, the mess looks far worse than it actually is, and once the blood is cleared up, I can see that the scrape is narrow and centred on the meaty part of my thigh.

"Moonwalking across the road, were you?"

I shrug. "Sliding tackle on a runaway suspect."

Chris grins. "Don't envy you lot out there. You got them, though?"

"We're questioning them now."

"Mm-hmm. And the stiff just reached the coroner. Poor thing. But at least we'll have a post-mortem soon."

That rage builds inside me again. I tamp it down with a fierce shove and concentrate instead on keeping my leg from twitching.

Soon Chris is rubbing a cold, white cream all over my thigh, then wrapping it with a light bandage. "Just keep it clean," they murmur. "It's not deep or infected or anything like that, but there's a lot of it. Mostly skin. You'll see some scabbing over the next day or two, so try to keep it dry. When you wash, just pat it clean."

"Yeah, yeah, I know the drill." This isn't the first time I've been hurt in the line of duty. Hell, I've been stabbed before. And shot. That last one isn't as impressive as it sounds, just a hot graze from a bullet flying past my shin. Barely even a scar to tell of it, even though it's pretty cool to tell everyone I've been shot.

"Fine, hardball. Then get dressed and get yourself out of here. Skip says you're going home?"

Ha, no I'm not, but I don't tell Chris that. Instead, I push into a sitting position and feed my leg back into my trousers. "Thanks for the help."

Chris makes a non-committal noise and a vague waving gesture as they settle down to fill in paperwork.

I leave them to it.

Barely realizing it, my feet take me back towards the interview rooms. It isn't hard to find the one housing the witch—it's the only one closed. I risk peering through the observation slot and see Hozier already in there with two other officers I don't know. The camera winks on its tripod, and on the table, a small voice recorder also flashes a red light at me.

The woman inside looks petrified.

Now I can finally get a semi-decent look at her, I can see just how pale she is. Her red hair is huge and curly, a halo of shiny red strands around her head. Most striking are those eyes, though, the brilliant, gleaming blue of one versus the warm, honeyed undertone of the brown one.

My hand is on the handle before I realize it.

Deep breath. Easy, Tina.

Loud footsteps from behind pull my gaze around. It's Vince, marching to keep up with yet another woman who seems to be making a beeline for the door.

She stops when she sees me, hands on her hips. "Is that the room?"

Her voice lashes with the whip of command, a woman used to being obeyed.

"Wh-what?"

"Is that Blake's room? Blake Allen? I need to see her immediately. I'm her representative."

Blake. So that's her name.

Vince cuts across the pair of us. "This is the room, Ms. Wesker, please just wait here a moment while I check in with my colleagues." He tries to step past me, but I can't move. I find myself staring at this woman and feeling the bottom fall out of my stomach.

Wesker. I know the name well. *April* Wesker is one of the reasons Nikolette and I have spent so much of our time sneaking around and avoiding detection. If Nikolette is nervous about her grandmother learning of her relationship with me, April is another reason why.

April Wesker is a witch. Not only that, she's the Mother of the Elm Stems.

CHAPTER NINETEEN

I back up, keen to give space to this powerful woman. She arches an eyebrow at me but says nothing, actually reaching around Vince to open the door to the interview suite and sweep inside.

I hear a gasp of relief, then confused murmurs, both of which cut off as Vince hurries in and shuts the door.

Again, I use the observation slot.

Damn it, Vince, move.

He's right in front of the door, but I can hear them well enough. April has introduced herself with the same power and authority with which she no doubt handles her coven, and Hozier is doing his best to keep up. I hear him stutter, then pause, then politely introduce himself as well as the other officers in attendance.

Not that it matters.

"Blake, get up." April's voice is sharp and clipped. "You're not being charged, and you're under no obligation to say anything more to these officers. Come, we're leaving."

What? How can she not be charged?

I can't help it, this time I open the door.

The room is packed, two officers, Hozier, Vince, April, and Blake all crammed into a space ideally designed for maybe half that many. I squeeze myself in and immediately find a glare from Hozier waiting for me.

I don't care.

Blake is already standing, her nervous hands playing in front of her as she waits for instruction from her Mother. The other two officers to either side of her seem poised, ready to take her by the arms, but

April cuts off all that with a sweep of her hand.

It's not a spell, of course it's not, but the authority of that simple motion almost makes the gesture feel like one.

"Unless you have an apology for Ms. Allen, then we'll be on our way. Thank you for your time, Officers." She gestures towards the door. Through me.

With short, nervous steps, Blake shuffles away from the two officers and scoots around the table. She seems to hug the wall as she goes, struggling to make herself as small as possible.

At the door, we meet face to face once more, and I glare with such venom in my heart I can feel it fizzing in my fingers. "Blake Allen," I murmur.

She winces.

"I'll be seeing you again." My voice is low, deliberately so, but I know she hears me. The little twitch of her right eyebrow tells me as much.

She turns sideways and eventually squeezes out past me, not that I give even the smallest shred of space.

Then April arrives at my shoulder, and I find myself leaping to one side.

Seconds later, the pair are gone, whisked away down the corridor as swiftly as April arrived.

"Skip!" The word bursts out of me. I can't help it. "Why didn't you charge her?"

He gives a weary sigh. One hand reaches up to wipe at his face. "Come on, Tina—"

"No, she was right there. *Right there*. And she ran. Clearly she knows more about this than she's letting on."

"Maybe, but that body had been there for at least a day or two. Surely you saw that when you first found it. Looks like Ms. Allen was just unlucky enough to stumble on it right as you found her. But there's nothing on her to suggest she was involved."

"What? I think—"

He raises a hand to me. "Stop. Just stop. Go get changed, like I told you, then meet me in the cafeteria."

"Skipper—"

"Tina. Do as I say."

Again that tone. I've pushed it too far. With a last glance at him and Vince—who looks more confused than ever—I whirl about and stomp back to the changing rooms.

❖

By the time I'm back into my own clothes, my mood has steadied enough to allow rational thought. I sit on the bench running down the centre of the room as I fiddle with my boots and try to think back to the scene.

It's all a blur now. My mind is too busy, my thoughts too rapid. And just thinking of it sends a fissure of pain and grief through me so strong that I can barely breathe.

Hyacinth. My Mother. My mentor. My friend.

A tear catches in the corner of my eye, but I dash it away. Now isn't the time. It can't be the time.

Step by step, I force myself to go back through my grisly discovery.

Entering the building, removing my hat as I passed through the first door towards the back, Anansi and Dink scurrying away up the stairs and—

Oh no.

My heart twists. "They knew."

Of course they did. Familiars are linked inexorably to their witch, matched to them in ways most people can't fathom. They must have felt traces of her presence and hurried away to investigate.

Their pain and sorrow must equal if not exceed mine.

I wonder where they are now. In the rush and frantic chase that followed I'd forgotten all about them. By now the area must be under full investigation, filled with officers, SOCO, photographers, and all the other professionals who frequent horrific crime scenes. I hope they're all right. At some point I'll need to go back and get them.

But Hyacinth…

I remember her body, the way she slumped so brokenly against that shattered table. The blood around her body, face, and clothes, so dry as to be a dark, rusty stain.

Hozier is right. Her body—cold, grey, and frighteningly light—had clearly been in that spot for at least a day. Maybe two.

I can hear the hiss of my own ragged breathing, the distant clomp of footsteps through the building, and the rumble of the air conditioning filling the space with cool, recycled air.

A shuddering breath escapes my lips.

Then I'm crying. And not a gentle tear down the cheek either, my chest heaves as the sobs grip me, and I crush my hands against my face as if that simple motion might shove the tears back in.

Hyacinth.

What happened? When? How? Why? And who? Who would do such a thing? Is this why the wards were gone?

Again I think of her limp and battered body. Though it wasn't entirely clear through the clothes, I know she had been stabbed. More than once.

She must have been in so much pain. So scared. And alone. Nobody was around to help her. She died in that cold, dark space with nothing but her own thoughts and the slow trickle of her lifeblood draining away.

"Tina?"

I bolt upright, immediately wiping at my eyes and cheeks.

"Tina, you okay?"

I gasp out a shuddering, "Yeah, what's up, Skip?"

"Can I come in?"

I shrug, but he can't see it.

Not that it matters, because a moment later, Sergeant Hozier creeps slowly into the space. He looks left, then right, then sits beside me. He doesn't speak, just waits.

My lower lip wobbles.

"Who was she?" he whispers. "You're going to have to tell me eventually."

"H-Hyacinth Dixon." I sniff again and, once more, swipe at my eyes. "She…she's…I mean, she was…fuck."

I can feel Hozier's gaze on me. I don't normally swear, not at work at least.

He puts a gentle hand on my shoulder. "Come on. You can't stay in here." He pulls, and I follow with no resistance.

He leads me out of the changing area, back through the main office, and towards the break area where the kettle is. He points to a low, squishy sofa, and I slump into it, elbows resting on my knees, face cupped in my hands.

The scent of sugary coffee fills my nostrils as he gently nudges a mug into view.

I take it. The fluid within is milky enough to make even his pale skin appear tan, but I take a sip anyway. "Thank you."

He nods and sits at the table opposite. He faces me with his hands clasped between his knees. "You know what I need to ask. You know how this works. But for now, we can go off the record. I know you've got a…sensitive personal life."

That's one way of putting it.

I breathe deep through my nostrils. "What did Blake say?"

"You know I can't—"

"What did she say?"

Long, taut silence.

"She said she was due to meet someone there. She went in through the back like she always does and found the body when she went upstairs. She had been about to call for help when she heard people downstairs, presumably yourself and Vince. Your arrival scared her, so she tried to sneak away and panicked when you began to follow."

"Why did she run?"

Hozier sighs. "We don't need to do this."

"Skipper. Why. Did. She. Run?"

"Come on, you saw the state of that place, a den if ever I saw one. Anybody caught in there would at the very least get written up, more likely charged with all sorts. Nobody wants to get nicked for those weird *edane* crimes. That doesn't mean she's a murderer."

The mug trembles in my hands. "But she was there. If she was already going to call for help, why did she run? She has to be hiding something. She must be."

"Enough. I know you're upset, but—"

"Upset?" My fingers flex and the mug hits the floor. The handle snaps and skids away beneath the table while the coffee within washes across the dull grey carpet. "Someone murdered my friend. Do you hear me, *murdered*. I'm more than upset, I'm fucking livid. And I want to know what she was hiding."

Hozier's face hardens. As he stands, I can all but hear the decision he makes in that moment to stop humouring me. "Go home," he mutters. "Take the rest of the day off. I don't want to see you here until you've had the chance to calm down. And keep your phone on you—I'm assigning you a support officer—"

"I don't need—"

"A support officer"—he raises his voice—"who will go through a health check with you. This is a shock, and you need support."

"Skip, please—"

He shakes his head. "No. We're done. I'll call a cab for you. Do *not* try to drive out of here. You're in no state."

I open my mouth to object again, but he spins and walks off before I can, leaving me in the break room with cool coffee soaking into the hems of my jeans.

CHAPTER TWENTY

While standing on the kerb outside the station, I try to keep my thoughts steady. I struggle to focus on one thought at a time, but the different words, questions, and feelings are moving too quickly in a soup of mental chaos. I can't focus on anything at all.

Thankfully, mercifully, my phone begins to ring.

Nikolette Mob.

Goddess. In the midst of everything happening today I'd forgotten about our argument. And the uncharacteristically apologetic text messages that followed. I still haven't managed to respond, and I have no idea what I'm supposed to say to her.

My thumb hovers over the square on my screen marked *Answer*.

I *want* to answer. I want to talk to her. I want to hear the silky smoothness of her voice and the calm it carries. I want her to tell me it's going to be all right and feel her arms around me while she whispers in my ear. I want her cool, calm presence and pragmatic reasoning.

The phone stops ringing.

Yeah. Maybe that's for the best.

After several long seconds of fretting, I see a car with a big sticker on the side proclaiming it a taxi for private hire.

The driver, a sprite with bright green skin, shiny with a sheen of pine needles, winds down their window. "You ride?"

I reach for the rear passenger handle. Freeze.

Do I really want to go home right now? *Can* I go home? Or will I simply sit there in the dark and fume over what has happened today? There must be something more I can do.

"Lady-lady?" The sprite leans over the seats to look at me. "Ride?"

I tuck my phone back into my pocket and shake my head. "No, thank you, I'm going to drive."

"Oh. Is shame. I'm sorry. Then goodbye, yes?"

But I'm already moving, walking left to enter the short fence that separates the grounds of the station from the public. It also provides access to the car park where I can already see my crunchy old banger waiting for me.

I know what Hozier said about driving, but this is one of the few decisions lately that I feel well equipped to make on my own.

I'm going to drive myself. And that drive is going to take me to Angbec General.

❖

On site, I settle my rucksack on my shoulder and gaze up at the tall squat building that makes up the rear of the hospital. The morgue is down here, an area I've visited several times in my career as an officer.

I hate it.

The double doors swish open as I approach, and the bright lights of the interior spill out. Somehow the sky is already beginning to darken, and I realize just how much of the day has already passed without me. Hard to believe it's the same one.

At the arrival desk, a woman looks up from her computer and gives me a neat, professional smile when I show her my ID card. "Hi, Officer, wasn't expecting you today."

"It's a fly-by," I tell her, wishing I could remember her name. "Can you tell me what room the latest has been sent to?"

"The Jane Doe?"

I bite my lip. So Hozier hasn't made it here yet. Good.

"Yeah. This afternoon. Older woman. Stab wounds."

"Yup"—she taps away at her keyboard—"Belmy Road. They've just started, actually, if you want to sit in. Check room six."

Oh. I hadn't expected to arrive while the pathologists were working.

A vague, queasy feeling ripples through my stomach, but I tamp it down, nod my thanks at the receptionist, then follow the corridor.

On my right, two sets of lifts form a route to the first basement level, but I ignore both in favour of the stairs. It's only a short distance, and the extra time will give me a moment to prepare for what I'm about to see.

The next level down is noticeably cooler. I'm not a fan of cold, but I prefer that to the alternatives that would no doubt include stuffiness, humidity, and horrible smells. This place already stinks as is, of death, preserving fluids, and misery.

Rooms two and four on the left stand doors open, lights off. I spot the examining tables as I pass, everything around them cold, metal, and glistening. The same is true of rooms one, three, and five. Room six has the door closed, and I take a moment outside to steel myself.

From within I hear the low murmur of a single deep voice, and I take the time to pin a bored, nonchalant look on my face. My reflection in the surface of the shiny metal door isn't convincing, even to me, but it's the best I'm going to get.

I open the door.

"...sixty to sixty-five years old. Obvious injuries in the form of multiple stab wounds across the chest, abdomen, and thighs." The voice stops.

I move deeper into the room and find a tall, broad figure stooped over the table. His skin is deep red all over, with huge barbs across his temples that resemble horns. Somehow, he has folded his colossal body into a stretched white lab coat, though his wings are exposed and curved over the top. His tail too, complete with a line of short stubby spikes, is exposed through a slit up the back.

Why even bother?

He smiles as he spots me. "Oh, hello, Officer."

"Hey, Xian."

The gargoyle clicks a button on the voice recorder hanging from a loop above his head. Then he pulls a white sheet up over the body.

The body.

"I wasn't expecting company today. Can I do something for you?"

I gesture to the table. "I'm the one who found her. Just wondered if there was anything you could tell me to kick-start the investigation."

He nods. "Well"—a sigh slips from his lips—"this one is nasty, but simple. Stabbed. Multiple times. She simply bled out, poor dear. I've only just cleaned her up enough to start, but I can already tell there's not much more to it than that. She's been dead for about two days, three at most, from the state of the body."

Three days?

But we had a conclave arranged yesterday. Does that mean she was dead even before then? Does that mean the previous morning, when I missed meeting her, she was already gone? I only left her three days ago, promising to see her shortly, so *when* on that third day? After I left her to meet Nikolette?

"It is weird, though," Xian continues without looking at me, his gaze all for the figure on the table. Good thing, really, because my mind is whirling, and I know it must show on my face. "With that many wounds, you'd expect to see some others, maybe across the hands and arms."

"Defence cuts?" I force myself to think clearly, to consider his words like a trained officer.

"Yep. But I can't see a single one. Nothing on her hands, forearms, fingers, or palms. It's like she just stood there, waiting to be stabbed."

That doesn't sound like Hyacinth at all. She is…was…rather like me, always moving, always busy. Even when cooking she would be shifting from foot to foot, dancing around or swinging her arms. In fact, the only time I recall ever seeing her still was because she was sleeping.

"Can I…can I take a look?"

"Sure." He starts to lift the sheet, pausing when I hurry in, hands raised.

"No, no, just the face. I don't need to see the rest."

Xian gives me a curious look. "Are you all right?"

"Y-yeah." I clear my throat. "Of course. I just thought I saw something, is all. I wanted another look."

He nods, but not as though he believes me. Carefully he steps back, his huge form moving easily and delicately through the tight space. One of the barbs on his head comes close to knocking against the light fixture, but he must be finely aware of his surroundings because he ducks under it with no apparent thought.

Hyacinth lies on the table, eyes closed and peaceful. If not for the location and the tiny scrapes on her cheeks, it would be easy to believe she was sleeping.

My heart gives a painful little twist.

I remember her eyes open, the skin around them slightly wrinkled as she smiled at me. I recall the way they sparkled with mirth and pride as she showed me a trick or spell that I picked up easily, the soft warmth of her voice as she talked me through a particular set of herbs or the benefits of one crystal over another.

In that moment I realize with a pang that I'm never going to hear that voice again. Never see those eyes again. Never feel her warm hand on my shoulder again.

I swallow hard over the sob rising at the back of my throat.

Xian shifts the sheets just far enough to gently pick up her right arm. He turns it slowly, showing off the bare skin. "See? But for a few bruises there's nothing here to suggest she put up any sort of fight." He lets that arm rest, then picks up her left. "Same here. I've not reached her fingernails yet, but if there's no sign of damage to her arms and hands, I find it hard to believe she was grabbing or scratching at anything either."

Though I believe him, I take care to look for myself. I may be a boring human, but I am a witch. Perhaps there's something on her that he's missed. But even as I run a practised gaze over her arms, I can tell he's right. There's not a single mark on them. All the damage seems focused on her centre mass.

What happened in there?

"Goddess, I'm so, so sorry." I reach for Hyacinth's face and tuck a curl of her greying hair back behind her ear.

A little jolt of energy pierces my fingers.

With a yelp I yank my hand away and rub it down my thigh.

Beside me, Xian offers a sympathetic look. "Are you all right?"

"Yeah"—I shake my fingers around—"just caught me off guard."

"There's a fair amount of static down here. Even on the cadavers."

Static? No, that wasn't static. That was a spell, an expired one, giving off the last traces of magic energy before fully dissipating.

I remember then how I felt it before, back in the shop when I turned her body over. I mistook it for static then, same as Xian assumes now, but without the stress and distractions of everything else, I can identify the true source of such a feeling. I frown down at my mentor. What spell could possibly be so strong that it's only fading now?

"Anyway, I'll have more to tell you later. First thoughts—victim may have been under the influence of drugs or alcohol and therefore caught off guard by the attacker. I need the blood work back to verify that speculation, though. I've found no bruising or marks to suggest restraints, and the wounds appear to be from multiple weapons. Attacker was likely right handed judging from the angle and depth, and I'm not yet sure if there was only one. I do know, however, that this lady was most certainly alive while the wounds were inflicted. And—"

I raise my hands. "Okay, okay. Enough, thank you, Xian."

He studies me closely. "Are you sure you're all right, Officer?"

I nod because I don't trust myself to speak.

"I'll send the report to Hozier when I'm done. It shouldn't take all that long, to be honest. Will you be around later?"

Mute shake of the head.

"If you're still interested, pick it up from him."

"Are there any similarities between this"—I swallow hard—"body and the ones found earlier this week?"

"Funny you should ask, I wondered that myself." He pulls the sheet back up and shakes it out to flutter down over Hyacinth's body. "No. Not a thing. For one, those bodies showed absolutely no external sign of injury, and I couldn't find anything internal either. For all intents and purposes, those other three just…died."

"Old age?"

Another shake of the head. "One was barely older than eighteen. The other two, late twenties. Do you need to see them too?"

I'd rather not, but something tugs at the back of my mind. Besides, it wouldn't hurt.

Xian beckons me out of the room and across the corridor into room three. It's even cooler here, and instead of a large worktable, the space is full of drawers that clearly extend a good seven feet back towards the wall.

He walks through, again ducking the light fixtures to study the tags hanging on each of the handles. He tugs out one near the bottom, a long, gleaming metal tray so long that he has to pace backwards to allow space.

Another white sheet, draped over the form of a lifeless body.

"Number one," he murmurs, pulling back the covering.

I gasp. He's right. This girl looks so young, I doubt she's even twenty. But for a faded scar on her neck and the odd shape of a birthmark on her left shoulder, there's nothing special about her. I can't see a single mark on her.

A glance at the tag hanging off her right big toe shows me a number. No name.

Xian turns and counts again, choosing another drawer. This one is slightly higher up, and the machinery inside the cabinetry whirrs as it lowers the open drawer to a more visible level.

Male, I think. Short, scruffy hair and tattoos everywhere. Holes from several piercings too, though I can see all the studs and loops have been removed and placed in a small, clear bag beside the body. The only thing remotely special about this body is the faint green tinge to the skin around the nose and upper lip.

I point to it. "Faerie dust?"

"Without doubt. I think that detail was left off by the press, but this person clearly used a lot of the stuff. I'd suspect their last hit was one too many."

I remember the reports well enough. I helped collate them. Which means the last body I have yet to see belongs to another woman, slightly older and littered with the scabbed-over punctures of vampire teeth.

The contents of the third drawer bear out my memory.

She was plump in life, with faded lines of wrinkles around her eyes and forehead. Laugh lines, my mother would call them.

The crook of her left elbow is the most dotted with little rings of fang marks, though I spy several more on her collarbone, her stomach, and even more on her inner thighs. High on her inner thighs.

I avert my gaze.

"But these aren't the things that killed them—the faerie dust, the vampire bites?"

Xian shakes his head. "From what I can find, their hearts just stopped beating."

Again I reach for a tag, this on the big toe of the woman with the bite marks. My fingers brush her skin as I turn the slip of card, and again, another jolt like lightning fizzes through my skin.

"Wow, it's bad in here today." Xian gives an apologetic smile. "Try pressing your hands against the handle on that trolley over there. It's a good way to get rid of built-up static."

But I don't. Instead I move back to the second drawer and touch the big toe. Then the first drawer. Each time I experience a little fizz of leftover magic, traces of something powerful and ancient that no mundane—or gargoyle—pathologist would ever be able to find.

Though I hide it better this time, my stomach begins to flip-flop with a cold, alarming understanding.

A witch was involved in Hyacinth's death, there's no doubt about that. But these bodies, found over the last couple of days, they have traces of magic on them too. I have no way of knowing if it's old or recent magic, but isn't that too much of a coincidence to ignore? Especially with no other signs on these three that might point to cause of death.

I exhale hard through my nose, then pull a calm, blank expression onto my face as best I can. "Thanks for indulging me, Xian. I think that's everything I need to see."

"You're sure? I have the copies of the paperwork if you want to go through them."

What's the point? I've already learned more from these quick glances than he possibly could have in hours of study.

"No, I'm fine, I—" My phone rings. Nikolette's ringtone.

Without looking, I shove my hand into my pocket and dismiss the call by pressing the button on the side. Later. I'll have to speak with her later.

Xian pushes the drawers, one by one, back into place. "Well, if you do, let me know. I'm here for the next hour or two, so I can go over anything you want."

Kind of him, but I don't need to see anything else. I don't *want* to see anything else.

He gestures back through the door, towards room six. "I need to get back to it, if I can't help with anything else. Have a good evening, Officer."

I nod, turn, and flee.

CHAPTER TWENTY-ONE

Cool air buffets my face and neck as I scurry back outside. I appreciate it after the close, medicinal stink of the hospital. The breeze lifts the scent of embalming fluid and scatters it, leaving me with the sweet, sweet smell of car exhausts and faded cigarette smoke. Even that is preferable.

Yet again my phone rings.

This time I yank it from my pocket and press it to my ear. "Can I call you back, Nikolette? I'm in the middle of something right now."

There's a long pause from the other end. "Nikolette? The Elm Stem? Why would she be calling you?"

I wince. "Iris?"

"Yeah, who did you expect?" Her voice is clipped and irritated. As usual. "I wanted to know if you're still coming tonight and if you've found out where Hyacinth has got to. We need to get this vote out of the way, so we can get on with other business."

No. Oh no, no, no, the Willow Barks don't know. *I'm* going to have to be the one to tell them.

"Tina? Are you there? Tina!"

"Yes, sorry, sorry, I'm here." I lick my abruptly dry lips. "We… um…we need to meet sooner."

"What do you mean?"

"Now, we need to meet right now. How soon can you get to the sanctum? Can you contact the others?"

She grunts. "Why can't you do it? You used the stones this morning, we all felt it. Just do that."

My patience snaps like a breadstick. I feel the horrors of the last few hours swell and touch a part of myself I thought buried long, long ago. "Gods damn it, Iris," I hiss into the phone. "Once, just once, help me the fuck out. Tell the others we're meeting now and that I'll see you there. Understand?"

More silence down the line, only this time it's stunned and wary. "I—"

"No, just say yes, then get on with it."

I hardly recognize my own voice. I'm not sure that she does either. Iris's breathing is low and quick, and my phone creaks as I tighten my grip.

"Do you understand?" I snarl.

"Yes, Tina."

"Good. See you within the hour."

I hang up.

Another gust of cool breeze chases dust and leaf litter across the ground. I turn my face into it, letting nature's breath sweep over me. It's soothing, it's gentle. It's a whisper against my senses that brings the smallest measure of comfort.

Then, like a tipped mug of coffee, my anger spills away and more tears slide down my cheeks. I gasp as I think about how I'm going to share this news with my coven sisters, how I'm going to tell them that our Mother is dead.

❖

I arrive at the sanctum, park in the usual spot, and make my way down the little path between the homes. At the back, as ever, is the lush green space we have decided to make our own.

Already I can see signs of other Willows having passed through—the grass is crushed in places, almost entirely flat. Up ahead, beneath the curtain of willow branches, there is a soft golden light. Someone has already lit a fire.

On any other day it would have brought great comfort to see my sisters. I could have smiled and put aside my nerves to simply enjoy being around them. But today…

I swallow back the lump of pain threatening to fill the back of my throat.

The murmur of soft voices greets me. As I lift aside the trailing stems to make my way beneath, the glow of low flames brightens just a touch. Gathered loosely around it are my sisters. There is no blood between us, no traditional family bond. But to join a coven is to join a new family, a chosen family, and to accept each person within as someone to love, honour, and protect.

Like a sister.

A refreshing ripple of cool washes over me, and I recognize the circle placed around us to prevent the nosy eyes and ears of mundanes. To an outsider, we might well be invisible gathered like this, and certainly unheard. Sounds from outside the curtain of the willow branches vanish into nothingness.

I know then that casting belongs to Chloe. Yes, she's young and timid but also skilled in a way very similar to Nikolette in her ability with circles, only she is able to make hers unusually small if necessary.

Iris looks up from her pensive glare into the fire. Her thin lips tighten when she sees me, but that's all, and she tucks a wisp of her stylish angled bob back behind her ear. To her side, Edith sighs deeply as she underhands little handfuls of dust into the flames. Her hands move deftly, despite the perpetual tremor in her fingers, obvious when she places a hand over her mouth to hide a huge yawn.

Away from the pair of them, the two younger witches, Chloe and Kiara, stand closely facing each other, clearly avoiding the older women as much as they can in this small shared space. Chloe, though taller, is hunched and round-shouldered, close enough to Kiara that she seems to hide behind her. By contrast, tiny Kiara has the presence of a grizzly bear and the temper to match. She could never hide behind anybody, even if she wanted to.

How did I become the centre point between these four women?

My feet sink slightly into the soft greenery of the ground beneath, so I kick off my shoes and peel off my socks. Not necessary, but I always feel better with a direct connection to the earth. I'm going to need that level of grounding tonight.

The others, spying my motions, quickly follow suit.

"Good evening, Tina," murmurs Iris. "I'm glad you could make it."

Well, well now. Seems that a sudden snap was enough to make the older woman behave herself. I regret it, but I also don't. Though I *do* prefer the way she looks at me now, wary but respectful, even stepping back ever so slightly to grant me space.

Almost a pity, therefore, that my furious, fiery temper from earlier is gone, because now I need it. And yet…

"Hi, everyone. Thanks for coming out." I hesitate. "Thanks also for coming here early, I…" I should say more. I *need* to say more, but my tongue is stuck to the roof of my mouth, and all of my words are trapped behind it.

Soft murmurs, then some none too subtle glances behind me.

"Well?" Iris raises her eyebrows expectantly "Where's Hyacinth?"

Not really much point in drawing it out.

I draw a long deep breath, then let it go as slowly as I can manage. My bottom lip catches between my teeth for a brief moment, and I use the stab of pain to ground myself. "She…she's dead."

The words slam hard and leave a tangible impact crater in the mood of the meeting.

More tears are creeping forward, but I force them back yet again. I can't afford to cry now. There will be time for that later, much later, when I've done my duty to my sisters.

"Excuse me?" Edith looks up from the fire and dusts off her hands. She tucks them into the pocket on her crumpled linen trousers, but I can still see them trembling through the fabric. "So sorry, Tina, I thought you said—"

"I found her today. On my beat. I found her body in the warded game shop on Belmy Road."

Gasps. Whispers. Soft murmurs of shock and fear.

"No way," snaps Kiara. She turns slightly aside from Chloe and faces me with her arms folded. "Belmy Road? You're having a laugh—she's got no need to be anywhere near that shithole."

"I saw her face. And her tattoo. It was her."

Chloe stumbles, then catches herself on a tree trunk before sliding fully down to her knees.

The fire roars as Iris jabs a finger at me. "No. It's a mistake. It has to be. What happened? She can't be dead. You saw her only a few days ago. And since then? What are you trying to say?"

I lift my hand. I need to say it all, and fast, before I break down entirely.

"I went to her house this morning, but she hadn't been there since my last visit. Her familiars were near reverted—both Loki and Seshat ran off when I entered. They probably won't have much longer left.

Anansi and Dink stayed with me and retained their senses. In fact, they were the ones to find her…the body. They recognized her."

"But what *happened*?" Edith steps around the fire to get close to me. She reaches out, as if to put her hands on my shoulder, and immediately changes her mind. "Did she have an accident?"

That lump is back. And so are the tears. I can't stop them any more. They fill my eyes and spill over, dribbling down my cheeks. "Someone murdered her."

More gasps. Little cries of shock. Chloe immediately bursts into tears, while Iris also hurries forward to join me.

"What are you talking about? Murdered? When? By whom?" Edith insists.

These are all questions I wish I knew the answers to. Goddess, I wish I knew those answers.

Once again, I try to speak, but the words are stuck.

I find myself thinking of Dink in that moment and even Anansi. I wish they were here, close enough to offer their strength and comfort. Is that what it means to have a familiar? Even if one is a huge, creepy spider?

I wipe my eyes with the heel of my palm.

Must keep going.

"I don't know yet. I don't have all the details, but I chased down a suspect at the scene. She was at the station for a while, but we didn't charge her—"

"Why the fuck not?" Rather than the shock and sorrow of the others, Kiara explodes with anger. Her eyes blaze. She lifts a hand, almost as though she intends to strike me, but at the last moment balls it up into a fist near her face. "Where is Mother now?"

"Angbec General morgue. I was leaving there when you called, Iris. I know you don't want to believe it, I know it's hard, but I saw her. I identified her myself. It was Hyacinth."

"But who would do such a thing?" Chloe speaks from behind her hands, which are splayed across her tear-stained face. "Who would hurt such a kind and gentle old lady? She never did anything to anybody."

Iris snorts. "Is that why we were talking about joining with another coven? Hmm? Because the sweet and innocent Hyacinth never did anything that might make somebody come after her? Suddenly it makes far more sense."

"Shut your fucking mouth about Hyacinth." Kiara squares up to Iris in an instant, finding no disadvantage in her diminutive height. "Just because you haven't the sense to accept change doesn't mean you get to talk like that. Have more respect."

"For the woman who went and got herself killed? Who knows what she was up to—she may even have brought it on herself."

Uproar.

Four voices all raised, all heavy with emotion, all trying to be heard at once. In the middle of it I flit from person to person, sister to sister, trying to make my voice heard above all the yelling and screaming. They can't hear me. I can't even hear myself. I can hear nothing but the roar of pain and anguish made real, and the buzz of it fills my ears.

I step away from them slightly, help myself to a small stump already starting to show shoots of new growth. I sit with my head in my hands and try to gather my thoughts enough to think.

But I can't. I can't think of anything. My mind is full of Hyacinth's smiling face, juxtaposed against the sight of her pale, limp body shredded from multiple stab wounds.

Truly, how could anybody do such a thing?

I think of Blake and her horrified face and try to imagine someone as apparently timid as that even raising her voice, much less lifting a blade. Then again, looks are deceiving. Kiara is tiny, innocent of face and voice, but she is more than capable of doing and saying incredibly cruel things. Blake could be just the same.

By the time I return my attention to the sanctum, the yelling has intensified. Chloe is openly sobbing, while Edith puts an arm around her, gently wiping at her own tears. Iris and Kiara have faced each other and now, with their height difference, are caught in the most visually bizarre of shouting matches.

"The force released her, but they don't know that there was magic involved. Or that the suspect is a witch. Maybe she didn't do it, but she definitely knows more than she's letting on."

More yelling, crying, screaming, pushing, and pointing.

No. That's it. I've lost them—if I ever had them to begin with.

I consider leaving. In fact, I even turn to do so, when a tiny money spider drops from the branches above me, dangling on a single silken thread. I can barely see it, so small is the creature, but the gleam of light on the web makes it just visible.

Hyacinth always liked spiders. Though she would never have admitted it, Anansi was her favourite familiar.

This one is too tiny to be much more than a nuisance, but somehow seeing it gives me a sense of calm, a fine contrast to what I might normally feel when faced with an arachnid.

"So this is the Willow Barks, hmm? That's...disappointing."

The new voice is barely audible over the din of my sisters, but it is so calm and gentle that somehow my ear manages to catch it as an anomaly amongst the rest.

I look beyond the spider and clench my hands into tight fists when I recognize April Wesker standing on the inner edge of our sanctum.

CHAPTER TWENTY-TWO

"What the hell are you doing here?" I snarl.

She smiles at me, friendly and open. Sympathetic, even. "I came to pay my respects. And to see if there's anything I can do to help."

I stare at April, my mouth agape. Around me, my sisters have finally noticed the arrival of someone new, and their arguments begin to fade off. Within seconds they're all gathered behind me, staring in confusion at our guest.

I wonder how many of them even know her.

"What you can do is take Blake back to the station to explain what she was doing in that building."

Soft murmurs from behind me.

April tuts and narrows her eyes at me. "Still wrapped up in that, are you? Surely you see she had nothing to do with the matter. She couldn't possibly."

"Then why was she there?" I snap.

Iris shoves up to my side and places her hand on my shoulder. "Who is this?"

Though part of me wants to fling Iris's hand far away from me, I force myself to take the contact as what it is intended to be, a gesture of solidarity and support.

"This is—"

"I am April Wesker." The older woman cuts across me like a piece of chipped obsidian, smooth and slick, but deadly sharp. "I lead the Elm Stem coven and have come to pay my respects to the leader of yours. I'm so, so sorry to hear about what happened. You must be beside yourselves with grief and fear."

Chloe gapes at April in poorly concealed awe. Her puffy eyes are round and wide, and she inclines her head at April. "Another Mother? Wow."

"Elm Stem, hmm?" Iris narrows her eyes, immediately on her guard. "Who told you where our sanctum is?"

"It doesn't matter." I scramble to regain the conversation. "What I've been trying to say is that the suspect I chased down today is a member of the Elm Stems. Her name is Blake Allen."

Even Edith, usually so placid and calm, frowns at that one.

Kiara lifts her hands. "Well, why the fucking fuck isn't she locked up yet?"

April glares at me, then raises her hand slowly, just to eye height.

Silence.

Wow. My skin prickles with a sudden sensation of unease.

April is a coven Mother, sure, but the fact that she can so easily subdue *my* sisters—even Kiara—makes me feel…strange. Not just because that's Hyacinth's job but because, well, that isn't an authority April has any right to exploit.

"Blake *was* arrested, yes," April continues. "Hastily so, I might add. But it is clear to anybody with two brain cells to rub together that she couldn't possibly be involved."

"What makes you so certain?" I shoot back. "Were you at the scene? Did you see what happened to Hyacinth, how many times she was stabbed? Were you the one who had to chase Blake across several busy streets?"

Edith's face is a queer shade of green. She looks about ready to be sick any moment. "Stabbed?"

"Multiple times," I murmur. "And she was alive while it happened."

Fresh heart-rending sobs burst from Chloe, who lowers her face into her hands.

April lifts her voice again. "Not least, no witch would ever harm another in so cruel and final a way. We all know and follow the Rule of Three, therefore to act so heinously is against the very fabric of our being." Her pause allows those words to sink in. "This is a truly awful crime, but I believe Blake when she tells me she was simply in the wrong place at the wrong time. I vouch for her. Besides, she also tells me that Hyacinth had been there for days already."

"And how did she know that?" Again I butt in. I can't help myself.

"Do you really wish me to be so graphic?"

I'm about to say yes, to insist that she explain exactly how she knows, but the sound of Chloe weeping is too much. *I* experienced that horrible sight, and there's no need to put my sisters through it, even indirectly.

As if my silence is an answer, April goes on. "To my mind, it is clear. Hyacinth stumbled on some wastrels who proceeded to kill her to protect themselves and their crimes."

I have so many more questions, but no space to ask any of them. They all catch in my throat when the curtain of the willow branches shifts again, and another interloper steps into our space. Thanks to Chloe's circle, I don't even hear her coming until it's too late.

"Good evening, everyone." Nikolette brushes a few pieces of catkin fluff off her shoulders, then positions herself closer to April. "I'm so sorry for your loss." She barely looks at me beyond a brief acknowledgement, but I can read the emotion behind her eyes. She's… scared.

I think again of my phone and all the missed calls I've ignored. Did she know April was coming here tonight? Was she trying to warn me?

Iris splutters through her building anger. "And who is *this*? When did our sanctum become a thoroughfare for all and sundry?"

April lifts her hand again. "This is Nikolette Christie. She joined me today because I have instructed that all members of the Elm Stems travel in pairs, at least for the foreseeable."

Oh. That I didn't expect.

Nikolette lowers her gaze and shifts from foot to foot. Though as ever, she is impeccably dressed, her hair smooth and shiny in a knot at the back of her head, she has never looked more uncomfortable.

"Murder is a serious crime," April pushes on. "Bad enough against humans, but against a witch? A sister more than capable of protecting herself? Alarming. But against a witch like Hyacinth Dixon, High Crone and perhaps the most powerful witch in the country? If she can be dispatched so simply, so firmly, and in so mundane a manner, we must *all* be more cautious. Which is why I've come to you."

I try to catch Nikolette's eye. I need a clue, something, anything, but still she refuses to look at me. Seems I'm on my own.

"Well, we don't want anything to do with you," Iris snarls. "This is private Willow Bark business, and you have no right to—"

"Iris." My voice is sharper than I intended, but her antagonism fills me with unease. The last thing I want is for her rudeness to drive away the only person who might be able to help me find out what Blake was doing.

"What?" Iris glares at me, lip curling back in a sneer. "Planning to yell at me again?"

Yeah. She won't forget that for a long time.

I raise a hand, palm out to her. "No, Iris. I just think we all need to calm down and take a breath. April is our…guest."

Iris opens her mouth again, very much as though she intends to shout me down. At the last moment she simply nods. Her fingers tighten on my shoulder and then she yanks me backwards so she can take my spot in front of April.

"April Wesker"—she raises her voice a little and adopts a more formal tone—"I welcome you to our grove, our meeting space and sanctum in Angbec."

Relief fills my belly. Good. I don't have the mind to be official and formal right now.

She goes on. "May our wards serve your safety and our fire warm your body as your *fortis* warms your soul. May our home be as yours for the pleasure of your stay, and let us all remember the Rule of Three."

"So mote it be," April murmurs in response. Is that a hint of amusement in the slight lift to her eyebrows? Surely not. "I, April Wesker, Mother of the Elm Stem coven, accept the gracious welcome to your meeting space and sanctum. May my will grant you strength and my intent match yours." If it was amusement, it's gone almost instantly. "Let us all remember the Rule of Three."

"So mote it be," Iris repeats. The faintest ghost of a smile plays around her lips as she spreads her hands. Clearly she has more to say, but even that faint smile is wiped away when April clasps her hands together and leans forward.

"With the formalities out of the way, allow me to be frank, girls." April looks at each of us in turn. Her gaze is heavy, and despite myself, I find my body sagging beneath it. "The Willow Barks are a small coven. More than once I discussed with Hyacinth the possibility of your coven joining with mine. She agreed, in truth, though I know she intended to speak with you about it before making the merger final."

I peer at her. Not only is that news to me, but I can't for a second imagine a world in which Hyacinth would agree to such a thing. The Elm Stems? Of all covens? No. That doesn't seem right at all.

At my side, I feel Iris stiffen.

But April hasn't stopped talking. If anything, she has taken the stunned silence as consent to keep speaking. "Clearly given the tragic learnings of this afternoon, there is no longer an opportunity for her to speak with anybody, much less address the subject of her plans to merge. So, I shall lay out the facts as I see them, the same way I once did for her."

Something at the back of my mind yells and screams in defiance, but with effort I put the feeling aside. I need to know what she has to say.

"Not only are you a small coven, but you are a weak one." April shrugs at the indignant scowls from Iris and Kiara. "Am I wrong? The majority of your power lay with your Mother, and she is now gone. The fact is that the Willow Barks are alone, vulnerable, and, in my opinion, in need of protection. Hyacinth, your Mother, our High Crone, was the victim of a terrible, terrifying crime. And it is a crime that could happen to *any one of you*. Were you to join *my* coven, you'd enjoy the instant benefit of the protection of my wards, my daughters, and my will. You would be safe."

The murmurs from behind me pick up again.

"Safe from what?" I venture.

April pins me with a long, calm look but says nothing.

I stare back, unsure but suspecting more and more that she knows more than she is telling me. I can't pinpoint what, but something about her demeanour and the words she chooses make me uneasy.

"Hyacinth stumbled onto a drug deal or something like that. Didn't you just suggest that? It's not common for us to go wandering alone in those sorts of places."

"No. It isn't."

There. Again. There are so many more words being said than the ones she speaks aloud. I wish I could figure it out, but I can't concentrate on anything but keeping calm in the face of this sudden shift.

I backtrack. "So you want to join covens?"

"Was that not already a point of discussion?"

I had thought the vote was private. Sure, I mentioned it in passing to Nikolette, but I didn't realize that anybody other than Willow Barks had any clue we were considering a merger. The fact that April was the one to suggest it in the first place is a surprise to me as much as anything else.

"Besides, I don't *want* you to join us, Tina. I *want* you to do what feels safe and right for you and your sisters. If I've understood Hyacinth and our past conversations correctly, she had every intention of passing the mantle of Mother to you when she could no longer bear it. You must have had these talks with her regarding the safety and the legacy of your coven."

Nikolette looks up sharply. For the first time she looks at me fully, and I see her dark eyes narrow. Her lips compress into a tight, thin line.

Damn. I didn't want her to find out like this.

But Nikolette is the least of my worries. Chloe has stopped crying in time to give me a disbelieving shake of the head. "But you're too young, Tina. You couldn't be Mother, could you? Would you know what to do?"

Iris is nowhere near as gentle. She spins back to face me and grabs my arm, pinning me in place while her incredulous gaze sweeps me up and down. "You? *You*? No. Never. Not in a million years."

"We discussed it. I mean, she mentioned it," I splutter, unsure of whose emotions I want to wrangle first. "We didn't agree on anything—I didn't accept—I don't even want to. I mean, it was idle conversation in passing…" I realize I'm babbling, but I can't stop myself. "There were no firm plans. And I didn't agree—I mean, she doesn't need me to do anything like that. The Willow Barks already have a Mother, and I—"

"*Had*," April interjects softly. "*Had* a Mother."

I can feel the anger building in Iris's grip.

Across the small space Nikolette stares at me so hard I fear she might burn a hole through me. Her body seems to hum with tension, and both hands are curled into tight, tight fists at her sides. This is going to be awful.

Iris shakes my arm. "How long has this been planned in the background, hmm? A new, barely present witch to become Mother of a coven as old and powerful as the Willow Barks?" Her fingernails dig into the flesh of my arm. "I'd rather chew dirt."

"I didn't agree to anything," I whisper, taken aback by the strength of her anger. "Please believe me when I say I would never do something like that behind your back. Neither would Hyacinth." I always knew Iris in particular would hate the idea of me taking over anything, especially since I, and probably everyone else, assumed *she* would be the one.

"But she *thought* about it. You. *You*, above all of us. Above *me*? Goddess, save me." Iris whirls around and marches out of the grove.

I try to follow, but Edith sidesteps into my path, blocking the way. "Why would you not tell us what Hyacinth had planned? Did you think it would be easier to take over if you acted in secret? Does this make you Mother now?"

My mouth drops open. "What? No."

This is spiralling faster than I ever thought possible. What is *happening*? One absent, throwaway comment from April, and suddenly my sisters have turned on me.

April takes another step into our sanctum. I feel her presence and her will pressing down on our space, the intrusion like to a broad, all-encompassing wave washing over a flat beach.

Though Nikolette follows, her presence is nowhere near as powerful or overbearing. If anything, she appears timid and awed when side by side with her Mother. Not a look I'm used to seeing on her.

April touches her bottom lip with the tip of her index finger. "Interesting. Edith, is it? You say all that as if Tina planned this. Surely you're not suggesting that Tina herself orchestrated this for the sake of power?" Her voice is light and incredulous, her eyebrows raised high.

Edith frowns. Kiara eyes me with fresh suspicion. Chloe cocks her head and stares at me through her mask of tears. Even Nikolette offers me a sideways look.

Slowly, Edith shakes her head. "I'm not *suggesting* anything. P-please don't put words in my mouth."

I try to speak, but my mouth feels as though it's filled with dirt, my throat lined with sandpaper. How could I possibly go from sobbing with the horrible news I have to share, to abruptly fending off thinly veiled accusations of a coup?

I force myself to breathe long and deep, to let my mind settle just long enough to string a coherent thought together. This can't be right. This must be a mistake, something, somewhere has gone horribly wrong, and all I need is to find the right words to make it right.

"I don't want to be Mother," I blurt out. "I never have. Hyacinth knew that."

Chloe nods, then lifts a trembling hand. "You said we would be safe if we joined you, Ms. Wesker. Does that mean we're in danger if we don't?"

"No, I—"

"Who can know?" April cuts me off, slick and quick. "I would assume not, but is it ever really safe to assume?"

"But then"—Chloe shares her gaze wildly between myself and April—"then what do we do? Do we join your coven now? We were going to vote anyway, that's why we're here. It was the Elms, the Chestnuts, or the Acorns right? So let's vote now."

"Not tonight." I make my voice as firm as I can manage.

"Why?" Chloe wipes her eyes and stares. "We're in danger—we have to do something. Why can't we vote now and secure that extra protection?"

"I said no."

Every witch turns to face me.

I raise my hands helplessly. "Come on, guys, think about it. Consider everything that's happened today. We've lost the very heart of our coven. Don't know about you, but I'm scared." The glares become looks of surprise, but I press on. "Aren't you? I'm scared and in shock, enough that I don't trust my judgement right now. I don't think this is the moment to be making big decisions."

Kiara shakes her head. "This is *exactly* the time. We're here, aren't we? We all know what's at stake. If anything this should push us to make the decision faster. We need to know where we stand, so we can be safe."

"Why wouldn't we be safe?"

"Someone murdered our Mother," she shoots back. "If someone under the influence of alcohol or drugs can kill Hyacinth, then what chance do the rest of us have?"

Edith sighs, then shares her weary gaze with each of us in turn. "I suppose this is the moment, then. Let's do it. We vote now: Do we join the Elm Stems or not?"

Chapter Twenty-three

I face my sisters, hands raised. "No. The vote was to decide on which coven to join or even if we should, not specifically to join the Elm Stems." I hope the reminder of that fact is enough to knock a little sense into them.

Kiara gestures to April. "Well, she's here, ain't she? No other sod showed up. They don't give two shits 'bout us, but I reckon April does."

Maybe my sisters don't know how unusual it is for a coven to intrude on another's meeting space, but I certainly do. Edith might understand, but she's too upset to care. And from the glare Iris gave at the start, she knows too, even if she was quick enough to take over and formally greet April.

There may be fancy, formal words of greeting in the odd case that it does happen, but one of the reasons both sides quote the Rule of Three is to remind everybody that to harm anybody else is to bring that harm back upon yourself three times. It isn't a senseless repetition of tradition, but a firm, dire warning of the consequences, should someone cause trouble.

"I'm sure we're grateful for April's concern"—I hope she can't hear the slight panic in my voice—"but we need to calm down and take a breather. Surely we can come back to this when we've all had a chance to process it."

Iris abruptly stomps back into the space beneath the trees. Her face is dark with anger, but her return is not without purpose. She carries a long, thick stick, about the width of her thumb, and uses it to drag a deep groove into the dirt near the fire.

With a glare she positions herself on one side of the line. "Whatever else is happening right now, giving ourselves up to the Elms isn't the way to solve it. I'm sure you already know what I think, but I'll make it formal now. We are proud and powerful and have no need of another coven to shield us. Maybe one day in the distant future we may consider joining another coven, but"—and here she tilts her chin to peer down her nose at April—"it will never, ever be the Elms."

From the corner of my eye I catch Nikolette bristle with anger, but April seems to take it in her stride. She gives a nonchalant wave of her fingers, as if flicking away the very obvious insult.

"Thanks, Iris," I sigh, "but I just said we're not voting tonight."

"I don't want to join *any* other coven." Edith raises her voice. "We're small, but we're strong. We should be asking covens to join *us*, not the other way around." She moves to the far side of the line to join Iris.

No. This can't be happening. Not now, with everything else going on.

"I want the protection." Chloe's soft voice carries surprisingly far. "I don't want to be scared and looking over my shoulder all the time. If that could happen to Hyacinth, we need the protection of a bigger coven, and the Elms are right here. I say we join them." Though her knees wobble, she steps right up to the line drawn in the dirt, then positions herself on the near side of it, directly opposite Iris.

"I appreciate this, sisters, but we can't vote yet. Think about what we've just learned. We need time to grieve."

Kiara approaches the line and without hesitation steps over it to stand beside Chloe. She puts her arm around the trembling girl and holds tight. "We can grieve and vote," she murmurs. "We ain't children—we can multitask. I put up a right fight earlier, but now it's bloody important."

April gives a little hiss of annoyance. I experience a moment of confusion before another glance at my sisters explains why.

Both of my younger sisters to the right, voting to join the Elm Stems. The older pair on the left, voting to remain, or at least to find an alternative. Two in favour, two against. An entirely even split.

With a sigh, April turns to me, her head cocked slightly to one side. "Then it appears that *you* are the deciding vote."

I fight the growing urge building in my belly that tells me to run away as far, hard, and fast as I can.

This grove, this beautiful pocket of nature and beauty, has always been a wondrous and beautiful source of peace and calm for me. Now I can't think of anywhere I'd rather be less.

"Me?"

All four of my coven sisters turn to look at me.

"Well," snaps Iris, "we've got this far, can we finally make a decision?"

"I—"

Chloe looks up from gnawing on her fingernails. "Vote to join. It will be better for all of us. Safety in numbers is real." She angles herself towards April. "How big is your coven, Ms. Wesker?"

With a start, as though surprised to be addressed, April smiles brightly. "Twenty-three," she says at once. "Then with myself and Nikolette here, that makes twenty-five, but please, you must simply call me April."

"Nikolette?" Iris throws me another sharp look.

I look away.

My girlfriend—ex-girlfriend?—has clearly gathered her composure. She shrugs her slender shoulders and adds, "Yes. Is there something you wanted to add?" I know her well enough to recognize the dangerous edge beneath her light tone.

"I've heard your name a couple of times today," Iris murmurs, "in places I didn't expect."

Pure, unflustered poker face. Nikolette doesn't even glance my way. In fact, she smiles. "Well I've not had the pleasure of yours. Please, indulge me."

"Iris."

The silence which follows is painfully taut.

April breaks it with a sharp clearing of her throat. "Tina. You have a decision to make."

"No. We can't do this now."

Iris drags her glare away from Nikolette to look at me. "Yes, you can. I'm sick of your shilly-shallying whenever we have something to do. You're young and weak, but you're not stupid. I hope. Don't vote to tie us to the Elm Stems who are elitist, antiquated, and out of touch enough to still quote sacrifices of goats and chickens."

"Where did you hear such nonsense?" April sounds amused. "We haven't sacrificed a goat in years."

They're staring at me. *All* of them—my sisters, April, Nikolette—

every single one of them has their gaze pinned on me, staring with such intensity that I can feel their *fortis* bristling and lapping up against me.

Still smiling, April folds her arms across her chest. I've no idea what she's thinking, but there's something smug and catlike about the way she avoids my gaze.

A little tickle draws my gaze down to the back of my hand. That money spider is back, speedily crawling across my wrist. With a yelp I flick it aside.

Iris rolls her eyes. "Get a grip, Tina, and answer the question. What are we going to do?"

Nothing comes to mind. No miraculous answer, no incredible plan. Even my own thoughts are a jumble, tangled in my feelings for Nikolette versus my loyalty to the word and will of the woman who took me under her wing and protected me when she had no reason to.

I sigh. "Nothing." When the gathered women prepare to rumble their complaints, I shake my head all the harder. "No. I can't do this. I've already said it, but this is too soon. We've all had a shock, I'm trying to grieve, and I think it's safe to say we're all scared. I won't be forced to make such a huge decision in this mental state."

Chloe gives a tiny whimper. "Then who's going to lead us?"

"I will." Iris steps forward at once, with her back straight and her head held high. "I'm the oldest and most experienced. It's my place."

Kiara gives a loud, unflattering scoff. "I'd sooner follow a lemming off a cliff."

Iris and Kiara square off, yelling with increasing ferocity. Chloe gazes at me, fearful and wide-eyed, while Edith shakes her head wearily and sags against a tree.

I sigh.

Was Hyacinth really the only thing holding us all together? There won't be much of a coven left if this in-fighting doesn't stop.

I spy Nikolette staring at me. Her gaze is firm and steady, her brows knitted. Though she says nothing, her hands are once again balled into tight, angry fists.

No magic required to know what she's thinking.

If this was her, she would snatch up the opportunity in an instant. Given the revelation that Hyacinth was considering me as a Mother of the future, Nikolette must be furious to see me say nothing.

But I can't.

April also looks at me, one eyebrow raised. I shrug helplessly.

Her gaze hardens. "Daughters," she snaps.

I wince, but my sisters immediately whip around to look at her. The title isn't lost on them either.

"Clearly we are at an impasse. Given your *unique* methods of negotiation and discussion, I'm hardly surprised, but I can't wait here all day."

Iris plants her hands on her hips. "And what does that mean?"

"It means we have to hurry," Chloe whispers. "We have to join now, or else we'll never get the chance."

Though she never makes it explicit, I also get the sense that April is laying an ultimatum on the table. I don't like it.

Finally I find my tongue. "No, no, Chloe, that can't be right." I turn to give April the best approximation of a smile that I can manage. "She might not be our Mother"—I take care to stress that part—"but she would never abandon fellow sisters at a time we need help. She's not cruel. She understands we need time to grieve and process. No one in their right mind would force us to have all the answers at a time like this."

April's mouth twists unpleasantly, but she doesn't fight me.

Inwardly, I congratulate myself. Did I just manage to buy us some time?

"Right mind or not, the fact is I have my own coven and myriad other responsibilities to take care of." April becomes brisk and businesslike. "Regardless of the situation today, I had thought this decision was made weeks ago. I've discussed this with Hyacinth at length and believed all that remained was to inform you of her intent. I see that isn't the case."

"Hyacinth would never have—"

"I can't afford to spend more time than I already have waiting for you to come to your senses." April bulls right over me without even looking my way. "My time is precious, and while I freely offer my resources, my time isn't one of them."

Chloe gives a little squeak of terror.

I face April.

She's so much younger than I first thought she might be. In my mind, the Mothers of the Angbec covens are all old and grey, wrinkled and wise. Perhaps because that is my experience with Hyacinth. But

April is barely in her sixties and looks good for her age. Her skin is smooth and even, her eyes clear and bright. She moves with the ease and comfort of a woman much younger. All of her age, her authority, her power, is in her eyes and her presence.

"How much longer are you willing to give us?" I murmur.

"I give *you* forty-eight hours."

I'm not slow to catch the emphasis she places on the word *you*. This isn't a deadline for the Willow Bark coven. Oh no. This is a deadline for *me*.

I push back the little burst of panic and nod. "Fine. If that's all you're willing to allow a grieving coven, I'll make my decision then." She sniffs, but I don't back down. Instead I step forward and allow her to see the fire I feel in my belly. "In forty-eight hours, I'll cast my vote and break the tie." With those words I face the others. "Is that okay with the rest of you?"

It isn't. Of course not, but nobody seems willing to say so. Even Iris has lost some of the wind from her sails and simply nods.

It will have to do.

"April Wesker," I mutter, "thank you for visiting our sanctum in Angbec. May our fire light your way and our wards guide your safe passage as we note and acknowledge the Rule of Three."

Her eyebrows rise. Maybe she didn't expect such a firm and obvious dismissal, but I don't care. I need to get her out of here before she causes any more damage. *I* need to get out of here. This night has officially become too much, and I need to leave before I break down entirely.

I know those aren't the right words either, but on the fly and under pressure, they're the best I can do.

"I observe the Rule of Three as I leave your sanctum, lit by your fire and protected by your words." She gives the smallest of nods. Perhaps a grudging display of respect? "So mote it be."

"So mote it be," I intone back.

And that's it. There's not much more to say.

April's eyes linger on me for long, awkward moments, before she finally lifts her hand to Nikolette. "You heard them. Let's go."

Nikolette loiters. Though she tries to hide it, her body is slightly too forward, her gaze lingering slightly too much on me. It's clear she has more to say, but also no idea of how to do so. In the end, with visible annoyance, she gives up and follows April.

And just as suddenly as they arrived, the two Elm Stems step back out of the circle of willow trees and off into the night.

I release a slow, shuddering breath.

Around me, my sisters break away from their voting spots and begin to gather themselves together. No one speaks. Perhaps no one really knows what to say. Perhaps, for the first time, what I said before the interruption from April is beginning to sink in.

Hyacinth is gone. Murdered.

"Take the time to mourn, guys. Please. Hyacinth is…was…" I take the moment I need to swallow back the reappearance of tears. "She was our Mother. At the very least she deserves acknowledgement of that."

Miraculously, no one argues. One by one they begin to file away, slipping off out of the trees in various directions.

Last to go is Edith, who stops by my side to place a surprisingly gentle hand on my shoulder.

"Take care of yourself," she murmurs. "She was our Mother, sure, but I get the feeling she was *your* mother."

The difference in title verses relationship is obvious.

"I'll be okay."

Her fingers tighten ever so slightly on my shoulder before slipping away. "Call me. If you want. If you need to, I mean. Like, if you need to talk."

I nod. Better that then burst into tears.

I want her to go. I *need* her to go. I desperately need to be alone so I can quietly process the insanity of the last hour.

At last, she too walks away, and all that remains with me is the sigh of wind in the trees.

I back up, sitting carefully on that stump I utilized once before.

A long, deep breath escapes my lips.

Goddess, please, please help me. What am I going to do now?

CHAPTER TWENTY-FOUR

I sit on the stump with my head buried in my hands as I try to work up the will to move. My body seems locked up tight, weighed down by grief and fatigue. But I can't stay here.

After several minutes I pick up my shoes and socks, slide them back on, and douse the fire. It doesn't take much—there's a bucket on hand filled with sand, and we always make the effort to kick out any embers before leaving.

Without the fire, the grove returns to a more natural spot of quiet and peace, and I take a moment to listen to the stillness.

I wish my mind would fall as quiet.

There are crickets somewhere nearby, singing their chirpy song in the darkness. Far, far beyond the grounds of the green space, I catch the vaguest hints of traffic roaring by on main roads. When I step out, the light changes, soft silver giving every edge a slight gleam. The moon is full now, and on its way into waning, but the light is so bright I can see clearly all around me.

A memory stirs inside me, Hyacinth throwing off her jewellery and clothes to race out into her garden and dance, barefoot and naked in the moon's light. I remember her beckoning to me, grinning, giggling, but always disappointed when I refused to join her in what she cheerfully called a moon bath. Time and time again I chose not to join her, and now I would never have the chance again.

I bite my lip to keep the tears back.

Bed. That will have to do instead. If I can just get home, I can tumble onto my sheets and bury my face in the soft pillows. The thought of mindless oblivion in the form of sleep has abruptly become deeply, deeply attractive to me.

I cross the field and make it back to the street where my car is parked. Just mine and one other, with a tree shaped air freshener dangling from the rear-view. I don't recognize it, but that's hardly surprising. There are plenty of residents parked in this area, as well as my sisters.

I stop outside my car with one hand resting lightly on the door handle. My vision needs to clear before I can even think about driving.

Someone moves on my right.

Perhaps the blurry vision is why I'm slow to spot her at first, but when I finally do, my heart skips once.

"Nikolette?"

She steps out of the shadows at the far end of the road and hurries over to me. The whole time she casts half glances over her shoulder, to scout out left, right, and behind. When she reaches me, she stops at the side of my car and places a hand on the roof. And stares.

I find myself smiling. "You waited for me?"

"I had questions," she murmurs. "And…and I wanted to say I'm sorry for your loss. I can't imagine what you're feeling right now."

"Oh." I nod. "It's not great, that's for sure."

"I'm so, so sorry," she whispers.

A pathetic hiccup of a sob bursts out of me. I can't help it.

There's a long awkward moment of Nikolette simply watching me, before I risk the step towards her. Then another. And a third. I press my head against her shoulder, and she lets me, eventually putting her arms around me.

I sigh out the breath I had been holding.

Her hand reaches the back of my head, stroking gently, and she whispers something soothing but no doubt nonsense against my ear.

And I cry. And cry. And cry.

I don't know how long she allows me to slump against her like that. All I know is that when I finally come up for air, my vision is blurry and her shoulder is a soggy mess of snot and tears.

Nikolette grimaces at the patch on her blouse, then returns her attention to me. "I can't believe you're going to be the Willow Bark Mother," she murmurs.

"No." At once I'm shaking my head. Maybe a little too hard, because my vision begins to swim, but I *need* her to understand how far from the truth that statement is. "No, I'm not. Hyacinth offered it, but I don't want it."

"But you didn't tell me. Why?"

"I had other things on my mind, Nikolette." A tiny fissure of irritation starts to force its way through the misery. "Besides, I never took the offer seriously. And I certainly didn't expect her to die."

She backs up. "Yes, you're right, I'm sorry. I…maybe this isn't the right time. Maybe I should go." Another step backwards.

Away from me.

I feel each step like a physical pang and experience a sudden stab of fear. I grab for her hand. "Wait. Please. Please don't leave me."

I can feel her hesitation.

"There's no one here." I hurry on, gesturing around me. "See? Look around, everyone has already left. Please, Nikolette, don't leave me to do this alone."

She sighs. "You're not alone. I wouldn't—couldn't—do that, I just…" Another sigh, bigger this time. "No. All you need know is I'm sorry. Mother April caught me off guard when she mentioned you becoming Mother, but it doesn't change anything. I do want to be with you."

Relief crashes over me like a tsunami. She puts out her hands, and I sink into her again.

My words stutter through fresh tears. Goddess, why can't I stop? "I th-thought you didn't want to b-be with me." Even to my own ears I sound pathetic and weak. But I don't care. "After yesterday I thought it was over."

Nikolette averts her gaze for the smallest moment. "Last night was a blip, and I'm not proud of it. And now you've even more to be worried about. I should have had more grace. But the fact remains, I…I care about you. I love you."

I feel my stomach flutter. "You do?"

"I do. I love you." Firmer this time. "I think it took something like this, something so horrible for me to realize it. But I want to protect you, and I can once you join the Elm Stems."

I rub my stinging eyes. "I'm not sure."

"Of course I can. I'll be able to keep you close to me and watch your back—"

"No, I mean I'm not sure we can join the Elm Stems. An Elm did this."

Nikolette frowns at me. "Didn't you hear Mother April? Crone Hyacinth passed long before Blake arrived."

"Then why was she there?"

"Why did *we* go there, Tina?" Nikolette spreads her hands. "Only this week we were in that same place. Blake could have a secret like ours."

I shake my head. "She knows something. I can feel it."

"Mother April questioned Blake herself, and if she's satisfied, then I am too. I trust her."

"But—"

"Didn't you trust Crone Hyacinth, even when things didn't make sense?" She stares into my eyes, even slips a finger beneath my chin to tilt my face. "Please, Tina. Please. I'm sorry you're in pain, but you need to focus your attention somewhere useful."

She's so close. Her mouth is slightly open and damp enough to catch the moonlight. I can see the pale pink of her tongue between her lips.

I kiss her long, hard, and deep, and by every Goddess of the moon and under it, she feels so good.

Her lips are soft and tender, tasting ever so slightly of mint. Her hand beneath my chin quivers, and in an instant her body melts against mine. Both arms snake around me, her lips part, and the tiniest tip of her tongue slips out.

She's hot and eager, all curves and softness, an exquisite femininity I long to stroke all over.

"Tina…" Her voice takes on the faintest edge of a whine.

I moan into her mouth, internally begging for the distraction to continue. So much easier to fall into her than to think about everything else right now.

"I fucking knew it." Iris's voice lashes out over the still of the air.

Nikolette shoves me back, and I stumble wildly, slamming painfully against my car door.

I look beyond her, straining to see where the other woman has so suddenly appeared. She's not hard to spot.

Iris stands beyond the narrow path that leads out to the grove.

It's dark there, cast in shadow from the two tall walls, but she marches out of it now with her arms folded tight across her chest. Her lips are twisted, nostrils flared as she glares at us.

I shove off the car and try to straighten myself out. "I can explain—"

"Explain what exactly?" Iris gives a horrid bark of laughter. "That you've been lying all this time?"

Nikolette wipes her mouth with the tips of her fingers. Her impeccable lipstick has smeared across her bottom lip. "Now, wait a moment—"

"Fuck off, *Elm*." Though Iris makes no gesture, her rage is suddenly palpable. I feel it against my skin like a wave of heat, and I know her *fortis* is burning. "Nobody asked you. Just like nobody asked for your busybody coven Mother to come and try to scoop us up like pebbles on a beach."

"Iris, please—"

"And *you*." She whirls back to me. "I don't care who you date—it's really none of my business—but I won't be lied to. If you're keeping something like this, how do we know what else you're hiding?"

"If you would let me explain—"

She shakes her head. "Don't want to hear it. But know this, Tina. In forty-eight hours, if you dare give us up to that bitch, April, know we won't be going anywhere without a fight. This isn't what Hyacinth wanted, and you know it. I only went for a walk before coming back to my car"—she gestures to the vehicle with the tree air freshener—"but now I'm glad I did." She shoots Nikolette the filthiest look, first up, then down. "Would never have known your decisions were being led by your libido."

Nikolette makes a sound rather like a growl.

Given that the jig is up, I put aside any attempts to be coy. "Nikolette has nothing to do with the decisions I make as a Willow."

"That so?" Iris sniffs. "Then why hesitate tonight? You could have ended this merging nonsense in an instant."

I feel Nikolette at my side, trying to lend her support to me, but I hold her back at arm's length. "It's not that simple. There's more to consider than where we have our sanctum, and I think we're all missing something. I need time to figure it out."

Iris glares at me, hands on hips. "Guess you'd better be quick because forty-eight hours is all you have, though maybe closer to forty by the time you're done getting your clit stroked."

I gasp.

Nikolette whips her hand up. A visible glow of blue sparks dances across her fingers. They're loud and bright, and though, in truth, the display is nothing more than a light show, Iris steps back in alarm.

"You wouldn't—"

Nikolette takes a single step forward. "You should be more respectful. She just lost her coven Mother. In fact, you *both* did. Go cool your head and begin your mourning before you do or say anything that you can't take back."

I put my arm out across the pair of them, but the damage is already done.

"Well," she murmurs, "I guess we know who's really leading the Willow Barks at the moment." With a slow nod, Iris unlocks her car and slides into the driver's seat, never once taking her eyes off Nikolette. "I'll be sure to let the others know."

Before I can say anything more, she slams the door and drives away.

❖

At my side, Nikolette shakes her hand around to dispel the sparks from her fingers. Such an open display of her *fortis* is unusual for her. I can imagine the whirlwind she must be experiencing right now, largely because it likely matches mine.

She blows out a heavy breath and looks across to me. Her perfect lipstick is still smeared. The little line of it smudges down her mouth corner and stretches towards her chin.

I can taste it on my own mouth, mingled with the flavour of her.

"I'm sorry." My voice is low and my eyes downcast. I can feel her gaze on me for long seconds before she speaks.

"It was bound to happen sooner or later, I suppose. Who was that woman anyway? She's awful."

"Iris." I sigh. "And yes, she is, but she means well. The coven is incredibly important to her, and all this must be quite a shock."

Another of those weird sounds like a growl from Nikolette. "It's a shock to you too. She won't be able to act like that under Mother April, that's for sure."

I blink at her continued assumption that the Willow Barks will be joining with the Elm Stems. "Nothing is decided yet. I have forty-eight hours, so I'm going to use that time to be certain that Blake is as innocent as April claims."

"Tina—"

I lift my hand to Nikolette. "Please let me do this. I know you have faith in your coven Mother, but I just lost mine. My heart is burning, and I need to do *something* before I can expect to get any sort of rest." As the words leave my mouth I realize what I need to do.

"*Something*? Like what?"

"My job." I straighten my back. "I'm a police officer, aren't I? And there's been a murder. I'm going to find out who did it."

Nikolette eyes me coolly. "You're a beat constable, not a CID detective."

Maybe not now, but years ago…

I tell her, "I'm also a Willow Bark witch." There's more bite in my voice than I intend, but I'm not sure I care. "There's more to this than the APD will ever understand without me."

Nikolette frowns. "What are you talking about?"

"I felt magic on Hyacinth's body. I don't care what April says—she didn't feel what I felt. I know there was a witch involved, I just need to find out who. And why."

Resolve solidifies inside me. Not quite *fortis*, but certainly a drive and determination I haven't felt in a long time. It doesn't have to be related to my connection to the Goddess to be real. I can feel it, a tiny flame inside growing brighter.

"More than that," I press on, "we were there only days ago, right? And it was fine—plain, comfortable, clean. But today there were gang signs all over it, old clothes, food, blood bags, faerie dust cartridges… It looked like a den more than six months old."

Silence stretches between us. Nikolette puts a hand to her mouth and tangles her other hand in her hair. She stands like that for long, long seconds, eyes darting as if to follow the path of her thoughts. "I don't like this," she murmurs at last. "What if poking around puts you in danger? Mother April already has us moving around in pairs."

"I'll be fine."

"Like Crone Hyacinth?"

She has a point. But what can she really do about it? As an Elm Stem she can't realistically be involved in an investigation into her own coven.

"I'll be careful. I promise."

Her eyes shimmer. It's clear she wants to argue, but Nikolette isn't, nor has she ever been, stupid. Getting involved would likely cause trouble for the pair of us, maybe even her more than me.

She nods. Backs up. Walks away.

I watch her go, wondering if this might be the thing that breaks us—not the secrecy, the sneaking around, or even the reticence of her family, but this entirely unrelated turn. There's only one way to find out.

I give her the slow count of five hundred, then slowly climb into my car.

CHAPTER TWENTY-FIVE

I don't go home. Instead I return to Belmy Road and the abandoned game shop. I'm forced to park half a mile away, but the walk back to the location gives me the time I need to rest my head.

As I approach, the black and white tape with *POLICE* marked across it in large letters slowly becomes visible, fluttering in the cool night breeze. It goes from drainpipe, to lamp post, to lamp post, to drainpipe, forming a large square that encompasses the exit, the narrow alley, the store's door, and its windows. Within stands a uniformed officer, yawning behind their hand.

I've never envied the night shift.

I formulate my plan as I approach on foot, wrestling into my pocket for my ID card. I hold it up as I slip beneath the flimsy barrier, aware of the immediate stand to attention. Across the road, the door of a grubby looking Volvo also opens. Oh. So there's plain-clothes officers here too?

"Tina Marks," I say. "I'm here to—Oh. Vince?"

My beat partner gives me a quick once over. "Oh, hey. What are you doing here?" He waves away the other officer approaching from the Volvo. I watch as the officer nods, then returns to the vehicle, though not without a curious stare my way.

"I wanted to check something."

"Playing detective now, are you? Looking for a transfer?"

"No. But I was first on scene. And I left pretty fast, if you recall. I thought I saw something, but I want to confirm before I start running my mouth."

Vince hesitates. "You cleared this with Skipper?"

I flinch before I can stop myself. "I—"

A nod. "Yeah. Didn't think so. He said you weren't supposed to be involved in this case. Something about a conflict of interest."

Well, that makes things harder than I was hoping. Better change tack.

"I'm not involved going forward. But I need to see if I was right, so I can let the team working this one know about it."

"What did you see?"

I'm quicker this time, the lie just sliding off the tongue. "Probably nothing, but there was a sign or symbol on one of the walls. I thought I recognized it."

He glances towards the door, which is hanging slightly ajar. "There was a lot in there. SOCO already have most of it, but there were bags and bags and bags of it. No way to tell what's related and what's not, so they took everything not nailed down. I doubt there's anything left."

"But they wouldn't have scrubbed the walls, right?"

"I guess not."

"I'll be ten minutes. Five. Maybe even two, but I can't shake the feeling it's important. You know how a hunch feels, right?"

A slow smile pulls at Vince's lips. "Working from the gut. That's why I like you. It's not always about what's right in front of us, y'know? Sometimes there's just a feeling deep down in the belly."

Couldn't have put it better myself.

He gestures to the car again, a quick circle of his index finger. Then he opens the door to the shop. "Five minutes, that's all I can give you."

That's all I need.

I smile my thanks at him and dart inside.

Immediately it becomes clear how right he was about the contents of the building. Most of the lower floor is undisturbed, though there is a narrow path on the ground marked with white tape, showing where it's safe to walk and where might still need to be investigated. The door at the far end marked *Private* is also open, and I make my way through.

"Dink? Anansi?"

No answer, but I don't expect to get one. The pair have either hightailed it out of here or hidden themselves thoroughly to avoid the many, many officers who would have been moving back and forth through the space. I hope they're close enough to hear me.

The air feels far less thick than before. Perhaps the passage of so many bodies has brought new, fresh air into the place.

"Anansi?"

Up the steps, around the corner to the left, and into the larger room.

Remnants of the search are still very visible. I can see the pieces of string used to mark out the quadrants to be searched and then more string splitting those into smaller squares. There are little plastic standees dotted about the space, folded yellow arches scribbled with marker pen. I know those mark out areas in the space containing evidence that can't be removed and taken off-site for further analysis, so I'm not surprised to see a large cluster of them around the dusty stains of Hyacinth's blood.

One step forward. And another.

I have to force myself to take these steps, willing myself closer and closer to the scene of my mentor's final moments.

Sickness bubbles within me, but I tamp it down. The last thing I need is to shower the crime scene with the contents of my stomach. Then again, would it really be noticeable amongst the devastation of the place?

"Dink?"

I hear the little squeak long before I spot the mouse. Eventually he hops into view from my right, though where he was hiding I can't be sure. He crawls over my boot, then begins the long climb up my trouser leg. I scoop him up to save him the trouble.

His tiny, warm body is easy to grip, and I do so now, turning him back and forth, to and fro.

Unharmed. Good.

"Anansi?"

Still no answer, just the murmur of voices from outside.

Then, at last, the near silent step of very many legs crawling over the hard and dusty floor. Behind me, from near the fire escape, the large spider skitters towards me with intent. She stops beyond my reach, twitching her front pair of legs at me in slow, forlorn circles.

"It's okay," I tell her, crouching down. "I'm so sorry. Come on. I've got you."

More hesitation.

Eventually I steel myself, breathe deep, and take a step towards her until she's close enough to touch. I still can't do it, can't quite touch her, but at least I can give her relative proximity.

She stands near my boot, and somehow, despite having no features with which to carry the expression, she looks incredibly sad.

"Both of you," I murmur, "I'm sorry. You can stay with me for now, okay? I'll look after you."

The pair stare at me, solemn and forlorn.

I have no idea if they understand me or not. I've never really studied familiars and their relationships with witches, but this at least feels right. I'm mourning, sure, but these two were linked to Hyacinth in ways I'll never understand. Her passing must be like a huge void within them.

"Let's go."

Dink immediately wriggles out of my hand. I clutch and grab at him, but he's fast and light, springing to the ground and away again. He scampers all the way up to the dusty, rusty stains on the ground, then stops, sitting beneath the arch of one of the large yellow evidence markers.

Fine. I can take a hint.

I crouch again and move my hand over the ground in a low sweep, not quite touching but *feeling* the air.

My fingers pass over the first of the stains, then the next, then the next. As I move, more and more I feel the lingering traces of Hyacinth on my skin. If there had ever been any doubt it was her, this proves it, at least for me. I feel her just as clearly and inevitably as I did in her home, because this is a very real part of her left behind.

A horrible stab of static cramps my hand. I yelp, frozen in place, my hand trembling but unable to move from that fixed spot. The sensation crawls up my hand as far as my wrist and then holds, tingling, cold, and painful.

Dink watches for several seconds, then zips forward to nip my finger.

The pain is sharp and sudden, but it breaks the odd paralysis instantly.

I drag my hand away, shaking it around as the last trace of magic fades.

If I needed proof that something strange happened here, that Hyacinth was no victim of a mere wastrel, I suddenly have it.

The last shredded traces of magic here and on her body aren't static, of course they're not. No, they're the last traces of a paralysis spell.

Someone was held here, in this space, likely against their will.

"Oh Goddess, no…"

The truth of it hits me like a truck.

No defence cuts on the hands or arms. No sign of any residue beneath the fingernails. No indication that Hyacinth did anything more than sit and wait to be murdered.

Hyacinth didn't fight back because she couldn't fight back. Someone, some *witch*, paralysed her in this disgusting, filthy pit and then stabbed her to death.

Chapter Twenty-six

I manage to reach home before I begin to dry-heave. I can't remember the last I ate—maybe the sandwich from Vince?—but my body and nerves are furious with me. My stomach muscles contract over and over, but there is nothing there to expel. Instead I retch and cough and splutter and cry, while clinging to the car door for support.

Dink rests on my shoulder, his whiskers twitching against my neck, while Anansi loiters in the pocket of the car door.

A small cluster of women, clearly recently finished at the pub, pause to eye me warily as I lean against the open vehicle.

I can hear them whispering, wondering if they should tell someone about this drunk woman clearly finishing up a drive.

Any other day I would correct them, perhaps even flash my badge, but I can't today. I need to get inside. I need to think.

I slam the door and lock it, checking for both familiars before darting over to my front door.

My home is a bland 19th century mid-terrace bore, but it's mine, and I can't wait to be inside it again. Which is why I'm annoyed when Dink bites my earlobe.

I lower my key from the lock to give him a poke. "Stop it. That hurts." Again I lift my hand to the door, and once more the mouse nips me. "What is your problem?"

He bites again, harder this time, and I'm pretty sure he's drawn blood.

I slap at him, forcing my key into the lock and turning it.

Several things happen at once.

From above the door, Anansi swings down on a fine length of thread and slams her hairy body into my nose.

Heat, blistering and painful, arches down my hand and up my arm.

Dink bites me yet again, swinging from my earlobe like a terrier.

The door explodes.

I scream.

The force of it, thick, fast, and sudden, hurls me back into the street like a rag doll. Shattered chunks of wood and plastic fly through the air and rain down around me while my head, back, and arse slam into the pavement, hard enough to force the air from my body. Stars dance before my eyes.

My door keys fly from my hand and vanish beneath a parked car while still more magic billows through the open door, a rolling cloud of sparkling glitter only I can see.

The alarms of several parked cars begin to scream into the night. Lights flick on in the surrounding houses. Doors begin to open.

Through the ringing in my ears I hear shouts and cries of confusion.

I blink up at the night sky, watching the stars, waiting for the pain to stop, for my ears to recover, for the heat from the spell to recede.

It takes several long, painful seconds.

By the time I manage to sit up, there are people hurrying towards me. I see a couple of my neighbours reaching down, concerned hands grasping for my arms and shoulders. I try to fight them off, mindful of the two familiars somewhere close by, but they seem to be gone. The concerned citizens pull me up, brush me down, start firing questions about what happened, if I'm hurt, do I want an ambulance?

No. I can't think of anything I want less than an ambulance. Back to Angbec General? No, thank you.

I push hard until I'm standing on my own two feet.

"I'm fine, I'm fine." Even to my own ears, my voice is slightly muffled. "I'm not hurt—just let me catch my breath."

Someone has already called for help. Far off in the distance I hear a siren. Perhaps two.

The explosion must have been incredibly loud.

Still fighting off concerned hands, I walk slowly back towards the door of my home.

I can feel it now.

Dink must have been trying to warn me.

Magic is heavy in the air, traces of intense, powerful *fortis* forced into a tiny space—my door. Even the residue is hot and painful on my skin, and I experience a small ripple of fear at the thought of what might have happened if I had walked through it.

A heavily breathing man, perhaps no more than eighteen, rushes up to my side. "Are you okay? Is this your house? I could smell the gas. It was so strong. I called the emergency line. You know, for gas leaks? But they ain't here yet. I called them ages ago."

Gas?

This wasn't a gas explosion. This was magic, pure and simple, a manifestation of *fortis* condensed into a horrible explosion.

Through the ravaged door frame I can just about make out some of the interior to my home. Carnage.

Debris everywhere, dust, pieces of wood and masonry tossed all over the place. Glass glitters in sparkling shards across the shredded carpet. Confetti fragments of paper, mangled plastic, and who even knows what else. Hard to tell what belongs to what when everything looks as though a giant simply shoved their hand in and stirred it around.

I finally gather enough of my senses to pull my ID card out of my back pocket.

"Back off, please." I raise my voice to be heard over the rumble of conversation. "Back off, everyone. This is the site of a serious accident, and you all need to keep your distance."

The young man who spoke about gas widens his eyes at me. "Are you from the emergency gas people?"

"I'm a police officer, and I'm telling you all to step back."

I scan the crowds, already on the lookout for someone or something suspicious. But I can't see anything beyond the morbid curiosity of my fellow humans. Something awful has happened—clearly it must be time to come and have a look.

❖

When the emergency responders finally do arrive, I have my head back on my shoulders. A good thing, because I don't have time to sit and worry, I need to be the voice of reason and authority. Somehow that's far easier to do among civilians than with my coven sisters.

I don't stop to think about why.

Instead, I greet each responder in turn and explain, over and over—and over—what I experienced when I opened my front door.

Of course everyone agrees that it was clearly an gas explosion. A small one, fortunately. I mention to the emergency gas engineers that the area is surprisingly free of flame for a gas incident.

"Oh yeah." The woman dressed in bright orange high-vis nibbles on the back of her thumb. "Explosions can kill off flames pretty easy. It's the pressure, you see. All that force, no way a fire can hold and spread. You might find a few charred bits in there, but likely nothing more. Just a mess."

I can't decide if that's good or bad.

Somewhere in the middle of it all I spot Dink hurrying along the edge of the pavement, and I scoop him up to deposit him in my car. After everything else today I don't want him getting trampled. Anansi is harder to find, but I discover her, eventually, swinging from the passenger side mirror of my car. She too hops inside and waits patiently as I lock the door.

Fire crews and gas services are already making their way inside. Soon there will be others to survey the damage to my home and those close by.

Unlike some explosions I've seen footage of, or even still photographs, the building itself seems largely unscathed. The roof is intact, and windows on the upper floor have somehow survived.

Then again, the explosion wasn't supposed to catch anybody *upstairs*, was it?

I answer more questions for people wearing high-vis. I leave my name and number for police. I insist to paramedics that I'm unharmed and in no need of a hospital visit. They are harder to reassure, but once I flash my badge and explain my job, they seem more inclined to believe me.

At least there are some perks to being an officer.

I finally manage to get myself free of all the questions and run my gaze over the crowds. Now with backup from other officers it's easier to keep people back. More of that black and white police tape and the physical barrier of actual officers keep back the crowds.

That's why I almost don't see her. It's also why I'm not quite certain that I *have* seen her. But towards the back of the crowds of people, all shoving and jostling to get a better view, I catch a glimpse of long red hair.

I'm halfway towards the barrier when Hozier shows up.

I eye him with surprise as he stops his car several feet away and then jogs over. He forces his way easily through the irritated crowd and beelines straight to me. "Marks?"

"Skip." I find myself looking beyond him as I speak, trying to spot the red hair again. Did I really see it? Was it Blake? Is she spying on me?

"What are you doing here?" The words are automatic. I don't even really want to know.

"I only just sent you home," he murmurs. "Were you caught in that?"

The words drag my gaze away from the crowds. I find him facing my home, eyeing the devastation of my front door with a stunned lift to his eyebrows.

"Almost," I tell him softly. "I got lucky."

"You really did. All the ground level windows are blown out. How close were you?"

"Close enough. It wasn't fun."

His gaze turns to me now. "Do you have somewhere to stay? I was coming by to check on you after, well, after today, but on the way I heard about this mess on comms. When I realized it was you, I moved faster. Are you all right?"

"Fine. Just sore."

"Did you get checked over?"

"Yeah."

He frowns. "And they didn't take you in? What about your hearing? Are you concussed? Did you hit your head?"

"Skip." I lift my hand. "I'm okay, honestly. Stop fussing."

"I'm worried about you." He leans in closer. "I got the report from the coroner. Seems like you were there earlier, paying a little visit."

I don't look at him, simply wait for him to continue.

"So you know how bad it is. You know what happened to that woman and—"

"Hyacinth."

"What?"

"Her name is Hyacinth Dixon."

He sighs. "Exactly. You know what happened to her. And now this. I was stopping by to tell you to take some leave. And…to ask some questions."

That catches my attention. "What kind of questions?"

His voice remains low and private. "Come on, Tina. You know we're drowning in cases right now. After all that vampire stuff, we have more on our plates than we can handle. I need a simple win here. But I get the feeling this isn't an open-shut murder case. I need to know what you know."

Finally I look at him. I take in his creased and weary features, noting with interest how tired he looks. I can't remember the last time I saw such heavy circles under his eyes. Has he not been sleeping?

"You don't have to tell me much," he hurries on. "All I need to know is if this is one of ours, or if I get to pass it on to SPEAR." There is the smallest note of hope in his voice when he says that. "If it's *edane* nonsense or something to do with…with…your condition, then we aren't equipped to deal with it. I can hand it over to the real professionals."

A stubborn streak of defiance fills my belly. "No. No way."

"Tina—"

"We take care of our own, Skip. That's it. If I have to work this on my own, fine, but I'm not letting some SPEAR who couldn't care less figure out what happened to my Mother."

He gapes at me. "Mother? She's your mum?"

"No, I…" Ugh. Now isn't the time to explain. "It's witch stuff," I murmur, using the phrase he picked out earlier. "All you need to know is that she's important to me. And if I have to find out what happened to her by myself, then I'm going to do that. Don't you dare take this from me, Neil."

Maybe it's the look in my eyes. Maybe it's the fact that I actually used his name. Whatever it is, Hozier's eyes widen as he stares at me, and he takes the tiniest of steps back. "You're too close to this. You're never going to see the wood for the trees."

"I'm the only person in the APD who can. Unless you have another witch tucked up your sleeve?"

He looks down.

"That's what I thought. Now it's late, and I need some rest. I'll talk to you tomorrow." I begin walking, halfway to my car before he stalks after me.

"You never said if you have somewhere to go."

I give him a dark, mirthless smile. "I think I do, actually. Probably the one place left I *can* go."

❖

This time, when I approach the gates, I hop out of the car to open them fully. The huge, iron hinges are smooth and slick, despite likely never being used. I get back into the car and ease it onto Hyacinth's drive and right up to her front door.

Then I close the gates behind me.

As if pleased to be home, both Anansi and Dink dart out of the car and towards the dark bulk of the house. The front door is locked, but both of them are small enough that such an obstacle is no problem to them.

I'm the one who has to open the door, and I do so slowly, pushing gently to allow myself entry back into the cool interior.

Everything is as I left it earlier that morning—partially cleaned, smelling faintly of lemon washing-up liquid and slightly musty food.

I dump my meagre belongings on the floor and trudge through into the sitting area.

The stairs aren't far off, but I can't face them right now. Besides, the only bed I know of in this place belongs to Hyacinth, and there's no way I can sleep in that.

No, I'm perfectly happy to lie on the long, lumpy sofa and catch some sleep there.

Everything else can be dealt with in the morning.

There's a large throw draped over the back of a huge winged armchair. It's handmade, knitted or crocheted—no idea which—with dozens upon dozens of bright coloured squares. On each square is a different flower or herb, finely crafted with such detail that I can tell exactly what each one is.

Thyme. Sage. Rosemary. Lavender. Fennel. Mint. Basil. Clover.

Some are simple and entirely mundane, others are not. All of them can be consumed in various forms, making the blanket resemble nothing more than a crafty chef's homage to food flavourings.

I pick it up and know immediately that Hyacinth was the one to make this.

The yarn is soft in my grip, and I press it to my chest, as if I might be able to catch more of the memory of Hyacinth by bringing it close.

I can't, of course. All I feel is pain. And anger.

Someone did this. And then someone went after me.

There's no proof the two events are related, but I'm not much of a believer in coincidences.

Two Willow Bark witches attacked with varied levels of success.

Is the coven truly in danger? Is this a sign of more to come?

I lie on the sofa and drape the handmade blanket over myself. I resolve to think about all the different clues and facts I have and pull them together into a tapestry as pretty as the one I lie beneath.

But sleep comes almost instantly.

Chapter Twenty-seven

I wake to the soft warmth of sunlight on my face and the brush of fur against my neck. Several seconds pass before I remember where I am, teetering on the edge of the sofa cushions. Dink is curled into a ball against the base of my throat, his whiskers tickling my skin. I move slowly, so as not to wake him, and cradle his tiny body in my hands as I sit straight. On the low coffee table, patiently waiting, is Anansi. I have no idea if she's asleep or not—how would I even tell? She's unmoving and silent, like a creepy, hairy statue.

A yawn stretches my lips, and I whisper some words of gratitude to my silent, tiny protectors.

Then…I sit.

I don't know the time, but it must be fairly early. My internal clock allows for a natural wake-up fairly close to six thirty, and the light is about right. Normally at this point in the week I'd be getting up and preparing for a slightly earlier shift, showering, eating, moisturizing my hair.

But there's none of that today. Just the quiet stillness of Hyacinth's home.

I remember sitting on this sofa, watching Hyacinth crush a sprig of whatever herb she had dried that week. I recall the deft, assured way her hands would move as she arranged crystals across that same coffee table for a scrying session. Even the tarot cards she would sometimes use—she had several packs, but her favourite was always the plain green set, with real leaves and flowers pressed into the fronts. The few times she ever let me touch them, I found that they were quite difficult to handle, but she would always tell me that the live nature of the components made them all the more powerful. And I never doubted her, because that deck had always been sassy and direct in scolding me for all the mistakes I was making.

I hunt for the deck now and find it tucked neatly away onto a shelf with all the others. The desire to touch the cards stirs inside me, but even as I reach out for them, I know I can't. Not yet. Despite everything, they still belong to Hyacinth.

I pick out a different set, also green, though with stylized pictures of insects across the backs.

By this time Dink is awake, and he watches with interest as I take the cards back to the table and begin to shuffle.

Reading these cards has never been a strong skill of mine, but I understand what to do and how. I close my eyes as I jumble them all up, focusing my will, my *fortis*, on my request. Clarity. Advice. Comfort.

The simple three-card-draw for past, present, and future is quite telling.

First to come out of the deck is Justice. I struggle to remember the number, but it doesn't really matter. I can just about recall what it represents, and the picture helps to get me there: a picturesque field lit by rays of golden light streaming down from a yellow disc. Behind the disc, however, are smaller, paler yellow circles, weak copies or imitations of the one in front. This card represents truth. But it comes out of the deck upside down, and I peer at it with a frown. I know darn well there are some lies to root out. This doesn't give me any sort of clue beyond confirmation, in a sense, that I'm right to be suspicious. But that has always been in my nature.

I think about where the lack of truth could have originated. Clearly with Blake. She's hiding something, and April, with her power as coven Mother, is doing a great job of glossing over that. Then again, I know Hyacinth would have moved mountains to be sure all of us were safe. I can't be surprised to learn that April would do exactly the same.

My second card is Ten of Swords. Again, no surprise there. I'm petrified, and this card, which features a spider with the body of a giant human skull, matches that sensation perfectly. Someone tried to kill me. I want to believe my house was torn to shreds by an unfortunate gas explosion, but the reactions of the familiars and the tingle of magic at the door are impossible to ignore.

Dink flops his tail onto my thigh, and I rub his head with the tip of my index finger.

Fear and uncertainty. A sensation of powerlessness.

Once more I find myself marvelling at the ability of a simple deck of cards to pinpoint exactly what I'm feeling or what is happening around me.

No advice in particular, but certainly some of the clarity I hoped for.

I pause before drawing the third card. What I really want is an idea of what to do, where to go next. Maybe even whom to trust. Far from my own home, surrounded by another person's things, I abruptly feel alone and trapped. I long for the safety of Hyacinth's smile, or the comfort of my own creaky sofa. But I have neither.

Anansi moves for the first time since I woke. She turns in a slow circle, then crawls off the side of the coffee table. I lose sight of her for several seconds before first two legs, then four, then the rest appear over the edge of the sofa. I tense, but she doesn't stray close to me, simply positions herself at my side before falling into stillness again.

"Thanks, I guess."

Third card.

Sixteen. The Tower. The picture on this card is another spider, tiny against the vast expanse of a crumbling wall made of rough, uneven stones. There is perspective in the image, which shows how far the spider has climbed versus how much further there is to go. The distance is about even.

Change. More uncertainty. Ruin and devastation.

My fingers tremble on the card. I've no way of knowing if this card refers to a future far down the line or something less distant, but it almost doesn't matter.

I think about my sisters and wonder how the events of the last day are going to crush my coven. Will we survive this level of upheaval? Are we equipped to survive without our coven Mother, or is her loss what brought about this card? So very many questions that I have no answers to.

It's a feeling of lost helplessness that I hoped I would never have to experience again.

Briefly I consider calling my mother, but somehow the thought of hearing her voice instead of Hyacinth's makes me recoil. Jasmine

Marks is my mum and will always be my mum. But Edith was right when she pointed out that Hyacinth was my mother.

Well, it's time to find out what happened to her.

❖

Now that I'm properly awake, I can think more clearly about what I need to get done. More than that, I realize that I probably can't stay here indefinitely. Much as I would like to, there will no doubt be officers here to scour the place once Hyacinth is officially identified.

That means I need to use the time I have quickly and effectively.

The first thing I do is move my car. Sure, Hozier knows, in a vague sense, that I am connected to Hyacinth, but nobody else does. I'm not sure I want to be involved with speaking to my colleagues until I'm certain of a few other aspects. So I hop in and drive the vehicle several streets away.

On the quick walk back I formulate a plan of attack for my search of the house. The mundane areas are unlikely to hold anything of importance. In fact, I can afford to leave those for the APD to search as they would any other crime victim. The places with the most information are going to be Hyacinth's spell spaces, like the attic and her bedroom. Maybe even the garden.

Back at the house, I close the main gate and help myself back inside. Though the house seems dead and lifeless, that other strange sense of magic in the air remains. I marvel at how powerful a ward it must be to survive the death of the caster. I allow myself to enjoy that soft, velvety feeling and realize then that the ward, whatever it is, is *welcoming* me in, not pushing me away.

Even from beyond, Hyacinth is looking after me.

I try not to tear up at the thought.

Given that I looked over the kitchen and sitting area yesterday, there isn't much to see beyond basic household odds and ends—cleaning materials, cupboard foods, clothes, books, furniture. The most interesting stuff is upstairs.

Dink joins me, riding my shoulder as I make my way up. Though she seems to want to follow, Anansi keeps a good distance back, crawling along the wall close to the ceiling.

First, the bedroom. The door is open, and again, sunlight streams in, pale gold through the net curtains. I step in and let my body become still, waiting for something to leap out at me. Nothing does, until Dink scrambles off my shoulder and down to the ground. He darts across the carpet and runs quick loops around something small and silver beneath the dresser. A tiny key, perhaps for a bike lock or a child's treasure box. But nothing in the room seems to match. I leave it on the dresser and continue to look around.

Shoe boxes, clothes, jewellery, and old cassette tapes. Fancy perfume bottles—mostly empty—and crystals either dangling from thin, near-invisible string or gathered together in small piles. And books. Not spell books and histories like might live upstairs, but fun, mundane ones.

It always amuses me to remember that Hyacinth likes—liked—manga and graphic novels. There are plenty of them, neatly arranged right to left on the shelves beside her bed. Beneath those are the romance novels she also enjoyed, as well as the eclectic mishmash of poetry and classic literature.

A jumbled-up library for a jumbled-up woman.

One section of the manga is related entirely to witches. I giggle, wondering if they amused her as fanciful representations of our lives as actual followers of the Goddess.

In the dresser, unsurprisingly, I find stacks of clothes. The top drawer has several small trinkets, including a feather, three jagged pebbles, and an orange so old it has become rock solid. There's also a small wooden box, with a tiny padlock on it.

I perch on the end of her bed with Dink sitting quietly on my knee and inspect it. The box is oddly heavy for something so small, dense in a way that makes me open it quickly. The key fits perfectly, and I pop it back into my pocket for safekeeping.

Inside is a single sheet of yellowed paper folded into a tight package. On one side I catch neat, precise handwriting spelling my name in glittering purple ink. The dried remnants of a yellow flower with red inside lies pressed between an outer fold of the packet. Verbascum, I think. The whole packet rustles when I shake it.

My throat constricts.

Verbascum is a flower usually used to symbolize protection and comfort, sometimes healing. Is this a charm, then? What was she trying to protect me from?

Another puzzle for later.

Though the box appears empty, there is still such weight that there must be more, perhaps a secret panel or hidden compartment. I turn it left, then right, upside down, then right way up. I run my fingertip along each edge inside and out until finally my fingernails catch the tiniest raised edge of an inner shelf. When I pull it out, sure enough, there is more beneath, tucked into a secret compartment.

Papers. No, *letters*. Dozens upon dozens of them, short, but meticulously handwritten. Some in a hand I recognize, others I don't, but seemingly just those two.

I pick one at random.

Sweetest Persephone, I missed you tonight.

How long will you make me wait before I kiss you again?

My hand trembles as I reach for another letter, different handwriting this time.

Pretty Flower, meet me tonight.

Under your willows or in our usual hiding place.

P

Love notes? Was Hyacinth seeing someone? I had no idea.

I pick up another and another, barely noticing as Anansi crawls her creepy way onto the pillows nearby. She watches as I read, and as I search, I simply find more of the same: loving notes between two women who refer to themselves with the nicknames *Flower* and *Persephone*. Flower is easy, that must be Hyacinth, but who is Persephone? A further curl of sadness coils through me when I realize that this other woman, whoever she is, has lost a lover.

Then again…

Most of the notes aren't dated, but those that are seem to spread across a number of years. After careful searching, the most recent I find is ten years prior, from Persephone to Hyacinth.

My Flower, you look so beautiful when you bloom.

You've reached heights one can only dream and you'll fly away into the stars.

Will you remember me when you soar above us?

P

I gather all the notes and place them back in the box. The secret drawer goes on top and then the charm on top of that. Part of me wants to keep it. The rest of me is uncertain that I should. I lock it back up and balance the key on my palm, considering how best to proceed.

Did Hyacinth place the charm for me on top of all those love notes to ensure I found them? Or was the box simply a convenient place to keep little treasures and trinkets?

A loud thud from downstairs drags me out of my thoughts.

Dink dives into my collar while Anansi immediately dashes up the wall, leaving me to check it out for myself. But there's no one else here, right? Seshat and Loki ran away, and I'm the only one here. Or so I thought.

That's why it takes every scrap of self-control I possess to muffle my gasp of shock when I spot Blake Allen standing at the bottom of the stairs.

CHAPTER TWENTY-EIGHT

I dart out of sight, rising onto my toes to avoid making too much sound. The house is old, but it isn't creaky, so I'm able to slip back into Hyacinth's room unnoticed, with my hand over Dink to keep him quiet. Anansi needs no such help, crawling straight up to the ceiling and simply waiting there, silent and frozen.

My heart hammers a samba in my chest.

What is *she* doing here?

Confusion melts rapidly to anger and on into a pulsing, red-rimmed rage.

That woman knows *something* about what happened to Hyacinth. And now she's here.

The internal war I experience is short, but intense: Confront her immediately and get the answers I so desperately crave? Or learn more about her intentions by watching and observing?

The soft pad of footfalls on the stairs quickly makes the decision for me. I drop to the ground and scoot under the bed, pulling my arms, legs, and Dink close.

It's dusty down there, with several shoe boxes spilling their contents through sides ripped and torn. Soft rolls of fluff and hair roil against my face, and I squint against them.

The footsteps approach.

By the time I open my eyes again, I see two feet lingering in the doorway. They are turned away, as if uncertain of entering, and I catch the sense of hesitation. Then they approach.

I watch the feet move around the bed, unwittingly following the same path I used only minutes ago. It's only when they pause near the dresser that I remember that I left the box on the bed.

Did I lock it? Did I finish replacing the notes? The charm? I have no idea. The key is with me, though, clutched tight in my hand, forgotten until that moment. I find myself hoping that I thought to lock the thing back up.

The feet move around the bed, leaving my line of sight briefly before turning up on the other side, where the bookshelves are.

I fight the urge to reach out and grab her ankle. Instead I tighten my grip on Dink, who shifts uneasily between my fingers.

I'll learn more if I watch and wait.

Blake sighs. I hear the faint vibration of a mobile and then rustling as the phone is retrieved.

Her half of the conversation is soft and halting.

"Hello? I—Yes…Yes, I'm there now. I don't know…Maybe, but I've just started…Are you sure?…Which room?…I'm there now, but I don't see anything, just a box…Small, wooden. There's a lock on it… Are you sure that…Yes, yes, all right, I've got it…No. There's no one here…I'm going to check upstairs as well…"

My hands are forming fists before I realize it. I bite my lip to stop the snarl of anger and gently flex my fingers. Dink takes that chance to slide out of my grip and scurry away. Can't blame him, really.

"Perhaps in some other rooms, but I'll keep looking and…" Blake's voice fades as she leaves the room.

I scramble crablike out from under the bed. As I suspected, the box with my charm is gone. I silently thank my idle hands for locking it, then creep towards the door.

Ahead, Blake stops briefly in the spare room. Then the bathroom. Then the study. She moves softly and quickly, catlike on her feet. Were she not in front of me, I might never have known she was here at all. Worse still, her furtive yet confident movements suggest she has been here before.

A shadow passes overhead, and I recognize Anansi slowly picking her way along the flowery cornice towards the next set of steps.

The last place is Hyacinth's sanctum, and Blake stops at the bottom of those stairs looking up. I see her hesitate and bite her bottom lip before she ascends.

I slide out of the bedroom to tiptoe across the landing and press my back to the wall by the stairs. I lean in an inch at a time until barely, just barely, I spy a sliver of Blake's form standing on the topmost step, observing the closed door.

She's just standing. Looking. Waiting? After long moments, she presses down on the handle.

I hold my breath, but the door remains shut.

Blake gives a tut of irritation. "Aperta."

I feel her *fortis* twist through the air as she tries the handle a second time.

Still it doesn't budge.

"Aperta," she says again, jiggling the handle.

I put out a hand, intending to recast my locking paltrick when I spot Anansi abruptly swing down from directly above Blake's head. She sways, long legs flexing in sequence as she inches lower and lower on a fine, near invisible thread of webbing.

I freeze. What is that creepy arachnid trying to do?

After two more attempts, Blake sighs and lifts the phone to her ear again. "One more room, but I can't get in…I think there's a spell…I already tried that, but it won't open…I don't see one, but I could look for a key…" She runs a hand around the door frame, particularly the top and sides. "No," she says at last. "But I have that box, isn't that enough? I…okay." She turns to leave, never noticing Anansi barely a foot from the top of her head.

I jerk back into the bathroom and wait until Blake's footfalls pass, descend the stairs, and head away. Only when the front door clicks shut do I make my way out of the bathroom.

My skin prickles, the air around me singing with rage on the verge of exploding outward.

I imagine doors slamming, walls shuddering, and pictures leaping off hooks. If poor Becca from the ComDis helpline thought she caused some damage, she has no idea what a seasoned witch can do.

Dink appears from the study, twitching his tiny nose at me. Anansi drops silently from the ceiling close by and considers me in her usual eerie fashion.

I ignore them both, scroll through my own phone, and tap *Dial* on a number close to the top.

Nikolette answers after the first ring. "Hey, Tina, how are you holding up?"

"Blake just robbed Hyacinth's house," I snap. "I need to get to April."

❖

Nikolette coughs and splutters down the phone line. "What? Slow down a moment, what are you talking about?"

"I'm at Hyacinth's house, and Blake just left. I saw her creep about the house, steal a trinket box, and then leave."

"When? How? Why aren't you at home?"

My heart aches at the sudden realization that Nikolette doesn't know what happened last night. "I'm sorry. I should have told you. You should have been the first to know. There was an explosion at my house."

"What?" The burst of sound from the phone forces me to temporarily lift it away from my ear. "Are you okay? What happened?" A gasp. And then, "There was a gas explosion on the local news. Was that you? That was your place?"

"It wasn't a gas explosion." Before I realize it, I'm pacing, doing circuits through all the rooms on the upper floor while Anansi and Dink watch from the top of the stairs. "I mean, yeah, there was gas, but it was a spell. Someone trapped my house."

Silence.

"Nikolette? Did you hear me?"

"Who would do something like that?"

I fight the urge to scream. "Blake. I saw her when all the emergency crews showed. She was lurking in the crowd, probably surveying her handiwork."

More silence, then rustling over the line. The jingle of keys. "I'm coming to you."

"No, you're not listening. I need to get to April so we can talk about Blake and—"

"You can't be alone right now," she snaps. "Someone set a bomb in your house."

"It was hardly a bomb…"

"Tina! April wants the Elm Stems travelling at least in pairs. Please say you at least have one of the Willows with you."

"I don't want to scare them when they need space to grieve. I'll tell them in my own time." Even as I glance around me, I realize that's only partially true. More than them needing space, *I* needed some time alone in this house, sitting with my quiet memories. "You're the only one who knows, Nikolette, and I want to keep it that way until I figure out more."

"Fine." The click of a lock. Nikolette has already left her home. "I'm still coming to get you. If you insist, I'll take you to Mother April, but I won't let you be out there alone." Another door slams as she leaves the apartment block. "Where are you?" The background sound around her voice changes, now filled with the rumble of rush hour traffic. "Tina?"

"Lower Mendyke," I murmur. "Sparken Drive."

The rumble of a car engine. "Good. Wait for me. Don't do anything reckless."

I nod even though she can't see me. "Look for the biggest house at the end of the cul-de-sac. One with a gated drive."

"I'll be there in thirty." She hangs up.

Chapter Twenty-nine

Thirty minutes are more like twenty. I've barely finished my second search of Hyacinth's spell space before I hear a car approach outside.

I'm not done, not by a long shot, but I don't want Nikolette in here if I can help it. Hyacinth's home has been violated enough.

As I leave, I try not to think about the fact that my mentor will never again give permission for someone to enter her home.

Nikolette has parked beyond the huge iron gates. Her face is oddly pale, her hand half raised towards me. "Wait," she murmurs, as I approach. "Don't move yet."

I freeze and watch her.

She shudders. "Can't you feel that ward? It's massively powerful."

"There were two. One broke and expired when I arrived yesterday, but there's also this one. I have no idea what it is."

"How can you stand to be inside it? The whole thing is so spiky and painful—like shards of glass." Nikolette gives another rippling shudder. "It's huge and it doesn't want me here."

I frown. "What are you talking about? It's a lovely ward, all cosy and buttery soft. Like warm fur."

She rubs her arms. "Not to me, it isn't. And without seeing the source point I can't know how big it is, but my guess is that it starts in the house. That means the ward covers the entire building and some of the main road. I'm certainly standing in it."

Yet another mystery I have no answers for.

Nikolette frowns. "Whatever Crone Hyacinth was protecting against, she didn't want it anywhere near this house. But apparently that doesn't include you." She lowers her hand at last. "It's…good to see you. How are you?"

I gaze at her. "Been better."

"I'm glad you're not hurt." She raises her eyebrows at me. "An explosion? Seriously?"

I step through the large gates. I don't want to bring her in, but I can't stand the physical barrier between us. "Everyone says gas explosion, but it's more than that. I know you have an aptitude with wards and circles, you'd probably be able to tell exactly what, but I *know* there was magic involved. Dink tried to warn me."

"Who?"

"Hyacinth's mouse familiar. Every time I tried to open the door, he bit me. Anansi too."

Another quizzical look from Nikolette.

"Anansi is a spider. Another familiar."

"You had a spider nearby and didn't lose your mind?" She gives an incredulous smile.

A shrug. "I've had other things to think about. Like Blake."

Nikolette's frown returns. When I don't back down, she leans back a step and folds her arms tight across her chest. "Fine. Tell me."

I cast an arm back at the house. "She was here. No more than an hour ago. I caught her snooping around, going into all the rooms. She even tried to get into the spell space."

"And you're sure it was her?"

"I. Saw. Her. I'm not stupid. I recognized her, and I—"

"I'm not calling you stupid. I'm just saying if you didn't speak to her, if you were hiding, how can you know for sure?"

Internally I count to ten.

"Because I know her face. And she was here before that too, yesterday." I feel a faint twitch of smugness at Nikolette's look of surprise. "When I came here yesterday morning, I nearly hit her with my car. I bet she was leaving the house."

Nikolette stares up at the building. Her eyes are busy, taking in every detail from the roof down. I don't know what she sees, but I get the impression that she's following the lines of something invisible to the naked eye. The ward, perhaps? "I don't understand," she murmurs.

"Me neither. And maybe I should have confronted her, but I thought I would learn more by seeing what she wanted. She was on the phone to someone—no idea who—and she stole a trinket box from Hyacinth's bedroom."

"There must be an explanation."

"Yeah, that she's a liar, a thief, and possibly a murderer." I step forward. "Will you take me to April or not?"

Nikolette gnaws her bottom lip. Her fingers shuffle awkwardly as she begins to pace. "Mother April vouched for Blake." Her voice is soft and timid. "Surely she wouldn't do that if there was any reason for suspicion." Not a question, but her tone makes it such.

"She's wrong."

"Was Crone Hyacinth ever wrong?"

That makes me snap my mouth closed. Long seconds pass before I dare speak again. "You really trust her, don't you?"

"Of course I do. The same way you trusted Crone Hyacinth. She's my Mother." For a brief moment, her lower lip quivers. "I can't believe she would wilfully lie about something like this."

I soften my voice. "What if she's not lying, then? What if she doesn't have the whole story?" I insist. "April can't possibly know about the protective wards around this place, or what happened at my house. She doesn't know what I felt on Hyacinth's body or the residue back at the game shop."

"What are you talking about now?"

"She was paralysed." Even saying the words aloud makes my body ache with anger and pain. "When I went back to the shop, I felt the remnants of a paralysis spell. Then, when I visited her…body… at the morgue, I felt the same thing. And on three other bodies found over the last couple of days. There's a witch out there so powerful that even Hyacinth couldn't fight them. She was paralysed so firmly that she couldn't fight back or defend herself while someone…" My voice breaks. Can't help it. "While someone stabbed her to death."

Nikolette's hand flies to her mouth. "Oh Goddess, no." The colour flees her face. "She was High Crone. Who could possibly be powerful enough to do that?"

"*Now* do you understand why I need to speak to April? You're right, I don't know if it's Blake, but isn't it a strange coincidence that she turned up here the day after I found her with Hyacinth's body?"

A sense of urgency seems to wash over Nikolette. "Let's go. Right now."

I dart back inside to grab my things.

Both Dink and Anansi scuttle to keep up with me. Their movements are jerky and uneven, both of them loitering at the edge of what I feel to be Hyacinth's last ward. They seem unwilling to approach Nikolette but equally uneasy about leaving my side.

As I walk, I scoop the mouse into my hand and pop him on my shoulder. I reach as if to do the same to Anansi, but at the last moment I yank my hand back. Nope. Still can't do it.

Back in the sanctum I take care to close the curtains and study the traces of chalk dust one last time. As the hours have passed, the sensation of magic in here has faded even more. While the rest of the house has become inert, I had hoped that this room would hold on to Hyacinth's aura or presence.

I barely feel anything now, and most of what I do feel seems to come from the altar. It takes only a moment longer to realize that the sensation stems from her book of shadows.

Is this it, then? Is this the last trace of my mentor left to the world, a heavy book filled with her thoughts and memories?

I run my hands over it, feeling warmth rise up from the cover.

Dink squeaks at me, then runs down my arm. He hops off my hand to the cover of the book, then onto my hand again, back and forth, back and forth.

He wants me to take it.

But to remove *this* book from *this* room is to admit, once and for all, that Hyacinth is never coming back.

Obviously she isn't, Blake has seen to that, but somehow I'm yet to admit that to myself.

Dink does his little back-and-forth dance a few more times.

Then a soft sound at the door brings my head around just in time to see Anansi make her slow, creepy way across the threshold. She waits between me and the door, waving her middle legs.

Again, I look at the book.

Am I *supposed* to have it? Is anybody supposed to take it from here? Surely it will be safe if I just lock the door again?

But then I remember Blake trying to force the door, manually and with spells. Is this what she was looking for?

I step out and stand in the doorway, looking in at this magnificent spell space.

Or what *was* magnificent.

It's just a room now, one filled with incredible knick-knacks and books, but still just a room. The life is gone.

I lower my head and pull the door shut. With my fingers loitering on the handle, I speak one word. "Clostra."

I don't use Latin very often. Not only do I know very little of it, but after all the rants on *Wood, Woof, and Wold*, something about it feels fake and performative. But this time, as a faint glow pulses briefly around the edges of the entire door, it feels right and proper.

Gently I push against it, but the door doesn't move. Even within the confines of the frame there is no movement at all, though I can see, just down the edge, that the locking mechanism is still open.

Nobody is getting into this room ever again. Not if I can help it.

Anansi begins her slow walk down the wall at shoulder height, and I take my time following after. She, as much as me, recognizes that our time here is over.

When I reach the car, Nikolette is on her phone. She gestures for me to keep my voice down, so I take the passenger seat without speaking.

Dink immediately crawls out of my pocket to take his place on the dashboard while Anansi crawls into the back and rests in the foot-well.

"But what do you want us to do in the meantime?" Nikolette's voice is softer than I've ever heard it. No, not soft, but respectful and… deferential?

I give her a quizzical look.

The voice on the other end of the phone is too low for me to hear, but Nikolette's expression gives me clues. Her lips are pursed, her brow furrowed. Her gaze keeps darting, first to me, then the road, and back again. If I didn't know better, I'd say she was nervous.

"Fine. I'll wait, but please, it's important, and I—yes…Yes, of course. Understood. Goodbye." She hangs up, a sigh puffing out her cheeks. She struggles to meet my gaze. "Mother April is in the middle of something and can't be disturbed. I'm to wait with you until she contacts me, and only at that point can we discuss when to meet."

My fingers curl down over my palms. "What could possibly be so important that she doesn't want to discuss a murder?"

Nikolette shrugs and starts the car. "No idea. But she told me to wait. So I'll wait."

"But—"

"Stop. Please. I don't have the same relationship with Mother April that you had with Crone Hyacinth. We're not friends, she's my coven Mother, and I do as I'm told. She's probably deciding the best way to keep everyone safe."

"But this would help her do that."

The car roars as she pumps the accelerator. "It can wait, and so can we." A brief pause. "Now, should we go to the park, or the coffee shop in Cipla?"

I stare at my hands as weariness settles on me. "I can't be around people right now," I tell her. "Seeing life just go on around me while Hyacinth is dead? Goddess, I…I want to go home."

Long, long silence.

Nikolette clears her throat. "I could take you to my place?"

Somewhere in the distance a car horn blares, but aside from that and the soft purr of the car beneath us, there is no sound. Just our quiet, gentle breathing.

She waits, not looking at me, though on the steering wheel, her knuckles are tight and pale.

A bead of sweat runs from my hairline down the front of my ear. I want to open my jacket or adjust my top, but my body is locked in place. Not a spell, but an abrupt arrival of nerves the likes of which I haven't felt since my teenage years.

"Yes, please."

There's a loud rush of air as Nikolette expels a deep sigh. Was she holding her breath?

"Okay. Let's go." She slips the car into gear and pulls away from Hyacinth's house.

As I watch the huge building slide out of view in the passenger window, I wonder if I'll ever be able to come back.

CHAPTER THIRTY

Princess is not pleased to see me. The fluffy Maine Coon arches her back the moment I step into the apartment, and even a shooing from Nikolette makes no difference to her mood.

She hisses as I enter, then more when she spots Anansi and Dink. The little mouse burrows deep inside my clothing to get out of sight, while Anansi springs from my bag to scuttle up the wall and to the ceiling where she crouches in a corner, well out of reach.

"You two behave," I tell them softly. "We're guests here."

Neither seems impressed.

The increasingly familiar prickle of a ward washes over my skin. This one is cool and almost damp, but watchful and curious rather than dangerous. I shoot Nikolette a questioning look.

"Someone booby-trapped your house," she says simply as she shuts the door. "I won't let anybody do that to mine."

Fair enough.

Off with the shoes and socks, as I always do when entering a witch's space. This time I leave them neatly by the door and follow Nikolette as she guides me to her living area.

Here are clear signs that she left in a hurry: a bowl of soup on the table beside half a slice of bread, a mug half full of something that is no doubt stone cold by now. She pushes all of it to one side and gestures for me to put my bag down.

I do. Then stand.

I knew it would be strange to be back in this space, but what I didn't realize was *how awkward* it would feel.

Clearly Nikolette feels it too because she clears her throat softly and lowers her gaze to the fluffy rug just beside the coffee table.

"Would you like a drink? I have tea."

"Maybe coffee, if you have it?"

Though she still doesn't look at me, a faint smile tugs at the corners of her lips. "Should have known. All I have is decaf."

"And *I* should have known. What kind of witch am I anyway?"

"A great one." She speaks firmly enough that I actually step back. Her gaze is hot and intense. "Stop putting yourself down. You're worth so much more than you seem to be believe."

With that, she steps out of the room, and I hear the familiar sounds of beverage production—cupboard doors, mugs clanking, spoons clicking, the kettle boiling.

Rather than standing stiff and uncomfortable, I move around.

This might be an apartment, but the rooms are spacious. This sitting area seems to serve as both dining room and living space, separated by twin rugs.

Closest to the window looking down on the street is the sitting area, with a low, squishy sofa, a tiny corner table, and the TV. On the table is a copy of a mystery book from some author I don't recognize and a small pad of paper beside the cordless landline. Beside the TV, a large, white pot homes a yucca plant with broad, sharp leaves, and to the left of the sofa stands a tall scratching post.

The scent of incense clings to the air, sandalwood this time. I inhale deeply to drink in the soothing smell.

"You're allowed to sit, by the way." Nikolette's voice from the kitchen. "At least *try* to be comfortable. I don't know how long we'll have to wait."

She's right, of course, but my body is tense from forehead to toes. Is it this space? The memory of my first and last time here? Or what I've learned about Hyacinth?

It could be all those things, it could be neither. It could simply be that Princess is glaring at me from the top of that scratching post.

Nikolette returns to the room holding two mugs. She aims for the coffee table with both, pausing just a moment to tilt her head. Before my eyes, two coasters slide from the stack on the corner and position themselves to accept the mugs she gently places on top.

At last, I sit, and the cushions of the sofa immediately swallow me in their softness. I'm not sure it will be easy to get up again.

Nikolette sits too, but right at the other end, staring at her fingers.

The gulf of space between us is so, so large. Is this really what we've become?

"Nikolette, I—"

"Tina, I'm so sorry—"

Our words mash together, crashing in the middle in a sudden burst of nervous, uneasy sound.

I gesture for her to continue.

At last, she looks at me. "I never should have said what I did," she whispers. "It wasn't fair, and it isn't true. You're not weak, and you're not a child. If anything, from what I saw, the old grumpy one is afraid of you."

"Iris? I doubt it. She just has a certain way of doing things."

"I saw her face when Mother April mentioned you becoming coven Mother. It doesn't matter how it comes about, at this point. All that matters is that you would be the one to lead, and she knows that."

This again.

I swivel my legs to face her properly. "I promise you, Nikolette, though Hyacinth talked about it all the time, I made my position clear. I don't want to be Mother. I don't want that kind of power ever again."

Her eyebrows twitch. "Again? What are you—"

I grab her hands. "I just need you to understand I wouldn't do something like that without telling you. Ever. I know what it means to you. And I understand the pressure from your grandmother—"

"Stop. It's okay." The corners of her mouth turn down slightly, while her fingers tense up in mine. When she smiles, her eyes remain cool and distant.

"*You* deserve it, Nikolette. We both know that. I don't have what it takes to be responsible for the well-being of anybody else. But you're kind and generous and powerful. You'd make an excellent Mother."

"I'm…" She breathes deeply. "I'm proud of you." The words stretch as though dragged slowly over sharp spikes. But when she says them, her body straightens. She treats me to a real smile. "I knew the High Crone only by reputation, but Mother April knew her well. And if she trusted Crone Hyacinth's judgement, then I do too."

I gaze at my fingers, still linked with hers. The words should be warming and soothing, but instead I feel nothing but the insectile prickle of nervous fingers teasing down my back.

No. I don't want it.

I cling to the subject that seems safe. "They knew each other?"

She nods. "She mentored Mother April, I think. Or they were once both part of another coven together. They were close once."

"Is that why she's so keen to take us in?"

Nikolette shrugs. "It must be. Why else would she visit your sanctum so quickly? Maybe she feels beholden to Crone Hyacinth's memory, or they had some if-anything-happens-to-me agreement. I don't know. But she wants to help you, Tina."

I sit back. "Hyacinth was very kind to me. She took me in when she didn't have to and has taught me so much. Maybe she saw something in me, but that doesn't change the fact that I'm not cut out to be a coven Mother."

She cocks her head. Licks her bottom lip. Her fingers play back and forth against each other, a gesture I'd normally attribute to nerves.

"I hope you're not doubting yourself because of *me*. I said some horrible things, Tina, but I was angry and…and jealous. You are just as capable as anybody else."

"I'm barely capable of keeping a date—"

"Stop that. Please." Her voice hardens for the briefest of moments as anger flashes across her gaze. "I know there's a lot you haven't told me about your past. That's fine." She holds up a hand as I try to intervene. "I don't care. It's not important. What *is* important is you and me right now. My raging perfectionism must make it so hard for you to just *be*. But now *you* need to understand something."

Again I open my mouth, but this time she shuffles forward and presses her fingers against my lips.

"My journey has nothing to do with yours," she murmurs. "Maybe my destiny *is* to be a coven Mother, but I can't let that rule every conversation I have with you. Nor can I let fear of *Yaya* get in the way of what I feel for you. I'm sorry," she whispers. "So, so sorry."

I gape at her. "I…me too. I mean, I said some pretty nasty things to you."

Again she moves closer. Our thighs are touching now, and the warmth of her body seeps through my clothing. I can smell her too, the fresh scent of vanilla clarifying shampoo and ocean breeze shower gel.

She stares deep, deep into my eyes, and low in my belly the flutter of butterflies the size of sparrows begins to rise.

"Nikolette…"

"I love you," she whispers. "I love you, and I want you, and I'm so sorry."

My throat seizes up. Her image blurs before me, and I realize that I've begun to cry.

She reaches out with the pad of her thumb, probably to brush the tears away, but I turn my face, to kiss it instead. She freezes, and I allow my lips to press against her skin.

She moans softly.

I draw her thumb into my mouth.

The moan hitches, and Nikolette presses down slightly with her thumb, nudging herself deeper and closer to my tongue. "Fuck."

Dink crawls out of my collar. Maybe he senses what's coming, or the heat coming off our bodies is too much. Whatever it is, he slips off my shoulder and down onto the arm of the sofa to vanish out of sight down the side. From the corner of my eye I notice Princess whip her head towards him, large eyes wide and unblinking.

I prepare to admonish her, or at least warn Dink, but suddenly Nikolette is all I can see, finally closing the small distance left between us to cup my cheek in her hand. Her eyes are big and round, near shimmering with a sudden flare of need that I feel rise within me to match.

"I love you too," I manage to croak out.

Nikolette shoves forward and crushes her lips to mine, snaking her other hand down to yank my hips to meet hers.

CHAPTER THIRTY-ONE

I'm lying flat on the sofa, lips fastened firmly to Nikolette's as she runs her hands up and down my body. Each pass of her fingers sends a pleasurable jolt through me, even through clothing, and I moan loudly against her mouth.

She angles her body over mine, using her weight to hold me in place as she thrusts her tongue greedily into my mouth.

By the time we come up for air again, the pair of us are panting.

"I want you," she hisses, never once breaking eye contact.

I nod. It's all I can manage, gazing into the pool of her eyes and finding a burning heat that matches my own. "Then take me."

"Fuck yes."

Nikolette's mouth returns to mine as she grasps at the button on my jeans. An instant later I feel the fabric give and the zipper slide down. Her hand dives inside the gap, playing over my stomach, the top of my underwear, teasingly lower.

I buck my hips, aware of how needy I've become and caring nothing for it.

Her blouse slips and slides between my fingers as I fumble for the buttons. My fingers are trembling, my breathing ragged, but I keep trying to work the tiny circles of plastic. One pops off and flies across the room. I hear it land, but I've no idea where. A second one loosens and dangles from a thread that catches on the skin of my paper cut from a few days before.

The little stab of pain slows me until Nikolette grabs both my wrists and presses them to the sofa above my head. "Stay."

"But I—"

"Stop. Moving. I want to touch all of you, a piece at a time." The sudden deepness in her voice sends a thrill through me, and I watch the shadow of her long lashes fall across her cheeks.

I nod. Can't possibly speak, so why try?

Then another blistering, breath-stealing kiss. Her tongue presses my lips apart, and I open to let her in. I catch the taste of her, tart green tea mingled with the exquisite flavour of *her*.

All the while, her hips grind against mine, pressing my body to the sofa, as sure as her hands tight about my wrists. "Stay," she says again.

Over the rise and fall of my chest, I watch her gaze travel down my body. She seems to be considering me, weighing me up, deciding which part of me she intends to devour first. Then she slips her forefingers into the belt loops either side of my hips and pulls.

My jeans slide off as though greased, all the way down to my knees, where she leaves them to trap my legs. Grinning now, she puts one knee between mine, on top of the denim, further trapping me against the sofa cushions.

"If I manage to let you up long enough," she murmurs, "I'll throw you over the sofa like I promised. As it is, I have other plans for you."

Through the partially open sides of her blouse I catch sight of her bra. It's olive green, lacy, and with such a daring plunge that I could lose myself in the shadow it makes.

I want to touch her. I want to taste her skin against my lips and tongue. I want to slip my fingers inside her and feel her perfect body move with me.

But I can't move. I don't want to move. Because her hands are on my hips now, gripping firmly to tug me a little further down the sofa. Then up, up, along my stomach, bringing the hem of my T-shirt with them.

The cool air against my skin brings out goosebumps that vanish immediately when the heat of Nikolette's hands follows after. She slides the soft cotton up some more—over my bra, past my shoulders, and beyond my head. Not all the way off, though. Instead she pulls it as far as my elbows and then flips the rest towards my hands, further immobilizing me.

Don't care. So long as she keeps touching me, she can do anything she wants.

"Nikolette…"

Another kiss to plug my words and her left hand gripping my

breast through my bra. Plain, black and simple, boring compared to hers, but from the look she gives me, it's as sexy to her as burlesque wear.

She squeezes gently and I buck my hips again, fighting to press myself against her. But her knee is firm between mine, using my own clothing to pin me in place.

Through the fabric, she strokes my nipple.

I give a needy, shameless whimper. The nipple stiffens against her touch, and she rubs a firm, possessive thumb over it, teasing through the bra.

"Please…"

She rubs again, still over the fabric, while her right hand traces slow, teasing circles on my hip.

I never imagined it could be like this. That the world would fade away to nothing more than the hotness of her breath on my skin, the heat of her body, and the faint scent of her hair. There is nothing in the world but Nikolette, her hands and her sultry, tempting smile.

Then at last she tugs my bra down, never mind the clasps at the back, simply pulls the cups down to free first one breast, then the other. She kisses each in turn, then runs her tongue in the slowest, most agonizing circles around my areole.

And still that other hand on my hip, across my stomach now, and along the top hem of my underwear.

I twist again, trying to push against her, to get close to her hand, to her hip, her thigh, anything.

My body is burning from the inside out, a need I've not felt in months. I long to feel the heat of desire and the passion of need fulfilled. More than anything, I want Nikolette to fuck me.

Another kiss, first against my mouth, then her lips scorching a path down my body—chin, neck, collarbone, breasts, ribs, stomach.

Her fingers wriggle into the top of my underwear and pull them down just a fraction. I feel her nails against my pubic hair and mewl my need. There's no words any more, no sense or reason, just raw, base need. Yet again I lift my hips.

My underwear butts against her chin, and I feel the warmth of her breath against me.

"Don't move," she reminds me.

"Okay," I whisper, unwilling even to nod if it might disturb her current path.

At last she lifts her knee off my jeans. The pressure fades from my thighs, and I slam down the urge to grind against her leg.

Nikolette smiles and then tugs the jeans off the rest of the way. At last my legs are free, but I can't use them. They're trembling, useless bends of boneless flesh that couldn't take my weight if my life depended on it.

Good thing I don't need to move.

Down again, eyes fixed on mine, she breathes over the top of my underwear, causing me to whimper and whine.

"I wanted to run my hands over every inch of you," she murmurs. "But all I can think of now is tasting you. But we might be here a while, so we can take our time, right?"

"Yes." My answer quivers out on shuddering breath. I'll say anything, agree to anything, *do* anything…

A contended sigh. Then she pulls my underwear down.

I watch her eyes widen, her pupils dilate. Her sweet, full lips part gently, and I watch the tiniest film of moisture stretch between them, then break as she inhales.

We are suspended in time, me gasping and waiting, Nikolette staring in wonder and arousal.

Then she lowers her head and puts her mouth on me and the entire world fades back into nothing.

We never make it off the sofa.

CHAPTER THIRTY-TWO

Damp. Hot. Sticky.

I glance at Nikolette and notice her ordinarily perfect hair is plastered to the side of her face and neck. Her eyes are closed, her breathing gentle, and though she might hate me for observing her in a less than pristine state, I can't help but stare.

Though her forehead gleams with sweat, the dampness around her mouth and chin are a decidedly different sort of moisture. So is that on her fingers and upper thigh. I don't quite remember grinding against her, but I suppose I must have.

We're tangled on the sofa, legs dangling towards the floor, upper halves barely on the cushions. Her head rests gently against my stomach while one hand toys with my nipples. I have my arms curled around her, gently trying to peel her hair off her face.

"We waited so long," she murmurs, into my belly. "So. Worth. It."

"I'm glad you think so. Maybe next time we can—"

"Next time?" Her head snaps up, and her eyes fix me with an expression so gleeful and childlike that she almost appears a different person. "Already thinking ahead?"

I nod slowly.

Though I resisted and worried and fought it, I realize now how much I needed this. How much I craved the tender touch of another, to be chased by the grip of someone near frantic with desire. I'd forgotten how good it feels to be wanted in that way. Needed. Craved.

"I'm sorry," I murmur at last.

The joyous expression stutters. "What's wrong? Why?"

"We could have had this weeks ago. I'm the one who made us

wait. I was the one so reluctant to visit your home that it took me *almost dying* to realize what I wanted."

"Tina—"

My phone rings.

"*Nooo*," she whines in a tone so unlike her usual that I catch myself laughing. "I don't want you to move. You're soft and sexy and beautiful and warm. And comfortable." She adds weight to that last part by nuzzling her face more deeply into my stomach.

I stretch my hand out, but my jeans are far across the room, hanging from the yucca where Nikolette tossed them after finally yanking them off my body.

"Let it ring," Nikolette purrs. "I like feeling you under me."

"I know you do, but I should get it."

"Mother April will be calling *me*. Who else would be calling for you in the middle of the afternoon?"

"I don't know, and I—"

The ringing stops.

Nikolette hums happily and resumes her lazy manipulations of my nipple.

A little shiver runs through me as the arousal begins to build anew under her steady, constant teasing. "Don't you want a drink first?" I ask.

She grins. "Got plenty to drink earlier, thank you. Though I wouldn't say no to more of *that* if you're offering."

The phone rings again.

I turn against the sofa cushions and tug her up to meet me. Our kiss is slow and languorous but building fast in heat as our tongues touch once more. My legs shift, and I slide one thigh between hers to allow our hips to connect.

We're still fondling, still kissing, still grinding, when the phone stops ringing once again, only to start immediately two seconds later. Someone really, really wants me.

"I'll be back," I tell Nikolette, gently easing myself from under her. "Keep my spot warm."

But she stands too, and sight of her body causes my skin to warm as she stretches both arms above her head.

"Bedroom," she says simply. "I have a bed to throw you over."

I almost follow her. Wouldn't it be so much nicer to forget the call and simply skip towards the bedroom for yet more passion and sex? But the phone is too loud and too shrill to ignore.

As Nikolette slips out of sight with a coquettish grin, I snatch up the little device and press it to my ear. "This better be good. I'm very, very busy."

At the other end of the line, Chloe gives a little gasp. "Oh. Oh no, I've done it again, haven't I? I'm so sorry."

"It's fine." I sigh. "Honestly, don't worry. Are you okay?"

"F-fine. I just wanted to, uh…" As she breaks off, the image of her gnawing on her bottom lip comes to my mind's eye. She is always so very, very nervous, even being on the phone.

But I don't have the patience for it right now. "Chloe?"

"I…no. It's nothing. Don't worry about it." Her voice is soft and hesitant. Behind it I catch the sound of many other voices; she's clearly in a crowded place. "I'm sure you have other things to do."

"Really? Are you sure? Because you're right, I am…occupied." I chance a look over at Nikolette's bedroom and see her watching me, one finger crooked towards me, beckoning me in.

"Um. It's just that I…"

I roll my eyes. "Good grief, Chloe, spit it out."

A little yelp, then a fumbling sound. I'd be willing to bet she actually dropped the phone.

"It's nothing. Nothing. D-don't worry about it. I'll see you later." She hangs up before I can say anything else.

I scroll through the options on my phone to turn it to silent, then drop it on the sofa. No need to risk further disturbances when I have such a wonderful distraction waiting for me next door.

Grinning now, I hurry into the bedroom, where Nikolette catches me immediately into her arms. With a giggle, she hooks her leg around mine and tips me hard onto the bed where I bounce against the soft duvet. At once she's on me, pushing my arms up again and laying kisses to the side of my throat.

"Now where were we?" she purrs.

I must have fallen asleep. That's all I can assume, because the next thing I know, Nikolette is gently shaking my arm. She's dressed again, more casually than before, but beautiful as ever, in tight black jeans and a baggy blouse stylishly tucked into the high waist.

"It's time to go," she says, handing me my clothes. "I just spoke to Mother April. She says we can meet her."

With a jolt, I'm bolt upright. "How long was I out? What time is it? How long has it been?"

Nikolette lifts her hands to me in a soothing gesture. "Only fifteen minutes, I promise. I was going to cook but I figured we wouldn't have much time, so I just cleaned up a bit."

She smiles gently, but my stomach tightens with an abrupt pang of guilt.

How could I sleep at a time like this? How could I forget, even for a moment, why I even came here in the first place?

When Nikolette touches my arm, I remember exactly *how* I could forget, but that doesn't stop the abrupt tightness in my chest as I pull on my jeans. "Where do we meet her?"

"The Elm Stem sanctum."

I pause, halfway into my T-shirt. "Will I be allowed inside?"

A curious glance from Nikolette. "Mother April herself invited you. I'm sure it's fine. Why?"

Instead of answering, I find myself gnawing my bottom lip.

"It's okay," she says. "I'll be right by your side, and if anybody has a word to say about it, they'll have me to answer to."

"You can't—"

"It's only a matter of time before everyone finds out about us." She touches my shoulder. "You've been so brave over the last couple of days, the least I can do is attempt the same. And don't worry, I'll protect you."

I must look decidedly goofy as I smile at her, but I don't care. Despite myself, I quite like the idea of being protected. By Nikolette, anyway.

Though her words are strong, there is something quietly anxious about Nikolette as she watches me. She fiddles with her hair and toys with the thin gold chain looped about her neck. When I try to step out of the room, she actually slides into my path.

"Can I say something?" Her voice hitches ever so slightly. "I know it isn't my place, but I…I have to." She doesn't quite look at me, instead fixing her gaze on the top of my left ear.

I pull her fidgeting hands into mine and squeeze before laying them over my chest, like I did so many days ago. "You can say anything you want to me."

A long, long pause.

"Take Mother April's offer. Please." Her words waver, but she doesn't stop. "I know your sisters are fighting you—that older one especially will likely never forgive you—but surely Crone Hyacinth would want you all safe and protected, rather than killed through hubris."

My fingers stiffen on hers, though I don't pull away. "Hubris? I wouldn't go that far."

She lifts an eyebrow. "Crone Hyacinth cast a protection circle around her house so strong it's active even after her death. She was worried about someone or something. And someone trapped your house."

"But I'm fine."

"And if the spell had been stronger? Or triggered differently? If those two familiars hadn't stopped you entering?" Her words begin to run together, her breathing quickening. "You could be dead." At last she meets my gaze, her own tight with anger. "*Dead*, Tina."

"Nikolette…"

"I can't save you if you won't let me."

Something inside me softens. "But you don't need to save me. I'll be okay."

Her eyes shimmer, though no tears fall. "I know you've worked with SPEAR, tutored with the best—even cast protective circles against a literal demon or whatever it was—but you're *one* person. And all it takes is *one* mistake. I couldn't bear it if something happened to you." She sucks in a deep breath. "Please, please let me help."

I kiss her. Not like before, but with tender understanding and gratitude that I can't quite put into words. Her lips are salty with the tears that finally begin to fall.

"I'll be okay. The Willow Barks are strong. Promise."

That deep breath whistles from her lips on a long, weary sigh. "Fine." She stands, wiping her eyes. "Fine." A moment later the calm, confident look is back on her face again. She clears her throat. "I shouldn't have said anything. What you and the Willow Barks do is up to you and your sisters, and I—"

"Nikolette." I wait until certain she hears me. "Thank you. Just… thank you. It's good to know you care so much."

She sniffs and fishes her car keys from a hook near the door. "I'll drive."

Guess that's the end of that.

Dink is already sitting on the doormat. He scurries up my leg as I approach while Anansi makes her slow, creepy way across the ceiling, towards the door.

Clearly they mean to join me, but then, who can blame them? The past two days have been a riot of change and disruption. I'm the only constant they have left. Makes sense that they'd prefer to stay close.

Which doesn't make it any easier when faced with a giant spider wanting to hitch a ride on my back.

CHAPTER THIRTY-THREE

When Nikolette starts driving, I realize I have no idea where the Elm Stems meet.

Each coven has their own preferred meeting space and area in the city attuned to them, their needs, and the style of magic they perform. Given that the Willow Barks are soft, gentle, and nature based, of course it makes sense that we would meet outside. But the Elm Stems are nothing like that.

Some of their rules and guidelines may be archaic and dated, but their living habits are not. With so many old families as members, they are a decidedly rich coven, and it is only as Nikolette turns onto the A-road that leads through Harmony Rise that I realize where she must be heading.

"I should have known."

She looks the question at me.

"Well, you certainly don't meet here." I gesture around me to encapsulate the area. "Harmony Rise may be rich, but it's too new—bachelor pads and bro caves, if I remember right. But *through* here? That leads to The Meadows."

Nikolette arches an eyebrow at me. "Is that a problem?"

"Of course not. I just…" I stare down at my fingers. "Don't worry about it."

"No, go on. Something's bothering you. Tell me."

I look around myself and feel a twinge of unease. "I don't think I've ever been to Rich Cunts' Drive before."

Her head whips round so fast I fear the car might leave the road. Too late I realize my mistake. This is Nikolette, after all, not my colleagues down at the APD.

"I mean, that's what they call it at work."

"I see." Her tone is abruptly frosty.

"I've never called it that, though. Why would I? That's mean. I settle for Money Boulevard since that's a bit closer." I'm babbling, but I can't help it. "Or Rosewater Meadows. I mean that's what it's actually called, isn't it?"

Nikolette stares straight ahead and points to one of the properties on the right, vast, sprawling grounds with a building more like a manor house than something belonging in Angbec. I catch sight of fields extending into woodland where the snobby owners can no doubt hunt grouse and foxes as much as they please. I don't see a stable, but that's probably because there are two around the back, as well as other luxuries like a tennis court, swimming pool, and manicured garden with a maze and fancy topiary.

"That's my parents' house," she murmurs blandly. "One of them, anyway. There's one more in Greece and another in Spain somewhere, though I don't go to those much any more. I grew up there before my mitéra died."

Heat rises in my face and chest so hard and fast I fear my skin might start to smoke. "I—"

"Never liked it much." She continues as though I never opened my mouth. "Comfortable, of course, and I do miss the horses, but suffocating, considering there's so much space. Mitéra never much enjoyed the idea of me living away from here, but I wanted to experience what it was like being a witch when and where it mattered."

I feel about six inches high. "I knew your family was well off, but I had no idea how much. Shit." I sigh. "Well, I'm a bitter, jealous bitch, aren't I?"

She chuckles. "A little."

A quick glance her way shows the smile, but I'm not entirely sure I believe it. "I'm so sorry."

"How were you to know? I don't talk about my family. Don't worry about it."

Oh, but I'm going to worry about it. I'm going to worry about it for the rest of the day and probably into the next one too. Oh well. At least my foot tastes good.

Nikolette slows, and I see a huge home on the right, slightly closer to the road than many of the others. The grounds out front are covered in sparkling white gravel from the private road, right the way up to the double front door. To either side of the door stretch four huge windows, and then wings that protrude forward. I imagine the same towards the rear, making it something of a large H shape.

As we pull in, I notice several cars on the right hand side, parked haphazardly atop the gravel. Nikolette eyes them suspiciously as we pass. So do I. None of them look like they belong here, and they stand out almost painfully against the obvious opulence of the building.

"Is this normal?" I point towards the cars.

She shakes her head.

I climb out, already on high alert. Dink and Anansi follow close behind, the mouse clinging to the end of my shoe, while the spider scurries at my side.

On my right, Nikolette gestures to the main doors, waving me in to follow, but I hang back just a moment longer.

Those cars certainly don't belong here. Each one looks about as out of place as mine would, but one of them seems very familiar. I peer into the passenger side window and spot a familiar green and brown shape dangling from the rear-view mirror: an air freshener shaped like a tree.

❖

The inside of this place is just as impressive as the exterior. The sound of my boots vanishes instantly into thick, plush carpets, my voice dulled and captured by the panelled walls.

The front door opens onto a long corridor that extends both left and right along the front of the house. Through the massive windows I can see the gravelled front, and opposite those are several rooms. Though I have only the quickest glance into each, I catch sight of rich furniture in tones of deep brown and gold, rugs more expensive than my entire home, and light fixtures broad enough to illuminate several rooms at once.

Nikolette grabs my hand and starts walking left, to an area where, instead of another room, a large open staircase leads upward.

Dink darts ahead of me while Anansi immediately skims up one of the walls and settles into a crouch high above my head.

More panelled walls, beautiful wallpaper, and then paintings in golden frames with little cards beneath them. I catch sight of one as we rush by.

I don't need to be a detective to figure out that these paintings are pictures of prominent witches, maybe even coven Mothers of the Elm Stems back through history. There's no doubt that this building has belonged to one of them or to the coven as a whole for many years.

Nikolette aims for the stairs, pulling me along after her, when a soft, familiar voice pulls us back.

"I'm down here, Daughter. No need to go upstairs. In fact, we're all here."

We turn as one, and though I try to maintain my grip, I feel Nikolette's hand slide out of mine at the sight of April Wesker.

The woman appears calm and entirely at her ease and not at all surprised to see me. She stands at the door beneath the stairs, holding it slightly ajar so she can look out at us.

I stare at her. "We? Who is we?"

"All those who seek protection of the Elm Stems."

The urge to roll my eyes rises within me. This woman could be a politician.

"And why is one of my sisters here?"

Again that smile. "Why don't you ask for yourself?" She pushes the door open wider behind her.

Back down the steps and round, I look past her into the room beyond and realize then why the cars outside looked so familiar.

Not just one of my sisters. All of them. Iris, Edith, Chloe, and Kiara, standing in a stiff, uncomfortable row at the back of the room. In front of them, between them and the door in fact, are dozens of witches I've never seen before. Elm Stems.

"What's going on?" I look back at Nikolette. "What is this?"

She lifts her hands slightly. "I don't know."

April lifts her hands. "Please, come inside. This has been long enough in coming."

I can't think of anything I want to do less than step into that room. With my sisters lined against the back wall like naughty schoolchildren, I can't help but liken this to some sort of weird, unbalanced disciplinary hearing. What are they doing here? And why did nobody tell me?

And then I remember the calls to my phone. Chloe's uneasy voice when I answered. The sound of many voices in the background. Was she already here?

I try to catch her eye, but Chloe has her gaze pinned firmly on the ground and seems unwilling to look at anybody, least of all me.

I leave Nikolette at the door and finally step into the room, aiming for Kiara. If anybody is going to give me a straight answer, it's the forthright and plain younger woman. "What's going on?"

"Where the fuck have you been?" Kiara snarls.

"Excuse me," April cuts in like a blade, "I'll not have language like that in my sanctum, Daughter."

Kiara turns, anger flashing across her features.

I step in quickly, my own quip teetering on the tip of my tongue. "This is the shortest forty-eight hours I've ever heard of, April."

"Things have changed," she says simply. "I found it necessary to bring forward my plans, and you would do well to do the same. Besides, if you speak to your sisters, I think you'll find that opinions there have changed too."

I can barely see my sisters past the wall of Elm Stems close around me. Still and silent, they press in from every side, their power so obvious and near visible in this place they call home. I shoulder my way through to reach them.

"Guys." I keep my voice as low as I can. "What's going on? Why are you here?"

"You need to learn to answer your damn phone." Iris puts her back to the gathered Elm Stems, then gives me her worst glare. "We've been calling you."

I think again of Chloe's call. Of how I immediately set the phone to silent after hanging up. "I…was busy."

"I bet you were." Her voice is icy, and I'm not slow to catch the flicker of her gaze towards Nikolette. "But you're here now, so stop this nonsense before it gets any worse. Talk some sense into these fools."

"But what's happening?"

Chloe smiles, grabs my hands, and squeezes my fingers excitedly. "April extended another invitation to us. We can join the Elm Stems today, Tina. All we have to do is say yes. Please say yes."

"But—"

Edith looks around her slowly. Her pale eyes are hooded and

weary, her forehead slashed with wrinkles I might swear were not there the last time we met. "While that would be easier, I don't think that's the best plan for us. Look around. This place is stuffier than a badger's backside. Do you really think we could fit in here?"

Kiara flicks her hair back over her shoulder. "It's not about fitting in. It's about safety. If whoever is out there could hurt Hyacinth, or Tina, then what chance do the rest of us have?"

"What are you talking about?"

Some of the excitement leaks from Chloe's features. "The magical explosion at your house. You could have died."

I frown at her. "How did you—"

"Daughters." A loud clap cuts across my question. April. She's walking through the crowd of her coven to position herself in the space between us and them. She faces the Willow Barks, arms spread, smile warm and inviting. "Esteemed guests, please, be welcome. Daughters?"

As one, the women behind her intone the words Iris quoted only a day before. "Willow Barks, we welcome you to our home, our meeting space and sanctum in Angbec. May our wards serve your safety and our fire warm your body as your *fortis* warms your soul. May our home be as yours for the pleasure of your stay, and let us all remember the Rule of Three."

Silence.

April raises a questioning eyebrow.

Kiara elbows me in the ribs.

"S-so mote it be," I manage. Then, as my brain kicks back into gear, "I accept—wait. We…I mean we, the Willow Barks, accept the gracious welcome to your meeting space and sanctum. May our will grant you strength, and our intent match yours. Let us all remember the Rule of Three."

"So mote it be," comes the rumbling response from everybody except a figure towards the back, shabbily dressed in a long, patchwork dress to match the hat perched on the fiery curls of bright, red hair.

"Now then"—another clap from April, as though to punctuate her words—"I accepted your request for an audience because I understand the gravity of your situation. I also take that to mean that you have come to a decision ahead of the deadline I set for you."

I tear my gaze away from Blake. "What are you talking about? We didn't request anything."

Chloe clears her throat. “It was me,” she murmurs. “I did it.”

I stare, open-mouthed. The others do too.

Iris looks about ready to spit bullets. “Why the hell would you do that?”

Chloe flinches, her face drawn and afraid.

I put my arm around her, alarmed to realize that she’s trembling. “Calm down, Iris.”

“No, she betrayed us. She went behind our backs and brought us all here to—”

“Shut up,” I snap. “Chloe? What’s going on?”

Tears fill her eyes. “I was so scared, Tae, I had to do something. First Hyacinth and then a magical bomb? I came to Angbec to be safe, and straight away I’ve lost my Mother and nearly my best friend.”

I don’t have the heart to ask who she’s talking about with that last comment.

“I can’t lose any more people,” she hurries on. “I just needed some guidance. Some help. So I called April. She said she would help me and invited me here, but I didn’t realize it would be a full conclave.” A pitiful sniff, then her words speed up, running into each other in her haste to get them out. “Iris, I’m sorry, I didn’t realize. It’s not a betrayal, I wanted to help. I just want us all to be safe.” She clings to me. “I tried to tell you, Tina. I called you, but you were busy, and I didn’t want to disturb you, so—”

I pull her into a hug. The poor thing is shaking, and her tears sparkle like sad little diamonds. She sighs against my shoulder and leans into me, holding tight as she trembles.

“It’s not your fault,” I tell her. “You were scared. So am I. But we’re together now, and we’re going to protect each other like always. We’ll all go home and then—”

April daintily clears her throat. She seems not to notice or care about the venomous look shot her way from Iris. “I’m afraid that’s not possible. Matters have become more urgent, and I have need to change my plans. But in order to do that, I must know what *your* plans are.”

“But we haven’t decided yet.”

“Then do so now,” she says coolly. “Will you or will you not join the Elm Stem coven?”

CHAPTER THIRTY-FOUR

I stare at April, aghast, but it quickly becomes clear that she isn't joking. She really means for us to vote right here and now.

"Can it wait, at least a few minutes? I came here specifically to speak with you." I try not to look at Blake, still standing by herself at the back of the room. "It's important."

"More important than the safety of your sisters?"

I lower my voice. "It's specifically about the safety of my sisters. And your daughters. And everyone else in this room."

She eyes me thoughtfully, staring so deeply into my eyes that I wonder if she's trying to unearth my very soul.

Finally, she shakes her head. "Whatever it is can't be more important than this. We're all in danger, and the sooner we accept that and takes steps to secure ourselves, the better."

I fight the urge to stamp my foot. "That's exactly my point. The danger is exactly what I need to speak with you about."

Iris leans in and snags my arm. "Let's get this over with. We all know how this is going to end, so formalize it so we can get out of here."

"But—"

Kiara nods. "The miserable old bat is right. Let's get it done."

"Wonderful. Then what is your choice?" April shares her gaze among the five of us.

I lift a hand at her. "One second." Then I turn my back on her and gesture my sisters closer to me, one arm still tight around Chloe. They huddle in, and Iris immediately hisses her anger into the circle of our bodies.

"What the hell were you thinking? Damn it, Chloe, why would you drag us all here when you *know* we have no intention of joining these people?"

As Chloe stiffens beside me, Kiara leaps to her defence. "You *don't* know that. Tina still hasn't voted. Accept that it's up to her now."

My mouth and throat resemble the Sahara. I don't want this. I don't want the fate of four others hanging on *my* decisions.

Iris glares. "I'll languish on the dark side of the moon before I let myself get swept up with these…these…" Her rage makes the words stick in her mouth. "Tina, see sense. You can't give us over to them. Grow a spine."

I rub my forehead. "We had forty-eight hours. I don't want to do this now."

"You have no choice," Edith murmurs, her soft voice giving way to uncharacteristic firmness. "I don't know why you're so afraid, but you have to make a decision. Think of Hyacinth—you knew her better than any of us. What do you think she wanted?"

I hesitate. The truth is, I'm not sure.

Sure, the history and traditions of the Willow Barks were important to her, but not for a moment do I believe she would ever choose a path of tradition over safety. Certainly not for us, her precious girls.

I close my eyes. I try to bring her face to mind: the gentle smile, the lively eyes, the pattern of that tattoo across her right cheek. With a jolt I realize that I never once asked her what it meant. And now I'll never be able to.

No parent should lead their child by the hand through all things, she said. *Their role is to teach a young one, furnish them with the tools to make informed decisions, and then allow them to do so. It isn't my place to do this for you, simply guide and support.*

"She wanted us to be happy and safe," I say at last, trying to ignore the way my voice cracks. "She trusted us to do the right thing with the information in front of us and act in the best interest of our sisters."

Kiara nods. "Then what's the problem? These women will help protect us."

"They'll strip us down to nothing and destroy us," Iris shoots back. "What becomes of the Willow Barks then? What happens to Hyacinth's legacy?"

Chloe whispers through her persistent tears, "There won't be much of a legacy if we're all dead."

More arguing.

Again I close my eyes and look for strength within myself. I search hard for the knowledge, power, and confidence Hyacinth always insisted I possessed deep inside.

But I can't find it. All I find instead is fear, regret, and uncertainty.

I. Can't. Do. This.

Movement close by catches my attention, a flash of red. Blake. She stands slightly apart from her sisters, watching us with her hands clasped before her face as though in prayer.

From this distance, can she hear us? Can she read lips? Does she know what we're saying right now? Does she know that the very second I have April in a quiet space, all her secrets will be revealed?

I grit my teeth against a surge of anger.

How dare she stand there, calm, safe, and alive? How dare she watch me or my sisters when she's the one who caused this mess in the first place?

The most un-witch-like thoughts fill my mind, cruel fantasies of torture and pain while she screams for mercy, the way Hyacinth no doubt ached to do while trapped inside her own paralysed body. The image makes me smile.

"Tina?" Edith's sudden hand on my shoulder shakes me out of it. "The last remaining vote is yours. Hyacinth ran our coven as a democracy, which means the majority vote wins. You have to decide."

"Daughters." April's voice breaks over us. Her eyes are narrowed, her lips tight. Something makes me think she isn't used to being kept waiting. "What is your answer? I don't have all day."

I can't look at her. Instead I search for Nikolette.

In the middle of her own sisters, my girlfriend stares at me with such longing in her eyes that I long to throw myself into her arms. She doesn't speak, but her lips move to form words that I recognize even without the benefit of sound. *Please. Let me protect you.*

I want her to. So, so much.

Edith's hand tightens on my shoulder.

April crosses her arms and drums an impatient rhythm on her elbow with the tip of her index finger.

I stand on the edge of a knife, balanced perfectly to the point that even the faintest breath of pressure would tip me one way or the other.

I close my eyes. Memories swim before me.

Dozens of women, their gazes turned to mine, naked bodies sheathed with sweat that makes their skin glow in the bright silver of the moon's light.

I stand in the centre of them, aware of the goosebumps prickling across my own bare skin.

Now isn't the time to worry about that, though. We have too much to do.

"If you're ready," I whisper, "we can begin."

Soft murmurs of assent from the gathered crowd around me—some nervous, some excited, all edged with the faintest rim of fear.

I smile. "It's okay. I'll protect you. Let's begin."

With a little gasp I shake myself free of the scattered remembrance and look once more to my sisters. They're staring at me. So too is April, and Nikolette and Blake and every other woman in this tastefully decorated room.

I have no choice.

I moisten my lips. "I see you, April Wesker." My voice trembles. I can't make it stop. "You and your coven extend a hand to us in our time of need and made clear that we would find safety among you. Protection."

Someone behind me whimpers. No idea who.

April's gaze becomes wary.

I clench my hands into fists to stop them shaking. "We are Willows. Like our namesake we are supple and flexible, we move with the storm and accept everything it gives us, knowing we'll come out the other end as strong and as powerful as ever."

Silence. The air is so thick I can practically taste it. It fills my throat, clogs my nostrils, makes every word struggle to leave my lips, but I push on. I have to get the words out. I have to do the right thing.

I look at my sisters, silently begging them to understand. "We *will* make it out the other side. But first, we must get through."

Iris shakes her head. She knows, Goddess help me, she knows what I'm about to say.

"But what does that mean, Tina?" April's patience visibly snaps. "Answer me now, or leave."

I close my eyes. "I vote to protect my sisters. I vote to join the Willow Barks with the Elm Stems."

CHAPTER THIRTY-FIVE

April presses her hands together in a sharp, single clap that seems to reverberate around the room like a drumbeat. "So mote it be," she murmurs, and a smile draws back her lips.

The Elm Stem witches begin to clap, polite and orderly, except for Nikolette, who looks ready to burst into tears.

And Blake. Closer now, her mismatched eyes are bright with horror and she spins on her heel without a word. Though I crane my neck to see which way she goes, the sudden rush of Elm Stems blocks her from my view.

Behind, Kiara and Chloe cling to each other, dancing on their toes like children. Edith looks as though she has taken a punch to the gut. She stumbles back to lean against the wall, clutching her chest. Iris stares at me as though she's never, ever seen me before.

"Guys." I reach out for them.

Iris leaps back as though burned. "Don't touch me," she hisses. "Don't touch me, don't talk to me, don't even look at me. How could you do this? Do you have any idea what you've done?"

"I've protected us—"

"You absolute raging coward," Edith murmurs. "I hoped for better from you, but you're a coward. What would Hyacinth say?"

Their anger is palpable, and I recoil two full steps, straight into April, who smiles as she places both hands on my shoulders.

"You've made the right choice, Daughter." She gives the word deliberate emphasis. "Just as I do all my daughters, I'll take care of you and your sisters with my life. Nothing will harm you ever again. We both know that's all Hyacinth ever wanted for you."

I nod, but the glares of stunned betrayal on the faces of half my sisters means I'm not sure I believe it.

The chatter in the room is excited and loud. Through it, I notice Kiara introducing herself and Chloe to some of the Elms, who welcome them warmly.

My chest feels tight, my limbs leaden. I blink hard and realize there are tears in my eyes. Did I get this wrong? Have I made a mistake?

"Wait, April—"

"This calls for a celebration," April calls over me and the excited chatter of the gathered women. "All of you, head into the ballroom while I have one of the dining rooms laid out for a feast. We'll celebrate our union with an offering to the Goddess, and welcome our new sisters."

"Please, wait. I think I made a—"

But she doesn't wait. Nobody does.

April reels off more orders, sweeping from the room with several of the Elm Stems hot on her heels, Nikolette among them. I catch sight of her walking after her Mother, face so filled with joy my heart begins to ache.

Later then. First, my sisters.

But Iris and Edith have already taken long, deliberate steps away from me. When I try to step closer, Edith raises a trembling hand to me, shaking her head. They refuse to even look at the Elm Stems, instead speaking softly and urgently in a corner.

Then the Elms close in around me, offering welcome while trying to share their names. They reach for my shoulders, my hands, my hair, soft fingertip touches that I associate with joy and welcome.

Then Chloe rushes to me. She flings her arms around my neck and squeezes hard. The relief is visible in her eyes and voice. "Thank you," she cries. "You've saved us all. I knew you would. I knew you would protect us."

I can't meet her eyes.

She doesn't seem to notice. "These women are so kind. Somebody, I think her name might be Kitt, was telling me about this house. Did you know it used to belong to the Crown before it was gifted to some noble years and years ago? Just so happens that noble married a witch, and when he died, she took on ownership, which was very strange for a widow back then. And then she managed to hold on to the land and the deed, even though dozens of men kept trying to take it away from her and—" She cuts herself off. "Are you all right?"

"Yes." I make my voice as bright as possible and focus my gaze on her left eyebrow. "Yes, I'm fine. Just overwhelmed. I need to sit down."

She squeeze-hugs all the tighter before pulling back. "I'm not surprised. It must have been a horrible couple of days for you. Where have you been staying?"

I open my mouth, then snap it shut again. I had been about to mention Nikolette, to say that I was safe and sound, but that doesn't seem like the best idea. Then for the first time, the words Chloe speaks seem to really sink in, and I remember my question from earlier.

"How do you know what happened at my house?"

"About the magical bomb? April told me."

I catch myself frowning. "*April* did?"

Chloe nods earnestly. "Yes. That's when I knew we needed help. If someone was trying to get you, then we were all in danger and I thought—" She breaks off, apparently noticing my unease. "Is something wrong?"

But I don't answer. I can't yet, my mind is racing too fast.

Put aside, just for the moment, that April went out of her way to gather in one of the youngest and most vulnerable of my sisters. How did she even know about the explosion? It isn't likely that Blake told her, given her part in the whole affair. In fact, the only person besides Blake to know it was anything other than a gas explosion is Nikolette because this morning when we—

Something in me seizes up.

I put out my hand, afraid I might stumble. My hand reaches the cool solidity of a nearby wall, and I lean there while my mind attempts to catch up with itself.

Nikolette. She was the only one to know. Certainly the only person to call it a magical bomb. Hozier wouldn't have called it that—he wouldn't have called it anything.

So did *she* tell April what happened? At once my gaze cuts across the room, searching, but of course she's gone. Something about a feast, right? But she wouldn't, would she? After I specifically asked her not to?

Chloe's forehead creases with concern. "Are you okay?"

"I—"

"Wait there," she says. "I'll get help, don't move."

Not sure that I could even if I wanted to.

When did Nikolette even have time to tell April? We spoke earlier in the day and then were together for the rest of it.

Chloe returns, dragging Iris by the hand, and the older woman looks me up and down with fury she makes no attempt to hide.

"What's wrong with you, then?"

I straighten. "Nothing."

Eye rolls. "So you're lying to my face now?"

"It's not a lie—"

"You said you would look out for us, but instead you sold us out because you're too much of a coward to step up. And to think I protected you."

Now what the hell is she talking about? I give her a look, then shake the thought aside. "I don't have time for this. I need to find Nikolette."

Her glare intensifies. "Oh, I'm sorry, am I in the way of you celebrating with your girlfriend?"

Chloe gasps. "Girlfriend? Tina, what's happening?"

But Iris won't be stopped. She stands with her arms folded tight across her chest. "Didn't you know, Chloe? She's been sleeping with the enemy. Literally. Didn't you notice that they arrived together?"

"What? The tall woman with the nice hair? The one who came to our sanctum?"

"Nikolette." Iris all but spits the name. "I caught them sucking face after everybody else left. Who knows how long they've been sneaking around. That's probably what she was so *busy* with earlier instead of answering her phone."

The confused stare from Chloe near breaks my heart. "I didn't know you were seeing anybody." Her voice is so tiny and confused. "You never told me."

"Of course she didn't," Iris rages, before I can get a word out. "Because she knew damn well it's frowned on. A Willow Bark and an Elm Stem? Please. How long have you been in their pocket, Tina? Good show, though, making us wait forty-eight hours before you betrayed us. But you couldn't even manage that. Did Hyacinth know what you were up to?"

I back off. Part of me longs to tell Iris she has it all wrong, but does she really?

"I need to get out of here." The words tumble from my mouth. The voice doesn't even sound like my own.

Iris calls something derisive after me, Chloe something fearful, but I don't hear either of them. I'm forcing my way through the excited crowd to get to the door.

As soon as I open it and stumble back into the hallway, I recognize how hot the room was. The air out here is clearer and cooler, and at once my head feels lighter. Anansi scuttles down the wall on my left, waving her legs in my direction. Dink skids and slides uneasily down the banister to make a daring jump down to my shoulder.

I feel better with the familiars close by. Their presence soothes me and reminds me of Hyacinth, which immediately brings a sense of calm to me.

I manage a smile. "I need Nikolette," I find myself saying, not even to them, but as if to speak the words aloud is to affirm my intent.

Anansi clearly takes that as an instruction because she climbs back up the wall quickly and onto the banister, where she waits, waving her legs at me.

"Did you see which way she went?"

Dink pulls lightly at the neck of my top.

"Fine, show me. Take me there."

Chapter Thirty-six

The upstairs of this place is just as grand and beautiful as the lower floor. Paintings of old coven Mothers line the walls, though now they are joined by intense watercolours of scenes featuring many people. Most seem to be old, from the clothing the subjects wear, but they all show scenes of important periods in history featuring witches. I see several of what I assume are the witch trials in America, as well as some scenes of what appear to be mobs in pretty, picturesque British countrysides. Other pictures depict lords and ladies in fabulously wealthy dress, and the last even appears to feature royalty.

My general knowledge of history isn't fantastic, but I'm fairly sure I recognize the grim-faced, smooth-haired figure with the veil and tiny crown. She stares out from a throne with her hands gathered in the lap of her rich and heavy black gown while the two figures before her, young girls in scratchy looking cotton and headscarves, lower their heads in supplication.

No time for that. Anansi has stopped outside a door far up the corridor and waits for me there, skittering back and forth. When I approach, she climbs up the frame and proceeds to dangle there from a long length of fine webbing.

The door is slightly ajar. I move closer, meaning to knock and enter, but the mention of my name makes me pause. It's April's voice, and she sounds happier than I've ever yet heard her.

"…to come here today. I'm so pleased you were able to talk some sense into her."

"I didn't do anything." Nikolette sounds almost bashful at the praise.

"You acted in a manner most becoming of my teachings. There's clearly hope for you."

"Hope?"

April chuckles. "I won't be here forever, Daughter. And I'd have to be blind to know nothing of your ambitions. What you've done here today puts you in excellent standing for mentorship. You're certainly strong enough. I imagine Diana would be most proud to learn that you're considered leadership material. Jasmine too, if she was still with us."

"It would be everything to her." A faint sniff from Nikolette. "It would be everything to *me*. It's all I've ever wanted."

Though I know I shouldn't, though the honourable part of me demands that I back off or simply enter, curiosity bests me. I crouch and inch forward on my toes to peer around the edge of the door.

In the gap I see April. She's sitting at a desk mostly obscured by the door, though I catch sight of her smiling face as she leans forward. In front of her, hands clasped at hip height, stands Nikolette with her head bowed. I can't see her face at all, just her back and the slight forward hunch of her shoulders.

"After everything you've done with that girl, you're on the right path. You've tamed her in a way I didn't think anybody could. Well done."

Tamed? I grit my teeth against a spike of irritation. Surely she isn't talking about me?

Nikolette shrugs. "Tina is a little wild, maybe, but she's a good person. She was always going to do the right thing."

"Not without your guidance. She's as stubborn as Hyacinth ever was." April sniffs and pushes something across her desk. Her voice gives an odd little wobble. "Tina must be brought under control before she causes trouble. Can I trust you to do that?"

"What do you mean? Control?"

"Modest as ever, aren't you?" April's voice is dry. "You brought her here right when we needed her. Not only that, but you did so with her in just the right mood to carry the Willow Barks into our waiting arms. The time you spent with her today was clearly well spent. Now I'll finally be able to move forward."

My body stiffens. I can't move. I can't breathe.

They're still speaking, but I hear them as if through clods of cotton wool.

Then I'm standing. My hand is on the door. With one mighty shove I slam it back, and the heavy slab of wood crashes into the near wall.

Both women jump as I stomp into what I now see is a small office.

Inside my collar I feel Dink shudder as he burrows deeper into my clothing to hide.

Nikolette's entire body stiffens as she spies my face, and her fingers immediately thread together, gripping hard enough to make her knuckles turn pale.

April reclines in her high-backed leather seat, her eyes narrowed. "You would do well to knock, Daughter." She peers along her nose at me.

"I'm not your daughter," I hiss back. Then to Nikolette, "What does she mean you brought me here *right when she needed me*?"

Both of them pause, aware that I overheard their words.

Nikolette wrings her hands again. "Tina—"

"Oh, would you look at this." April chuckles. "You *do* have your work cut out for you, Nikolette. Though they hide it well, I know that Willow Barks are a challenge when it comes to matters of love."

I gape at Nikolette. "*She* knows? You told *her*?"

"No." Nikolette's hair flies as she shakes her head. "I didn't, I swear." The words are quick, her breath shallow. "I was praying for guidance and wisdom from the Goddess, and she overheard me."

"When?"

She hesitates. Looks away. Cold fills my stomach.

"Several weeks ago," says April. "Long enough to offer plenty of advice on how to handle you. And she has done so admirably."

I step back. "Weeks? Nikolette, weeks?"

She tries to speak, but the words seem stuck. Her eyes are shiny and glassy now.

"Weeks? So while you raged at me about Hyacinth, while we met in the game shop, while I comforted you and told you to take your time, she already knew. Does your grandmother know?"

A mute shake of the head.

I turn aside. Lower my face to my hands. Pace. Freeze when the horrible truth settles over me like ice. "That's why you took me to your place instead of coming straight here. You had to stall. You needed to give April time to gather up my sisters and bring them here."

Nikolette rushes to me, reaching for my hands. "No. Goddess, no. Please, Tina, let me explain."

I jerk away. "Please do. Explain how long you've been reporting back to her? Telling her everything we've discussed?"

"Stop, please. It's not like that."

Tears blur my vision, frustration, anger, and hurt all gathered into one painful ball of betrayal at the back of my throat. "Isn't it? I know how much you want to be Mother, but I never guessed you'd use me to score brownie points."

Tears spill over and course down her cheeks. "No, I want to protect you. I love you. That's all I've ever wanted. Please, Mother April, tell her."

April slowly stands. She rearranges an empty cup and two small saucers on her desk. Both saucers are filled with piles of wet tea leaves. "Calm yourself, Daughters. I won't have raised voices in my office."

Rage bristles inside. "I'm not your—"

"Oh, but you are. By your own vote, I'll have you remember. As such I expect proper decorum in my sanctum."

I plant both hands on the desk. "No. Not after what you two have done. The Willow Barks will never join you, not now, not ever. We're leaving."

She smiles at me. I don't like it. The gesture resembles one I imagine a cat might give a small sparrow, trapped and helpless, unable to fly.

"The Willow Barks are no more, Daughter. By your word they are joined with the Elm Stems. Were you not paying attention?"

I fight to keep my hands to myself. "What are you talking about?"

But instead of answering, April looks past me, towards Nikolette. "*Propira Potentia*," she murmurs.

Nikolette's hands fly to her mouth. "No. You didn't. You wouldn't do that, Mother April? Not without telling them?"

That maddening smile persists.

My patience snaps. "If you two are going to talk in riddles, have at it, but I don't have to stay and listen. I'm taking my sisters and—"

"Tell her, Nikolette."

Long, long silence.

"Screw this." I head for the door. "And I'm not a fool—I know what personal coven powers are. I don't need a history lesson."

"Do you know what the Elm Stem *Propira Potentia* is, Daughter?"

My fingers flex in and out of tight fists. "Call me that one more fucking time…"

Nikolette flinches as April's gaze slides back towards her. "Our coven power is immutable circles, Tina. Goddess, I'm so, so sorry. I didn't know. Please, please believe me."

April makes no attempt to hide her smugness as I whirl around to face her.

"Bullshit." My words tremble. I fight to keep my breathing steady. "Nobody can cast those circles any more—it's not a thing."

"It is most certainly *a thing*, Daughter." April's eyes sparkle with triumph. "All words spoken in such a space are binding, such as the agreement to speak only truth. Or…?"

Nausea rises within me. "Or the decision to merge my coven with yours."

Her eyes take on a wicked, wicked gleam. "Correct. When I spoke of celebration, it was not idle chatter, nor was it speculation when I spoke of the importance of your decision. Your words bound your coven to me from the moment you spoke them. It cannot be undone."

"Bitch!" I'm halfway around the table, anger burning, hand raised, before I come to my senses. Or maybe my senses are brought to me because my body stops dead with an alarming jolt. I struggle to move, to speak, but my legs may well be severed entirely from my mind, such is the effectiveness of my attempts.

I stand frozen by the table while April considers me, eyeing me up and down the way a student might consider a sample they've been tasked to dissect.

My skin prickles with fizzing, sizzling energy, like electricity has been pumped through my feet to lock them into place. I can't move even my smallest toe. Both feet are just stuck to the floor as though welded. It doesn't stop the rage, though.

"I don't take kindly to threats," she says at last. "Come back to me when you've calmed down and not a moment before. If you're going to act like a child, then I'll treat you like one, Daughter. And this naughty child is in time out. Get out of my office. And take that disgusting insect with you."

The moment she finishes talking, the odd sensation ends, and I stumble forward half a step before catching my balance. I look towards where her gaze has landed, and I see Anansi hiding in the corner, crouched high against the ceiling on a line of webbing.

She came to support me after all.

Behind, the door sweeps open again, as clear a *You're dismissed* gesture as the one I gave only the day before.

Beside it, Nikolette stands silently, tears streaming down her face.

I look first at April, then my girlfriend. Then back again.

"This isn't over," I tell her.

"Get out," she says again. "I have a celebration to organize, and by the Goddess of spring herself, I'll not let you ruin everything I've worked towards. Out."

I stomp to the door. As I reach it, Nikolette reaches for me, but I wrench away from her grip. "Don't touch me," I hiss, "ever again. I'll never forgive you for this."

And I flee, with the faint scuttling sound of Anansi chasing me out.

CHAPTER THIRTY-SEVEN

Back in the hallway, I'm not sure which way to go. Part of me wants to leave and never come back, while the rest longs to rush down to the spell space, gather up my sisters, and haul them out with me. Whether they want to or not.

Instead, I stop and take a long slow, steady breath while fighting to keep my anger down.

I've been tricked. Played for a fool. Manipulated by the woman I thought truly cared for me, and for what? Why is April so desperate to gather in my sisters? Protection? Well I certainly don't believe that any more.

There is something else going on that I need to get to the bottom of, and all my police instincts scream for me to stop and go right back to the beginning. There must be something, a detail, a word, an action that I've missed. Something that will make all of this slot into place.

Back downstairs. At least that way I can be with my sisters and keep an eye on them.

I turn and barrel straight down the steps, around the corner, and into the room I now understand to be a spell space. But it's already empty.

"Damn it."

The ballroom, right? But this house is huge. Am I really going to have to search from top to bottom?

Anansi pauses in the doorway. She turns slowly on the carpet, first left, then right, her middle legs reaching out. Part of me wonders if she knows where everyone has gone. Might I be able to follow her?

"Do you know where everybody went?"

The massive spider turns in another slow circle, then walks up the wall once more. There are no quick darts in any direction or even gestures like before. It seems she has as much of a clue as I do. There's no movement from Dink either, except a faint twitch of his little nose against my chest.

Fine, I'll look myself. I'll search the whole house if that's what it takes. I won't abandon my sisters now. Never again.

I decide to scan the lower floor first, but I barely make it out of the room before I step straight into another woman on her way in. A woman with a shabby-chic aesthetic and mismatched brown and blue eyes.

"Blake." The name hangs on the edge of my lips as we stare at each other in a moment that extends into forever.

She holds up her hands. "We need to talk."

No. No more. No more manipulations or lies or flowery words to put me off the truth. After so long worrying and avoiding my own ability to do so, it's finally time to act.

I push her. Hard.

Clearly she doesn't expect it because her balance is gone and she stumbles hard against the wall. I follow, scrabbling for her wrists in an attempt to wrench her arms behind her back. "How do you fit into all this?" I snarl. "Were you working to manipulate me too?"

Her eyes are huge and round, her mouth open in an fearful display as she struggles to keep her hands free. "Wait, please. You don't understand—"

"How long have you been working with April? Is that why you trapped my house?"

"It wasn't supposed to hurt you."

I stare at her, alarmed. "Wait, so it *was* you?"

"Yes, but not like you think. You need to listen to me."

Again I reach for her hands, aiming for a police officer's hold. "I'm done listening to you people."

"I'm so sorry, Tina," she murmurs, eyes downcast.

"Damn right you are. All this began because of you. Because *you* decided murder was a fun and exciting pastime. I'll make sure you're locked up for the rest of your life."

"Not for all that. For this." She stares me dead in the eyes. "Relligo."

My throat closes up. Or rather it feels so, words locking in my mouth on a strangled exhalation of air. A bolt of *something* tears through my body, cold, tingling, painful. It starts in my fingertips and toes, then speeds inward, leaving a trail of prickling, electric pain in its wake.

I tumble bonelessly to the ground close to Blake's side.

Carpet mashes against my eyes and nose, half blinding me, stoppering my breath until Blake tucks a hand beneath me and flips me onto my back.

What the hell have you done? I yell. Or try to. No sound comes out. Not even the smallest whisper leaves my lips, and as the cold settles over me I realize that I recognize this sensation.

Touching the bloodstains on the ground of the game shop felt like this. The tingle of static in my fingers from each of the four bodies in the morgue is but a shadow of the feeling cloaking my entire body right now.

I'm paralysed.

Blake scrambles to her feet. Her breathing is quick and harsh, her movements jerky, as she grabs me by the shoulders and rolls me to my side. With speed that suggests experience, she grabs my arms and legs to shift me into the recovery position, gently tilting my chin to prevent me choking on my tongue.

I can't see her from this angle, but I hear her steps on the carpet, feel the vibrations as she hurries over to the door. There's a pause, a soft whisper of "Sero," and then the door slams shut. I hear the click of a lock sliding into place.

Goddess, no. What's happening? What is she going to do?

A faint *flumph* sound reaches my ears, and I catch sight of several slender legs darting past me and across the room.

Anansi.

I strain to speak, to move, to anything at all, but my muscles are locked. Each time I strain against the invisible bonds holding me, the icy prickle of magic stings harder.

Does the spider know what's happening? Does she recognize the magic binding me as the same that trapped and held her old mistress? I've no way of knowing or even seeing where Anansi has gone. She's crawled right across my field of vision and away, but she must be gone because Blake apparently hasn't noticed her either.

A pair of feet step into my field of view. They're small, with flat shoes made of brown leather and tatty fabric. They move back and forth in front of my face, left, then right, then left, then right. Pacing. Blake mutters to herself, a debate only she is allowed space in.

I want to blink. My vision blurs as the air begins to dry my eyes from being so long exposed to the elements. Is it possible to go blind like this? Am I going to lose my sight before Blake follows through with whatever plan she has in mind?

I hope it's quick at least. Unlike for Hyacinth. At least if it's quick, whoever eventually finds my body won't have to suffer the way I have.

I tune back into the room in time to hear Blake's voice growing softer and shriller before she eventually stops pacing. "Can't believe this is happening. What am I going to do? How do I fix this? How do I fix this huge mess?" She bends, and I first see the thick curtain of her curly red hair before her face joins it. "I'm going to let you speak," she whispers, "but you have to promise not to yell. Please give me a chance to explain."

I hope I'm glaring at her. I hope the venom of my thoughts is visible in my dry, itching, unblinking eyes. Clearly not, because she nods and rubs her palm over my face.

The tingling sensation melts away from the neck up, and my eyes automatically flutter closed. The relief is intense. I inhale sharply. "Help—"

She slams her hand to my mouth. "Guess we're not doing that." She presses in briefly, and the frozen sensation returns to my mouth, though thankfully, blissfully, my eyes continue to move. At least I can look around now.

Blake bites her lip. "If you can't be reasonable, you're going to have to stay like that because I need you to listen."

Fuck you. I'm chanting it over and over again, my mind screaming, raging, yelling, bellowing. *Fuck you. Fuck you. You'll pay. I'll make sure you pay. This isn't over.* My head begins to pound with the force of my anger, building with no way to escape. *You'd better kill me before I get loose because you damn well won't get another chance.*

She heaves me into a sitting position, then tucks her hands beneath my armpits. Her breathing hitches with the strain, and then she's dragging me across the floor towards the furthest wall.

I watch the door recede from me, as I beg it to open. Someone *must* be nearby, surely. Someone must be able to see. Surely someone must be wondering where I am by now?

But even as I think it, I realize that's likely not true.

Iris and Edith are furious and never want to see my face again. Chloe and Kiara are so thrilled and relieved to be in a place of *safety* that looking for me won't cross their minds. In fact, the only people who may want to find me are Nikolette and April, and I didn't exactly leave them on the best of terms.

But why would they care? This is clearly part of their plan.

Again my body slumps, gently though, as Blake releases me with one hand. I catch a sense of her pushing against something, muttering low words. Then I hear low rumbling, like stone or brick grinding together.

Another pause, then more movement, still being dragged backwards, though now at a downward angle. Soon we pass through an arch built into the panelling of the room, and my heels scrape on the threshold. Then a thick wall grinds across to block the gap.

A secret passage?

Bump. Then bump again.

I can tell Blake is trying to be gentle, but I must be heavy. My heels slide then bump, slide-bump, slide-bump down a set of shallow steps into the depths of the house.

Around me the walls are bare, thick, grey stones pressed together with such precision that I wonder if magic is involved. A faint glow emanates from them, vaguely white with a hint of pale green.

Strange gusting sounds come next, and as I'm bumped further down, I realize there are candles tucked into recesses in the walls, bursting with flame as we pass.

Neat little paltrick. But if there are candles ready and waiting, this space has been previously prepared, and I'm an expected guest.

A shard of panic rises in my belly.

Does this mirror Hyacinth so many days ago? Did she too feel doom rushing towards her, knowing there was nothing she could do?

Movement inside my top drags my thoughts away from whatever nightmare awaits below. Dink crawls out through my collar, his tiny claws digging in as he tries to keep his balance on the bumpy ride my body has become. Tiny, beady eyes, glittering like chips of mica, consider me from his cute furry face.

Run, I try to tell him. *Escape and be safe.*

He stares at me long moments, then scampers down my chest,

across my stomach, and off my right hip. I catch sight of his tiny body hitting the floor before he scurries away, back up the steps and out of sight.

Good. Hopefully he'll meet with Anansi, and the pair of them will find a way out of this wretched house.

At last my heels stop bouncing as they leave the last step, and I watch the room slide through my vision in reverse.

The stairway widens into a broad, stone space lit with more candles. The scent of sage, rosemary, and perhaps a little cinnamon clings thickly to the warm air. A low table on my left, draped with a white cloth, homes a book, a pen, and a familiar looking box made of dark, shiny wood. Hyacinth's trinket box.

I spy smudges on the floor, a mix of crumbled black charcoal and dusty white chalk. They make the vague shape of a curve, exposed more and more as Blake drags my body over it.

But not all the way. She stops me in the middle of the dusty circle, then props me up against the legs of a rickety chair.

My hands flop uselessly beside me.

Silence.

Then Blake starts walking around me, her steps slow and purposeful. Her hand dips into a little cup, and she sprinkles something fine and white around us. Salt. She's trapping me in a circle.

The magic swells against my skin like a cool breeze, and I spy the milky-white haze of the circle rise from the ground. It domes near the craggy ceiling of the room, trapping me inside.

No. Not me. *Us*.

I notice Blake is standing within the hazy whiteness, breathing hard, brushing sweat off her neck and forehead with the back of her wrist.

She looks at me. Up the stairs. To me again.

"Alone. Finally. This was too long coming." At last she sits cross-legged across from me and places her hands on her knees. "It's time to listen, Evangelina Marks, and finally learn the truth about Hyacinth Dixon."

CHAPTER THIRTY-EIGHT

The realization that Blake knows my full name is a shocking fact entirely eclipsed by the rest of her words.

She stares at me for a full ten seconds, and when I still can't speak, she goes on. "No one can hear you here. No one will think to look for you here. Only two people know of this space, and one is me. I made this circle using our *Propira Potentia*, which means every word we say here is true and binding. Do you understand?"

I don't move. Of course.

Blake sighs and gives the fingers of her right hand a little flick.

My jaw loosens, and the locked-in sensation vanishes from my face. I can't move the rest of my body—probably for the best—but at least my mouth can move.

"I understand that after your first sample, you developed a taste for sick, twisted torture."

"Tina—"

"No! Why, Blake? What did Hyacinth ever do to deserve what you did? And how did you best the most powerful witch in the city?"

"She wasn't the most powerful."

For some reason, that hurts more than anything else, and fire swells in my belly. I scream one short, loud, wordless note and clench my hands into fists.

Blake stares at me, and in the same moment she does, I realize what I've done.

Fists? I thought I was paralysed.

"You're so strong," she murmurs. Is that a note of fear in her voice? Oh, I damn well hope so.

"Not strong," I shoot back, "pissed."

"Same thing." She uncrosses her legs and folds them the other direction. "Anyway, she wasn't the most powerful. Maybe in raw *fortis*, but power isn't just strength of will. It's about what you're willing to do to get what you want."

I snort. "Oh, so obviously *you're* more powerful? Because you want things so badly? What is it you want anyway? That's what I don't get. What could Hyacinth possibly have worth killing for?"

Her eyebrows lift. "I didn't kill anybody—"

"Fuck you," I spit the words. "You've paralysed me with the same spell I found on her body. Was that the only way you could do it? Pathetic."

"No." She narrows her eyes and a prickling rush of power pans off her body. "I adored that woman. I would never, ever have raised a hand to her."

I long to look away or punch or kick, but my hands remain locked into impotent fists. Even my head relies on the chair to stay upright.

Words, then. "You murdered her. You paralysed her on the floor of that abandoned shop and stabbed her while she couldn't fight back. You are *disgusting*. How dare you call yourself a witch?"

Blake gazes down at her fingers. For long seconds the only sign she is even breathing is the faint sway of her hair as she exhales. "It wasn't me," she says at last. "I already told you, I walked into that shop a few minutes before you, and I found her like that."

"Liar—"

"Think about where we are, Tina." She gestures around herself. "I knew she had been meeting someone secretly, but I wasn't sure of who. I went there to look for clues. It was a long shot—everybody knows why we use that space—but I found her on the ground maybe five minutes before you arrived." She leans forward, expression earnest and intense. "I would have explained, but I was terrified. I had no idea who you were or if *you* were the one who did it. So I ran."

"Don't give me that—you'd met me before."

"Yes, when I was leaving her house. But I didn't recognize you as the same person until much later. How was I to know? You stomped into that shop, stinking of magic, and there was Hyacinth, clearly hurt by magic. What else could I think but that you had done something awful?"

Again I strain to lift my arms. Nothing happens. "Awful like you, you mean? Why were you at her house that morning? You're an Elm Stem, what the hell were you doing in Willow Bark territory?"

"Territory? We're not werewolves." She snorts. "But if you must know, I hadn't heard from her for a day or two, so I was checking on her. I was worried."

I cast my mind back to that morning, to leaving the quiet house filled with my own worries about the missing familiars. A little rush of guilt shoots through me when I think of Seshat and Loki. I still have no idea where they are.

By now, without their witch, they must have reverted back to their mundane selves, a ferret and a barn owl with no connection at all to the witching world. I hope they find themselves loving homes. They deserve it after everything they've been through. Anansi and Dink too—I hope they've made it out of this horrible place.

As if to think her name is to call her to me, I spot a glistening line of silky thread waving from a spot in the ceiling. On the end of it swings the giant, hairy spider, legs curled upward towards the thread to hold her bulbous body steady. She moves silently but quickly, inching lower and lower towards the intangible surface of the circle.

What is she doing? Why didn't she run?

I bite my lip. Whatever it is she's doing, it's vital that I keep Blake from noticing her. She might be a familiar, but she's still only a spider. If Blake can paralyse me and even Hyacinth, then what chance does the little arachnid have?

I return my attention to Blake. "Worried about what? How did you even know her?"

This time when she looks at me, it's with a strange, considering sort of look. As if *she's* uncertain if she can trust *me*.

I wait. Not too much more I can do.

Blake chews on her bottom lip. "You knew she was dying?"

"Of a cold or summer flu? You're deluded. She wasn't that old."

Her hands fly to her mouth. She closes her eyes. "Goddess…she never told you."

The pit of my stomach flutters with panic. "Told me what?"

She picks at her fingernails. One of them cracks, and I watch her peel the offending slip of keratin and flick it away. "Tina, she had cancer."

My hand flexes again, but I'm too stunned to celebrate. "No." That flutter in my stomach intensifies. "No. She would have told me. She would have. You're lying!"

"Think about where we are—"

"I don't care where we are, you're lying. You're trying to trick me—"

"I can't lie in this circle," she snaps. "Didn't you hear what I said?" She gestures to the ring of salt around us. "This is an immutable circle. I told you that. I've done nothing but tell the truth since I brought you here."

Tears gather in the corners of my eyes. I can't stop them.

"But Hyacinth…"

I remember thinking how frail my mentor was when last we sat together, how her motions were slow and her body so thin and light. I recall thinking even the faintest of breezes might blow her off her feet were she not supported well enough.

Then I think back to her book of shadows.

The sickness is spreading faster than I anticipated, she wrote. *Soon. Perhaps within the next two days I must reveal all.*

"N-no." It's stupid, I know it is, but I can't help fighting Blake's words. If I believe this, then I have to believe everything else, and I can't possibly do that. "There was no chemo or there was no treatment. She had all her hair…"

"Do you really think she would have stopped long enough to accept treatment? Maybe you didn't know her as well as I thought."

My mind slips back to the last time Hyacinth was injured in a significant way. Even then, she refused to visit the hospital. I had personally bandaged her hand, cut after she mishandled a paring knife. Part of me had been afraid she would lose the use of her pinkie finger, but there was no convincing her to visit A&E. Instead she insisted I bind the wound, then went right back to chopping her leeks and onions.

A flash of movement catches the corner of my eye. Not Anansi this time. She's still hanging in the air directly above Blake's head. No, this is Dink, carefully flopping his way down the steps one at a time.

He stops halfway, peers at me, then continues a little faster, scurrying off under the table after reaching the bottom.

Blake, with her back to the stairs, notices nothing.

Again I resolve to keep her gaze on me. "How do you know that? How? Who are you?"

"No one notices me," she whispers. "Here with the Elm Stems, the coven is so big and grand, everyone expects the members to be grand too. So when you're as quiet as me, as soft and *timid* as me, it's easy to be forgotten and unseen. But Hyacinth never forgot me. She *saw* me in a way no one else ever did. Did you know she wanted me to join the Willow Barks?"

"No." My voice is soft this time. Somehow, I find that I believe her.

"I resisted at first, but the more we talked, the more she taught me, the more I knew it was the right move. But now I'm trapped here, and there are no Willow Barks. You gave them up." Her voice cracks. "How could you?"

"No. No, no, don't turn this back on me. Don't forget about what *you've* done. Explain away the coincidence of Hyacinth being trapped by exactly this paralysis spell, and three other mundane humans."

"Three mundanes?" She gasps. "When? Did they die?"

Someone shouts, far out of sight, near the top of the stairs. I don't understand the words, but I feel *fortis* as surely as I feel my own skin.

An eruption of brick, dust, and stone rockets down the stairs, followed by the stomp of hurrying feet.

Blake spins around, and I see the hazy dome of the immutable circle waver.

Sensing weakness, Anansi flings her legs out and drops off her web thread straight through the winking dome of the circle. Her vast, hairy body lands directly on Blake's face.

She screams, flailing, and the circle flickers several times before winking out completely.

From the left Dink darts out from beneath the table, straight up the leg of my jeans and into my lightly furled hand where he chomps down hard on my finger.

It hurts and that entire hand jerks reflexively against the hold of the spell. Not enough to break me free, it's a start.

Through more screams, Blake grabs Anansi around the abdomen and hurls her away. The huge spider slams into the far wall hard and thuds to the floor, all eight legs curling in.

"No," I scream it, just as Nikolette dashes into view at the top of the stairs, her right hand gleaming with bright golden light.

She takes it all in with her mouth open wide, then directs her gaze at Blake. "You?"

"I can't move," I yell. "She paralysed me."

Blake finally stops screaming. "No, wait—"

Nikolette thrusts out with her hand, sending a shower of golden sparks directly at Blake's face. The sweep of *fortis* catapults Blake across the room. She slams the wall headfirst, and then, just like Anansi, she crumples to the ground.

I throw my will into fighting for freedom, pushing harder than I ever have. My *fortis* meets Blake's enfeebled will and overwhelms it with a skin tingling burst, like static. The hold on my body gives, then breaks entirely. For the first time in what feels like hours my body moves freely.

Dink clings to my sleeve, squeaking loudly until I snatch him up. "You stupid, stupid rodent," I tell the tiny creature. "Why didn't you run?"

He slips free of my grip, then scampers up my arm to dive back inside my top. Fine. He can stay there.

Instead I look at Nikolette as she walks further into the room, her fingers still bright with golden light. "Are you okay?" she murmurs.

In turn I test my arms, my legs, my hips, my neck, my head. I am. I *am* okay. Despite the confusion and anger of the last few minutes, I don't appear to be harmed.

I step away from her. "How did you find me?"

If Nikolette notices my motions, she keeps her feelings to herself. Instead she keeps her gaze on Blake. "April and I fought. She sent me away, and when I left, I found your familiar outside."

"I don't have—"

"The spider. That huge hairy thing came running up the stairs shooting web all over the place and wouldn't stop until I started to follow. She brought me all the way back to the meeting space and then disappeared through a crack in the wall." For the first time she looks around the room. "I had no idea this was down here."

Wait, Anansi. Oh no.

I rush over to the spider, wincing at the sight of her crumpled tangle of legs lying at the base of the wall. She isn't moving.

"Anansi?" I reach out to touch her, but I can't quite make my hand move the last few inches. Her thick body is so round and fat, her legs covered with visible hairs.

But then I think about her bravery, her dedication to me, a witch she has no actual ties to.

I pick her up.

So light. Like handling a large clump of hair.

"Anansi? Please move. Do something, please."

One of the legs twitches. Then another. And another and another.

Soon, in the warmth of my hands, the huge spider unfurls like a weird, black flower and turns over to a standing position. She rests on my outstretched hand and flexes her legs one by one before facing me.

Relief washes over me.

"You reckless jerk," I whisper, alarmed to find tears running down my nose. "You could have died."

She shudders, then hops off my hand by way of another of those fine, shiny threads.

"Is she okay?" Nikolette calls from across the room.

"Fine. Just stunned, I think."

"Good. Anybody would think she was *your* familiar from the way she was acting. The mouse too. But I'm glad they came to find me." Finally Nikolette looks at me. Her lips are pressed into a tight, thin line, her brow deeply furrowed. "I'm glad they did because I had no idea my *stalker* was down here."

CHAPTER THIRTY-NINE

"Stalker? What are you talking about?"

Nikolette glares across the room before turning her attention back to me. "We used to date. Long ago. But just recently I've been seeing her following me around. I was scared she was following you, that she would do something to you. Seems I was right."

I try to focus through the mind-numbing nature of this latest revelation. "You never told me that."

"Why would I? I'm sure there's plenty from your past you haven't told me about. Certainly you've never mentioned your exes."

I try not to let my memory take me back to pale eyes, sweat-slick skin, whispered promises of a future I was never destined to have.

"Fine. Table that for now. I think we should—"

Blake's low groan cuts off my words. She drags herself into a sitting position, with her right arm limp and awkward at her side. With a faint sense of horror I realize that she may have dislocated her shoulder.

At least that should stop her casting more spells.

With the paralysis gone and the haze of the circle shattered, I can finally see more of this room. In times long past, it may have been used as storage or a panic room, because in the walls I can see divots, holes, and nails marking areas where shelves or cupboards once were. There's even a grated vent set into the wall at floor height near where Blake crouches.

Nikolette's past romantic entanglements later. First, this.

I march to Blake and stand over her, hands on hips. She seems dazed, but that's fine by me. I have more questions, and I can't focus on them if I'm worried about what she might do.

The chair she used to prop up my limp body is more than enough.

With Nikolette's help, I drag her into it and then shoot a questioning look at Anansi.

"Are your webs strong enough to hold a person?"

The spider stands motionless for several seconds before scuttling across the floor and up into Blake's lap. Then, with speed and skill I've never seen up close, she begins to spin, forming long lengths of glistening thread that wind round and round Blake's body. It only takes a few minutes for Anansi to wrap the woman from shoulders to hips, trapping her arms by her sides.

Wow. That can't possibly be natural.

I'm beginning to appreciate Hyacinth's choice in familiar.

Only when Blake is restrained does Nikolette allow the golden glow to fade from her fingers. She grabs at me, yanking me into a hug so tight, so fierce that for a moment I can't breathe.

I let her.

Despite my anger and the sense of betrayal, I don't know where I would be if she hadn't thought to follow the familiars.

When she tries to kiss me, though, I pull my head away.

She nods and backs off a step, though her eyes shimmer with hurt. Then, as if in need of somewhere to direct her frustration, she rounds on Blake. "What were you trying to do? Why did you bring Tina down here? What even is this room?"

Blake blinks blearily. "The winds of change blow hardest in spring." Her head lolls.

Nikolette sighs and snaps her fingers in Blake's face. "What are you talking about?"

But I freeze. Not a spell this time, but my own jumbled thoughts. I've heard that phrase before, from Hyacinth. A number of times, in fact, usually when explaining something to do with desire or need. She said it especially often during our talks about the Elm Stems.

Spring is a time of renewal and rebirth, three months early in the year in which promises are made, new alliances are forged, and covens gather together to make offerings to the Goddess of the season.

"Persephone." I form the word almost silently, but I know Nikolette hears me. She looks the question at me.

I lower my head to my hands. How could I have been so blind? How could I miss something so obvious?

"Tina, what is it?"

I face her. "Persephone is the Goddess of spring," I tell her.

"Yes, I know. And so?"

"Spring," I say again, "three specific months of the year—March, April, and May. *April.*"

Nikolette stares at me as though I've lost my mind. "Are you okay?" Again she tries to touch me. "Did you hit your head?"

"Flower and Persephone," I insist. "Hyacinth had a lover called Persephone, and she was the Flower. But they broke apart when Hyacinth took her own coven."

"Tina, speak sense."

"You told me she and April were once close, you said that."

Nikolette nods. "I did. But what does that have to do with anything?"

"How close, though?" I face Blake. "Did you ever find out who Hyacinth was meeting at the game shop?" From behind, Nikolette gives a soft gasp. But I ignore it and wait for the answer. The horrible, dreadful, damning answer.

I see it in Blake's eyes before she speaks. She nods. "April," she murmurs. "Hyacinth was meeting April."

I cover my mouth with my hands. "Goddess, no."

Blake's lower lip trembles. "At the time I didn't understand the significance. When April asked me to visit Hyacinth's house, I assumed it was a simple errand. She would send me to do all sorts of odd jobs, and this was nothing new. That was how I met Hyacinth in the first place. But that night I arrived, and there was no answer. I didn't want to enter without permission, so I left. But as the hours went on and I didn't hear from Hyacinth, I knew I had to check. That's when I found you, the following morning."

Nikolette steps forward. "What's happening? What are you two talking about?"

"Two nights before the Willow Bark conclave, Hyacinth and April met at the gaming shop," I murmur, piecing it together as I go. "A day after the conclave, Blake and I found Hyacinth's body in that same game shop. I think the last person to see Hyacinth alive was April."

"What are you saying?" An edge of ice creeps into Nikolette's words. "That April killed her? Don't be ridiculous."

"I saw something." Blake cuts across the pair of us. Given her painful dizziness of moments before, she appears calm now. Her hands are relaxed, and she makes no attempts to wriggle out of the webbing stretched around her body.

"Hyacinth always encouraged me to read tea leaves. She said I had an aptitude for it."

I stare at her. "So *you* were the one she was teaching? I knew there was someone else, but she wouldn't tell me who." I remember Hyacinth's quiet avoidance of my question when last we sat together. Could this be why?

"Yes. She wanted you to learn to but made do with me." A faint smile plays briefly over her lips. "She had so much faith in you."

I look away. "What did you see?"

"Danger," she says. "But tea leaves are imprecise and vague, so I never knew more than that." Blake gives a one-sided shrug. Her right arm sags at her side within the sticky web bindings. "Danger. But there was one clear thing I managed to read out of that messy lump of Earl Grey—Willow Bark intervention."

Nikolette steps even closer. "What did you do?"

"What any good little witch should—I told my superiors. First Hyacinth, who was…well, she was *Hyacinth*." A crooked smile lifts her lips. "She told me not to worry and that everything would be fine. But when I told April, she was terrified. She wanted more information and made me read again and again, but the only message I could see was *danger*. And that the Willow Barks were key in saving us."

Nikolette offers me a sceptical glance. "So?"

"So April became obsessed with the Willow Barks joining the Elm Stems. She would regularly visit Hyacinth to make her case, but Hyacinth always refused. Eventually she pushed so hard that Hyacinth agreed she would ask the coven to vote."

There *had* been talk for several months about joining another coven, but Hyacinth never specifically mentioned the Elms Stems. When we discussed it, she simply said that a small coven like ours might benefit from joining with another.

I sniff back the prickle of tears. "She refused to press her will on us or force us into anything. She was happy for us to decide as a group, even if it didn't match what she wanted."

More of the pieces begin to slide together. "So before our conclave, when we would finally vote, Hyacinth agreed to meet with April at the gaming shop so they could discuss it together?"

Blake nods.

"Nonsense," Nikolette scoffs. "Both Mothers of their respective covens, why would they meet *there* of all places?"

I think back to the little wooden box I found in Hyacinth's drawers. "Because there was more to their meeting than business. They loved each other, Nikolette. Hyacinth and April, Flower and Persephone. They wrote each other dozens upon dozens of love notes."

Blake nods her head towards the trinket box on the low table that makes what is clearly an altar. "She's right, I've seen them. The voices of true love speaking to each other, captured on paper forever." Her gaze flickers briefly towards Nikolette. The sneaky glance is so brief I might have missed it had I not been looking right at her.

I remember her carrying the box out of the house after snooping through all the other rooms. "You had no right to take it. I should have stopped you when I saw you."

Her head whips up. "Can you hide your aura?"

"Not that I know."

"I had no idea you were there. But those notes…maybe after all this time, after talking so long about the welfare of the covens, they were starting to rekindle something."

The certainty rises in me like a kettle beginning to bubble. "But Hyacinth refused. She must have. In all our conversations she never expressed a desire to join the two covens. And April killed her for it."

"I don't believe that." Nikolette immediately shakes her head. "We have to be missing something. Mother April would never *kill* someone. None of us would. The Rule of Three—"

"Hyacinth is dead," I snap back. "She was bound by paralysis magic. Someone stabbed her multiple times—"

"*She* can cast paralysis magic." Nikolette jabs a finger at Blake. "She cast it on you. She's been following you. Who knows what she's capable of?"

Blake eyes Nikolette for long seconds, then gives another of those passive nods. "We're not in the circle any more, but I've no reason to lie about what I can do. April taught me that spell. I could never cast it as strongly as her—you would never have escaped if she cast it, Tina. The few times she demonstrated on me, I couldn't move at all. I thought even my heart might stop beating."

I gape at her. "She could do that?"

"Certainly, if she wanted to. But paralysing the body's functions—lungs, heart, brain—that would kill someone."

I cast my mind back over the three other bodies in the morgue. The bodies with no outward sign of injury. Did they die because they were paralysed from the inside out?

Upstairs, before I came downstairs, my body had locked up in April's office. Paralysed.

My mouth floods with the bitter taste of fear saliva. "We need to get out of here." I rush to Blake, meaning to untie her. "We all do. Now. None of us are safe."

Nikolette grabs my arm, sighing when I wrench away. "There has to be more to it than this." Her voice takes on a pleading edge. "Mother April has protected this coven since she took over. She wouldn't hurt anybody. You can't possibly believe Blake over her. Over me?"

No idea what that means, but now isn't the time.

"After what I heard upstairs, you're lucky I have other priorities. At least Blake was upfront about the immutable circle she put us in."

Again she reaches for me. "I had nothing to do with that. I didn't know. Please, Tina, do you really think so little of me?"

I give her the weight of my anger. "I believe becoming a coven Mother is so important to you that you insisted we lie about our feelings for each other. Is it such a stretch that you would do whatever April asked to get you there?"

At last her hand drops away from me. Her eyes shimmer. "I would never do anything to hurt you. Ever."

"Save it, I'm leaving."

"None of you are going anywhere." This new voice comes from the top of the stairs, and I whirl to face it with my hands raised.

I don't know what I planned to do, maybe throw a punch or hurl a paltrick of some sort. But none of it matters.

Because even as I turn to face her, April Wesker raises both hands to shoulder height, then slams them down as though swatting an insect.

Crushing force slams into my back and shoulders, and though I fight it with everything in me, a heavy, invisible force shoves me to the ground and pins me there.

CHAPTER FORTY

Nikolette cries out as she too hits the floor. To the side of us, Blake wobbles dangerously in her chair.

Movement inside my top tells me I've half crushed Dink. I try to lift my chest to give him space, but I may well be fighting with the weight of a boulder for the good it does.

"Murderer," I bellow. "How could you? How could you do that to her?"

Tiny sparks of silver fill the air around April's hands. Her hair rises on the rippling current of her own *fortis*. "How dare *you* accuse me of something so ridiculous? You have no idea what you're talking about."

"You paralysed Hyacinth and killed her!"

Time stretches, one single moment in which I meet her gaze and fill mine with every ounce of fury I can muster. I live an entire lifetime in that moment, watching April's features slowly morph from rage, to uncertainty, to fear, and finally…

"You don't understand." Her voice quivers, then breaks. Each breath as it leaves her lips trembles audibly.

Again, I fight to lift myself, but the weight of her *fortis* is just too much. "What's to understand? You murdered your only obstacle, duped me, and now here we are. I walked the Willow Barks right into your arms."

"Mind your tongue." Her chin tilts ever so slightly as she scrambles to regain any shred of authority she has left.

"Mother April, please"—Nikolette's strained voice suggests she's trying to lift her head—"tell them they're wrong. Please. You haven't killed anybody, you wouldn't do that. Please. This has to be a mistake."

"There *has* been a mistake." April walks slowly down the steps. The sparks around her fingers fade as she reaches the bottom step. "Perhaps the largest, most significant of my life."

Again, I fight the force pinning me flat. "Murderer's guilt?"

Her eyes harden. "I think I've had enough of you, Tina Marks." April sweeps her hand in the air.

My entire body rises with that gesture, sliding off the floor and hurtling towards her like a rag doll. I hang suspended a full foot off the ground, body locked into place while my feet dangle.

Nikolette screams, "No, please!"

I grit my teeth.

April brings me close enough that I can see the very whites of her eyes, the flare of her nostrils. I watch the anger burn inside her and wonder if I'm about to experience what those three nameless people in the morgue did.

"There are words for witches like you," I hiss. "Slayer."

"Don't you dare call me that." She glares with such heat in her gaze that I can almost feel it. "I didn't kill her. I…it was an accident."

Silence. Nobody moves. Perhaps nobody can.

Through the stillness, I hear the house settling, the far, far distant sounds of excited voices preparing for a feast, and the faint click as Anansi steps lightly towards Blake's chair.

April looks at the ground. "I loved her more than anything in the world—despite her Goddess cursed stubbornness." Her back and shoulders slump forward. "I should never have left her."

The magical hold on me breaks, and my body crashes down in front of her.

I yelp as my legs hit the floor but scramble up as fast as I can. I need to be agile, mobile. Ready.

Behind me, Nikolette makes a sound rather like a whimper. "Mother April? What do you mean *left her*?"

April rubs her nose. Is she…crying?

I flex my fingers, the words of a paltrick for darkness just ready on the tip of my tongue. "What are you talking about?"

"She was so stubborn." April sniffs again and gazes at her hands, though not as if she really sees them. "I just wanted her to listen. She *needed* to listen. If only she would have listened, then I wouldn't have—" Her head snaps up. "I've done nothing but protect the health and livelihood of my daughters. You must understand that. Everything I've done, everything, was to protect those in my care."

"I know you want to protect us. You're my coven Mother, and I trust you." Nikolette's voice wavers so much I've no idea who she's trying to convince.

It works on April, though, who straightens her back as she recovers herself. "Good. You should trust me, I *am* Mother." She faces me. "You more than most know what she was like. Hyacinth rarely listened to the desires or opinions of others."

I pat down Dink as he pokes an indignant paw out the neckline of my top. "She did nothing *but* put others before herself. If it was up to her, we never would have considered joining your coven. But she let us decide."

That seems to catch April off guard. She eyes me carefully. "She had no part of the vote? Never exercised her right to veto?"

I scoff. "If you have to ask me that, then maybe you barely knew her at all."

April stares at me, then off at something in the distance. She seems to be gazing into herself, at something only she has the ability to see. "Then this was all for nothing."

Nikolette reaches my side. Her gaze is fixed on April. "Mother, please, what did you do?"

"Nothing." April breaks out of her reverie. "My paralysis spells are harmless—she was perfectly safe. If only she had agreed, I wouldn't have had to leave her where those…those…*humans* could find her." She spits the word as though it tastes bad. "*They* are the ones who stabbed her—*I* did nothing wrong!"

Gasps from Nikolette and Blake. Probably from me too.

With two long strides I'm back in April's face, close enough to feel her breath on my nose. "You have three seconds to tell me what the hell you're talking about."

"Or what?" Her expression wavers between anger and fear. It's a split-second flicker, one I might have missed were I not right in front of her. Then brisk efficiency slips back into her voice. "Was that a threat, Daughter?"

"Does it need to be?" I shoot back.

Her eyebrow rises. "Hyacinth and I met at that disgusting game shop to decide, once and for all, what to do about the approaching danger. I offered her coven protection, and she refused. Prideful woman. So I…" She clears her throat. "So I paralysed her, meaning to keep her with me until she would see sense."

Another little whimper from Nikolette. "Mother, no…"

"I knew nobody would disturb us in that shop. I knew she would be safe."

"Safe from what?" I say carefully.

"Anything. Nobody enters that space but other witches, we all know that. You young ones think you're so clever"—she cuts a glance at Nikolette—"but I *know* what happens in that shop. I knew it was perfectly safe to leave her while I checked her house."

"But you removed the wards." I cast my mind back to the strange, empty feeling at the door the day I found Hyacinth. "Aren't they part of what keeps the space safe?"

She twitches her shoulders. "Perhaps, but a ward as strong as that was incredibly uncomfortable. Besides, what need of it while we were there?"

"Wait, you left a sick, paralysed old woman alone in an unwarded space?" For the first time Blake speaks up. Her eyes are wide and round, her mouth hanging open. She seems not to notice the way her shoulder sags within the confines of her web bindings. "How long were you gone?"

"An hour at most." Again, April affects a brisk, businesslike tone. "I wanted to find whatever protective artefact she had squirrelled away and use it to protect *all* of us. After all, why should the Willow Barks be the only ones who are safe?" She sniffs. "But at the house, even more wards. I couldn't get in. So I returned to the game shop and I…" Again her words falter. She exhales a shuddering breath.

"What, April?" Nikolette's voice has an edge. It's the first time I've heard her use it directed at her Mother and the first time she's neglected to use her honorific. "What happened?"

"They'd made such a mess of her. Those mundane wastrels. They must have thought she would turn them in. Or perhaps they were so mindless from whatever drugs they took that they had no idea what they were doing." Her eyes narrow.

Blake gives a low moan of horror and grief. I fight the urge to copy her.

Nikolette advances on April and gently nudges me aside. I let her, too stunned to resist. "And after that?" she whispers.

"I showed them what it's like to suffer." April's voice darkens. "I hunted down those putrescent sacks of waste and imprisoned them in their own filth. And then I left them for the Goddess to judge."

I step back from April as the true horror of her words sinks in. "You paralysed them so completely that their hearts and lungs stopped." Disgust bubbles within me. "You killed them."

"I did not, nor have I ever killed anyone." The sparks are back at her fingertips, and she screams the words with such force that I feel them in the very air. "I'm not a murderer and certainly not a *slayer*. I'm guilty of nothing but misjudging the worth and morality of humans."

Tears shimmer on Nikolette's cheeks. She turns aside with a choked-up gasp, and for the first time I realize that she has been betrayed just as much as I have. Maybe more so.

April seems not to notice. "Since that awful day I've done everything possible to move forward. And it's working. You're here now, Tina, and you're safe. All of you. We're together, Daughters, and we can take care of each other."

From her chair, Blake gasps as the web bindings around her arms and chest break away. I see Anansi clinging to the back of the chair, clearly removing her handiwork. When the silk is loose enough, Blake brushes it away with her left hand, then stands. Though she wobbles slightly, her voice and expression are firm.

"There *is* no artefact." Her soft voice is harder than I've ever heard it. "I told you that before, after you sent me to look. No artefact, no spell, no special item, just an old woman's home filled with herbs and books."

"You didn't get into the spell space, Daughter. You can't know for sure."

But *I* know.

Hyacinth's spell space was beautiful and powerful, but there was nothing especially potent or special inside it. Every source of power in that house came from Hyacinth herself.

Dink nuzzles himself into the hollow at the base of my throat, and

I place a gentle hand over him. How much of this does he understand? Does he know we've figured out what happened to his mistress? Does he realize that the woman in front of us is responsible for her death?

Blake cradles her right arm against her body. "But Hyacinth told us both there was no need to worry. Why couldn't you just trust her?"

"Because she's wrong." April glares. "Hyacinth *refused* to take the matter seriously, telling me that we should have faith. But I've seen what we're up against. And so have you." She jabs a finger at me.

"What are you talking about?"

"The creature you pulled out of that SPEAR agent last year. If a thing like that exists in our world, we *must* protect ourselves at all costs."

The ache of the senseless loss settles low and heavy in my belly. "Even if that cost is leaving someone to die in the dark, alone and powerless?"

April grits her teeth. "Hyacinth was my precious Flower, and she's gone forever. Don't you think I've suffered enough? Even dressing that horrible gaming shop to resemble a vampire den. I've paid enough by keeping the police from investigating any further. Now that it's a crime scene, no witch need dirty themselves with such a place ever again."

Mention of the police stirs something low in my belly.

Blake touches my arm. "We have to get out of here. We have to go to the authorities."

I hesitate.

"Tina"—she grips harder—"four people are dead. She has to meet justice."

Nikolette leaps to her feet. With one smooth motion she sidesteps to put herself between us and April. "Wait. Please. Both of you. Before you do anything rash, consider the effect on the coven. Consider the circumstances. It was an accident."

"Paralysing someone until their heart stops isn't an accident," Blake snaps. "And what about the coven? You mean, they'll no longer be led by a murderer and a slayer? Good. We deserve better. We deserve Hyacinth."

April's eyes blaze with rage, but Nikolette gets in first. "April has looked after us for years, put everything on the line for us again and again. You'd throw that all away now?"

"To honour Hyacinth? In a heartbeat. Tina"—Blake tilts her chin, still holding her limp right arm—"you're an officer, aren't you? Arrest her."

Nikolette puts out her arm, as if to shield April. "No, you can't. Let's think about this."

"Don't worry, Daughter," April snorts haughtily. "I am Mother of the Elm Stem coven. No mundane human order of law has any authority over me."

Again that stirring in my belly. Stronger now, blending with a prickle in my fingers.

"Wait. All of you—"

"No, Tina." Blake begins to fumble in her pockets. "I'm calling this in right now. I'll testify, I'll give any statement you could possibly want, but you have to arrest her. Now." She awkwardly tugs a phone from her pocket and begins to dial.

April smiles. "And what then of you, Daughter? Do we arrest you too? There's no law to cover the magic of it, but arson is still a crime."

The beeping from the phone stops. Blake looks up, sudden fear in her eyes.

I focus on April. "What are you talking about?"

The smile grows wider. "Ah. So during your little heart-to-heart she neglected to mention her role in destroying your home? How convenient."

In the midst of everything else I had forgotten that confession. "Why, Blake? Revenge? A bad day? Why destroy my home?"

She shrinks away from me. "April told me to make sure you had no choice but to come to us. I had to make it look like you were in immediate danger. But I never wanted to do you harm."

"You nearly killed me—"

"No." She tucks the phone away. "I would never. Please believe I did what I thought I had to."

Another of those infuriating snorts from April. "So *you* may act on your beliefs, but *I* may not? I do so despise hypocrites."

Blake tries to speak but breaks off with a cry of pain. Her forehead is shiny with sweat, and still she grips tight at the elbow of her right arm. Her shoulder must be incredibly painful.

Rage over my ravaged home fades as I stare at her pitiful state. "Come here, let me help."

"No"—she hops back—"I know what to do." With her teeth tightly clenched, she bends at the waist, then grips her right wrist with her left hand and yanks down. Hard. With a loud click her shoulder joint pops back into place, and she lets out a sharp cry from behind the cage of her teeth. Her face is pale beneath the vibrant red of her hair, and though she sways slightly, she refuses to fall.

"Are you okay?"

She ignores the question in favour of a shake of the head. "I'm so, so sorry. I've handled this badly, I know that. I'll make up for what I did. But please let me start now by doing the right thing. We *have* to take April to the police."

Nikolette clenches her fists. "No. No police."

I stare at my sometime girlfriend. "What are you saying? That she should get away with all this with no consequences?"

"Of course not. But we're witches. We're Elm Stems. There are ways we do things, and involving human law enforcement is not it. The Elm Stems have to handle her."

The three women before me share glances, then turn their attention to me. With a jolt, I realize with alarm that they are looking to me for a decision. Me.

As if noticing my anxiety, April spreads her hands before her in a wide gesture. Her knowing, almost smug smile persists. "Well then, *Officer*, I suppose you'll be taking me in?"

Chapter Forty-one

April's stare is cool and unruffled. She stands at ease, watching my face, but I see, from the corner of my eye, the way her hands curl into tight fists.

"April Wesker, you're under arrest for—"

Nikolette grabs my arm. "What are you doing?"

"My job." I shake her off. "What else do you think?"

"You'd give her over to humans?"

"I'd give her to law enforcement officers." I try to ignore the increasing discomfort intensifying around my belly. The flutters there resemble bouncing basketballs more than butterflies.

"Tina, please." Tears shimmer in Nikolette's eyes. "Think about this. You can't do this. What about the coven? What about me? What about all the sisters who depend on her? You can't just take her away."

"She killed four people."

"She's all I have." Her voice cracks.

I stare at her, really look her over.

Nikolette's eyes are wide and haunted. Her hands shake as they reach for me. Even her ordinarily pristine hair has flyaways that give her a wild, desperate look that I've never seen before. "Please…"

"You have so much more than you think. You're so much more than whatever she's made you believe."

The tears free-fall down her cheeks now. "There has to be another way. What if we—the Elms, I mean—we could handle it amongst ourselves. We have rules and laws, right? We can handle it together."

Across from us, Blake sighs as she gently tests her right arm. "Your ambition knows no bounds, does it? You'd prevent us going to the police just so you can keep playing favourites?"

Nikolette buries her face in her hands. "I know what you think of me, but it's not like that. I'm not that cold or callous."

"You were to me." Blake's voice is low and hollow. "I was never good enough for you. My ambitions were never bold enough or strong enough. I was beneath you."

A stifled sob floats through Nikolette's fingers. "Was I so bad that you think I'd condone murder?"

Silence. I catch Blake silently shaking her head.

I look at Nikolette—her damp, blotchy face, her streaked make-up. She looks like a child I want to scoop into my arms and protect with a layer of softest cotton. "You really didn't know about the immutable circle, did you?"

She looks up, wilted and pitiful. "Of course not. I thought I was guiding my girlfriend to something good. I would never do anything to hurt you. Ever." She turns to April. "And I never believed you would either. Please, Mother, explain this. Make it make sense. What did you do to those people?"

Long, tense silence.

"I gave a trio of murdering humans to the Goddess for judgement. Whatever happened after that is between the Goddess and their souls."

Blake gives me a meaningful look.

Again I step up to April. "Turn around."

She glares at me. "Whatever for?"

"You're under arrest, April Wesker, under suspicion of the involuntary manslaughter of one Hyacinth Dixon, as a result of gross negligence—"

"Don't be foolish, Daughter. You don't really want to do this."

"You aren't my Mother, April." I fight the urge to slap her. "If you call me that one more time, I'll—"

"What? You'll what? Throw another tantrum, then spend three days thinking about what to do? Child, you haven't been *listening*. There is *danger* out there, and we're ill-equipped to fight it. Blake saw it, Hyacinth disregarded it, but *I* know it is there. All you have left to guide you through is me."

"You're going to prison."

A smile, slow and sad. "Is that right? Very well." April lifts her hands, wrists together. "Arrest me. Cart me away. But then who will look after the Elm Stem coven? Who will look after your sisters?"

I hesitate. That thundering sensation in my belly becomes a crescendo.

"Nikolette can lead them," I blurt out. "She's clearly strong enough."

"Pathetic," April snaps. "I have known you only a short time, but I've known *of* you for considerably longer. And your behaviour over the last two days only proves my first impression. You are weak and cowardly—you are so afraid of making a choice that you paralyse yourself with the very thought of it." Her eyes blaze. "You would arrest me, take me away from my daughters, and then leave my Nikolette to pick up the pieces? Pathetic."

I sense rather than see Nikolette react. She's talking quickly, low and soft, but I can't hear her over the thundering in my belly, which now reaches my chest, my throat, my head. The memories crash down over me, a tsunami that brings back another night far in my past. A night in which screams of fear, anger, and pain filled the night sky like church bells.

They stood before me, patient and silent, waiting for my word, my command, that would bring everything crashing down. One word. That's all they needed.

A older woman of the large group stepped forward. She touched her lips, then her forehead with the edge of her index finger, a classic sign of deference. "Are you all right?"

"Fine, I—"

"We don't have much time. What do you want us to do?"

The air was electric with the weight of their expectation, their need. As one, all eyes turned to me and fixed me with quiet, trusting stares.

"Go," I whispered. "Do it."

No hesitation.

As one they raised their hands. Bright white light filled the air, the power of dozens upon dozens of witches directing their fortis *at a central point. And at the centre of it, bound and helpless, the figure trapped within tossed back their head and screamed their agony to the pale, unyielding sky.*

I shake myself free of the memory and back into the room in time to hear April hiss, low and angry, "I'll never understand what Hyacinth saw in you."

No reaction from Nikolette or Blake. Clearly those words were intended just for me.

In my mind's eye, Hyacinth's image swims before me. Her gentle smile, encouraging voice, and odd, cryptic words. I miss her more in this moment than I've ever missed anyone, her wisdom, her guidance, her knowledge. I'm not like her. I never have been, not in my past, nor now.

"I don't know what to do."

April is on me in an instant, her arm slithering around my shoulders. "Of course you don't, that's not your job. It's *mine*. I'm here now, and I'm going to take care of everything. I promise, you and your sisters will be safe."

"No." I shove her away from me, until that moment unaware I'd said the words aloud.

I *don't* know what to do. I can't figure out how this is going to go. I have no idea what Blake saw in those leaves and why Hyacinth was so adamant that we would all be fine. But I *do* know that I trust my Mother, more than I've ever trusted anyone. Certainly more than myself.

"No. You're a citizen of Angbec as much subject to the laws of the country as any other being. You're not special, April. You're not above anyone. You're going to prison."

To my side, I catch Blake smiling, nodding silently, urging me on.

Nikolette looks…defeated.

April tilts her chin at me, her expression haughty. She opens her mouth as if to say more, but Anansi chooses that moment to spring off the ground, directly at her face. Threads of webbing fly through the air, and Anansi swings on them like an acrobat to lay them across April's mouth.

Her eyes flash wide, both hands fly up, but I'm faster. I snatch at her wrists and pin them behind her back.

"You're coming with me. Blake, get the door."

"Gladly." Even with her injured arm clearly causing pain, she bounds past me towards the stairs and darts up them two at a time.

Anansi finishes her binding of April's face with a flourish in the form of two jaunty kicks from her middle legs. When next I look, April's mouth is covered in white sticky strands, plastering her hair to her ears and cheeks. Her eyes blaze with fury.

Nikolette wipes her eyes. The tears keep coming. "What if she's right? What if she's the only one who can protect us against what's coming?"

"Hyacinth didn't think so," I murmur. "Come on. We need to get out of here." I give April a shove to get her walking, then follow close behind, my hands still tight on her wrists.

Several seconds pass before Nikolette follows.

Chapter Forty-two

I stand in the kitchen of Hyacinth's home, looking out the large windows towards the garden as it wraps around the side of the house. Still beautiful, still colourful, and no doubt still smelling as sweet as ever, though I can't catch the scent from indoors.

On the sideboard, Anansi sits—stands?—facing me, silent and still as a plastic figurine. Dink sits on my shoulder, his tiny body pressed tight against my neck.

I'm still not used to being here—the air isn't right, the mood is all wrong. I know it's because Hyacinth is missing, but it isn't just her presence that the house pines for. It's the sound of her moving through the kitchen, gently singing or whistling old 50s tunes in a most unladylike manner. The scent of her cooking, rich with roasting vegetables smothered in garlic oil or spicy chilli. Even the heat in the air, left over from her magic as she performed little paltricks to make life easier—sweep the floor here, dust a shelf there.

It will be a long time before this place feels like a home rather than just a house.

It's dusk, a time I truly love, when night creeps in to overtake the day. Part of me comes alive at this hour, the mundane, everyday police officer stepping aside for the dark, silver-rimmed glory of a moonlit night.

Maybe I'll go for a walk. Maybe I'll take a moonbath.

"Are you even listening to me? Hello? Tina?"

With a jolt I remember that I'm supposed to be on the phone. I adjust the Bluetooth earpiece and clear my throat in what I hope is an apologetic way. "Sorry, Nikolette. Miles away. What was that about the coven?"

She sighs. "I know you don't want to think about it. But you have to. *We* have to."

"There's not much more we *can* do until—" I glance upward at the sound of a soft bumping sound somewhere above.

Perhaps mistaking my distraction for irritation, Nikolette softens her voice. "I know, I know. But, please, give me a few more days. I need to get my head straight."

"Fine…" I turn, shoulders tense. Dink and Anansi mirror my anxiety.

Neither of them have been far from my side in the last few days, as though uncertain of my safety. At any other time I might have been annoyed at the constant, mismatched shadows, but instead I cling to them as the last living traces of Hyacinth.

"Don't *fine* me, Tina. Come on."

Dink adopts a more ready position on my shoulder, while Anansi takes off along the floor, scuttling across it at high speed before climbing up the wall of the stairs.

I follow, the phone still loose in my hand. "While the Elm Stems don't know what's going on, they have no reason to vote for another leader. Why do you keep pushing me on this? Don't *you* want to be coven Mother?"

"More than anything." The misery in her voice is almost palpable. "But I can't. Not like this and—"

"Stop that." I pause halfway up the steps. "You didn't know. April manipulated you as much as anyone else. Maybe more."

"But I should have seen it."

"You've been training for leadership since you were old enough to speak. This was *made* for you. Besides, the Elm Stems are *your* sisters."

"And yours now."

A tiny fissure of anger runs through me, quickly suppressed.

Yes, mine too. And Edith and Iris and Kiara and Chloe, if the former pair will ever speak to me again. Though I know my Elm sisters resent it, I can't help but consider my Willow sisters an entity unto their own. Though we've joined the Elm Stems, we will never quite be part of them.

I sigh and adjust my voice to be reassuring. "How about we all take some time to get used to that first?"

Another bump from upstairs encourages me to keep going, and I hurry up towards it.

The bedroom door still lies open, the bed within still neat and tidy. Across from it, the spare bedroom shows signs of my presence in the form of rumpled sheets and a large carry case with a small supply of clothes.

I catch the sounds of ceramic clinking and the rumble of a kettle coming to the boil. Nikolette is clearly home and making herself something to settle with. She tuts softly under her breath. "Last time you were here, in my apartment, I mean, we were talking about coven Mothers."

"Yes?" I say with caution.

My steps take me to the bottom of the stairs leading up to the sanctum. It's dark but a quick light paltrick on my palm is enough to get me safely to the top. Tripping on Anansi once already was enough to teach me that lesson.

"You talked about responsibility, and you said you didn't want it. Again. You said *again*."

I wait, breath tight in my throat, locked there as surely as the door before me.

"Were you a coven Mother before coming to Angbec?"

I can't think of an easy way to answer that without lying, so I don't try. "I love you, Nikolette, despite everything. And believe it or not, I trust you. But there are some things I just can't share right now."

"Can't or won't?"

Another soft bump. This one for sure from beyond the sanctum door.

"When Blake and I told you we need to explain to the Elm Stems what April has done, you asked for more time. You asked us to let you get used to it before tarnishing April's memory to everyone who cares about her. Think of my past like that."

"You're tarnished?"

"In my eyes."

She pauses, considering. And then, "Do you want company tonight?"

I do. Goddess, I do. With this house so empty and lifeless I can hardly stand it, but other parts of me can't bear to leave. "You'd come here? Even with the ward?"

"I'd try." Though she tries to hide it, I can still hear the uncertainty in her voice. "Is it any different today?"

"Not that I can tell."

Just like before, when I pass through the ward, my skin comes alive with the sensation of warmth, love, and welcome. Nikolette has no such luxury and complains of the oppressive, angry nature of the ward against her skin.

I want to help her, but all I know is that the ward is one of the last things Hyacinth cast before she died, and that it doesn't seem to welcome anybody but me. A ward that seems to originate from the room in front of me.

"I'll try tomorrow, then. I want to see you."

"I want to see you too."

A pause, then the faint cooing sound of her fussing over Princess. "How long do I have before the police go public?"

I shake my head, even though she can't see me. "April must have excellent legal representation because the entire case has been set under a superinjunction. No news articles, no interviews, nothing. No one will ever know."

She gasps. "But then *we* would have to tell the Elms?"

I brush my hand over the door handle to dissipate the spell. No need to speak the words any more. The heavy wooden door simply swings open before me.

The curtains billow softly towards me as I stand in the doorway, gusting on a breeze from windows I'm certain I closed days ago.

I step into the room, then stop as a soft chuffing sound floats through the air.

A ferret, long, brown and fluffy, stands in the middle of what was once Hyacinth's casting circle. She eyes me curiously as I step deeper into the room and rises briefly onto her hind legs.

"Oh Goddess." I clamp a hand to my mouth.

"What? What happened?"

A soft trill from the ferret. Then she scurries over to me, making a curious, breathy, panting sound as she darts back and forth around my ankles.

"Loki?" I whisper.

Where did she come from? Where has she been?

I crouch so I can pet her head, marvelling when she lets me. For at least three seconds, she pushes her head more firmly into my hands before bounding over to the altar, with little squeaks of pleasure.

Only then do I notice the other occupant of the room.

A barn owl. Soft, beautiful, silent, and powerful, the bird blinks slowly at me as I approach.

"Seshat?"

She clicks her beak at me.

From my shoulder, Dink gives the tiniest of squeaks, while Anansi finishes her path along the walls to swing down from one of her usual threads.

"Where have you been?" I murmur.

But they don't answer. Of course they don't—they're animals. Perhaps I'll never know what adventures Seshat and Loki went on, but the fact that they knew to return here fills me with quiet joy. They haven't forgotten Hyacinth, as I feared they might. As all familiars eventually do, they have returned to the home of their witch to be in companionable service.

"Tina?" Again Nikolette's voice fills my ear. "What's happening? Are you okay?"

"I'm fine, but the familiars are back."

Her voice becomes urgent. "Do you need me to come over? I will, right now, I—"

"Not this time." I make my own voice soft and soothing. "Thank you, truly, but I think they're here for me."

"Keep me in the loop?"

I smile. Not long ago that would have been a demand, not a request. Maybe she really is changing. "Of course. I need to go, though. I'll speak to you tomorrow."

She returns the farewell and hangs up.

I look across the spell space.

All four creatures—ferret, bird, mouse, and spider—gather around the altar now, clustered close to the book of shadows I have been unable to move from this space or even touch. They stop and look at me.

"You want me to read it again?"

Silence, of course. But the air becomes abruptly heavy with the weight of expectation.

I reach for the book.

Warmth rushes from it, rather like last time, but instead of resentment and uncertainty, this time I feel eagerness and excitement. Hard to place, coming from a book, but the sensations are so real that I know they're true.

"I don't understand," I murmur.

The book opens of its own accord, the front cover flipping back before several of the penned pages follow suit. I watch it skip through the pages, the physical representation of Hyacinth's life flickering before me. When it stops, I note that it does so on the page I previously marked with the piece of bark. The same page into which is tucked the little wooden ring, dangling on a piece of thread.

Again I read Hyacinth's words.

Oh, Tina. My dearest Daughter, I am so very sorry.

I must also give her the ring. I have no use of it now.

Perhaps I can disguise it as a gift and later leave instruction on how she can—

A gift. I remember my previous reluctance to take the little band, hoping that Hyacinth would be able to hand it to me herself.

This time, I take hold of the ring and tug until the thread breaks. Easy, and at last the wooden band is free to examine more closely.

Just like before, I see the script etched delicately into the inner curve. I have no idea what it says, or if it says anything at all, but the symbols are thin and beautiful. The outside is plain, but for the natural grain of the wood.

Slowly, I slide it onto my finger.

More warmth rushes over me, from the ring outward, billowing from my finger like a cloud. For a moment I almost see it, soft green and sparkling. Hyacinth's favourite colour. It washes over my face and hands, and with it I catch the scent of flowers: rose, lavender, and—

"Hyacinth?"

In that moment I feel her presence as surely and clearly as I see the four familiars. They clearly do too because they become excited and animated, hopping about on the altar in a chorus of animal sounds.

I spin around, suddenly captured by the wild thought that I might see her. I would give anything to see her smile again, watch her flick greying hair off her face or scratch the little tattoo on her right cheek.

But of course there's nothing. Just the five of us.

I sigh and return my attention to the book.

The page is filled with writing.

Not the writing of Hyacinth's previous entry—that seems to be trapped beneath. No, these words float off the surface of the page, thin and delicate, but very much another example of Hyacinth's writing.

Dearest Tina,

My heart catches in my throat. I want it to stop, but the words keep forming, line after line, appearing then vanishing like a magical teleprompter.

> *If you are reading this message, I am gone.*
>
> *I hope I found time enough to avail you of the true nature of my condition, but if not, I am so dearly sorry.*
>
> *Though my spirit is strong, my body has weakened and can no longer carry me forward.*
>
> *None of us are long for this world, and I had the distinct pleasure of living in it longer than most.*
>
> *But my time is over.*

I press my hands to my mouth, transfixed. Loki chuffs and bumps her head into my ankles again. Even Dink returns to me to press his tiny body back into his favourite spot at the side of my neck.

> *Despite that, you know as well as I that my next journey begins now.*
>
> *Cry not for me, my child, for I am flying among the stars, dancing in a field of the most colourful flowers.*

A tear slides down my cheek. An image shimmers before me, Hyacinth with her hands raised, her lips parted in laughter. She is barefoot and dressed entirely in white, spinning on her toes across a grassy plain, with flowers springing up in each of her delicate footprints.

> *Look instead to your own safety, Daughter, and that of your sisters.*
>
> *For there is a terrible danger approaching.*

I wish I could explain more fully, but I do not yet understand it myself.

And now, I never shall.

But I do understand this: You are strong and capable.

Your sisters will need you in the days ahead.

When the time comes, I trust you to protect those weaker than yourself as you have done so mightily in the past.

The beautiful image of Hyacinth fades away, and I'm left to myself and my own trembling hands. My past is a dark, murky shadow, one I've worked hard to put behind me. I don't want to think about it or do anything remotely like what I did back then. But the words keep coming and, with them, a slow sense of dread begins to build within me.

Be not afraid.

Do not falter.

Trust in your own fortis, *Evangeline, and wisdom will one day be yours.*

This house and all it contains, I gift to you.

May all my treasures serve you as well and as fully as they served me.

My friends will care for you as they did me. Be sure you care for them in return.

Seshat hoots as at me, as if she knows she is being discussed. Anansi waves her legs at the floating words, passing through them like fingers through a hologram.

So the familiars really are mine now.

Goodbye, dearest Daughter. May the Goddess guide and protect you always.

The words fade away, sinking into the pages like motes of dust. No sign of them remains.

I stand at the altar, staring down at the book of shadows, fighting to keep the tears from blurring my vision. It doesn't work.

As the sun dips fully below the horizon and the moon begins to rise, I stand and walk to one of the open windows.

I still don't know who opened it, but given what I just saw, maybe I *do* know. Hyacinth's familiars are to care for me, just as they did for her. Little wonder they returned to this room to begin that mission. Maybe that was her last physical act in this world, to open the windows to let both ferret and owl back into the house.

No, not *the* house. *My* house.

Hyacinth gifted not only her familiars to me, but this entire house too.

I have no idea how the legality of such a decision works, but if I know anything about Hyacinth, I'm pretty sure she would have done the groundwork.

"This…is mine?"

A gust billows through the windows and flutters the thick curtains. Another breeze seems to roll across the ground, tumbling the old salt and crushed herbs across the floorboards.

"Mine."

Another gust, and with it, a smell, so familiar, so unexpected, so out of place that I can't help but laugh out loud.

I inhale deeply, smiling and filling my lungs with the delicious scent of dry-roasted, freshly ground beans.

Well, I always was more of a coffee person.

About the Author

Ileandra Young writes urban fantasy novels, has an unhealthy obsession with vampires, and would gleefully pick a sword over any other weapon. Yes, even that one.

She spends far more time in fantasy lands than the real one, since her hobbies include LARPing, TTRPGs, and more recently *Stardew Valley*, *Minecraft*, *Balder's Gate 3*, and of course, *Animal Crossing*. If she does graciously deign to visit the real world, you'll find her sitting in a corner, crocheting something weird or cooing over the latest addition to the family; a beautiful Russian dwarf hamster.

Visit her website at www.ileandrayoung.co.uk.

Books Available From Bold Strokes Books

Across the Enchanted Border by Crin Claxton. Magic, telepathy, swordsmanship, tyranny, and tenderness abound in a tale of two lands separated by the enchanted border. (978-1-63679-804-2)

Deep Cover by Kara A. McLeod. Running from your problems by pretending to be someone else only works if the person you're pretending to be doesn't have even bigger problems. (978-1-63679-808-0)

Good Game by Suzanne Lenoir. Even though Lauren has sworn off dating gamers, it's becoming hard to resist the multifaceted Sam. An opposites attract lesbian romance. (978-1-63679-764-9)

Innocence of the Maiden by Ileandra Young. Three powerful women. Two covens at war. One horrifying murder. When mighty and powerful witches begin to butt heads, who out there is strong enough to mediate? (978-1-63679-765-6)

Protection in Paradise by Julia Underwood. When arson forces them together, the flames between chief of police Eve Maguire and librarian Shaye Hayden aren't that easy to extinguish. (978-1-63679-847-9)

Too Forward by Krystina Rivers. Just as professional basketball player Jane May's career finally starts heating up, a new relationship with her team's brand consultant could derail the success and happiness she's struggled so long to find. (978-1-63679-717-5)

Worth Waiting For by Kristin Keppler. For Peyton and Hanna, reliving the past is painful, but looking back might be the only way to move forward. (978-1-63679-773-1)

All For Her: Forbidden Romance Novellas by Gun Brooke, J.J. Hale & Aurora Rey. Explore the angst and excitement of forbidden love few would dare in this heart-stopping novella collection. (978-1-63679-713-7)

Finding Harmony by CF Frizzell. Rock star Harper Cushing has to rearrange her grandmother's future and sell the family store out from under her, but she reassesses everything because Gram's helper, Frankie, could be offering the harmony her heart has been missing. (978-1-63679-741-0)

Gaze by Kris Bryant. Love at first sight is for dreamers, but the more time Lucky and Brianna spend together, the more they realize the chemistry of a gaze can make anything possible. (978-1-63679-711-3)

Laying of Hands by Patricia Evans. The mysterious new writing instructor at camp makes Grace Waters brave enough to wonder what would happen if she dared to write her own story. (978-1-63679-782-3)

The Naked Truth by Sandy Lowe. How far are Rowan and Genevieve willing to go and how much will they risk to make their most captivating and forbidden fantasies a reality? (978-1-63679-426-6)

The Roommate by Claire Forsythe. Jess Black's boyfriend is handsome and successful. That's why it comes as a shock when she meets a woman on the train who makes her pulse race. (978-1-63679-757-1)

Seducing the Widow by Jane Walsh. Former rival debutantes have a second chance at love after fifteen years apart when a spinster persuades her ex-lover to help save her family business. (978-1-63679-747-2)

Close to Home by Allisa Bahney. Eli Thomas has to decide if avoiding her hometown forever is worth losing the people who used to mean the most to her, especially Aracely Hernandez, the girl who got away. (978-1-63679-661-1)

Innis Harbor by Patricia Evans. When Amir Farzaneh meets and falls in love with Loch, a dark secret lurking in her past reappears, threatening the happiness she'd just started to believe could be hers. (978-1-63679-781-6)

The Blessed by Anne Shade. Layla and Suri are brought together by fate to defeat the darkness threatening to tear their world apart. What they don't expect to discover is a love that might set them free. (978-1-63679-715-1)

The Guardians by Sheri Lewis Wohl. Dogs, devotion, and determination are all that stand between darkness and light. (978-1-63679-681-9)

The Mogul Meets Her Match by Julia Underwood. When CEO Claire Beauchamp goes undercover as a customer of Abby Pita's café to help seal a deal that will solidify her career, she doesn't expect to be so drawn to her. When the truth is revealed, will she break Abby's heart? (978-1-63679-784-7)

BOLDSTROKESBOOKS.COM

Looking for your next great read?

Visit BOLDSTROKESBOOKS.COM
to browse our entire catalog of paperbacks, ebooks,
and audiobooks.

Want the first word on what's new?
Visit our website for event info,
author interviews, and blogs.

Subscribe to our free newsletter for sneak peeks,
new releases, plus first notice of promos
and daily bargains.

SIGN UP AT
BOLDSTROKESBOOKS.COM/signup

Bold Strokes Books is an award-winning publisher committed to quality and diversity in LGBTQ fiction.

www.ingramcontent.com/pod-product-compliance
Lightning Source LLC
Chambersburg PA
CBHW021959010726
47494CB00003B/804